HER
BETRAYAL

BOOKS BY EMMA TALLON

Her Revenge

Her Rival

Runaway Girl

Dangerous Girl

Boss Girl

Fierce Girl

Reckless Girl

Fearless Girl

Ruthless Girl

EMMA TALLON

HER BETRAYAL

bookouture

Published by Bookouture in 2022

An imprint of Storyfire Ltd.
Carmelite House
50 Victoria Embankment
London EC4Y 0DZ

www.bookouture.com

ISBN: 978-1-80314-031-5
eBook ISBN: 978-1-80314-030-8

For the two greatest loves of my life, Christian and Charlotte.
Everything I ever do is all for you.

PROLOGUE

Her hearing was in two hours. Right now, she knew the legal team would be gathering everything to put before the judge. Soon, before she was escorted to court, she would be taken back to the interview room to write her statement. Her confession. She closed her eyes as a wave of sickness threatened to overwhelm her. She couldn't believe it had come to this.

They would be surprised to hear her confess to the murder, after all this time spent vehemently denying her involvement. She'd decided to keep the admission of her crimes to herself until the last possible moment, until it was absolutely necessary. But now her time was up and there was no longer any way out of this. She was going to prison, but she still had a chance to save her family. As long as she played things just right, they could still make it out of this.

He'd make sure to rub in his victory, she knew, after the runaround she'd subjected him to. But much as she hated it, he *was* the victor. For the first time in the history of the Drews versus the police, the Drews had lost. *She* had lost.

ONE

Lily laced her fingers together and put her clasped hands to her mouth, staring off into the distance, not really seeing. Her usually calm and collected demeanour had disappeared, a wild, haunted hollowness in its place. The image of Ruby's face at the window as she screamed for help, the all-consuming fear as she panicked, was seared into the walls of her mind, and Lily closed her eyes against a fresh wave of pain.

There had always been risks in this life. The underworld was unforgiving, and its rules were harsh. The threats of imprisonment, violence or death were always hovering. Those were the risks they took. It was something she'd prepared herself for, prepared the whole family for, for as long as she could remember.

Stay alert, she'd told them. *So long as you keep your eyes open, your guard up and your mind sharp, you can stay ahead.* And she believed that, truly, down to her core. There were peaks and troughs, highs and lows, the same as in any game. But if they kept their wits about them, they'd end up on top.

Yes, Lily had always accepted the inevitability of the lows. But she had never in a million years expected to be faced with watching one of her children trapped in a burning building. She had never counted on being put in a position where she was so utterly powerless to stop what was happening. She had never counted on a rival quite as psychotic and as evil as Grace Dupont.

A spark of anger broke through the numbness and ran through her body as her thoughts turned to Grace. She'd watched Lily run to the burning building, towards her screaming daughter. With the reflection of the flames dancing in her gleaming eyes, Grace had smiled at Lily. The smile had been cold and triumphant, and was the worst thing Lily had ever seen in her life.

But that was the image that spurred her on. It was the rage that it incited which would help her get through this awful time, that would keep her strong enough to fight the overwhelming sense of pain and fear and other weakening emotions. Because now was not the time to be weak. Now was the time to stay strong and work out what their next move would be.

A knock on the door roused Lily from her dark thoughts. Her son Cillian walked in, closing the door behind him and blocking out the hum of general chatter and noise from the hospital hallway beyond. He sat down next to his mother in the other high-backed wooden armchair beside the bed. The steady beats of the heart monitor filled the long silence as they both stared at the burned, lifeless-looking girl hooked up to it.

'Any change?' Cillian asked.

'Not yet,' Lily answered.

When the firefighters had finally managed to get to the office where Lily had seen Ruby, they'd almost been too late. She had already passed out from smoke inhalation, and the fire had blown through the door as they tried to move her out. Her back had taken the brunt of the explosion, but the flames had caught her neck and one side of her face too. If she pulled through – and it wasn't the strongest *if* – she'd be scarred for life.

Lily reached forward and stroked her forehead, careful not to touch her burned cheek. Her fingers moved over her hair, resting on the singed ends of her tight red curls.

'I want you to get Roxanne in here tonight,' she said suddenly.

'What?'

'Roxanne. From the salon. Tell her to bring her scissors. This side of Ruby's hair is all burned – she'll need to cut it shorter to neaten it out and make it look nice.'

Cillian frowned. 'Mum, I really don't think Ruby's *hair* is our priority right now—'

'If Ruby wakes up—' Lily snapped, then paused. '*When* Ruby wakes up,' she corrected, 'she's going to have a lot to process. She's got to deal with what's happened and with her burns. The last thing she needs is to see her hair half burned off too.' She exhaled exasperatedly. 'We're just sitting here, *waiting*. I just...' Her hands flew up into the air and then back down into her lap defeatedly.

Cillian was quiet for a moment and then nodded. 'OK. I'll sort it.'

Lily nodded. She knew that this wasn't their biggest priority – of course it wasn't. But she needed the distraction. Every second that passed with Ruby still lost to them in this coma felt like a decade. Every second added to her mounting fear that her daughter would never wake up.

The doctors had said only time would tell. The smoke inhalation had done a lot more damage than Lily had previously thought possible. There was a good chance she'd wake up and start down the path of recovery, but there was also a good chance that she'd never wake up at all. She'd felt like wringing the doctors' necks at one point, as no matter how many questions she asked, they were never directly answered. All they kept saying was that they would monitor her and that they'd just have to see how things went.

'We need to talk about Grace,' Cillian said quietly.

'What is there to say?' Lily asked, staring bleakly into Ruby's ravaged face.

'What are we going to do about her?' he responded. 'What she's done needs to be answered for.'

'And she will answer for it,' Lily replied.

'How?' Cillian turned to face her. 'Tell me how, and we'll sort it.'

Lily's jaw clenched as she watched Ruby's frail chest rise and fall in time with the beeps of the heart monitor. 'I can't tell you how yet. It depends.'

'On what?'

'On whether your sister lives or dies.'

She turned to face her son, her deep brown eyes cold and unforgiving. 'We need to know exactly how much that bitch has to pay for before we go charging in. Because I intend to take that payment in blood. And I refuse to be even one drop short.'

TWO

Scarlet pushed her hands down into the pockets of her long, thin jacket and looked up at the broken bones of the building she'd once thought of as her second home. Pale wafts of smoke still rose here and there from the blackened remains, creeping out of jagged holes where windows had once been. Metal barrier fencing had been erected around the site, and the police tape, tied like bunting from post to post, fluttered in the wind.

She still couldn't believe it was gone. All her father and her aunt had worked so hard for over the years, torn down in minutes by one vindictive enemy. Well, not all, she mentally corrected. Financially this was only a percentage of their income. But the factory had always been at the heart of every-thing they did. All their illegal enterprises had been run from those offices. A lot of their money had been laundered through the accounts. They'd hosted poker nights and undertaken all sorts of other dark and dangerous tasks in its vast, noise-proof basement.

But most of all for Scarlet, the factory had felt like her last real connection to her dad. It hadn't even been a year since he'd been murdered and it was still the first thing that hit her as she woke every morning. There was always a brief moment between sleep and wakefulness where everything was peaceful and all was OK with the world. And then reality would come crashing in and her heart would drop like a rock through the ocean. But every day up until two days ago, she'd at least been able to get dressed and go into the office that had once been his. She'd been able to sit in his worn leather chair and work at his desk. She'd felt close to him, as she'd taken her place in the business he'd built up from nothing with his bare hands. And now that place, that sanctuary from the deepest levels of her grief, was gone.

Grace had certainly known where to hit them the hardest. They'd half expected this last move, realising midway through their last job that she was vindictive, cunning and fearless, in equal measure. Grace wasn't someone they'd accounted for, when they'd put their last job into motion. Her husband was just a rich, bored idiot they'd met one night at a big charity event who'd tried to force himself on Scarlet, and after she'd fought her way to a narrow escape, they'd come up with a rather lucrative plan for revenge.

He'd drunkenly revealed a black market painting he had hidden away, one of the lost treasures of the art world. They'd put together a team, stolen it and made all the right connections to sell it back through the black market. He wasn't able to call the police, as it was already hot property, and they were too organised for him to catch up. It was the perfect plan. But they hadn't counted on Grace, his wife. She was the real brains behind their wealth, the cold, hard businesswoman who kept things moving in the higher echelons of the black market whilst maintaining a flawless mask in front of society. They hadn't seen her coming, and when she came, she came with force. Burning the building down had been her revenge, when they'd turned in the painting for the five-million-dollar reward the FBI had outstanding on it. She'd thought Scarlet and Lily were inside, her plan being to burn them alive. But they'd anticipated that move and had watched from a distance. It all would have been fine, if Ruby hadn't gone looking for her mother that night. The factory would still have been gone, but no one would have been hurt.

Scarlet's expression grew heavier as she thought of her cousin. She and Ruby had never seen eye to eye, but they were still family. And Ruby hadn't deserved her fate.

As her gaze moved across the fragile shell that still surrounded the burned-out chaos inside, her vision blurred and she sniffed, blinking hard to dispel the threatening tears. She wouldn't shed even one more than she already had. She refused to. Grace didn't deserve it. No. Grace didn't deserve anything except retribution.

'Oi, Miss? Excuse me.' A voice broke through her thoughts and she turned towards it. One of the firemen was approaching her, wiping a streak of soot from his tired brow. 'Miss, you can't be 'ere. It ain't safe.'

She realised, as he spoke, that she was clutching the top of one of the rails surrounding the building and had pushed it forward. She immediately let go and stepped back. 'Oh, sorry. I didn't mean to... I'm not trying to come in.'

'Like I said, it's dangerous. It's still going in places.' He glanced back. 'Could collapse any minute, so best not to be even this close. Smoke's still sooty too. Don't want to dirty your nice clothes,' he added with a half-smile.

Scarlet smiled back, the action not quite reaching her eyes, and he saluted before heading back the way he'd come, his message delivered. Her cold smile faded as she watched his retreating back.

Don't want to dirty your nice clothes. The words echoed in her mind. He'd meant it kindly enough, but he had no idea who she was. She'd dirtied worse things than her clothes these last few months. She'd dirtied her hands, her heart, her soul – and she planned on all of those things getting dirtier still before this chapter of their lives was through.

She stared up at what was left of the factory once more and her gaze hardened. Grace had a lot to answer for.

Her phone buzzed in her pocket and she tried to shake off her dark thoughts. Hopefully it was John, her new boyfriend – the only positive thing to have entered her life recently. The only thing that wasn't destroyed or tainted by the dangerous life she led. Her solace from all of this.

She turned away from the ravaged remains of the building and pulled the phone out of her pocket, glancing expectantly at the screen. When she saw the number flashing up, however, her heart plummeted. It wasn't John calling to brighten her day. It was a call she'd expected and dreaded in equal measure, and one that there was no avoiding. With a deep breath she closed her eyes and answered.

'Hello, Detective.'

THREE

Connor pushed through the door of Salon Red, nodding respectfully to his aunt standing behind the reception desk. He was about to look away but glanced back, aware that something looked different about her. She smiled as he neared and he clocked the bright red lipstick and the shiny gold earrings below her styled updo.

He smiled back, pleased to see this change in her. Cath had always enjoyed dolling herself up back when his uncle had been alive, but since Ronan's death, his vivacious, bubbly aunt had gone into her shell and become a pale echo of herself. It was nice to see her colours begin to shine back through.

'Alright?' he greeted her and leaned forward over the tall reception desk as she tidied away some bits into drawers.

'Yeah, good, you? How's your sister doing?' Cath's smile faded into a look of concern.

'Same,' he replied with a sombre look. 'I don't know what Mum's going to do if she don't pull through. I've never seen her like this.'

'I have,' Cath replied.

Connor gave her an enquiring look.

'When you two were little, you both came down with chicken pox. You were alright, happy enough, even covered in spots with oven mitts gaffer-taped to your hands.'

'What?'

'Well, you wouldn't stop itching no matter how many times you were told and your mum didn't want you scarring, so she bought two new pairs of oven gloves and taped them onto your hands. You tried your hardest to get them off, but she secured them good and proper. There weren't no way you were going to defy her wishes and scar yourselves.'

'That sounds about right,' Connor agreed, thinking about his mother's iron will and how fiercely she protected her children – even from themselves.

'*You* were fine, but your brother, he got really ill. Ended up in hospital with his fever raging out of control.' She sighed at the memory. 'Me and your uncle came over to look after you and your mum stayed in hospital with Cillian. Wouldn't leave his side, not for a minute. Nothing else mattered, nothing else existed.' She stared off into the distance. 'She had that same look then. That same anger towards what was hurting him, and the same fear and helplessness as she waited to see if he'd turn the corner.'

'That may be true, but chicken pox ain't a person,' he replied gravely. 'She might have been angry at the wind then, but Grace is flesh and bone. I just worry that if Ruby don't pull through this, she might do something reckless.'

Cath shook her head. 'Your mother's not done one reckless thing her entire life. She ain't gonna start now. Don't worry about that. Anything she does will be done with purpose.' She eyed him and pursed her lips, then reached over and squeezed his arm. 'And as for Ruby, she's a fighter. More than anyone gives her credit for. She'll pull through. You'll see.'

Connor searched his aunt's face for any sign that she was

just trying to placate him, but she stared back at him resolutely. 'You really think so?' he asked.

'I do,' she responded. 'Now, why don't you tell me what you're here for. I assume you haven't just popped in for a natter.'

'Oh, yeah, I um...' His gaze landed on the stunning tall blonde assistant manager. 'Just need to talk to Sandra about something.' He sauntered over and gave her a winning smile as she glanced up at him from the pot of colour she was mixing for one of the stylists.

'Alright?' she asked, resuming her focus on the colour.

'Yeah, yeah, good thanks,' he said enthusiastically. 'And you? How's it hangin'?'

'Slightly to the left,' she answered, not missing a beat.

'What?' Connor pulled back, confused.

Sandra chuckled. 'I've never really understood that greeting, you know. I mean, how's *what* hanging? I can only assume it's meant for the guys as girls don't exactly have much that hangs.'

'Oh.' Connor frowned and glanced down at the skinny jeans she was wearing. 'But you're not like...' He pulled a face as she stared at him. 'You know...' he floundered and glanced down at them again.

'Oh, for Christ's sake, Connor!' she exclaimed, rolling her eyes. '*No.* I think you might have noticed something like that, don't you? I just mean... You know what, never mind.'

'You never know – people can change all that these days, can't they...' He trailed off as she just stared at him.

She walked over to one of the stylists and put her client's colour down on the trolley, then marched into the back room. Connor followed her in, and she frowned as she began clearing the dirty colour pots into the dishwasher.

'Did you want something?' she asked.

'Oh, yeah,' Connor said, glad of the prompt. Something

about her always made him forget himself. 'Mum asked Cillian to find out if Rox could go over to the hospital after work to sort out Ruby's hair. She don't want her waking up and seeing it all burned like it is.'

'Oh.' Sandra's face softened. 'Yeah, I'm sure she'll be happy to.' She put the last bowl in and shut the dishwasher door. 'Why you asking me though? She's out there – you could just ask yourself.'

'Well, you know, I just thought because you'd be able to see in the client diary.'

'For after hours?' She raised an eyebrow.

'Or that maybe, you know, you might just know—' He began to stutter and clamped his mouth shut, annoyed at himself.

'Right.' Sandra nodded slowly and crossed her arms. 'I don't,' she said bluntly. 'And even if her personal life was in the client diary, that's out there with your aunt. Not in the back room with me. And also, if your mum asked Cillian to ask Rox, how did *you* end up in here asking *me*?'

'Well...' He shifted his weight from one foot to the other, flustered as his thinly veiled excuse to talk to her was scrutinised. 'Mum asked Cillian and Cillian asked me to come in and ask Rox, but obviously I didn't want to disturb her when she's with a client.'

'OK.' Sandra held her hand out to cut him off. 'I'll just get her to call you when she's done. Alright?'

'Perfect,' he replied, relieved that the inquisition was over.

She started to walk out and he quickly blocked her way. 'Er, as I'm here,' he said, giving her his best smile. 'I was just wondering if maybe you fancied meeting up again sometime?'

Sandra raised an eyebrow and gave him a hard look. 'I don't work for you anymore, Connor. I work for your cousin. And *this* job don't involve all *that* kind of stuff. So I don't have to do any of that with anyone anymore. Even you.'

'Nah, I don't mean like before. I mean like, you know... For free. I wanted us to go out for free, no payment.'

Sandra arched her brows in derision as she stalked off. Connor closed his eyes and ran his hands down his face. With a sigh he turned and left the salon, waving goodbye to his aunt as he passed.

Sandra had been one of their high-end escorts for a few years, prior to working for Scarlet in the salon. Occasionally Connor had hired Sandra for his own evening pleasure, making sure to pay well so that she didn't feel as though he was taking advantage. He wasn't exactly a regular. He had no need to pay for sex – he was attractive and notorious enough to get as much female company as he wanted. But he'd had a thing for Sandra from the moment he'd met her. Now that she was no longer an escort, he'd been plucking up the courage to ask her out on a real date, but it hadn't come out the way he'd planned.

He descended the steps to the busy main road below and got back in the car where Cillian sat waiting in the driver's seat. Cillian turned to him and pulled the toothpick he'd been chewing out of his mouth.

'How'd it go?' he asked.

'Fucking terrible,' Connor said with a groan.

Cillian frowned. 'What, she said she wouldn't do it?'

'Eh?' Connor looked at him with a frown of his own. 'Oh, you mean Rox. She's gonna call us in a bit when she's done with her client, but Sandra reckons she'll be fine to go.'

Cillian pulled off down the road. 'So what was fucking terrible?'

'Me, trying to ask Sandra out.'

Cillian glanced at him and a slow smile crept over his face. 'Did ya really?' he asked, unable to contain his amusement.

'Yes, I did and it went down like the bleedin' *Titanic*,' he replied, annoyed. 'She hates me.'

'What do you mean? What did you say?'

'She assumed when I asked about meeting up that I meant like before, so I said nah, not like that, like, for free. And then she stared me out and walked off.'

Cillian turned towards him, his eyes widening and his mouth forming a wide, round O. '*That's* what you said?' he asked incredulously.

'Yeah, and she just walked off. She hates me,' he said glumly.

'Nah,' Cillian replied, turning away for a moment to hide his face. 'Nah, not at all.'

'You don't think?' Connor replied hopefully.

'Nah, she's just playing hard to get. She wants you to keep trying,' he said in a serious tone. 'Honest. You should definitely keep trying. She's into you. She tries to hide it but I can see it.'

'Yeah?'

'Oh yeah.' He nodded vehemently. 'Keep at it. Stress again how you mean you want to meet up for *free*, so she totally understands,' he continued, biting his lip with a slow nod.

'You think?' Connor was reassured by his brother's words. 'Maybe you're right. No point giving up so quickly. Especially if you think she really does like me.'

'Oh definitely.'

Connor looked out the window at the passing traffic, spurred on, totally missing the silent mirth that creased his brother's face.

FOUR

Scarlet sat down heavily on the plastic chair at the table in the cold, clinical interrogation room and suppressed a shiver as the door banged shut. She hated this room. She'd spent far too much time in it already, but at least this time she would be allowed to leave afterwards.

When they'd found out, a few months earlier, who had killed her father and how it had been in cold blood, they had taken their retribution as a family. It was black and white in the underworld. An eye for an eye, a life for a life. She'd been the one to put the bullet in his brain. It was the first time she'd ever taken a life. The only time. It had left her feeling a strange swirl of emotions. Guilt mixed with satisfaction, fear mixed with peace. Mostly she'd felt strong. She'd taken the final step over the threshold into their world and knew that from now on she'd be able to handle anything, whatever challenges lay ahead.

But then the police had found a link between her and Jasper, the man she'd killed. He'd accidentally cut himself with a knife he'd planned to use on her; it had ended up with both their prints on. Scarlet's lawyer had got her off, but only just. The evidence wasn't enough to convict her, but it was enough to convince the police of her involvement, and now they hovered like vampires, ready to strike and suck away her life the moment they got the chance. But she wasn't going to give them that chance. Not now. Not ever.

The door opened and she looked up expectantly. As she saw who it was, her expression dropped into a frown. 'You're dealing with the factory fire?' she asked in disbelief. Surely she couldn't be that unlucky?

DC Jennings sat down with a smirk. 'That's no way to greet an old friend,' he said, his tone mocking.

She narrowed her gaze. 'Except we aren't old friends,' she said carefully, stifling the urge to shudder. He gave her the creeps.

He watched her with a predatory gaze for a few moments. 'No, we're not,' he agreed. 'But I am here out of concern for you,' he added, his tone softening to a more friendly level.

Scarlet blinked, not sure what to make of this sudden change of tack. As the main officer on Jasper's murder case, he'd been nothing short of ruthless in his questioning of her before, making his disdain for her and her family known. Why would he be concerned for her in any way now?

'What do you mean?' she asked.

'I'm concerned that someone's trying to hurt you,' he replied solemnly. 'Whoever set that fire meant business and meant to kill whoever was inside. I think they thought *you* were inside.'

Scarlet was careful to keep her poker face in place as she waited for him to get to his point. Her guard was now well and truly up. What did he know about the fire? Did he know about Grace? Why was he even in here?

It was at this point she realised he'd come in alone and that the tape wasn't rolling. Her gaze flickered up to the camera in the corner of the room. That was on. He was trying to lure her into a false sense of security perhaps.

'Look, I know we don't see eye to eye,' he said, holding his hands out, palms facing up, 'but the most important part of my job is to keep people safe. And that means all people. Including you. So you need to help me out here. Do you know who caused the fire?'

Scarlet's gaze held his levelly as she considered her answer. 'No,' she said, after a short silence.

He leaned forward over the table. 'A retribution attack of this size would have to have been organised carefully. It would have likely meant a chain of people involved, all of whom are still very much a threat to you.'

Scarlet blinked. 'Retribution attack?' she asked.

'Jasper's father may be in prison, but he still has all his contacts. It wouldn't take him much to have set all this up, but if we can figure out just one of the links then we can stop them coming back to finish the job. We can keep you safe. But you need to tell me everything you know.'

It finally clicked, what DC Jennings was trying to do.

Scarlet pulled herself up in her seat, fury filling her expression. 'You are *unbelievable*,' she spat. 'I've told you before, I had nothing to do with Jasper's death – his *suicide*.'

'Let me help you, Scarlet. This time you were lucky, but next time he could send someone to your home, to burn you in your bed.'

Scarlet sighed, leaning back in her chair. Jennings was fishing with what he thought was live bait but was really nothing more than pink string. He thought he could scare her into a confession, but he couldn't have been more wrong – on so many points. The fire had nothing to do with Jasper. He'd taken a gamble, hoping it might have been, but he was barking up entirely the wrong tree.

'I didn't come here to be questioned about Jasper Snow,' she said. 'And if you intend to go down that route again then I'm not speaking to you without my lawyer.'

Jennings' jaw tightened and he pulled back, putting his

hands up in defeat. 'I was just trying to help you, Scarlet,' he said in a falsely casual tone. 'And if you change your mind, you have my number.'

'Where's the officer I'm supposed to be talking to?' she countered, totally ignoring his last-ditch attempt. 'Are they coming? Because if not then I have other places to be.'

Jennings stood up with a sigh. 'I'll go get him. I'll see you again soon.'

'Hopefully not,' Scarlet replied.

He stared at her for a few moments, then turned and left the room.

Scarlet felt the weight she always carried on her shoulders bearing down on her. Irritated, she stood up and crossed her arms, pacing across the room, back and forth, as she tried to shake the unexpected conversation off.

They didn't have anything on her – nothing that would stick anyway, she reminded herself. She just needed to keep her cool and focus on what she was really here about. The fire. Her aunt had already spoken to the police. They had been into the hospital to speak to her the day before. It was obvious that the fire had been purposely set, not least because Grace had chained all the exits first in order to keep whoever was inside from leaving. But the police had no clue as to what had actually happened.

Scarlet wasn't sure how they were supposed to explain it, but Lily had told her to play ignorant. So long as Grace hadn't left her own trail, the case would continue to go nowhere and they'd be forced to turn it over as a cold file.

She reached the back of the room, slowing as she approached a pinboard with various battered leaflets attached. She eyed a domestic-abuse-hotline flyer overlapping a social-services card. Her eyes swept over the rest of them and she pulled a face. All in all it was a pretty depressing display.

The door opened behind her and she heard someone walk in.

'Miss Drew, sorry to keep you waiting. My name is DI Richards – I'm the DI in charge of the case.'

Scarlet turned around, at first feeling a sense of relief that it wasn't DC Jennings back for another round of attempted trip-up. But as her gaze focused on the new person in the room, her feeling of relief swiftly morphed into one of shock and then horror. Her eyes met his and she saw the same spark of shock and realisation fly through his expression. For a long moment everything around her seemed to fade to a grey hum.

This didn't make sense. The new arrival, now staring at her as though she was a ghost, was John, the man she was *dating*, the man she'd started to really like. What was he doing there?

Her mind searched frantically for some answer that would make sense, to figure out the mistake that had led him here, but there was nothing. This was no mistake. He really was a copper. And all the time they'd spent together must have been his attempt to set her up. John walking up to her so casually at the bar that day, the dates they'd been on where he'd avoided all talk about work, the way he'd manipulated her to open up to him – it had all been fake. A story, an attempt to gain her trust and trip her up about Jasper's death.

He'd been working with Jennings all along.

FIVE

They stared at each other for a few long moments, his piercing green eyes locked onto hers, and then the door behind him opened once more. A short red-haired female officer walked in and cleared her throat. Scarlet tore her gaze away from John to look at her.

The break in eye contact seemed to spur John into action and he turned towards the officer in a sharp awkward motion. 'Er, right. So, as I was saying, I'm DI Richards and this is DC Ascough, who will be sitting in with us today.' He gestured for her to sit and then took his own seat on the other side of the desk next to DC Ascough.

Scarlet's gaze flickered between them, then she slowly walked over and sat down. So this was how he was going to play it. He was going to act as though they had never met before. Part of her, the newly angry part of her, wanted to put an end to this little charade immediately and demand to know who the hell he thought he was. Clearly, he'd been assigned this case in error as he was already working undercover in relation to her elsewhere. The shock on his face when he saw her had told her that. But her aunt's voice niggled in the back of her mind.

Wait and watch, it said. *We learn more by letting a situation play out than stopping it in its tracks.*

'Thank you for coming down to the station today,' he continued. His words were smooth and calm, which only served to infuriate Scarlet further, but she kept her poker face intact. 'We've had a conversation with your aunt, Lily, but just want to get an overview of everything that happened from you too; to ask a few questions.'

'Fire away. *Detective*,' she added in a loaded tone.

DC Ascough frowned but didn't say anything.

John cleared his throat. 'Where were you when you first noticed the fire?' He looked up at her properly for the first time since they'd sat down, his keen green gaze piercing hers intensely.

'With my aunt at one of our worker's flats, just down the road,' she answered levelly, keeping to the story she and Lily had agreed on. It was always better to stay as close to the truth as possible. Less to remember. 'Danny. He hadn't been well. We took him over some food.' Danny had worked with them for years and was someone they trusted implicitly. He knew the game, and he'd give the police the same story as they had, should they want to check it.

John bit his lip and looked down to the file in front of him. 'Do you do that with all your workers when they're ill?' he asked.

'The long-standing loyal ones, yes,' she replied. 'He's been with us for many years. A family friend.'

John nodded and exchanged a brief glance with DC Ascough. 'It was very late to be dropping off food. Nearly eleven, I believe. Wouldn't Danny have been trying to sleep at that time, being so ill?'

Scarlet frowned. 'We had only just finished work. Which is why it was such a late call. And good job we finished when we did, or we would still have been in there and I likely wouldn't be here to talk to you now.' She glared at him defiantly, every cell in her body urging her to scream at him, demand to know how he could dupe her the way he had.

John nodded and sat back. 'Yes. Good job indeed,' he agreed.

Scarlet decided to channel her anger into the conversation they were able to have. 'Look, if you're looking for someone to pick apart, *Detective*, then go find whoever just burned our livelihood to the ground,' she snapped. 'Don't sit here wasting time trying to find holes in *my* story. We lost everything in that fire.' Her clear grey-blue eyes burned into his. 'A lot of people did. Do you know how many people work for us at that factory?' She lifted one eyebrow in question as he flipped the pages of his file looking for the answer.

'Fifty-seven,' she continued. 'Fifty-seven men and women, some of whom have worked for us their whole adult life, and who now have no job. No income, no security, no familiar place to go to every day.'

John nodded. 'It has affected everyone involved, of course it has. I mean you no offence.'

Scarlet stifled a snort.

'But it's our job to look at all the angles.'

'And this angle you're looking at now – questioning whether we were doing what we said we were, treating us as if somehow *we* are the criminals – how is this helping you find the arsonist?' she asked. 'Or is that it? You think *we* did it?'

She glanced from John to DC Ascough and back again in question. 'You seriously think we would set fire to our own factory, destroy everything our family has built up over decades?'

She shook her head in disbelief. 'Let me guess, you're wondering if it was an insurance job, yeah? For starters, my aunt wouldn't set fire to a building with her own daughter trapped inside. And as for the insurance, ha!' She barked out a bitter, humourless laugh. 'The insurance won't cover what we've lost, not by a long shot. We had a thriving business – a solid work-force, long-term clients, a well-oiled operation that practically *churned* money. The insurance might cover the cost of some second-hand machines and the bricks and mortar, but it certainly won't compensate us for anything else.'

She sat back and closed her mouth, aware suddenly that she'd gone off on a tirade. She shouldn't have said anything that they didn't force out of her with their questions. Not that she'd said anything incriminating this time, but it was too easy to slip up when spilling thoughts like that. He'd got to her. John's pres-ence had totally thrown her and caused her to forget herself. But that wouldn't happen again.

'No one is suggesting that, Ms Drew,' John replied, watching her levelly. 'We just have to look at all the details. Now, can you run through with me what happened when you initially saw the fire?'

Scarlet closed her eyes, suddenly very tired of the whole thing. She had enough to deal with already with the factory gone and Ruby in hospital. The last thing she'd needed was to find out her new boyfriend was an undercover detective. She felt sick.

'Lil saw something out the window,' she said. 'We realised it was the factory and we ran out of the building and down the road. Ruby was leaning out the office window shouting for help and Lil tried to break through the front door but couldn't because of the chains.'

The memory of that night flashed through her head. The searing hot flames roaring behind her as she tried to push Lily back to safety, the black smoke that surrounded them like a blanket of hate, the fear that consumed her body and mind making it hard to think. She tried to keep her head in the present.

'The next thing I know, firemen were running towards us.

My aunt told them Ruby was still in there, then we were moved back out of the way so they could do their job. That's it. There's no more I can tell you that Lil hasn't already.'

'OK.' John picked up his pen and began tapping it on the file in front of him.

DC Ascough shifted in her seat and leaned forward. 'Do you have any idea who may have started the fire?'

'No,' Scarlet replied, turning her attention to the other woman.

'None at all?' DC Ascough pushed, lifting one eyebrow.

Scarlet frowned. 'No. Like I said already.'

'Could it have been a disgruntled business associate? Was there anyone who might have cause to want to hurt your family this way?' she asked.

'You're asking me if there are any clients who were so unhappy with the small plastic parts we produce for them that they wanted to burn down the factory with us inside? No. Funnily enough, I can't think of anyone.' She gave her a withering look.

DC Ascough sighed. 'What about your other business associates?'

Scarlet looked at her sharply and DC Ascough returned a challenging stare. She knew what the other woman was asking. She was being direct enough without outright saying it.

'I don't know what you mean,' Scarlet said calmly. 'We don't have any other business associates.'

'No, of course you don't,' Ascough replied, an edge of irritation in her tone.

John was still tapping the pen, looking down at the file, and Scarlet's anger resurfaced. How could he sit there so calmly, as though he hadn't just blown his cover? As though nothing had ever happened between them. How could he have gone out with her the way he had, got so close and personal? He'd even kissed her – looked her in the eye and put his lips to hers, pretending to feel something.

She felt sick to her core and suddenly unable to continue this charade any further. Standing abruptly, she almost knocked her chair over. John and Ascough peered at her, surprised by the sudden move.

'I have a lot to do, so we're done here,' she said curtly. She needed to get out of this room before her anger took over and she said something she'd regret.

'I just have a few more questions—' Ascough began.

'I've told you everything I know,' Scarlet snapped, cutting her off. 'There's nothing more to discuss. So unless I'm suddenly under arrest for some reason, I'm leaving. In case you've forgotten, I have a cousin in hospital, a salon to run and a whole lot of paperwork to fill out for the insurance company. I can't afford to sit here wasting time with you two.'

Ascough looked over at John and his eyes narrowed, but he gestured towards the door. 'You're free to leave whenever you want. I'll show you the way out.'

'*No thank you,*' Scarlet said with feeling. The last thing she wanted to do was be alone with him, to hear whatever lies he would come up with next. She might have fallen for it before, as he tried to worm his way into her circle, but luckily he'd got nothing. And now they'd messed up and blown his cover there was no way she was going to allow him anywhere near her again. She swept round the desk and towards the door with a glare before he could even stand. 'I'll find my own way.'

SIX

Scarlet marched down the street towards her car and ran her hands back through her long dark hair in agitation.

'Shit, shit, *shit!*' she growled, kicking her front tyre angrily.

She turned around and sagged back on the bonnet for a moment, closing her eyes. How could this have happened? How could she have been so blind?

Opening her eyes, she caught an odd look from a passing pedestrian. Suddenly aware that she was still very close to the police station, she unlocked the car and slipped into the driver's seat.

The more she thought about it now, the more she realised how stupid she'd been. Right from the off the situation had been unusual with John. He's turned up out of nowhere, insistent on talking to her despite the fact she'd just been trying to have a peaceful drink on her own. She hadn't been trying to draw attention, but he'd given it to her anyway. He'd quickly won her over with charm and humour and had steered well clear of any talk surrounding their careers. At the time she'd just been thankful that she hadn't had to lie and hide who she really was. But now it was clear that he'd just been trying to keep the conversation away from his own line of work. And had used it as a tactic to lure her into a false sense of security too.

Checking her mirrors, she pulled off and headed in the direction of the hospital with a grim expression. This was the last thing Lily needed to hear right now, but she was just going to have to.

Half an hour later she sat in Ruby's room across the bed from Lily, who was holding her daughter's hand and staring at her bandaged face, as if doing so might somehow rouse her from her coma. Scarlet swallowed, hating herself for being the person who was about to add to her aunt's mental load.

'What's happened?' Lily asked, without looking round.

Scarlet glanced at her, surprised. How did she know something had happened?

'I've known you from a baby, Scar – I know when you're in trouble. What's up?'

'Er...' Scarlet blew a long heavy breath out through her cheeks, unsure where to start. 'I've just been by the police station.'

'And?' Lily asked, her sharp gaze turning towards her niece. 'What did they say?'

'Jennings tried it on first. Pulled the concern card.'

'Concern?' Lily frowned, confused.

'He was hoping the fire was a retaliation for Jasper's murder. He played the whole thing out, trying to trip me up.'

'You shut him down?' she asked.

'I did. He gave up easy enough. I guess he knew it was a shot in the dark to begin with.'

'He's like a dog with a bleedin' bone that one,' Lily grumbled.

Scarlet nodded. 'He ain't gonna give up either. I can see it when he looks at me. He knows I did it and won't rest until he proves it.' She stifled a shudder of dread. When his dead grey eyes settled upon her, Jennings had a look of determination so strong it was almost feral. Those eyes seemed to follow her around these days, wherever she went. They haunted her dreams.

'He won't prove it,' Lily claimed. 'There ain't no proof to find. Don't worry about it.'

Scarlet cast her eyes away and worried her bottom lip with her teeth as her thoughts moved back to the reason she was here. 'Jennings might not be our biggest problem right now, where the Old Bill's concerned.'

'What do you mean?' Lily shifted in her seat to better face Scarlet, her hand still holding Ruby's.

'That guy I mentioned to you.' Scarlet paused and pushed a stray lock of her raven hair behind her ear. 'The one I met at that pub the day we went to that meeting with Arj.'

'What about him?'

'We've met up a few times and talked a lot over messages too. Well, we've been dating really.'

It was something she'd kept to herself, the fact that she and John had grown closer. She hadn't kept him a total secret, but she'd downplayed it and kept her comments casual, not ready to have her worlds mingle.

'I, um...' The anger, betrayal and shame she'd been feeling rose up again. She didn't want to have to tell her aunt this, didn't want to admit her stupidity. 'I started to have real feelings for him. Thought it was the start of something special. And I thought the feeling was mutual.'

'And it wasn't?' Lily asked, clearly unsure as to where this was going.

'It seems not,' Scarlet replied tightly. 'I found out today that he's a copper.'

Lily gasped.

'He's the lead DI on the fire. Seemed surprised to see me. I guess someone messed up when they assigned him to the case. Must not have realised he was already undercover.'

'Shit,' Lily exclaimed, her expression grim.

'Yes. Shit,' Scarlet replied, feeling her cheeks warm. 'It's my fault. I completely ignored the signs, and they *were* there, looking back,' she admitted. 'He was just so on his game and came from nowhere.'

'He didn't come from nowhere, Scarlet,' Lily snapped, her tone firmer now that they faced such a close threat. 'He came from the fucking police station. I thought I'd taught you better than that.' She glared over the bed at her niece. 'I've told you, you don't get close to *anyone* on the outside, not without vetting them first. Fuck's sake. What does he know? What have you talked about?'

'Nothing incriminating,' Scarlet replied hurriedly, her cheeks burning with shame. Her aunt was right. She'd been an idiot and there was no excuse for it. 'He insisted we don't talk about work, said it was boring. I was glad, thought it made it easier for me. But he got personal really quickly. Gave me some shit about losing his mum, to make me open up about Dad, gah.' She made a sound of frustration and leaned back into the chair, running her hands down her face. 'I can't believe I fell for it.'

She looked away, unable to meet Lily's eye, remembering John's open face, the fake pain, the well-woven story that had made her feel so aligned with him in her grief. She'd trusted him, a complete stranger – not with the business, but with her own feelings. And the betrayal of that felt almost overwhelming.

'This personal stuff, how much did you tell him?' Lily demanded.

'We never talked business,' Scarlet assured her. 'He must have been trying to line me up for it though.'

'You said you talked about Ronan,' Lily pushed. Her eyes searched Scarlet's face. 'What did you say specifically?'

'Just that he'd died. I didn't say how or go into detail, just that it was recent.' Scarlet swallowed the lump that rose in her throat at the memory of her father.

'You're sure there's nothing you've given away that might lead him in a direction we don't want?' Lily pressed. 'We need to know now, Scarlet.'

'No, there's...' Scarlet trailed off as one thought suddenly occurred to her. Her heart began to sink as she thought through the implications.

'There might be one thing,' she said, her voice lowering to almost a whisper in dread.

'What?' Lily demanded.

'The newspaper, the article I found about Harry's death. It was on the bench we were sat on. I picked it up and saw it, and... I don't know how much he saw. I ran off – I wasn't thinking straight.'

They'd strolled in the park a couple of weeks before, the day they'd talked about Ronan. She'd glanced at a discarded newspaper and saw a face she recognised all too clearly. It had been Harry, Grace's husband, the man who'd tried to rape her and whose painting they'd stolen. Except it hadn't been his. The painting had belonged to Grace, and when she'd discovered he was the reason it had been stolen, she'd killed him. The article was about his death.

'If he did notice how strangely you acted and saw the article it could create a link between us and Grace,' Lily said.

'I don't think he did. But I can't be sure.' She kicked herself again, as the situation continued to spiral downwards. 'I'm so sorry, Lil. I've really fucked up.'

'Yes, you have,' Lily replied. She eyed her niece hard. 'But we ain't out of the game yet. Call the boys – get them in here. He might have had the upper hand to begin with, but the tables turned when you found him out. So now we've got some work to do if we're going to make sure it stays that way.'

SEVEN

Cillian rubbed his head and began to pace up and down between the side of Ruby's bed and the window. Connor stared at Scarlet in disbelief. Lily sat watching them both, her expression grave.

'You had *no* idea?' Connor asked incredulously. 'None at all?'

'Obviously not, Connor,' Scarlet replied, annoyed. 'Or I wouldn't have been dating him.'

'This is really bad, Scar,' he said, glancing back at Cillian. 'This could really fuck us over.'

'Really? Could it?' she snapped, with irate sarcasm. 'I had no idea. I thought maybe we could invite him on our next job for a ride along.'

'That's enough,' Lily said, her quiet voice holding enough authority to silence the pair. 'This won't be resolved by bickering between yourselves.' She eyed them both hard.

'Right.' Cillian pinched the bridge of his nose. 'We're assuming he's undercover for what exactly?'

'Ain't that obvious?' Scarlet asked.

'Not really. It could be about Jasper, or it could be about the painting. The FBI have just handed over five million for a painting you supposedly found in the back of an old lock-up. That ain't small change. I'd be looking a little closer at the situation if I were them.'

The stealing and selling-on of Grace's already stolen Rembrandt hadn't gone as planned, and they'd had to put Scarlet's backup plan into play. Instead of selling the painting on through the black market, they'd handed it back to the FBI for the outstanding reward, setting it up as a sudden find in an old lock-up they had bought.

'It could even be to infiltrate the family as a whole,' he continued. 'It ain't like we're off the pigs' radar, Scar. They've pulled us for all sorts over the years. They just haven't managed to pin anything solid.' His deep brown eyes bored into hers with fierce intensity. 'You're assuming that because it's you it's about Jasper, but it may be because they see you as a weak link. You're the youngest, the newest to the firm.'

'I'm no weak link,' Scarlet replied stubbornly.

'I'm not saying you are. I'm saying they might *think* you are.' Cillian pushed back his dark tailored suit jacket and put his hands on his hips, turning to look out of the window down to the busy London street below. 'We can't assume anything yet.' He rubbed the dark stubble growing over his chiselled jawline. 'We should have checked him out sooner than this. I hadn't realised it was anything serious. We need to pay him a visit.' He turned back and directed this last comment at his mother.

'Do it,' she ordered.

'Do you know where he lives?' Cillian asked.

'No, we never talked about that sort of stuff. Maybe we could get George or Andy to follow him home?' Scarlet turned her gaze towards her aunt.

'I think we'll have to. It's going to be the simplest option,' she agreed.

'They won't even know what he looks like. And what are

they supposed to do, hang around the station and hope he doesn't notice when they trail after him?' Connor interjected. 'Ain't there a better way?'

'Not without getting technical and doing things that could land us in even hotter water than we're already in, no,' Lily replied.

'I can show them a picture. He has a profile pic on his WhatsApp. Here...'

Scarlet pulled out her phone and unlocked it, flicking through her apps until she found the right one. She opened it and scrolled down to his name, clicked into the chat and was about to lift it up to show everyone, but then her hand faltered and her hopeful expression faded. Where once his face had beamed out at her, there was nothing but a grey circle. Everything on his profile had gone.

EIGHT

Lily was roused by the sound of knocking on the door and sat bolt upright, quickly regretting such a swift movement when a muscle in her neck twinged painfully. She rubbed her eyes, trying to clear the bleariness and squinted at the clock. It was almost eight in the morning. She must have been exhausted to have slept this long around the loud noises of the hospital breakfast period. Then again, she'd been awake thinking and analysing the newest threat to the family for hours after the last visitor of the night had left.

Her eyes instinctively turned to Ruby, searching for any change. There was none, which was expected but didn't lessen the blow any more than it had the last hundred times she'd allowed herself a sliver of hope.

The knock at the door sounded again, reminding her of the reason she'd woken up. She rubbed her eyes once more and tried to flatten her ever wild curls into a socially acceptable position. She failed, and they bounced straight back, as they always did.

'Come in,' she said, clearing her throat.

The door opened and a petite blonde entered, a warm smile

on her face as she juggled the box she was carrying on one hip then closed the door behind her. Lily's resentment towards the girl did a flip in her stomach, and she tried to keep it from showing on her face.

'Hiya,' came a friendly voice. 'Hope I'm not intruding. It's not time for her check-up or anything, is it?'

'It's not time for her check-up, no,' Lily said in a clipped tone, ignoring the comment about intrusion.

She glanced sideways at the girl, not sure why she was here. She wasn't family, she didn't know Ruby, she was just Cillian's latest fling. Billie, her name was. She'd met her just a few days before. So much had happened since then, she'd all but forgotten her.

'I thought you might be hungry,' Billie said, placing several Tupperware boxes on the small table that sat at the end of Ruby's bed.

'I'm not,' Lily replied coldly.

Billie didn't seem fazed by her rudeness, which both surprised and annoyed her. She was purposely being rude hoping that the girl would take the hint and just leave. She didn't have the strength right now for anything else. Ruby's life still hung in the balance and she was barely even awake yet.

Her eyes slid sideways at the Tupperware as Billie turned back to her box and rummaged for something. There was a fresh fruit salad, croissants and what appeared to be bacon sandwiches in one steaming box. Her mouth suddenly ached for the fruit salad. She was hungry after all. She looked away though. As petty as she knew it was, she couldn't take Billie's food. Because that would signify acceptance. And she did not accept Billie one bit.

Finally, her temper snapped and she rounded on the girl. 'Why are you here?' she asked hotly.

'Because you're my boyfriend's mum, and your daughter's in hospital, and hospital food is shite,' she answered bluntly. 'I wouldn't feed that crap to a dog, to be honest. So I figured I'd bring you something decent to eat instead.'

'But why?' Lily pushed. 'Why you? You ain't family, love. You're a complete fucking stranger to me, to be honest.'

She knew she was just venting at the girl, aiming all her anger and frustration and devastation at her, but she didn't care. She didn't want her here. She wanted no one other than her family around – the people who cared, who really mattered.

Billie nodded and glanced away, her expression unreadable. 'You're right, I'm not. I'm sorry if I overstepped. I don't want to take up your time, I just wanted to bring you these.' She finished unpacking the rest of the Tupperware and put the box away to the side of the room. 'There's Tuscan chicken and rice for lunch and some snacks and drinks. I'll leave you to it.'

Without waiting for a response, Billie shot her a smile and left, closing the door quietly behind her.

Lily bit her top lip, willing the tears that were pricking at her eyes to go away. She was harder than this. She'd never felt guilt at telling one of the boys' bits of skirt to piss off before. Why would she? They were ten a penny, clinging on to their arms for the notoriety and the money until the boys grew tired and moved on to the next. So why was she suddenly feeling uncomfortable now?

Because Billie is different, a small voice in her head whispered.

She shook it off, annoyed. Billie wasn't different. She'd watched a decade of insipid Barbie clones come and go – why would one of them suddenly be different now?

Cillian had turned up to Sunday lunch with her in tow, the sacred weekly family gathering which no one outside of the Drews was allowed to attend. It had upset and enraged her. She'd made it very clear over the years how important Sundays were. It was the one time each week they spent as a family, all together, not because of work or because they needed to, but because they *chose* to. It had been that way for as long as they could remember, since she and Ronan had been just two kids struggling through the world alone. Family was everything.

It was never OK to bring an outsider to the family lunch. But he had, and what's more, he'd insisted she be allowed to stay despite Lily's adamant protests. He'd never done that before. None of them had. So why start now?

The voice began to pipe up again, the little whisper of doubt getting stronger, but she silenced it. Billie couldn't be different. Lily knew her boys, she knew the kind of girls they liked and she knew they were about as serious as clowns when it came to relationships. They had always put the family and the business first. They didn't want to get serious with anyone. They didn't want to settle down.

Did they?

Another knock sounded at the door and she turned as it opened. What was wrong with the girl? Did she not understand it was best to just retreat?

Cath walked in and stopped with a start as she caught the full force of Lily's glare. 'Christ alive, if looks could kill! What's happened?'

'Oh, nothing,' Lily grumbled, turning back to face the bed again and gesturing to the seat next to her.

'Yeah, looks like nothing,' Cath replied sarcastically. She sat down. 'How's Rubes doing today?'

'No change yet,' Lily replied, not able to hide the crushing disappointment in her tone.

'Was that Billie I saw just on her way out?' Cath asked.

'Mhm,' Lily responded through tightly pursed lips.

'Ooh, did she bring all this?' Cath asked, suddenly noticing the boxes of food. 'Looks lovely. You won't be needing this then.'

She was about to place the big bag of food she'd brought with her on the floor, but Lily grabbed it and opened it before she could.

'I certainly will,' Lily asserted. 'I ain't touching her shit. I don't know who she thinks she is, trying to play house with me. Thanks for bringing this in, Cath.' She pulled out some boiled eggs and bit into one hungrily.

Cath shook her head. 'Lil, you're going to have to give the girl a chance at some point. This is a nice gesture.'

Lily swallowed down the egg and sighed, staring unhappily at her motionless daughter. 'Cath, I don't have the energy to give some girl I don't even know a chance right now. I have my own little girl to worry about.'

The tears prickled at her eyes again, and she blinked rapidly to dispel them. She sniffed and held her chin up in defiance against her escaping emotions.

'Look at her, Cath.' Her voice wobbled. 'In all the years I've been chasing her from hellhole to hellhole, cleaning up her messes, watching her destroy herself, I've never seen her like this.'

Ruby had been a nightmare from the moment she'd entered the world. The screaming baby had turned into an unruly child, the child had become a destructive teenager and then a self-sabotaging adult addicted to heroin and bad men. Lily had pulled her hair out over the years, desperately trying to keep her together, and it had seemed like they were finally getting somewhere before all this had happened. Ruby was clean, she'd moved home and had even started working for the family business. But then Grace had locked her inside the factory and left her to burn.

'She was turning a corner, Cath,' Lily continued, the tears now beginning to fall unchecked. 'She was really making a go of it this time. Something in her had changed – I could see it. But now...' She closed her eyes, unable to finish the sentence.

'Now we just have to wait, while her body recovers enough for her to wake up,' Cath said gently, touching her shoulder in a gesture of support.

'She ain't waking up, Cath,' Lily said bleakly. 'It's been three days and there's been nothing.'

'That don't mean anything, Lil,' Cath replied. 'I've read that this is just what the body does when it's gone through something bad – it shuts itself down so it can concentrate on healing.'

Lily stared at Ruby's face. Her porcelain skin was so colourless that the deep red of her wild curly hair looked stark and harsh against it. Her closed eyes were sunken, and the one cheek that showed was gaunt, the other hidden under the layers of bandages protecting the burn beneath.

'She was a livewire from the off, this one,' Lily said as the memories of Ruby's childhood played out in her mind. 'Redfaced and screaming the second she drew breath. Always shouting, always fighting.' She half smiled as she remembered the way she'd boss round her two older brothers. Then the smile faded as the silence of the room became too heavy to bear. 'I've never seen her so quiet.'

'She's going to pull through this, Lil. She will,' Cath said, turning to look her in the eye. 'Right now she just needs you to believe in that. To believe in *her*, in her strength. Come on. You need to be brave, for her.'

Lily blinked, suddenly aware of how weak and pathetic she must look. It didn't matter that Cath was family – this wasn't acceptable. She could never be seen as weak. Even if she was. And for the first time in her life, she really was. No matter what life had thrown at them in the past, she had always taken it on the chin. She was hard. She could take absolutely anything.

Anything except the loss of one of her children.

She sniffed and straightened up. 'Yeah. Yeah, you're right. She's tough, our Rubes.' She forced a quick smile at her sister-in-law.

Cath searched her face, only half convinced. 'Do you want me to sit with you today?' she asked. 'Sandra can watch the salon. She has the other girls there. They can cope without me.'

'Nah, I'm fine. Honestly. The boys will be popping in and I've got work to do to keep me busy. I'll let you know if anything changes with Ruby,' she said.

Cath seemed to debate it for a few moments. 'Are you sure?'

'I'm sure. Go on – you'll be late,' Lily urged.

Cath looked troubled at the thought of leaving, but with no other option she slowly stood up. 'OK, well, if you need me back just text, yeah? I can come any time.'

'I'll be fine. I'll call you later.' She held the fixed smile on her face until Cath disappeared, then let the mask drop into an expression of defeat and worry.

Turning once more to Ruby, she grasped her limp hand between both of her own and pulled it to her cheek. She closed her eyes, willing some of her own life into her, even though she knew that will couldn't really do anything. Ruby had to return to them herself.

'Please come back to me, Ruby,' she whispered. 'I've only just got you back. I can't lose you.' She squeezed her eyes as the tears flowed freely. 'I *cannot* lose you.'

NINE

The rain streamed mercilessly down the windows of the café, beating out a sharp rhythm on the pavement beneath. Scarlet stood with crossed arms and stared out at the market, not envying the stallholders as they tried to avoid getting completely drenched.

'Why do we stay on this miserable island?' she asked. 'Why are we not living in some foreign country where it's always sunny and warm and never rains?'

'Because underneath the rain and the soot, London is the beating heart of this world,' Cillian answered from his seat behind her. 'There ain't nothing like it, and when you belong to it like we do, you can never really leave.'

'That's depressing,' she said, turning round and walking back over to the table where he sat waiting, playing with his ever-present toothpick.

Cillian shrugged. 'I don't think so. There's something to be said about belonging to a place. About it being a part of you.'

The door opened and the sound of the rain was instantly magnified until it slowly closed behind the tall broad man who'd just dived in. He pulled his sodden hat off his head and gave it a regretful look before pushing it down into the pocket of his equally sodden coat.

'Hey, Sid,' Cillian said as the man ambled over to his table.

Scarlet leaned on the table next to her cousin and smiled warmly at the newcomer. He smiled back and his gaze darted between the two of them for a few seconds.

'Alright? I got the message to pop in here to see you. What's up?'

'We just wanted to make sure you're doing OK,' Cillian said, offering him a seat. Sid sat down. 'You alright?'

'Yeah, I mean' – Sid pulled a face – 'I'm OK. Gutted about the factory. I guess it will probably be a while before the insurance is sorted and you can rebuild.' He looked down, a heaviness to his expression.

Scarlet nodded. 'Possibly. And we know you can't afford to sit and wait, so we've brought you this.' She reached into her large handbag and pulled out a thick brown envelope with his name on it. She handed it over, watching his eyes widen in surprise.

'What's this?' he asked.

'Two months' pay. We should be operational by then, or at least we hope we will be. If we're not then you'll get a further packet to tide you over until we are.'

Sid's jaw dropped open. 'Are you sure?' he said, looking from one to the other.

''Course,' said Cillian. 'You've been with us years, and we value you. We don't want to see you leave because you have no choice. You've got a family to feed – we appreciate that. We've got you covered until we can get things back up and running.'

'Thank you,' Sid said in a heartfelt tone. 'I really appreciate that.' The worry he'd been carrying in his shoulders dropped. 'I'll be honest with ya, I'm glad I don't have to go try my luck down the job centre. The missus has been on at me about it the last couple of days, but eighteen years I've been with you. I really didn't want to have to start over somewhere new.'

'Now you don't have to,' Cillian replied, shooting him a grin as he popped the toothpick back between his teeth.

'Thanks,' Sid said again. 'I mean it.' He stood up and nodded his gratitude once more to each of them. 'I'll catch you later. Let me know when there's any work to do.'

'Will do.'

Sid opened the door and with a cringe stepped out into the pouring rain. The cousins exchanged a look as the door shut.

'One more left,' Scarlet said.

Over the years, Lily and Ronan had built up so much more than just a factory. They'd created a loyal, steadfast workforce. Not everyone was as valuable as the likes of Sid. Some people were newer and didn't really have a clue about the other side of their business. These people, sad as it was to lose any, could be replaced. Indeed, a few were dead weight that they weren't sad to see the back of. But there was a core of staff who had been fine-tuned to perfection over the years. These people were loyal, hardworking, smart assets. They ran the factory with the utmost efficiency and with little need to bother their bosses. And on top of that, despite not actually being a part of the underworld, they understood exactly who their employers were and could be counted on to keep secrets and provide alibis when required. That was worth more than any amount of money. Loyalty and dependability could not be bought, so they had to protect what they had.

Scarlet folded her arms and approached the window, feeling restless. She was trying to focus on the task at hand, but it was going slowly and her mind was wandering towards other things. Things she didn't want to think about. She sighed and tried to focus on something else.

'I hear Billie popped in on your mum this morning?' she said.

'Oh?' Cillian glanced at her, his dark eyebrows raised in surprise.

'You didn't know?' Scarlet asked, equally as surprised by his reaction. She pulled a face. 'Didn't go too well for her, from what I hear.'

'And what *did* you hear exactly?' Cillian asked, settling back in his chair and watching her carefully with his dark brown eyes.

'Only that she turned up with some food and your mum wasn't too happy about it. Told her to do one apparently.'

Cillian nodded, as if this wasn't unexpected. 'She's tough, Billie. She can handle Mum.'

Scarlet's eyebrows rose in shock and she laughed. 'Christ, she must be made of solid steel if Lil don't have her quaking. You know how much she hates the girls you date.'

'Billie ain't just another girl,' Cillian replied. 'She's something else.'

'She must be.' Scarlet looked Cillian up and down critically.

He was a handsome man, physically fit with a well-defined face and a cheeky smile she knew caught a lot of female attention. Of her twin cousins, he was the more confident, always a beat or two ahead of Connor. She hadn't thought he was in the market to find an actual relationship. He'd always been all about work and play in equal measure, but he never took any of it too seriously.

'You know, you might want to talk to your girlfriend from time to time, so you know if she's planning on visiting your mother. No relationship lasts without basic communication,' she said.

'Advice on relationship communication from the cousin who didn't know she was dating a copper?' Cillian said with a small sound of amusement. 'What is the world coming to?'

Scarlet felt her cheeks flood with colour and she turned to look back out of the window. 'Well, I'm not dating him anymore, am I?' she snapped.

'Oh, don't get the arse – I'm just having a laugh,' he said.

It was a fair cop, Scarlet supposed, and she knew she'd also laugh about it one day. But not yet. Right now it was still too raw and she still felt like a total idiot.

'You heard anything from him?' Cillian asked.

'He's tried calling a few times,' Scarlet said with a sniff. 'But I ain't answered.'

Lily had told her to ignore any calls, asking her to wait until after the boys had paid John a visit. It would be easier getting information out of him and securing his future lack of public interest in them if they had that conversation at a place and time where they held the cards. Allowing him to feed her empty lies down the phone whilst he stood prepared and safe, far away, wouldn't help matters at all.

As if he somehow knew they were talking about him, Scarlet's phone suddenly lit up on the table and his name flashed up on the screen. She ignored it, every ring cutting through her like a knife. Every ring a reminder that he'd played on her emotions like a pro and that even now she felt some sort of bizarre loss for the person she'd thought he was. For a person that didn't even exist. She closed her eyes, hating herself for being such a fool.

Cillian glared at the phone with ill-concealed contempt then glanced up at her as the call went through to voicemail. 'They're following him today. With any luck we'll have his address in an hour or two and Connor and I can pay him a visit tonight,' he said.

'Good,' Scarlet replied. 'Do me a favour would you, while you're having this conversation?' She thought back to the tender kisses they'd shared, to the feeling of his warm lips lingering on hers, to the feelings that it had stirred within her. Her gaze burned into his. 'Make him sorry he ever tried to play with me the way he did. Make him pay. Make him pay in a way he'll never forget.'

TEN

John rolled his head back and rubbed his neck. He'd just finished a particularly gruelling late-night session at the gym and it was tight. Working out that hard was often the only thing that helped him focus when life was stressful and he needed to think. But even that hadn't helped much tonight. Because he was in a predicament. One he'd never encountered before. One he wasn't sure how to deal with.

The last person he'd expected to see when he'd entered that interview room was Scarlet. When he'd seen her face, seen the recognition and the horror in hers, he'd instantly realised the level of shit he was in. He'd kicked himself, wishing he'd paused for a second to check the file before going in. He could have had someone else take over, hidden away so she wouldn't see his face. But he hadn't had time to open the file and check who he was dealing with.

His time was stretched across several cases, all of which were highly demanding. For this latest one, the arson case, he'd had his team do all the evidence gathering and interviews so far. Aside from the initial brief look at the building itself, that was the first time he'd turned his personal attention towards it.

Having dragged himself away from a homicide case which was getting more and more complex by the minute, he'd only had time for Ascough to give him a brief rundown first. And then he'd seen *her*. The fierce and beautiful Scarlet Drew, in all her glory.

Her shock had been intense – and swiftly replaced by cold fury. Her big grey-blue eyes had flashed dangerously at him across the room, and he figured he could guess what was going through her mind. He'd been stuck like a deer in headlights for a moment as he panicked, not sure how to play it. This was a catastrophe of the highest degree, a huge conflict of interest, considering who she was already to him. But there was no police handbook in the world which outlined this particular scenario. And so he'd winged it, playing out the pretence as Ascough joined them, buying himself some more time.

It had been over quickly. She'd floundered, confused, and left the station. Now, he had some explaining to do. And after thinking it over carefully, he knew exactly what he was going to say. But now that he had it all figured out, she was dodging his calls, and his frustration was at an all-time high. He needed to get to her, to try and smooth things over and make sure he hadn't completely blown it. But how?

Slinging his gym bag over one shoulder, he pulled his keys out of his pocket and unlocked the front door to his small one-bedroomed flat. It wasn't much, his current home, but it was all the space he needed for himself and Poirot, his cat. Poirot was a surly old thing, not the friendliest of felines. But John had raised him from a kitten and was the one person he'd grudgingly curl up to on the sofa and accept the occasional pat from.

Closing the door behind him, John hung the keys on one of the coat hooks and threw his bag into the bottom of the airing cupboard in the hallway. He frowned and paused, wondering why Poirot hadn't immediately come running into the hall to demand his evening meal.

'Poirot?' he called out, listening for the telltale wail that usually returned.

The sound did come, but it was more muffled than expected. His frown deepened and he headed for the bedroom. 'Where are you?' he asked.

The sound came again and he realised it was coming from inside the wardrobe.

'How on earth did you manage to trap yourself in there?'

As he instinctively went to the closed wardrobe, it took a second to realise that there was no way his cat could have pulled the doors shut on himself. He tensed and coiled, ready to turn, but it was a moment too late. Something blunt and unforgiving smashed against the side of his skull, and a searing pain erupted through his head before he passed out.

Cillian walked through the tiny flat, ignoring the low growls from the grey fluffy cat that glared at him from the back of the sofa. He wasn't sure what he was looking for exactly. It wasn't like there would be a big file just sitting in the man's living room, marked 'Drew Family'. But out of habit he looked things over anyway, just in case.

There was very little at all in the flat to indicate that he was a copper. Only the badge inside his wallet and a caricature-esque plastic policeman on a shelf, obviously given to him as some sort of joke gift at some point. The whole place was very minimalist and neat, giving nothing away about its occupant.

In the small kitchenette he reached up and opened each of the cupboards until he found the glasses, then pulled down a pint glass and filled it with water from the sink before heading back through to the bedroom where Connor was watching John.

'Nothing?' Cillian asked.

'Nothing,' Connor replied with a shake of the head.

Cillian shrugged. 'OK.'

Walking over to the inert figure sprawled across the bed, he launched the pint of water into his face.

Immediately John came to, spluttering and pulling back, then groaning and putting his hands to his head as the pain set back in. Blood from the blow Connor had inflicted earlier covered one side of his head and dripped down his neck. He pulled his hands away, saw that they were slick with it and sighed with a note of annoyance.

To his credit, Cillian noted, he didn't panic as many would have done. Instead, he eyed them hard and inched up into a seating position, only half able to hide the pain he was in. He leaned back against the headrest and took in the pair, a flicker of recognition flashing across his face before he could mask it.

Cillian gave him a cold smile. 'Yeah, you know who we are, don't you?' he said quietly.

'No,' he replied calmly, not missing a beat. 'Why would I know who you are?'

Cillian rolled his eyes. 'We don't have time for this game. You know damn well we're the Drew twins.'

John looked surprised at the bold statement.

'We ain't trying to hide our identities, mate. We'd have at least worn masks, if we were. So, you know who we are, and we know who you are. And let's be honest, we all know why we're here.'

Connor nodded and stared across at John. 'I bet it was a surprise, seeing our cousin in that room, wasn't it?'

John's gaze moved from one to the other as he clearly deliberated over his response. Eventually, he nodded. 'It was,' he said frankly.

'Yeah. Someone fucked up there, didn't they? Blew your cover,' Connor continued in a hard tone.

'There was no cover,' John insisted. 'I had no idea who she was when I met her.'

'Fuck off,' Cillian said with a disgusted expression. 'You really expect us to fall for that? 'Course you're going to deny it. To the bitter end too, I'd imagine, if you're actually worth your salt.'

John sighed and made to move, but Connor stepped forward. 'You'll stay right there, unless you want this around your nut for a second round.'

John's eyes slipped down to the dumbbell in Connor's gloved hand, and he sat back with a bitter sound of amusement. 'You realise you're both in serious shit the second I get out of here?' he said. 'You can't break into a DI's house and assault him without serious repercussions.'

'There won't be any repercussions,' Cillian replied. 'We were never here.'

'Except my account of things is slightly different. Unless you're planning to murder me and silence that. Is that it? I won't be around to tell the tale?' He looked at Cillian and then back to Connor, studying their expressions with interest. 'No, I don't think so. What would you be doing me in for? Dating your cousin?'

'Nah, people don't get murdered just for *dating* my cousin.' Cillian paused, the memory of Jasper's dead body surfacing. Scarlet's track record wasn't exactly the greatest, he thought wryly. 'No, if we were here to do you in, it would be for *using* her to get information to fuck our family over. Dating her ain't a crime, but using her to get to us is pretty fair grounds for retribution. Wouldn't you agree?'

'I never *used* her for anything. I actually care for Scarlet,' John argued.

'Yeah, 'course you do,' Connor replied. 'What do you get exactly, for the whole set?'

'The whole set?' John seemed confused.

'The whole family. Scarlet, us, our mum. The full deck. What was the arrangement? You get in with Scarlet, get enough dirt to send us all down, then what? Do you get some sort of promotion?'

John rolled his eyes with a deep groan. 'For fuck's sake, I wasn't undercover. I wasn't trying to do anything other than date Scarlet because I *like* her.'

'Well, you ain't seeing her anymore,' Cillian said. 'She don't want nothing to do with your kind.' He looked the other man up and down, anger warring with his need to be sensible.

He sniffed and turned in a small circle. 'We ain't here to murder ya,' he said in an almost regretful tone. 'But you ain't going to tell anyone we were here anyway. Way I see it, you weren't too sensible with where you left these weights. This dumbbell was on that shelf there, above your bed.'

He pointed to the shelf above John's head, and he twisted to look.

'It fell on your head, giving you a nasty gash and causing you to spill your glass of water all over yourself.'

He saw John's eyes flicker down to his gloved hands and annoyance flash across his face. There would be no fingerprints on the glass or anywhere else – the twins had made sure of that.

'We also have watertight alibis for tonight and a reason to believe that you have a vendetta against us. Because you're a scorned man, whose new girlfriend found him out for what he really is and ditched him. So you trying to set us up would obviously just be you seeking vengeance on poor Scarlet. You'd look like a prize prat.'

John smirked without humour and shook his head. 'Nicely done,' he said flatly. 'Much as I'd like to, I guess I can't argue with that.'

Cillian held his gaze, the other man's eyes glinting with fury, despite his calm words. It wasn't fear that made him hold his tongue; it was intelligence. And his head must have been pounding from the blow but still he sat straight and proud, holding his own with no show of fear whatsoever. Cillian could see what had drawn Scarlet to the guy. Strength was always drawn to strength.

'Here's what's going to happen,' Connor said, staring John down with naked hatred. 'You're going to stay away from us. You're going to shut down your undercover operation and back the fuck off. If we see your face again, if we catch even a sniff of you lot tracking or recording us, we'll be back for another visit. But next time won't be so friendly. Do you understand?'

John stared up at him with a mixture of contempt and anger but didn't answer.

Wise, Cillian thought. He surveyed the damage they'd inflicted. They'd left a huge gash across the left side of his forehead, going back into his hairline. Blood painted the side of his face and stained his white T-shirt crimson. It must be hurting badly and would also probably need stitches before he lost too much more blood. He nodded to himself. His job was done.

'We can find you anywhere at any time,' Cillian threatened, holding his gaze menacingly for a few moments. 'So I suggest you take this chance while you can.'

It wasn't strictly true. If the police decided to put him into a safe house, they'd have no chance. They didn't have anyone on the inside to feed them that sort of information. But he hoped the threat would worry him enough to believe that they did.

Turning towards his brother, he tilted his head towards the front door. Connor fell into step behind him, and without a word, the brothers left the building as silently as they'd arrived.

ELEVEN

Connor entered Ruby's hospital room and closed the door, sitting down opposite his mother. She briefly looked over and nodded in greeting, but her eyes instantly shot back to Ruby's face. She clutched Ruby's hand so tightly her knuckles were white.

His gaze moved over his mother critically. She was pale and drawn, dark circles ringing her tired eyes. Her wild hair was dull and her clothes hung loose. He shook his head and bit his lip, feeling a wave of guilt wash over him. They should have been paying closer attention to her, these last few days.

'Mum, you need to go home and rest,' he said. 'Get some proper sleep, eat something.'

'I'll decide what I need, thank you,' Lily snapped. She glanced over at him, and after studying his face, her tone softened. 'Ruby needs me here. I'm fine. It's your sister we all need to be thinking about.'

'And we are,' Connor replied. 'But you ain't gonna be much use to her when she wakes up if you don't look after yourself.'

'I'm fine,' Lily managed to say calmly. 'Stop wittering about me. If you want to help, just keep doing what you're doing. Keep things rolling.'

Connor sat back in his chair, accepting defeat. There was no point arguing with his mother. No one could make that woman do something she didn't want to. Not even God himself would be able to tear her from Ruby's bedside right now, he'd wager.

'Update me,' Lily continued, stroking back a wisp of hair that was out of place on Ruby's head. 'You sorted that rozzer out?'

'Yeah. Left him with a scar to remember and a reason to watch his back. He shouldn't be a problem anymore.'

'No one saw you?' she asked.

'No, we were careful. Alibis are tight too. Cillian was with Billie having date night, and I was playing cards with Andy and George,' Connor answered.

'Good. Keep an eye on him. You may have warned him off but this is far from over. Pigs don't give up that easy, especially when they've spent time and effort undercover. What about the other thing?' Lily's jaw pulled tight as she asked.

'She's moving about, but she's always guarded closely and stays under cameras where she can, even when she leaves her estate. It's not going to be easy to get to her quietly.'

Connor and Cillian had been following Grace, trying to work out her routines. They were looking for weak points, time periods where she was vulnerable, but she'd upped her game. Day and night since the fire she'd had at least a handful of her men keeping watch, and even when she went out there was little opportunity for an ambush.

'There has to be a window somewhere. Find it,' Lily responded.

Connor scratched his head. 'We'll keep looking. She's smart though, Mum.'

'She is,' Lily agreed. 'But she also knows it. And smart people who think they can easily outsmart others always get too comfortable. It will happen. You just have to make sure you're there when it does.'

'What's the plan then?' he asked. Usually, their mother kept them in the loop when she was planning a job. It was better that way. Everyone was on the same page and knew what they were doing. But this time she hadn't told them anything.

'It all depends on Ruby,' she replied, giving nothing away once more.

'What do you mean?' he pushed.

Lily was silent for a few moments. 'It depends if she wakes up. I have something in mind. But if Ruby doesn't make it, and it's looking increasingly possible that she won't...' Lily had to stop momentarily. 'Then I'll be dealing with this one on my own.'

Alarm bells started to ring as he watched Lily's expression contort. In all his years his mother had never scared him as much as she did in this moment.

'What you on about?' he asked, his eyes widening. 'You can't mean that. We do things as a family. We're *stronger* as a family. We'll deal with this the way we always have.'

'No,' Lily said adamantly, shaking her head. 'Not this time. This one, if it comes to that, I'll be dealing with alone.'

'You can't—' Connor started to protest but Lily cut him off.

'I can and I *will*, Connor,' she said in a firm, deadly voice. 'I am still the head of this family and you will follow my instructions to the letter, the same way you always have.' The emotion in her voice was raw and strong. 'If that's how it goes, you will not disobey me – you will do as you are told. And you will keep this family going. No matter what.'

Connor felt his blood run cold and dread settle into the pit of his stomach. If Ruby died, Lily would find a way to get to

Grace. But if she insisted on going in alone, that meant that whatever she had planned, she had no intention of coming back out.

TWELVE

The salon door opened and Cath rushed back behind the reception desk.

'Welcome to Salon Red. Have you booked?' she asked, flipping to today's date in the diary with a wide smile.

Scarlet smiled. Cath had been like a new woman these past few days. She was obviously worried about Ruby, the same as everyone else, but now that Scarlet had hired her and she had a sense of purpose again, it was as though she'd been reborn. Bright new fashionable clothes had appeared, alongside her favourite old red lipstick. She was up earlier, chirpily flying around the kitchen in the mornings talking at a million miles an hour instead of tiredly forcing a coffee down her neck as she glumly tried to fill her day. And she'd taken over all the managerial duties in the salon as though she'd been doing it all her life.

Scarlet couldn't believe she hadn't thought of offering the position to her mother before. Now she realised how blind she'd been. Cath got on famously with Sandra too. Between them they were running the salon, managing the stylists and laundering money through the books as smoothly as she could ever have hoped.

Sandra took a coffee over to one of the clients with a smile, then she called across to Scarlet, 'You got a sec before you go?'

'Sure, what's up?' Scarlet took one more gulp of her own coffee. She'd been up late the night before, moving money and dealing with issues. It seemed to be a lot slower and harder to run things now that they'd lost their hub. Everything was scattered around, meaning more trips and less time. There was also a lot more to sort out without Lily at the helm, and she was starting to feel the pressure.

'Two things.' Sandra flashed her a dazzling smile and flicked her golden hair back off her face. 'Firstly, those products Natalie ordered in.' She wrinkled her nose. 'They're shit. Now, I know I'm no expert, but I've been trying out some of the things all these salesmen keep trying to peddle here meself, and there's one brand that I think is much better than the others. It's not as well known, but it's not so expensive. I think we should switch and try their wider range of products – but I don't know, what do you think?' She suddenly looked unsure, her confidence faltering.

'I think that's a great recommendation,' Scarlet replied. 'I'd rather go with something my staff have tried than something just because it has a better-known name. Go for it. What's the other thing?'

'Well, um.' Sandra glanced over at one of the stylists and back again. 'You know how I sort of accidentally ended up here, and what I did before and all that?'

Scarlet nodded. Sandra had worked as one of their high-end escorts for a few years until an unfortunate chain of events led to them having to let her go. She'd been lost and bewildered with nowhere to turn and Scarlet had taken pity on her, offering her the assistant manager job in the salon just to keep her afloat. She hadn't expected Sandra to enjoy it or to stay, but to everyone's surprise both had happened.

'Well, thing is, I really like it here. And it got me thinking that I'd quite like to train as a stylist.'

She took a breath and shifted her weight onto the other foot awkwardly, then carried on hurriedly, her words almost tripping over each other in the rush.

'I mean, obviously I'd pay for meself and everything, to go on a course, but I'd need to go into the college one day a week and I'd need a mentor here. Rox said she'd do it, if it was OK with you. It wouldn't take up much of her time or anything. It's just that you'd need to sign off on it and I'd need that day release.' She came to a stop and bit her lip. 'I mean, I totally get it if you need me here and it's not the right time. So I understand if it's a no.' Her cheeks flushed crimson.

Scarlet frowned. 'I hadn't realised that would be something you'd want to do,' she said slowly, thinking it over. 'OK.' She twisted her mouth to the side. 'There's just one part of all that I'm not OK with.'

'The day release thing?' Sandra asked, cringing. 'I know. It's too much to ask. I shouldn't have even brought it up. I'm sorry. And with Ruby in the hospital and everything with the factory, the last thing you need is—'

'Sandra,' Scarlet interrupted her forcefully and put a hand on her arm. 'The bit I'm not OK with is you paying for your own course.' She waited for realisation to dawn and then smiled. 'I think it's a great idea. Get all the details together for me, I'll sign what you need and you can start.'

Sandra blinked in shock. 'Wow. Oh my God. Thanks, Scarlet.' A slow smile crept over her face. 'Are you serious? You've done so much for me already. And now this. I don't know how I can ever repay you.'

'Maybe you will one day,' Scarlet replied. 'And until then, you can just owe me a favour.'

Leaving Sandra still smiling, she took one last gulp of her coffee and then waved goodbye to her mother before walking out into the bright sunshine.

As she made her way towards her car, she filed that favour away in a mental box for later.

Lily had taught her very early on – years before she'd even considered joining the family business – how valuable it was to look after the people around you and collect favours. You never knew when you were going to need them. It was a ruthless strategy, but a useful one. Maybe she'd never need to call on Sandra for help. But if ever she did, if ever she was caught in a dark corner with nowhere to go in years to come, she would be able to remind the other woman just how much she owed her.

She turned into the dead-end road where she'd parked her car an hour before and rummaged in her bag for her keys. She was about to open the door of the sleek black Mercedes that used to be her father's when a man in a hooded top appeared from the mouth of the alleyway and made a beeline for her. The sudden move caught her off guard, and she stepped back, startled. She was about to turn when she realised there was something familiar in the half-hidden face below the hood. She paused as he pulled it off and stood upright so that she could see him properly.

Still wary, she untensed and surveyed the damage her cousins had done with awe. They'd made quite a mess of one side of his face. One eye was almost swollen shut with a huge gash a couple of inches above. Fresh stitches sealed it shut, but the bruising and swelling had travelled significantly. Her first instinct was to feel sympathy for the pain he was in, and a strange protectiveness pulled her towards him. But she quickly reminded herself that this was the man who'd stalked her like prey, who'd manipulated her emotions and taken advantage of her personal trauma to get to her family. And her heart instantly hardened, beating with fresh anger.

'Not fun to look at, no?' John asked accusingly.

'Why wouldn't it be?' she snapped. 'It was me who ordered it.'

It was John's turn to step back in shock, and he did so with such a look of hurt that for a moment Scarlet felt her resolve quiver. But only for a moment.

'*You* asked them to do this to me?' he asked. He shook his head and let out a small laugh of disbelief. 'Wow. OK. I guess the stories really are true then.'

'What stories?' Scarlet asked indignantly.

'The stories of you being part of an organised crime ring. The stories that you're as hard and ruthless as they come. That wasn't the girl I met in the pub.' He shook his head once more in disappointment.

Scarlet's rage intensified. 'How dare you?' she seethed. 'Why are you even here? You *lied* to me. You *used* me to get close and bring my family down, and now I've found you out you're – what? Trying to lie even better so you can continue?' She ran her hands through her hair in agitation.

'I was never trying to get to your family,' John stressed. 'I had no idea who you were. I still don't.' He put his hand to his forehead, wincing in pain. 'It was nothing to do with work.'

'I don't believe you,' Scarlet replied. 'You were adamant you didn't want to talk about work from the off. *Life bingo*, you called it. Too boring. I should have realised something was off from that. Who doesn't ask about that sort of thing when they're getting to know someone?'

'Me!' John shot back. 'I don't. I don't like talking about my job, because when I meet new people they either ask too many questions that I can't answer, or they're put off by it.'

Scarlet's face acknowledged the truth of that last part.

'And it wasn't like you were exactly desperate to talk about your line of work either, though I'm beginning to understand why.' John looked up to the heavens with his one good eye.

Scarlet clamped her mouth shut, realising that this was probably just another way to draw her into conversation about her family. Perhaps he was even wearing a wire, some sort of last-ditch attempt to get whatever information he'd set out to acquire.

'Why are you here, John?' she asked levelly.

'I'm not entirely sure myself,' he replied, his tone falling tiredly flat. 'But I walked into that room and saw you there, and then I read your file and learned who you were – *you*, the girl I was dating, and...' He raised his hands then dropped them again to his side. 'I don't know. This has all been a shock for me too. And you weren't answering my calls and then your cousins turned up...'

A sliver of guilt made its way into Scarlet's heart at how helpless John sounded. Right there on the street before her he seemed completely lost and genuine, and part of her yearned to believe him. But she couldn't. It was all an act – none of this was real. He was still playing her, even now. But she wasn't going to fall for it this time.

'I was a fool for falling for your bullshit,' she said, her voice shaking with emotion, her cool façade shattering into a hundred sharp pieces. 'A complete idiot.'

She stepped forward with a pained glare. 'I *liked* you. I really, *really* liked you. I told you things I hadn't told anyone; I opened up about the death of my dad and what it did to me. You even made up a whole story about yourself to get me to do that. I mean, Christ!' She turned in a circle, running her hands down her face with a groan. 'Who does that? Who is that heartless?'

'Scarlet—' John started forward, but Scarlet pulled him up short, holding her finger out warningly.

'No.' She forced herself to regain her composure. 'No,' she repeated. 'You played me and you're still playing me now. And I can't do this.'

Backing away from him, Scarlet got into her car and turned on the engine. John didn't try to stop her, and she forced herself not to look back as she drove away from him and out of the road.

THIRTEEN

The wind blew through the copse of trees where Cillian and Connor stood watching the quiet country road. They kept to the shadows, mostly hidden behind the ancient trunks, enveloped in the deeper darkness the canopy above them provided in the swiftly fading light of the day. The car was hidden nearby down a farm track, behind a tall hedge.

Connor reached into his inner jacket pocket and pulled out a packet of cigarettes, but Cillian stayed his hand with his own.

'They'll see the smoke,' he warned.

Connor sighed and put the packet away. 'Fuck's sake,' he muttered. 'We've been out here for hours. I need a fag.'

'Hopefully we won't be here too much longer,' Cillian replied.

'Yeah? And what am I supposed to do till then?' Connor asked moodily.

Cillian shrugged and reached into his own pocket, where he stashed the toothpicks that kept his nicotine cravings at bay. He held one out to Connor with a grin. Connor looked down at it then up at his brother with a withering look.

'Those fucking things are the bane of my life,' he said flatly.

'I find them everywhere. *Everywhere,*' he repeated with a glare. 'I sit in my car and they're on my seat. I go to my kitchen and they're on my sideboard. I've even started to dream about the damn things. So no, Cillian, I do not want one,' he finished with an accusatory look.

He moved a couple of paces away and folded his arms, staring down the road towards the gated entrance to the estate. 'I liked you better when you smoked,' he added under his breath. 'Fucking pansy.'

'I hardly think avoiding a long painful death by lung cancer makes me a pansy,' Cillian retorted. 'But whatever.' He shot his brother a look. 'How's it going with Sandra? You been to see her again yet?' He hid the smile of amusement that so desperately wanted to curl across his face.

Connor never usually had to try to get the girls that caught his attention. Neither of them did. They had the classic tall, dark and handsome looks of their Irish heritage, which, paired with their notoriety, meant they had more than enough interest thrown their way. But of course, Connor had gone and developed an interest in the one girl who had absolutely no interest in him whatsoever.

'Not yet,' Connor replied. 'I'll pop in tomorrow, see if I can catch her in a better mood. I think maybe I just caught her on a bad day.'

Cillian turned away to hide his smirk. 'Yeah, that's probably what it was.'

'Hey, look.' Connor ducked further behind one of the larger trees and nodded towards the gate.

The glow of headlights shone through the wrought-iron bars, and they began to slowly open. Three black Range Rovers drove out onto the road in convoy, and they could just make out the outline of two people in each one.

'Six of them this time,' Cillian confirmed. 'Two less than yesterday.' He checked his watch. 'Another dinner out, it looks like.' Grace seemed to have an aversion to eating food in her own home and had gone to a different restaurant each night at roughly the same time.

'Come on, let's tail before they get too far down the road,' Connor said, agitated.

He set off back to the car and Cillian followed, filing his observations away for later. The good thing was that there was a pattern emerging, and whilst he wasn't yet sure how, he was certain his mother would soon work that to her advantage.

'We should go check out whether DI Dick's at home after,' he said as they got in the car. He switched on the engine and turned the car around. 'Start mapping out his coming and goings.'

'You don't think he's got the message?' Connor asked.

Cillian considered it for a moment as he pulled out onto the main road. 'I'm not sure. He got his claws into Scar, and there's something about him that just makes me think he ain't prepared to let this angle go that easily. I wouldn't give up at the first hurdle, if it were me.'

'But he ain't you,' Connor replied.

'No, but still. We need to keep an eye on that situation. A close one.'

Cillian thought back to the look in John's green eyes the night they'd paid him a visit. There had been no fear there, despite the violence and intimidation the brothers had doled out. No fear, just a cold hard glint of something dangerous. It could have just been pride. It could have been determination. But whatever it was, the man was stronger than he'd anticipated. And something told him that this particular problem was far from over.

FOURTEEN

John stared out of the window next to his desk into the cloudy sky beyond, absentmindedly swivelling his chair to and fro with one foot as he circled the issue that had plagued his mind for days. Scarlet.

'Any chance you'll give that pen a break any time soon?' came a slightly irritated voice from one of the other nearby desks.

He tuned in for long enough to realise he'd been tapping his biro on his desk. He stuck the lid back on and put it to his mouth, chewing the end of it, unable to just sit still.

'What's wrong with you today anyway?' the same voice asked, a little less abrasively. 'Other than your face, I mean.'

John looked over at DC Ascough, who grinned to let him know she meant no harm by her comment. He forced a smile back and sat up in his chair. He liked Ascough. She was efficient and helpful and had been one of the friendlier people on this team when he'd moved over from Essex a couple of months before. He was still finding his feet here, but she'd eased his transition a lot by showing the rest of the team that she accepted him as their new leader.

'Nothing, just thinking about a case,' he said dismissively.

He tapped his keyboard, bringing his computer screen to life and pretended to read something so she wouldn't probe any further. He'd explained his head injury away the way the twins had said. There really was no point reporting it. Aside from the fact that he couldn't actually prove it and they'd secured alibis, it would only jeopardise what he was trying to do. And that was much more important.

He'd found himself in a corner he hadn't expected and now he needed to come up with some sort of plan to redeem himself, but it was proving tricky. No matter what angle he tried, the outcome would be the same, and that wasn't good enough. He needed get things back on track, but how?

The door to their office opened and Jennings appeared, then made a beeline for his desk. As Jennings clocked his face, he made an expression of surprise.

'I know. Unfortunate incident with a dumbbell,' he said before the questions began.

'Ouch, looks bloody painful,' Jennings replied with a cringe. 'Listen, you got a minute?'

'Sure. Come through.' John stood up and gestured for Jennings to follow him to a private meeting room.

John closed the door behind them and took a seat at the desk, waiting until Jennings had sat down opposite him. 'What's up?'

Jennings leaned forward eagerly. 'I need access to your arson site, the Drew factory. Is there a safe way of me getting down to the basement?'

'Possibly. They've made it as stable as they can but I'd have to check about the basement. Why the basement?' he asked, curious.

'The Jasper Snow case I'm working on, the one we've linked Scarlet Drew to. There was some residue on the blade that had both their prints on that we couldn't place. It's some sort of chemical that's used in certain industrial paints. I have a hunch that whatever happened between them happened in that factory, and if I could link that chemical to the paint used for the walls and floors, that would give me enough to tie them all together. And I was hoping to get in the basement as I imagine that's the only area where the paint may still be intact after the fire.'

John's mind raced and his heart quickened. Was Scarlet really a cold-blooded killer? Her face flashed before his eyes the way he'd last seen it. Cold and unforgiving. Could there really be proof still in that building? Could this be his way back to redemption?

'Why haven't you been in there before now?' he asked.

'The chemical is fairly common,' Jennings admitted. 'Too common – considering her lawyer's harassment claim – to be able to get a warrant.'

'But now that it's a crime scene under my jurisdiction—' John said slowly, catching on.

'All I need is your permission,' Jennings finished smugly.

John sat back, the possibilities opening up in front of him. They swirled around his mind and he smiled. He'd let Jennings in and he'd stay by his side while he searched for this evidence. And if Jennings did find what he was looking for, then he would be right there with him when he did. This would be his way back. This would be how he redeemed himself.

'I'll take you down there myself,' he said decisively and stood up. 'Come on – let's grab what we need and head there now.' He paused, waiting for Jennings to react. 'Unless you have somewhere else you need to be?'

'No,' Jennings said hurriedly, standing up to join him. 'Not at all. I just hadn't expected the assistance. Thanks.'

'Well, it's all linked, isn't it?' John replied as he led the way out the door. 'And we've got to stick together, eh?'

He grinned and marched forward determinedly. If there

was any evidence left in the basement that could link Scarlet Drew to that murder, it was going to be found today. And John was going to be right there when it was.

FIFTEEN

Lily stared at Ruby's face, silently begging her to wake up, the same way she had every day since the fire. With each passing hour, their hope was diminishing, and the chances of her waking up were slimming. Her eyes slowly closed, the tiredness she felt beginning to press down on her like a weight. When she reopened them, the Bible Father Dan had brought with him when he'd visited caught her eye.

'What did I do, Lord?' she whispered. 'What have I done to deserve this?' She bowed her head. 'I may not follow the law of the common man, but I'm a faithful woman, and anything I've ever done was for the love of my family. Every eye I have taken is only to replace one they've taken from us, the way you commanded.'

Her words were met with silence, the way she knew they would be, and she sighed. Lily and Ronan had been born of devout Catholic parents and they'd both continued to be strong in their faith after their parents' deaths. Every Sunday morning, before the family lunch, Lily went to church to listen to Father Dan's sermon and to give thanks. Cath went too, and when she could collar them, so did the boys. Though, like Scarlet, she knew it was mainly out of respect for her.

Right now, more than ever, she needed God to hear her. But the question of why He would allow this to happen played on her mind. Was this a lesson? A punishment? If so, what for? Father Dan hadn't been able to answer her in any way that helped. He'd told her exactly what she knew he would. That God worked in mysterious ways and that she just had to trust in His judgement. It hadn't eased her fear or frustration in the slightest and that unnerved her.

God was as unreachable as Ruby right now. And if Ruby died, that meant she'd have been abandoned by them both. Which led her to the most terrifying question of all. Without faith or family, what was the point of life?

A knock at the door pulled her out of this vortex of horrifying thoughts, and for once she was grateful for the intrusion. That feeling was short-lived, however, when she saw who it was.

'I won't stay; I just wanted to drop these off to you,' Billie said respectfully as she walked in with two bulky zipped-up bags in her arms.

Lily glanced at them. 'What are they?' she asked.

'Just a few self-care bits. You've been in a few days – I thought you might want to freshen up properly instead of with the cheap nasty stuff they have here.'

Lily barked out a short laugh of disbelief. 'Self-care? My daughter is in a coma, and you thought I might want some fancy bubbles for my shower, is that what you're telling me?'

'Not just you,' Billie replied, casting her eyes down but pushing forward with a level tone. 'This bag's for Ruby. I thought her skin looked a bit dry so there's a body butter in there and some oil. You could rub some into her skin. When she wakes up, she'll feel a lot better for it.'

'Why are you doing this?' Lily snapped.

Part of her warned that she was being unfair, but another part of her was still too suspicious to take this at face value. Everyone kept telling her that this girl was different, yet here she was trying to suck up, just like the others. A schemer trying to worm her way into the family at the top of the tree.

'Like I said, I'm doing this because you're my boyfriend's mum and kindness don't kill anyone,' she replied.

'Come on, be honest,' Lily retorted. 'It's more than that, right?' She raised an eyebrow and held the girl's gaze.

Billie stared at her for a long moment. 'OK, fine. It's more than that. I admire you,' she admitted.

Lily offered a bitter smirk. 'Yeah, I'm sure you do. I'll tell you now, the respect I'm shown, the nice cars, the money, the businesses, this ain't happened overnight. It took years. Decades. And if you think—'

'I don't mean that,' Billie said, interrupting her with a deep frown. 'I couldn't give a shit about all that, to be honest.'

'Oh please,' Lily scoffed. 'You're all the same. All wannabe gangsters when you see the highlights, with no idea what it really means.'

'That ain't me at all,' Billie insisted. 'I'm happy with my life; I don't need to go envying yours. I enjoy what I do. I like where I live, I have great friends – a great boyfriend,' she added. 'All I meant was I admire you as a mum.' Flustered, she walked over to the window. 'Ruby's lucky.'

'Lucky?' Lily asked.

'Yeah, lucky to have *you*.' She stared at her again, looking suddenly tired. 'Not everyone has a mum as devoted as you. As loyal and steadfast.' She turned to gaze out of the window. 'Some of us weren't that lucky.'

Lily felt her natural aversion to the girl weaken as a wistfulness took over her expression. She watched her critically for a few moments, searching for any sign that this was just an act. But she appeared to be genuine.

'Any mum would be doing the same as I am,' she said.

Billie laughed under her breath. 'You'd think,' she said, an edge of bitterness entering her tone. 'The last time I was in hospital, my mum was nowhere to be seen. She's not talked to me or shown up in years.'

'What happened?' Lily asked, the arms she hadn't noticed folding relaxing into her lap.

Billie shrugged. 'We were close once. There were good times, good years. She can show a great deal of love when it suits her. But she also has to win at everything and at all costs. She plays a lot of games. For years, if I called her out or didn't agree with something she wanted me to, she'd twist the tables and make me out to be a problem to anyone who'd listen. Turn herself into a victim or martyr, all while throwing me under the bus. And for years – for the sake of peace – I'd accept the blame just to move on. Because it was always the same – whatever it was about didn't actually matter; her being right did. Even when she wasn't.

'But there comes a point when you can't just accept that anymore. And I reached it a few years ago. She'd started some trouble and it backfired, and instead of apologising or making things right, she threw me in to take the blame.' She shrugged. 'It was nothing new. But it was a big one, and I ain't heard from her since. Not even when I really needed her.'

She twisted her mouth and looked away, blinking hard. 'I've gone through some of the hardest times in my life without her, because it meant more to her to play the victim and act out the tragedy than to fix things and be my mum.'

Lily pursed her lips in disapproval. She thought about her own three children and knew she could never do that to them. Even when she disagreed with them, even when they'd done terrible things – and all of them had at one point or another – she couldn't dream of doing anything but support them. She'd lie for them, steal for them – she'd argue their cases with the devil himself, if she had to. Acting the way Billie's mum had went against everything she believed in. Even the *idea* of a wedge between her and her babies sent a shiver down her spine. They were her life.

'Maybe she'll come round one day,' she offered, not sure what else to say.

Billie smiled sadly. 'No. I'm not the first person she's cut off for not taking her shit anymore. It's just the way she is.'

'But you still miss her,' Lily observed.

'Every single day,' Billie replied, a stray tear escaping and rolling down her cheek. She wiped it away. 'Sometimes I let myself hope her good side will override the rest, that she'll turn up and set things right. But I've never seen her take responsibility or apologise for a single thing in her life. So it's highly unlikely. Anyway. I didn't mean to go into all that. You don't need my problems – you've got your own.'

Lily looked over to Ruby, feeling a sudden rush of pity for Billie. She knew how it felt to go through life without parents. It was as though you lived with a huge gap in your soul. But her parents had died, so she'd at least known that she and Ronan had been loved. They hadn't chosen to go. She couldn't imagine how it must feel to have a parent choose self-righteous stubbornness over being a part of your life.

Perhaps she had been wrong about the girl, she grudgingly thought. The protective side of her personality reared up at the thought. There was bound to be something wrong with Billie, it whispered, and she needed to find it before she could hurt Cillian.

She forced it away. Protectiveness had always been her overriding instinct. But maybe this time things were different. Maybe this time she needed to step back and give the girl a chance. Billie's outburst had revealed a lot. She wasn't after their money or status. She was drawn to them because deep down she was seeking a family. Somewhere she felt she could belong, be anchored, now she'd been set adrift by her own kin.

Lily couldn't give her that, because however much the girl wanted a family, theirs wasn't hers But now she'd realised she wasn't the threat she'd initially feared, she could at least give her a chance. For Cillian.

She moved her gaze over to the zipped-up bags Billie had placed on the table beside her and picked one up. Opening it, she reached in and pulled out a tub of body butter.

'Eucalyptus and lemongrass,' she read. She pulled a face of approval.

'They're both good for mental stimulation. I thought maybe, you know.' She shrugged. 'For Ruby.'

Lily nodded. 'I'll put some on her skin after the next doctor's round. He's due soon.' She glanced at Billie. 'It is a bit dry, like you said.'

It was a subtle shift but they both recognised it, and Billie gave her a small smile. This was to be a fresh start between them. Lily just hoped she was doing the right thing.

'I'd better go – I have a client due soon. There's an oil in the bag for her face too, when the bandage comes off.'

Just then there was a strange sound and the machine that was attached to Ruby began to beep at an alarming rate. Lily's heart paused in her chest and her eyes grew wide. What was happening?

She stood up abruptly and sent the chair skittering backward. 'Nurse!' she shouted, looking over her shoulder to the closed door. 'Quickly. Nurse!' she yelled again, as loud as she could.

'I'll get help,' Billie said, running towards the door. But as she touched the handle, the door burst open and a nurse flew in, the doctor hot on her heels.

The nurse swept Lily out of the way, gently but firmly, so that the doctor could get to Ruby's side. He glanced at the machine and then checked her pulse and shone a small light in her eyes. He pulled her hand up and began rubbing it – hard. 'Ruby? Can you hear me? Ruby?'

'What's happening?' Lily demanded, her heart hammering inside her chest as terror took over.

Was this it? Was Ruby dying?

The machine's beeping rang like a fire bell inside her head, screaming out its warning. Lily tried to push forward, cold terror seeping into her bones.

'Please, what's happening?' she begged. 'Let me past.'

The nurse held her back, despite her struggles. 'Let the doctor do his job,' she urged, not unkindly.

Lily felt her fear spiral, and with it came a flurry of anger towards the nurse. She just wanted to get to her daughter. Who the hell was this woman to get in her way?

'I said let me through,' she shouted, fighting against the woman barring her way with more determination than before.

'Mrs Drew...' the nurse began, holding her ground.

'Let me through, for fuck's sake!' Lily's voice rose as she began to panic. 'Let me see my daughter!'

'Mum?'

The word was quiet, the wobbly voice tired and raspy. But it was enough to stop her in her tracks. Her pounding heart skipped a beat and soared.

'Ruby,' she whispered reverently.

The doctor stepped back and the nurse moved aside, and Lily stared as Ruby's eyes fluttered open and searched the room for hers. As their gazes met, Lily fell to her knees next to the bed with a sob and grasped Ruby's hand as though she would never let go.

SIXTEEN

Cillian ran his fingers lightly down Billie's bare back as she lay in the bed next to him, content and replete. Her big blue eyes held his gaze and the corner of her mouth turned up into a slow, lazy smile.

'What are you thinking about?' she asked.

Cillian bit his bottom lip and trailed his hand further down over her buttocks as he considered deflecting with a flirty joke but then decided to answer her. 'That plod who went under-cover to get Scarlet. It bothers me, that he got so close.'

'At least you found out before he got anywhere. That's the main thing, right?'

'Technically. But we were lucky. They fucked up at the station, blew his cover by accident. If they hadn't, we still wouldn't know. She'd still be dating him, growing closer, sharing secrets.' He shook his head. 'We've never been infiltrated that closely before. She dropped the ball; she was stupid.'

Billie's eyebrows shot up accusingly.

'Look, I love her to bits, but when it comes to boyfriends, she's totally blind. And it makes her vulnerable. All of us.'

'Doesn't love and lust do that to everyone?' Billie asked.

'No,' Cillian replied with a shake of his head. 'The rest of us have always been careful. We have to be.'

'Is that right? How do you know *I'm* not a copper?' Billie asked, her eyes dancing with mischief. She twisted onto her side to face him and ran her nail down his chest. 'I could be undercover. How do you know I've not just dazzled you into a false sense of security so I can learn all *your* secrets, hm? How do you know I'm not building a case against you right now?'

Cillian grabbed her wrists and pushed her back roughly, pinning her arms above her head and straddling her. He put his face close to hers with a dark, menacing expression. Her breath caught in her throat as she stared back at him.

'For both our sakes, I hope you're not,' he whispered in a low dangerous tone. 'Because if I found out you were, I'd kill you.' His intense gaze burned into hers as his grip tightened on her arms. 'I wouldn't want to because I've genuinely grown to love you. But if I found out you'd played me the way that copper did Scarlet, if I found you trying to take us down, I'd take you out first. I wouldn't have a choice.'

The truth in his words scared even him, as he realised for the first time that this would be exactly what he'd have to do, if he found himself in that position. His eyes searched her face as a seed of doubt crept into his mind for the first time. She was just joking around – she had to be, he assured himself.

'Cillian...'

Billie's voice broke through his thoughts, and he realised he was still squeezing her arms. He released them gently.

'Did you just say you love me?' she asked.

Cillian blinked, going back over his words. Had he said that? He hadn't meant to. It was too soon, and it was something he'd never said to a woman before. But Billie seemed to bring things out in him in a way no one else ever had.

'Yeah, I guess I did,' he said slowly.

Her blue eyes crinkled up warmly as she smiled. 'Good,' she

replied. 'I was beginning to worry you were just using me for my essential oils.' She pulled a face and Cillian laughed.

'I have taken quite a fancy to the lavender,' he replied.

He bent his head down and kissed her deeply, pushing his naked body even closer to hers, and Billie wrapped her arms around him. He trailed his kisses down her jawline and over her neck. Her breathing quickened and her body responded to his touch as he moved down and ran his hands down her sides.

'Cillian,' she breathed.

'Mm?' he murmured, reaching her stomach with his mouth.

'I love you too.'

Cillian grinned with triumph. 'Good,' he said, lifting his head to look at her for a moment, a devious glint in his eye. 'Because I'm about to ruin you for any other man ever again,' he promised, grabbing her legs and pulling her sharply up towards his face. He lowered his mouth, holding her gaze as she began to moan.

'Oh my God.' She threw her head back and gave in as he worked her body the way he knew she liked. 'Ruin me, I don't care. Just never stop that. Never.'

SEVENTEEN

Scarlet took her time to study some of the market's produce. A couple of the stallholders nodded to her, one tipping his hat in respect. She nodded back but didn't stop to talk, wandering instead from one stall to the next. Pausing, she picked up a hat and pretended to study it, angling herself so that she could see behind her in the long mirror standing to one side.

Clocking a middle-aged man in the distance with his hands pushed down deep in his jacket pockets and a cap pulled low over his face, she made a sound of angry frustration. For the past couple of days, Jennings had been turning up everywhere like a bad penny. Clearly, she wasn't being tailed officially, as it had only been him and she was pretty sure this was below his pay grade. If it had been on the record, he'd have had members of his team do the groundwork.

No, this was his own little mission. His hatred towards her was evidently so strong that he couldn't bear to leave her to roam free. But it was starting to cause problems, restricting her and forcing her to hold fire on so many pressing jobs.

Looking around the busy market, she pondered what to do. She tried to come up with a decent angle, but whichever way she looked at it the answer was the same. She'd have to leave here empty-handed today and just hope that one of her cousins could pick up her slack. This wasn't ideal as they were all already so stretched, but she couldn't let on to Jennings why she was really here. He could never know about the money they laundered through these stalls.

She placed the hat back on the counter and turned away from the stall, walking slowly down the middle of the wide pathway. Their first stall came up on the right-hand side and the stallholder caught her eye. She subtly shook her head, a warning look. The woman immediately turned and busied herself.

Scarlet's eyes searched the sidelines until they rested on Jamie, their watcher. Jamie was a young man of eighteen who they paid to watch over their stalls when the police or the market inspectors came sniffing around, among other things. Casually drawing her hands together in front of her where Jennings couldn't see, she flashed him three fingers and then four. A clear simple code that relayed a warning.

The young man's head barcly moved as he gave her one small nod of understanding, then he pulled down his cap over his spotty young face and began to type out a text. Scarlet breathed in deeply and forced herself to relax.

She saw the next stallholder in their line-up glance down at his phone and then turn pointedly away from her. The warning had been received. And Jennings was none the wiser to any of the communication that had gone on right in front of his eyes.

Stopping at a fruit and veg stall, Scarlet bought some oranges. She took the brown paper bag and received her change, then turned and walked back towards where she'd left her car. Jennings quickly dived behind one of the stalls, still convinced he hadn't been spotted. She would have laughed, had the situation been less dire.

As she passed his hiding place, she stifled the urge to turn and glare at him, knowing she had to keep up her pretence if he wasn't going to suspect foul play. As far as he knew, she'd come here for the fruit, nothing else. He should leave the place alone.

The busy chatter of the market faded away behind her as she reached her car and got in, dumping the bag of oranges on the passenger seat. Yes, he should leave the market alone, but what about her? He had it out for her, and despite the lack of evidence, it appeared he was never going to stop. Was he going to follow her around forever? What did he think he was going to find exactly?

She turned the car around and sped off down the road, annoyed that her attempts at collecting the money off the market had been thwarted.

How was she supposed to work like this? There had to be a way to make him stop. To get him off her back for good.

But how?

EIGHTEEN

It had been several days since Ruby had come out of her coma. Exactly how many, she wasn't sure. All the days seemed to blur together, between doctors' rounds and sleep. It seemed crazy to her, because she'd just woken from what was effectively a marathon of a sleep, but Ruby was still completely exhausted. Each day was a little less tiring, which was something, but the pain hadn't lessened much yet. The raw skin on the side of her face and neck still burned and stung no matter how still she lay. But they'd told her this would start to ease soon. Apparently, the real damage had been on the inside. The reason she'd fallen into the coma in the first place had been due to the smoke inhalation. The smoke had filled her lungs and there hadn't been enough oxygen. The doctors had told her she was lucky she'd not suffered brain damage. That the coma had been her body's way of protecting her until she was out of that danger.

Lucky. She thought the word over with bitterness. She felt anything but lucky right now.

Lily placed the last of Ruby's things in the bag and zipped it up, handing it to Connor. Ruby ignored the very final sound for a few moments, continuing to stare out of the window.

'Rubes?' Cillian asked gently. 'You ready?'

She wanted to say no but knew she couldn't. They'd discharged her already. She no longer had a place here. She nodded, despite her true feelings, immediately regretting the action as the tight new skin on her neck pulled. Cillian grasped the handles of her wheelchair and swung her round towards the door as she swallowed down the pain.

Unlike her burns, her chest didn't feel too awful. Which was surprising, considering the damage the doctors described. It seemed the coma had worked its magic, helping her heal quicker than she otherwise might have. She couldn't breathe in too deeply or her chest felt tight, as though she'd had an infection, and there was a sensitivity that hadn't been there before when she pulled in each breath, but otherwise she felt almost normal.

'I can walk, you know,' she said quietly as they entered the hallway.

'Yeah, I know,' he replied. 'I reckon you just faked it all really, so you could get me to push you around.'

She heard the smile in his tone as he joked and tried to force one on her own face. Once more, fresh pain rippled through the ravaged side of her face and her spirits sank.

They moved together as a family unit, Lily at the front with Connor, and Cillian and Ruby bringing up the rear. Lily talked on, reminding Ruby of all the doctor had said she must do, but Ruby tuned out. She already knew what she needed to do. They'd only been reminded by the doctor half an hour before.

They soon reached the front entrance of the hospital, the sunny sky outside beckoning them, and Ruby felt a sudden sense of panic overwhelm her. She wasn't ready to leave this place. She felt safe here, looked after. In here, the outside didn't exist. Time, days, responsibilities, no matter how small, just all disappeared. In here, she was just a patient getting well, but out there she would have to face the real world once more. Out there, she would have to be Ruby Drew again, except now she was an even more damaged version than before. And what's more, everyone would be able to see that.

She grasped the arms of the wheelchair in a tight grip and locked her jaw, the panic turning into a strange feeling of grief and loss as they passed through the doors. She closed her eyes, feeling more vulnerable than she ever had in her life. But she knew she couldn't utter her protests out loud.

'You OK?' Cillian noticed the change in her stance.

'Yeah—'

Lily stopped talking and walking and turned around to look at her, a flash of fear crossing her face as she searched to see what was wrong. Her mother had been like this from the second Ruby had woken up. Anxious, worried. The fire had done something to them all, it seemed.

Ruby forced her body to relax. 'I'm fine. Just tired. Looking forward to being home,' she lied.

'Yeah, 'course,' Lily said, looking relieved. 'I bet you are after being stuck in here for so long. Let's get you back and settled into your room, eh? Connor...' Lily turned her attention to her son. 'Go get the car and meet us here, save Rubes the trip to the car park.'

'Will do.' He took the keys from her outstretched hand and set off.

Lily turned to Ruby with a smile. 'Not long now, love. We'll get you home, you can have a rest and then we'll have a nice dinner together as a family tonight, yeah? Get your aunt Cath and Scarlet round. That will be nice, won't it?'

'Yeah,' Ruby replied. She looked away, hiding the ever growing feeling that she was sinking into a dark and endless abyss.

NINETEEN

John made a beeline for the coffee machine in the shared kitchen down the hallway from his office. It had been yet another sleepless night of tossing and turning as he thought about Scarlet Drew and the conundrum he was now in. Not that this had been the only thing keeping him up. All his cases were heating up, and juggling them was proving to be a round-the-clock task. He'd be happy when at least one of them was wrapped up and off his plate.

A box of donuts sat on the kitchen side with a note telling people to help themselves. He eyed up a vanilla ring. Perhaps something sweet would pick him up and help him feel a bit more on the ball. He picked it up and took a bite, savouring the sugary dough and licking the sweet powder from his lips.

'Hey, guv,' came a voice from behind him. He turned to see that Ascough had walked in with a file. 'The initial crime-scene photos came in from the Heath murder. It ain't pretty.'

On instinct, John looked down at the open file she pushed towards him and immediately wished he hadn't. 'Jesus!' he exclaimed, pulling back.

'Yeah, like I said. It ain't pretty. We're going to have our work cut out for us solving this one,' she replied.

John looked at the donut in his hand with a regretful sigh and put it down. Suddenly he wasn't in the mood to eat. 'We'll go down and take a look in a bit – I just need to tie something up here first.'

'OK, guv.' She smiled up at him. 'I was just going to make myself a coffee. I'll do yours,' she offered.

'Oh, no need—' he began.

'No, it's no trouble,' she insisted. 'I'll bring it to your desk.' Her blue eyes held his for longer than they needed to, and he pulled his gaze away with a look of acceptance.

'Well, thank you,' he said walking out of the kitchen.

He turned down the main hallway, away from his office, DC Ascough still on his mind. She'd been nice to him from the off, having his back with the team as he got to grips with this new station. He'd assumed it was just kindness towards a newbie, but was it more than that? She was always smiling and going out of her way to do things for him, like just now. Was she flirting with him?

Reaching the bank of lifts, he shook it off. Of course she wasn't flirting with him. He was her boss. She was just doing her job and working towards her own future. He'd got his boss coffee many times. It was just good sense to make yourself useful, to make your record stand out from the rest.

John travelled down a level and walked through the busy floor towards Jennings' office. It had been three days since they'd carefully climbed down into the basement of the Drews' factory. The place had been in a state, steel beams had collapsed down through the ceiling and piles of rubble littered the floor, but other than that the basement had been mainly intact. The upper floor was all but gone, just part of the shell remaining. The ground floor was covered in debris and twisted lumps of metal where the machines once stood.

The firefighters had cleared a path through the middle as they worked on clearing things up and had managed to unblock the way down to the basement. Initially they hadn't wanted to allow the two detectives access, claiming it still wasn't safe enough. But after some persuasive conversation, they had given them hard hats and escorted them down.

Jennings had scratched the paint up from the floor in several places, where it was clear enough to do so, whilst John had watched with bated breath. If these samples showed the same chemical as they'd identified on the knife, then that would potentially be enough to put Scarlet away for the murder. They'd taken it straight to Forensics and had been told it would be back with them today. So far he'd heard nothing from Jennings, and the suspense was beginning to wear on his nerves. He knew it was likely because there had been nothing yet to share, but he figured it wouldn't hurt to go and check anyway.

As he approached Jennings' office, he could see the other man through the glass wall and open blinds within. He was on the phone and his expression seemed excited. John sped up a little, his heart matching his step.

As he reached the office, he saw Jennings' expression turn to one of victory and his fist slam down on the desk with a cry of glee. He opened the door and leaned in expectantly.

'Yep. Yep, OK. Email me the results and get the evidence back in the locker. Thanks.' Jennings put down the phone and turned to John with shining eyes.

'We've got her. We've fucking got her,' he cried, his smile lighting up his entire face.

'The chemicals match?' John asked, his heart now racing.

'More than that, Richards,' Jennings replied. 'Not only do the chemicals match, but they've found traces of Jasper Snow's blood. We've hit the evidence jackpot.'

He grabbed his jacket and moved around the desk. 'I'm heading over to arrest her now. And this time she's got no way to wriggle out of it. Not now we've got proof that both he and the knife with her prints on were there that night.'

His cold grin widened. 'I'll have her sent down by the end of the week.'

TWENTY

Scarlet crossed the road quickly, weaving between the flow of traffic. She held her bag close to her side. Inside was the takings from a number of their protection clients, ready to be laundered through the books at the salon. She'd actually managed to collect them today, unfollowed for a change.

Cath was now running the books behind the scenes, with a little help from Sandra. The pair worked well together, and despite her general outspokenness and tendency to speak before she thought, Sandra had displayed a subtle tact towards Cath, helping her to gently ease into the underworld she'd avoided for so long. She understood, to a surprising degree for someone who hadn't known Cath for very long, how hard it was for her to make this transition and seemed to be trying to make it as easy as she could. Scarlet was eternally grateful to her for this. It had taken a huge weight off her shoulders.

Sirens blared in the distance as she reached the other side of the road and climbed the steps towards the higher-level pavement. Scarlet heard them but paid no attention. This was London. It was an odd day if there weren't a few sirens screaming away in the background. But as she reached the salon, she heard them draw closer and she looked back with a frown as the glass door shut behind her. Blue lights appeared at the end of the road and came hurtling towards them.

'Hello, love,' Cath said warmly as she entered. 'Fancy a cuppa?'

'Not just now, Mum,' Scarlet answered, distracted.

She watched the car draw closer. Only one, but it was certainly in a hurry. Sandra wandered over and stood next to her, glancing out at the road and then back to her with a questioning expression on her pretty face.

The car screeched to a stop on the road below and as Scarlet caught a flash of Jennings' face through the windscreen, she instantly jumped back away from the door.

'Shit,' she cursed. Her heart began to race. Whatever was going on, it wasn't good. And she had thousands of pounds of hot cash on her. She quickly turned and marched towards the back, opening the bag.

'What's happening?' she heard Cath ask.

Sandra hurried after her and fell into step.

'Take this and go – quickly,' Scarlet ordered, pulling out the bulging plastic bag full of cash. 'You know what to do. Wait for me or Lil to contact you.'

'Got it.' Without hesitation, Sandra grabbed the bag and ran through the back room out the fire escape and into the car park beyond. The door swung closed behind her and Scarlet let out a breath of relief before turning back towards the front of the salon with a grim expression.

She had no idea why Jennings was there, only that he had it in for her. For all they knew, this could be a spot raid and the last thing they needed was for that money to be found. They had a contingency plan in place just in case things like this happened, and she was glad now that they did. Sandra would hide the money in a specified location and leave it there until one of them let her know the coast was clear. With that out of the way, there was nothing left on site that could incriminate them. Or at least she hoped there wasn't. She racked her brains, mentally checking everything off, hoping there was nothing she could have forgotten.

'Scarlet...' Cath had left the reception desk and was hurrying towards her, looking worried. 'What's going on? Tell me.'

'I don't know,' Scarlet admitted. 'But if they ask, Sandra was never here. OK?'

'OK,' Cath replied as the door swung open and Jennings marched in. Crawley followed close behind.

'Scarlet Drew, I'm arresting you on suspicion of murder. You do not have to say anything—' Jennings started, walking towards her with open cuffs.

'Oh, not this again,' Cath snapped loudly, talking over him as he continued with his statement. 'What is wrong with you people?'

He continued regardless, ignoring her as he slapped the cuffs over Scarlet's wrists.

'Are you fucking kidding me?' Scarlet demanded hotly. 'We've been over this.'

He continued talking and she felt her temper rise. 'Didn't my lawyer already put in a complaint of harassment? This is getting ridiculous now. You don't have anything on me.'

'We've always had something on you, Scarlet,' he replied. 'It just wasn't enough. But that's all changed.' He grinned at her, the action cold and unnerving.

Scarlet shivered, suddenly uncertain. 'What are you talking about?'

He pushed her forward and out of the building. 'You'll see soon enough.'

They descended the steps to the road, and Crawley ran ahead to open the car door. Pushing her head down, Jennings manoeuvred her into the back seat. Scarlet swallowed, her panic rising. What could they possibly have on her? They already had the knife and luckily it hadn't been enough. What more could they have found?

Jennings paused and considered her with contempt. 'You really should have cut a deal with me when you had the chance,' he said. And with that he slammed the door.

TWENTY-ONE

Ruby woke suddenly, unsure what had roused her from her dream. It wasn't entirely unwelcome, as the dream had been more of a nightmare. She'd been stuck on a merry-go-round, unable to get off. The lights had flashed, and painted horses had danced, but it never seemed to stop. All around there was glass, stopping her from joining the world beyond. It had felt lonely and frightening, the attractive ride not at all as fun as it looked.

She slipped off the bed, careful not to pull her aching wounds. She'd heard it said that dreams were a reflection of your subconscious thoughts. Did she believe that? She wasn't sure. But either way, she was glad to be awake.

She blinked away the sleep and glanced out of the window, drawing in a careful breath to test the pain in her lungs. It wasn't too bad, still tight, but no worse than before. Her bedside lamp was on, but outside it was dark. She must have been asleep for hours. With a frown she checked the clock and saw that it was almost midnight.

Walking over to the mirror on the wall, she forced herself to look up at her face. They had taken off the bandages today and the devastation beneath had almost killed her to look at. But she had to look at it. Because whether she liked it or not, everyone else would see it.

A lump formed in her throat as she stared at the raw rippled red skin that stretched from one side of her forehead down over her cheekbone. It trailed from there down her neck and continued over her shoulder.

They'd told her she was lucky, that she must have somehow protected the rest of her head and face before the flames could reach further. *Lucky*, she thought bitterly. There was that word again. People kept throwing it around like confetti since she'd woken up, as if somehow it made her new hellish reality any better. It didn't.

Her eyes moved to her hair. It was a lot shorter than it had been before. Her wild tight red curls stood out proudly from her head, too short for gravity to pull them downwards anymore. It suited her angular face, softening it somehow. But despite that, she still felt bitter. She shouldn't have had to have it cut. She knew there had been no choice, but still. It was just another reminder of all that had been taken from her in that fire.

Voices drifted up from the house below and she turned towards the partially open door. This must be what had woken her up. She moved to the door and listened. A man whose voice she didn't recognise spoke and she frowned. Who was visiting the house at this time of night?

She left her room, padding softly along the thick carpet, careful not to make a noise, crept down two-thirds of the stairs and then took a seat, pulling the long sleeves of her loose jumper over her hands and wrapping her arms around her legs. She could hear clearly enough from here without having to let anyone know she was there. Whoever it was, she didn't feel like seeing or talking to anyone right now.

'It's bad news, Lil,' the male voice said tiredly.

'Robert, just spit it out,' Lily said, barely managing to hide her irritation.

Ruby placed the voice as soon as Lily said his name. Robert Cheyney was the family lawyer. A man who was very good at his job, and, luckily for them, as bent as they came. *Why was he here?* she wondered.

'When the fire turned the factory into a crime scene, the site moved under the jurisdiction of the DI in charge of that case,' he began.

Ruby shivered and squeezed her eyes shut as his words triggered the memory of being trapped in the office with smoke all around and no way out. Blazing hot air filling her lungs, the sensation that she was somehow burning and drowning at the same time. She forced herself to breathe slowly and open her eyes. She was home. She wasn't there. She was safe now.

'This meant that DC Jennings was able to go on site in search of evidence for *his* case, with just that DI's approval.'

'But he had no warrant,' Lily replied, alarm in her tone.

'He didn't need one. Like I said, it's not your call right now.' Robert sighed. 'He collected some samples from the floor of the basement. Unlike the other levels, the basement was fairly well sealed, so it didn't sustain the same level of damage. They were able to get a fair bit of evidence.'

There was a long silence, and Ruby tried to piece together what was happening. The clock in the hallway ticked on, seeming louder with every passing second as she waited for her mother or anyone else in the room to respond.

When Lily spoke, her voice was heavy with dread. 'They found Jasper's blood, didn't they?'

'They did,' he confirmed.

The sound of someone breaking down in tears came into the hallway and for the first time Ruby was aware that her aunt Cath was in the room too.

'That *cunt*,' Cillian spat. 'It was *him*, in charge of that case. Lover boy. John Richards. *He* let Jennings in.'

'We should have killed him when we had the fucking chance,' Connor added angrily.

'Along with his blood, they found traces of a chemical that was also found on the knife,' Robert continued. 'It ties everything together. The knife was found with both their prints, they tied that same knife to a nick on his hand made not long before death, and now they have both the knife and his blood in the Drew factory basement. The only thing more condemning at this point for Scarlet would be an outright confession.'

'So what can we do?' Lily asked.

'Right now, with all of that against her, there's nothing we can do. I've advised her not to say anything for now, but to be honest I can't see any way out. No judge in the world could ignore that much evidence.'

Cath's sobs increased and then became slightly muffled, as though she'd turned her face into someone's shoulder for comfort. Ruby blinked, her brow furrowing even despite the pain it caused. Was her cousin really going to go down for murder? She'd never liked Scarlet. Indeed, she had daydreamed countless times about bad things happening to her, but she'd never really meant it. Whilst she wanted nothing more than to put the stuffy little cow in her place, she didn't wish her a life sentence for murder.

'What if they did ignore it,' Lily said slowly. 'What if they were paid off to ignore it. Do we have a way of making that happen?'

'We've never tried to get a judge in hand before,' Robert replied, his tone uneasy. 'That sort of thing would likely take months and a very cautious approach. And even then, only really if we'd identified someone with a weakness that could be manipulated to our advantage. It's no easy task even with all ducks in a row. Getting a pocket plod is hard enough, but judges...' He trailed off and made a sound of uncertainty.

'We have to try,' Lily replied. 'We can't just sit here and do nothing. Can you at least look into who she's likely to get?'

There was another silence and Ruby strained to hear.

'I'll find out what I can, but this isn't a plan to rely on,' he eventually said. 'You need to think up a plan B or start coming to terms with the fact that Scarlet isn't getting out of this one.'

There was a small noise and then Cath moved into the hallway, rubbing the tears that were falling freely from her cheeks. Her face was distraught and pale, and she didn't notice Ruby huddled up on the stairs as she made her way into the kitchen. The fridge door opened and closed, and Ruby heard her pour out a glass of wine.

'We're not coming to terms with anything,' Lily said, her tone hard. 'We didn't get to where we are as a family by rolling over every time we found ourselves in a corner. There is always a way out. *Always*,' she emphasised.

'And I understand that completely, but this time is different, Lily. She isn't in a corner, she's in a *cell*.' His voice grew more strained with every word. 'And they have everything they need. There's no smidgen of doubt to manipulate or inside person to utilise.'

'What about if we paid someone to take her place, to say they did it?' Connor piped up. At least Ruby assumed it was Connor. It was hard to tell the twins apart from voice only at times. 'There must be someone we can find, desperate enough for the money for their family or something.'

'They'd see straight through it,' Robert said dismissively. 'Maybe if they didn't have her prints, but they do. Look...' Ruby heard the sound of springs creaking as he stood up. 'I'll see what I can find out and get the information to you. We'll just have to take things from there.' His voice grew louder as he approached the hallway, and Ruby shrank back against the wall.

Surely there had to be more to it than that? Like her mother had said, there had to be a way out. Wasn't there? All her life the police had never really scared her. She'd always been wary of them of course. That was the way she'd been raised, to steer clear and stay off their radar. But in the back of her mind, they were never a very real threat. They might drag one of them in for questioning now and then or throw them in for an overnighter to scare them, but they always let them go. The Drews were too smart to ever be sent down. They were always two steps ahead. Or at least they had been up until now. Was Scarlet really going to be sent down for murder? Was their family really that vulnerable?

'I'll walk you out,' Lily said.

Robert appeared in the hallway then paused, turning back to face Lily tiredly. 'You know I'd do whatever it takes if it were possible. I've pulled you and Ronan out of all sorts of charges over the years. But you two never faced a case with so much stacked against you.'

Ruby could just see her mother's folded arms and the front of her golden curls move as she nodded.

'I'm sorry,' Robert said with a regretful shrug. 'I'll be in touch.' With that, he walked to the front door and left.

Lily stepped forward into the hallway, her eyes trained on Cath as she reappeared from the kitchen. Her face was drawn with grief and she opened her mouth to speak, but Lily got there first.

'We'll get her out, Cath,' she said with more conviction than she could possibly have felt. 'I promise you.'

'How, Lil?' Cath shot back in a wobbly voice. 'She's fucked. He's told you that to your face. Even you don't have the power to override all that she's facing.'

Lily's mouth opened to answer, but for once no words came out.

Cath closed her eyes in despair. 'Exactly,' she whispered. Turning on her heel, she disappeared back into the kitchen.

Lily's stricken gaze followed her for a moment, then Ruby's

breath caught in her throat as her mother's head swivelled to lock eyes with her. She showed no surprise to see Ruby there, like she'd sensed her all along. Lily always seemed to know when someone was watching. She always seemed to know everything. But as Ruby stared into her mother's horrified expression, she realised that Lily wasn't as all-knowing as she'd always thought. For the first time in her life, this was something her mother couldn't fix.

TWENTY-TWO

Lily closed her eyes and exhaled slowly through her nose, trying to calm the worries that raced around and around in her head. She'd been up half the night with Cath, trying to come up with some sort of plan to get around Scarlet's dilemma, but she'd hit nothing but brick walls. Short of stealing a tank to smash into the prison to break her out and go on the run, there was nothing they could do. Even that idea had a million pitfalls.

She took one last drag on her cigarette and then chucked it out of the car window. It was early, barely seven, and the morning air was clean and crisp around them. Not something they were used to, living in the city. Birds sang and the leaves on the trees around them rustled lazily in the breeze. She could see why Grace enjoyed living out here.

'Are you sure you want to do this right now?' Cillian asked from the seat next to her. 'We could wait until a better time.'

'There's never a good time,' Lily responded. 'There's nothing we can do for Scarlet until Robert comes back with the name of the judge. What do you suggest we do until then, sit around and twiddle our thumbs?'

She thought back to the wobble in Scarlet's voice when she'd called from the station. The one call she'd been allowed after being arrested. She'd sounded so scared, despite trying to hide it. Only Robert had been allowed in to see her, and it cut her to the bone, not being able to talk to her in person, assure her that everything was going to be OK.

No, she couldn't bear the thought of sitting around waiting. Time moved slower and worries grew into monstrous beings. She had to keep busy, keep moving forward, no matter what. And when the time came when they could do something to help Scarlet, she would be ready.

Cillian held his hands up in a gesture of defeat. 'I was just saying.'

'Well, less saying, more doing, yeah?' She opened the car door. 'Come on.'

Stepping out, she waited for Connor to get out from the back and for Cillian to join them on their side of the car. She stared through the trees that hid their car to the tall wall a few metres away. The twins had identified a weak spot in Grace's impressive estate. The cameras would have still picked up their approach, but they'd been careful to arrive in the early hours when it was likely the surveillance wouldn't be too closely watched. Cillian had also moved the camera that focused on the locked side gate just enough to give them a blind spot to hide the car and to cover their entry.

'Are you ready?' Lily asked, glancing at each one of them in turn.

Both Connor and Cillian had guns in their hands and Connor cocked his as she spoke. They weren't usually so tooled up, the penalty for being caught with a firearm being anything from five to fourteen years inside. But in this particular instance the threat of Grace and her men weighed heavier, and Lily wasn't taking any chances.

They made their way towards the side gate. Cillian swiftly picked the padlock and looked up at Lily.

'They could just be waiting for us to get inside,' he whispered.

'They could be,' she agreed. 'But either way, it doesn't matter. What matters is sticking to the plan. OK?' She gave each of them a sharp glance and they nodded.

Within seconds, the gate was open and they silently filed in. Lily led the way down the edge of the large Jacobean manor house and stuck to the shadows as they made their way towards the back. There was no one waiting to jump out at them and no thudding footsteps running their way, just the sounds of the world coming to life around them.

Lily slowed to a stop as they neared the back and heard the low rumble of voices in quiet conversation. A teacup clinked onto a plate and a chair creaked as someone shifted their weight just around the corner. She took a long, slow breath then turned and nodded to the twins.

They fell in behind her, one each side, and she stepped out into the bright sunlight covering the breakfast patio. At once the two men sitting at the table with Grace jumped up, one of them equipped with his own firearm. He lifted it swiftly and pointed it at Lily, but his gaze darted uneasily between Connor and Cillian as he realised he was outgunned.

Grace was facing away and had paused as her men jumped to attention, the teacup in her hand suspended in mid-air. She half turned towards the noise of their approach then placed the cup carefully back in the saucer.

'It's not very good manners to interrupt someone's breakfast this way,' she said, her smooth, eloquent voice cutting through the air.

Lily stepped forward, carefully rounding Grace's men at a distance as Connor and Cillian followed, their guns trained on their opponents' faces.

'It's not very good manners to burn someone's business to the ground, but there we go,' Lily replied, coming to a stop on the other side of the table where she could face the woman.

Grace's pale blue eyes held hers coldly but gave nothing away. 'We could go back and forth with these examples all day, but I doubt you came all this way for small talk.'

'No. I didn't.' Lily carefully stepped forward and took the seat opposite Grace, just vacated by the man without a weapon.

He looked at Lily, then at Connor's gun, then turned to Grace for instruction. She narrowed her eyes for a moment, clearly deciding what to do. Lily held her gaze boldly and waited. After a few moments, Grace lifted her hand to tell her men to step back. They fell in behind her, the way the twins stood behind Lily, and all the guns remained tensely pointed at the other party.

'The girl lived then?' Grace asked, her tone lazy and uninterested. She picked her tea back up and sipped it as she watched Lily across the table.

'She did,' Lily replied. 'You wouldn't be sat here now if she hadn't.'

Grace's face creased up into a mocking smile. 'What an interesting thought,' she said in a clipped tone. Her gaze narrowed. 'Why don't you tell me why you're here? It's not to kill me, which is wise on your part. You'd be dead before the bullet could reach me, were one of your sons to pull the trigger. But of course you know that. Which begs the question as to what you could possibly gain from this forced meeting?'

Lily took a deep breath and sat back, resting her elbows on the arms of the comfortable wicker chair and lacing her fingers together. She bit her upper lip and looked away for a moment before she spoke.

'I don't like you,' she stated bluntly. 'You don't like me either. And each of us have our reasons. Very good reasons. But what I think we do, or should, have for each other is respect.'

Grace laughed out loud in disbelief. 'Respect? For *you*?' She laughed once more.

Lily leaned forward. 'We got a Rembrandt out of your safe and out of your home without leaving a trace. We duped you *twice* and made off with five million right under your nose, and there wasn't a thing you could do to stop us. And you really did try.'

Lily pulled a face and watched as Grace's laughter ceased and a flush of anger crept up her neck.

'Now, you can hate us for that. But if you're sitting there telling me that that hasn't earned an inch of your respect, however grudging, then you're a bigger fool than I'd pinned you for.'

Grace's face contorted, anger vying with humiliation and hatred as Lily poured salt on the wound. Her cold mask fought to regain its composure, but the flush of fury still remained in her cheeks.

'Tell me,' she hissed nastily, 'is she badly scarred? I heard she was quite excessively burned.' Her cold eyes danced mockingly as her words hit their mark.

Lily's jaw clenched and she felt her raw anger swell into a tsunami that wanted nothing more than to break free. But she forced herself to stay on the path she'd set out on and resisted reacting the way Grace so badly wanted her to.

'I have a proposition for you,' she said sharply, refusing to acknowledge Grace's words at all. 'The past is done and there's no changing that. We can move on as enemies or we can move forward working together to the betterment of both our situations.'

'You want to *work* together?' Grace asked, the surprise evident in both her tone and on her face. She sat up and placed her tea down sharply. 'You're joking?'

'I don't joke when it comes to business,' Lily replied. 'When we broke in here – the first time that is,' she added, 'and we took the Rembrandt, we didn't know who you were.'

'Clearly,' Grace said.

'But now we do. You're an art dealer who supplies the rich and bored with high-value black-market paintings. The socially acceptable go-between, so that nobody feels as though they're dealing with anyone as common as a thief or a fence. Is that about right?'

Grace studied her for a moment. 'That's a fairly accurate summary, yes.'

'And you've been doing this for a very long time,' Lily continued. 'Years of placing high-value, non-reportable paintings in houses just like this one around the country.'

'So?' The interest in Grace's tone began to cool.

'What if you could make more money on the same paintings?' Lily asked.

'What is it that you're suggesting?'

'I'm suggesting that we go into a partnership. You tell us what paintings are in which houses and when there are social events that we could intercept. Perhaps even push to arrange a social event, if there isn't one. We plan and undertake the heist – all whilst you're in plain view, of course, so that you can't be linked – then you sell it on through the black market to a collector elsewhere in the world and we split the money. They're none the wiser as to how it happened and they can't report it to the police as the paintings are already illegal.'

'Steal back items I've sold to loyal and trusting clients, to *friends*? Do what you basically tried to do to me?' Grace asked incredulously. She paused and pursed her lips as she thought about it. 'Even if I did want to do that, why would I need *you*?'

Lily leaned forward. 'Because your men can't even keep you safe in your own garden for breakfast,' she said. 'Let alone pull off an intricate heist like that.' She sat back again with a smug look.

Grace shot a scathing look at her man with the gun and his cheeks coloured. 'I don't know.' She stared off into the distance for a few long moments. '*If* I were to consider this arrangement – and that's a huge *if* – then I'd be bringing the lion's share to the table. I'd expect a sixty-forty split, in my favour.'

'We'd be the ones taking all the risk,' Lily reminded her.

'Well, those are my terms,' Grace responded, staring at her with a steely expression. 'If you want what I've got, you'll have to pay what I want.'

Lily nodded slowly. 'If you deliver on your side of the deal then I'll accept that.'

'I'll need to think about it,' Grace said. She lifted the napkin from where it had been resting on her lap, folded it and placed it on the empty plate in front of her, making it clear the conversation was now over.

Lily stood up. She'd done what she'd set out to do – there was no need to linger. 'You have my number.' She gestured for Connor and Cillian to retreat.

'This has certainly been an interesting meeting.' Grace's cool voice held a note of malice. 'Though it really is a pity your daughter survived. I think I'd have enjoyed your begging to work with me more had she not.'

Lily paused and turned back, her gaze cold and dark as it rested on the person she hated most in the world. Grace's lips had curled up into a cruel, mocking smile. The smile of a viper.

'There would have been no offer had that happened, Grace,' she replied. 'If Ruby had died, I would have made sure to get to you alone, in the middle of the night. No cameras or walls or men or concern for potential consequences would have stopped me. I would have held your mouth shut as I cut your throat. And I'd have cradled your head as you struggled to take your last breath, while making sure you knew exactly why this was happening to you.'

The way she said it was so calm and so sure that even Grace with all her hard confidence finally faltered.

Satisfied that Grace now understood, Lily turned and exited with her sons in silence.

TWENTY-THREE

Lily turned into her street with a yawn and quickly tried to conceal it. There was no time to be tired. Everything was still falling apart around them and she was the key to holding it all together. Scarlet was facing a life sentence for murder, the factory was nothing but ashes, Ruby was awake, at least, but still in a bad way. And on top of all that, their clients still depended on them for protection, their businesses still needed running and now more than ever they needed to show a strong front. It was common knowledge that they were wading through tough waters – the last thing they needed was another firm believing they were weak enough to be overtaken. And it would happen, if they weren't careful. The underworld was a dangerous place at the best of times, but especially at times like these.

'Connor, I need you to show your face around the area today and put a hard word in here and there,' she said, pulling to a stop on the road outside her house. The boys' cars were taking up the driveway. 'The Italians will be watching closely at the moment – make sure they remember who we are.'

There were a few other firms that ran various illegal lines in the vicinity and they all kept out of each other's way. Most were smaller enterprises than the Drews', but there was one Italian family that rivalled them in size and had often pushed the boundaries looking for a weak spot. To overtake the Drews would double their presence and secure their hold on the east. Similarly, if the Drews decided to overtake them, it would secure *them* as the strongest firm in the east, but Lily didn't believe in stealing business that way. Not from another within the underworld. Anything they had was earned, and it would always be that way.

'Cillian, you need to go and collect the new routes from Ian. We're running short on hot stock in the market so let's get another truck identified to hit over the next few weeks. Go and meet Sandra afterwards to get that cash Scarlet sent her to hide. Split it between the regular laundries this time. They'll just have to swallow the influx. Tell them we'll make it worth their while.' She didn't like to push much more than usual through the other laundries, but while Scarlet was under scrutiny, it was best to avoid using the salon.

'Oh, er...' Cillian shifted in his seat and she saw him exchange a look with Connor in the rear-view mirror. 'Connor's probably closer to grab that cash and distribute it if he's doing the rounds to show his face.'

'Yeah, I'll pick it up. No problem,' Connor replied quickly.

Lily shook her head. She'd given up on trying to work out their private communications years ago. 'Whatever, as long as it's done. Cillian, if you're back in time then meet up with me to look over these new sites this afternoon. Can't hurt to have two sets of eyes on them.'

She'd identified a few potential sites to rebuild the factory. The insurance money hadn't come through yet, but due to their last job proving to be so fruitful, and the reward money for the painting being actually above board for a change, they were luckily in a position to plough forward with their plans.

'Will do.' As he spoke, his tone lowered and his dark eyes focused on something in the distance with a steely glare.

Lily frowned and leaned over to look down the road at what he was seeing. Her gaze landed on a big black car parked a little way down, the engine idling as its occupant waited. Cillian locked his jaw grimly and gave her a loaded look.

'Come on, Connor,' he said gruffly. 'Let's go.'

As they got into their own cars, Lily exited hers and waited for them to drive off down the road before she approached the waiting vehicle. Her high stiletto heels clipped out a rhythm on the pavement as she walked, and she lifted her chin as she reached the passenger door. She opened it and slipped inside, then placed her feet together into the footwell and closed the door behind her.

'Lil…' Ray Renshaw's voice was husky with emotion as he turned and put his hand on her cheek. He searched her face, a warm smile on his own. 'You alright?'

'Yeah, I'm fine,' she replied, placing her hand over his and squeezing it.

He glanced in his wing mirror at her house behind them. 'How's she doing?' he asked.

'She's not great,' Lily replied honestly. 'I think she's still in shock at the moment. She ain't said much since she's been home. But she's home, which is the main thing. She's alive.'

Ray nodded. 'I hated the thought of you sat in that hospital by yourself, all this time. I really did.'

'I know,' Lily replied. 'But it was for the best. If she'd woken up to see you there…' She trailed off.

'Yeah, I know,' he replied grimly.

Ray and Lily had been in love for thirty years, give or take. They'd been in a relationship for most of that but had always maintained their independence from each other at the same time. Lily had her family and the firm to think of, and Ray had his own even larger firm south of the river. She believed the two burdens of responsibility could not be run from one place. They each needed to be in their own corner and to prioritise their roles above all else. Ray had wanted to settle down and had tried to persuade Lily many times over the years, but she'd steadfastly kept their arrangement as it was. It suited them both, even if Ray couldn't always see it. And despite the casualness of their relationship, they were as loyal to each other as they were to their firms, but not everyone understood their strange set-up.

Connor and Cillian had never understood why they lived the way they did and were not Ray's biggest fans as a result. Ruby had always been indifferent, until recently when Ray had dragged her off the street and forced her clean from the drugs she'd been slowly killing herself with. He'd done it for Lily, so she wouldn't have the heartache of burying her child, but the way he'd done it had been brutal, and he and Ruby had not parted ways as friends. Ray had threatened her into staying clean, and Ruby had gone home sober but deflated. Or at least Lily assumed he'd threatened her; Ruby had never actually told her the ins and outs of what had happened, but she couldn't see any other reason that her wayward daughter would stick to her promises. She never had in the past.

Now, Ruby hated Ray with vehemence. And Lily had taken her side for a while. Until she'd cooled down enough to see that she couldn't stay angry at the man she loved for trying to save her child forever. However badly he'd gone about it.

When Ruby had ended up in hospital, Ray had rushed to be by her side, but Lily suggested he keep his distance until she was out of the woods and home at least. He'd done as she'd asked without question, the way she'd known he would. But now here he was, waiting for her in the shadows. They were never able to keep away from each other for too long, always drawn together like moths to a flame.

'I hear Scarlet's had a capture,' Ray said, changing the

subject. He picked up a packet of cigarettes from the centre console and held it out in offering.

'Good news travels fast,' Lily said grimly, taking one.

He lit Lily's cigarette and then his own. 'What happened?'

Lily took a deep drag and blew her smoke out of the window before answering. 'They gathered enough evidence to bag her for Jasper's murder.' She took another drag, the weight of Scarlet's predicament resettling heavily on her shoulders.

Ray frowned. 'What's your lawyer saying?'

'That there's nothing he can do,' she lamented.

'Surely there must be something?'

'Not this time.'

Ray swore under his breath. 'Is there anything I can do?'

'Not unless you have a judge in your pocket,' Lily replied, already knowing the answer.

'A judge, no. Plods, a couple, but not up here.' He grimaced and looked out of the window. 'You're still close with the Tylers, right? Maybe try Freddie. If anyone's got a judge tucked away, it will be him.'

'He was my first call,' she admitted. 'He has one, but she's on long-term sick leave and even if she wasn't, she'd be unlikely to get onto this case. The lawyer reckons they're going to push this through fast.' Lily closed her eyes for a moment, feeling utterly helpless. 'Look, I'm sorry to cut this short but I've got to go. I've got a lot to sort out today.' She leaned over and kissed him deeply on the lips. 'I'll come by tonight,' she promised.

'Go safe,' Ray called as she stepped back out into the morning sun.

She flicked away her cigarette and pulled herself up to full height, forcing herself to approach the house with a confidence she no longer felt. For her entire life she'd fought for and protected every member of her family. She'd always kept them out of jail and on the up – because that was her job. But now she found herself powerless. How was she supposed to face

Cath today? How was she supposed to look any of them in the eye again now that she'd failed to protect Scarlet? Because the stark truth was that Scarlet Drew was going down for a very long time. And there was nothing that she or anyone else could do to stop it.

TWENTY-FOUR

Connor slammed the car door shut then paused as he saw his brother's vehicle swing in behind him.

'What are you doing?' he asked as Cillian got out. 'You're supposed to be headed to the depot for the routes.'

'I'll get there,' Cillian replied, pulling a toothpick out of his inner jacket pocket and placing it between his front teeth. 'I saw you headed this way and figured I'd join you first.'

Connor frowned. 'Why?' he asked, suspicious.

''Cause Mum ain't the only one's who's heard rumblings about the Italians.'

'What do you mean?' Connor fell into step as Cillian moved forward through the alleyway towards the row of high-street shops beyond. 'She's just being cautious, ain't she?'

'Nah.' Cillian shook his head with a frown. 'That Luca Romano's been sniffing around the shops, asking about the laundries.'

'What?' Connor asked, outraged. 'Is he having a giraffe? He's fucking brave, ain't he?'

'Exactly. So I put everyone on alert the other day and I've

just had a text from Ash in the takeaway saying he's down here right now, so I figured I'd come give you a hand.'

'How's that going to look?' Connor replied, put out by the inference that he needed the help. 'I can handle roughing up one little Italian on me own, you know.'

'I know,' Cillian responded. 'But also I like the tuna melts from that café on the corner and I'd already arranged to meet Billie there for brunch, so it's all worked out quite nicely really.'

'Oh. Fair enough then, I guess,' Connor replied with a shrug. He glanced sideways at his brother. 'You've got a right thing for this one, ain't ya?' A smile crept over his face and he dug Cillian in the ribs.

'Oi, get off.' Cillian sidestepped another jab. 'Yeah, I do. She's something special.'

'How so?' Connor asked.

Cillian allowed himself a smile as he thought of all the ways that she was ever so uniquely special. Most of them he couldn't ever voice out loud, as discussing the sort of intimacy they shared would be nothing short of disrespectful.

'There's just something about Billie. She's a good girl. And you wouldn't think it to look at her, but the way she thinks, we're just, like, on the same wavelength,' he said.

'What, violent and unpredictable?' Connor joked.

Cillian nodded, not laughing. 'Kind of, yeah. She ain't scared by this life. I've turned up covered in blood with no explanation and she didn't bat an eyelid. Straight up just asked me what the cover story was, didn't miss a beat. She ain't distracted by all the shiny bits either. She knows the score. And deep down I think she actually likes it.'

Connor pulled an expression of surprise. 'That's a first,' he said. 'She related to another firm or something?'

'Nope. Clean as they get. Hard-working honest people, her family.'

Connor nodded. 'So what you're telling me is you've pulled a psycho.'

Cillian punched him on the arm. 'No. What I'm telling you is I've pulled a fucking diamond. When was the last time you went out with a bird who wasn't in it for the money and the status?'

'*All* birds are into us for the money and the status,' Connor replied.

'Billie ain't.'

They marched through the run-down high street and Cillian pointed towards a small record shop in the distance. 'Ash said he saw Romano heading in here.'

They reached the shop and pushed through the door, causing the little bell above it to tinkle, announcing their presence. Penny, who ran the shop, seemed anxious, her arms folded and no smile on her face as she faced the handsome young man leaning over her counter. They both turned at the sound of the bell, and the man smiled broadly, revealing a set of bright neat teeth and two perfectly positioned dimples.

'What a surprise this is, to find *you* here, Luca,' Cillian said sarcastically.

'Yes, coincidental timing, it seems,' he replied with a forced laugh. His demeanour remained casual, but the sharpness in his dark eyes gave away the tension he felt underneath. 'You're also shopping for records?' he asked.

'Oh, he's shopping for *records*, Connor,' Cillian said in an exaggerated manner. 'And there we were thinking you were shopping for something else.' He stepped forward with a predatory smile. 'Which one was it you were after?'

'Hmm?' Luca asked, straightening up and glancing between the two brothers warily.

'Which record? You're at the till talking to Penny here, but I don't see any purchases, so I can only assume you're asking about something specific. Is that right?' Cillian asked, slowly moving closer.

'Of course,' Luca replied, trying to brazen the situation out. He turned towards Penny with a winning smile, a bead of sweat starting to form at his temple. 'I was just asking you, wasn't I? About the er, the, the...' He moved his hand in a tight circular motion in the air as if trying to remember. His eyes pleaded with Penny to help him across the counter, but she ignored him and turned to the brothers.

'I'm sorry, I did try to tell him,' she said, her tone apologetic.

'Don't worry about it,' Connor replied. 'You can't help it if vermin find their way in here. We'll get rid of the problem for you. Wouldn't want an infestation, now would we?'

He stalked forward and grabbed Luca's arm roughly. Luca tried to pull away, but Cillian gripped the other arm and between them they marched him forward and out of the shop.

'Hey, get off me,' Luca growled. 'Get the fuck off me, both of you. How dare you handle me like this.' He kicked out and caught Cillian on the leg.

In return, Cillian twisted his arm up hard behind his back, causing him to cry out in pain. They marched him down an alley to the side of the shop, ignoring the quickly averted gazes of the people around them. Everyone knew who they were around here. This had been their patch for years. They kept the high street safe and dealt with any issues. That was what they were paid for. So no one would pay any mind to their business today.

As they neared the dead end, edged with bins and empty crates, they stopped and slammed Luca against the wall hard. Cillian pushed his face closer to the other man's.

'I'll handle you how the fuck I like when you come sniffing around here, Romano,' he said in a low growl. 'What do you think you're doing, trying to talk my clients round to using you, eh?'

'Think you're big, do ya, boys?' Luca sneered back, ignoring the question. 'Two against one. Too pussy to come at me one on one.'

'See,' Connor tutted, annoyed, and turned to his brother. 'I told you I should have just dealt with this.'

'Ahh, big brother here don't trust you to do it right?' Luca taunted. He laughed a cold, ugly laugh. 'Wise.'

'Shut up, you piss-taking cunt,' Cillian said in an irritated tone, slamming him back against the wall once more and sticking his finger in his face. 'He's actually the older one by seven minutes, not that it makes any difference.' He turned to Connor. 'I can leave, if you want,' he offered.

'Nah, you're here now,' Connor replied dismissively. 'Right,' he roared, keeping hold of Luca's arm with one hand and grasping his neck viciously with the other. He pushed him up the wall and off the ground. Luca's eyes suddenly bulged in surprise. 'We've got better things to do than teach *you* a fucking lesson. So why don't we cut to the point. Why are you out here taking liberties?'

Cillian stepped back, allowing Connor some space, and pushed his hands down into his trouser pockets. Luca struggled for a few moments and grunted uncomfortably. He seemed to be trying to speak, but his jaw was locked tight under Connor's grip.

'Maybe let him down a bit,' Cillian suggested. Connor eased him down to the ground but kept his hand firmly on his neck.

When Luca regained the use of his mouth, he spat in the direction of Connor's face. Luckily he missed, but, enraged, Cillian stepped forward and punched him hard in the face. Luca's head snapped to the side and his lip split open.

Righting himself, he doubled his efforts to get out of Connor's grip. Connor shoved him to the side, letting go and stepping back to stand with Cillian, shrugging agitatedly. Luca righted himself once more before sneering at the pair of them in turn, breathing heavily through his pain and anger.

'Come on then,' he taunted. 'Let's go.' He rushed at Connor, but Connor pushed him away easily.

Cillian stepped forward and grabbed him by the shirt with both hands, slamming him back against the wall. 'Big words for someone who can't even land one. Now we'll ask you again, *why* are you here trying to steal business, eh? This ain't your turf. This ain't even your area of expertise, so what's going on?'

Luca kicked out and struggled, but Cillian held him fast.

'You're on the out,' Luca spat. 'Word's got around, you can't look after your business anymore. Fuck, you can't even look after your own family. You've lost your edge, all of ya. You two, your mum, that cousin of yours. And your sister's been a liability for years. You couldn't save her from herself, let alone that fire, could you?'

Seeing red, Cillian pulled his fist back and punched him in the face again viciously. This time he let go and Luca slumped backward. He kicked him in the stomach, sending him sprawling.

'Can't look after our business or family? What d'ya call this then, eh?' He took his leg back and kicked him again, slamming all his body weight into the action.

Luca tried to get up, but still stung by the comment about Ruby, Cillian didn't give him a chance, laying into him with all he had.

'That's it, stay on the fucking floor,' he yelled, spit flying from his mouth as he trembled with anger. 'You piece of shit.'

As the red haze began to wane, Cillian reined himself in and stepped back. He wiped his mouth with the back of his hand, pacing for a moment as he tried to get control over his emotions. Luca attempted to stand, but not ready to let the man off just yet, Cillian shot one more carefully aimed kick straight into his face. Blood splattered outwards as his nose broke, and he fell back, cradling it.

'Hey,' Connor whistled a low warning.

Cillian swung round to see Billie making her way carefully down the alley towards them. She paused a few feet away and looked down at Luca.

'Hello, babe,' Cillian said, pacing up and down next to the groaning man, trying to sound casual and in control. Billie had been amazing so far, but what would she make of this scene? he wondered. 'I won't be long.'

'I'll go get us a table,' she said, as if nothing was happening. 'And a couple of tuna melts.' She turned to Connor. 'You joining us?'

'Oh, er...' Connor looked at Cillian, clearly surprised by her calm in the face of such violence.

'Yeah, you'll join us, won't ya?' Cillian asked, raising his eyebrows in question.

'Um. Yeah, go on then. I am a bit peckish as it happens,' Connor replied.

'Lovely. Fancy a tuna melt?' Billie asked.

'They do make a very good tuna melt,' Cillian added seriously, nodding.

'What the hell are you—' Luca began.

Cillian instantly turned and kicked him hard again in the stomach.

'Shut the fuck up. Can you not see I'm having a conversation?' he exclaimed, annoyed by the interruption.

'Yeah, alright. I'll have the tuna melt,' Connor decided after a few moments of thought.

'Great. I'll go order. See you in a minute.' Billie grinned and set off towards the high street.

As soon as she'd disappeared from view, Cillian leaned down close to Luca's face and pulled a flick knife out of his pocket. He grabbed the front of his shirt and pressed the blade up against Luca's cheek.

'You listen here. This family is as strong as ever and we ain't going nowhere. You tell that to whoever gave you the go-ahead for this little excursion. And if I see you around here again, I'll be using this to teach you a harder lesson. You understand me?'

Luca glared at him but offered no comeback.

With a sniff, Cillian stood up and straightened his jacket, putting the knife back in his pocket and leading the way out of the alley.

Connor fell into step beside him as they walked out of the shadows and into the bright midday sunshine. 'She's alright, your Billie,' he commented.

'Yeah, she is, bruv,' Cillian answered. 'She is.'

TWENTY-FIVE

Grace stood at the window looking out across the patio and long, manicured lawn, a brandy in one hand and the other crossed, tight and tense, over her stomach. She was dressed for bed, her cream floor-length satin nightie covered by a matching dressing gown. Her light blonde hair was pinned up softly on top of her head, and her pale face was devoid of her usual make-up. Anyone looking upon her might have compared her appearance to that of an angel. Anyone who knew her could have told them she was anything but.

A tentative knock sounded at the door behind her and she turned towards it expectantly.

'Come in,' she said, her voice heavy with the weight of her thoughts.

Duffy, one of her men, walked into the room. 'The last of the security upgrades have been completed,' he told her. 'It's all now linked to the tablets around the house, and notifications will flash up whenever there's motion around the perimeter.' He held out one of the new tablets and she waved it away.

'Show me tomorrow. It's been a long day,' she said tiredly. 'It's set to the highest setting?'

'It is, but I was going to speak to you about lowering it slightly. Any movement at all, every bird, cat, squirrel will—'

'I don't care,' she snapped, shooting him a glare that would turn any man's blood to ice. 'I want to know every movement that goes on anywhere near us from now on. I don't care if it's a damn spider, if it's on my property, we need to check.'

'Sure,' Duffy replied dutifully. 'I also copied that list for you, from the files in the bunker. All the items you've sold prior to two years ago, all in date order. I took the liberty of ringing a few that could be good targets for this thing with the Drews.'

Grace frowned and took the piece of paper he offered. She ran her gaze down the list, pacing back and forth across the room as she calculated each option in her head. She paused on one that he'd ringed.

'Marie... Her Fall Ball is coming up soon, isn't it?' she asked.

'Yes. It could be a good opportunity. Lots of people around, and her security is practically non-existent. She shows that piece to anyone and everyone.'

'True,' Grace mused. 'We'll go with that.'

She scrunched up the paper in her fist, moved to the fire that crackled away in the old fireplace and threw it in. Taking a sip of her brandy, she watched as the flames licked at the corners and took hold, burning the page to a blackened pile of dust.

'Do you not want to keep that?' Duffy asked in surprise.

'Why?' she asked.

'That's just the first option. This partnership with the Drews is ongoing, is it not? What about the second job, and so on?'

Grace felt her rage swell up like a ball of fire from the centre of her stomach, and she turned and launched her glass at him across the room, as hard as she could. He ducked just in time, and it hit the wall, smashing into shards which clattered onto the hard wooden floor.

'*Ongoing?*' she yelled. 'Those scumbags broke into my home and held me at *gunpoint*. The same scumbags who recently stole my most valuable possession and gave it to the FBI for a measly five million, a *fraction* of its value. Five million, I might add, that they're living the life of fucking Riley on, whilst I sit here with nothing. My *life savings* went on that painting. It was my retirement plan.' She stepped towards him with a cold, feral look in her eyes and he lowered his head, watching her warily. 'And you think we're going to work with them long-term?'

'Clearly I misunderstood the plan,' Duffy said, trying to keep his voice level.

'*Clearly*,' she hissed. 'We'll do this one job, use them, take the money and then kill them.'

Duffy blinked and looked up at her in surprise. '*What?*'

'Oh, don't pretend you're above all that now,' she said witheringly. 'You were more than happy to help me get rid of Harry, weren't you? 'Well, now we need to get rid of *them*. We just need to lull them into a false sense of security first. It will make things easier.' She retreated to the window, her anger subsiding to a gentle simmer as she thought about her end goal.

Duffy stared at her and ran a hand down his face. 'Grace, Harry was one man, and we staged a hit-and-run. There's a big difference between that and killing a whole family. A whole *criminal firm*. And they're not stupid. Look at the fire. They knew we were coming – they predicted everything.'

'Then we just have to make sure we're not predictable,' Grace replied, turning to look at him. 'They'll expect us to push back at first, so let's give them that. We'll show ourselves slowly softening and then once we've all settled into playing happy families and we've pulled off one successful job, *that's* when we'll strike.' Her cold eyes flashed with menace. 'And we'll make sure they don't suspect a damn thing.'

TWENTY-SIX

Scarlet paced her cell with one arm folded tightly across her middle and gnawed on her nail in a way that under normal circumstances she wouldn't dream of doing. But now, for once, she couldn't give a shit about keeping her manicure in order. Right now, things like that, things that usually seemed so important, were completely inconsequential. Her make-up had long gone, her usually styled long dark hair was tied back in a loose bun and her clothes were crumpled.

It had been twenty-four hours since they'd arrested her and she knew her hours in this holding cell were now numbered. They wouldn't keep her here for much longer. They would be making arrangements to move forward with getting her charged.

She'd had her one call which she'd used to speak to Lily, but since then she'd had no contact with her family. Robert had come swiftly, though he hadn't been able to work his magic the way he had last time. He'd told her in blunt terms that there was no way out of this one. There was enough evidence to charge her immediately, once they got round to processing her. She'd be taken to the Crown Court for the initial hearing and charged for Jasper's murder. Once that happened, she'd be sent to the nearest prison, where she'd stay on remand until the trial. That would take months, and in this case, Robert had explained, the trial would be merely a formality. The odds were stacked against her. There would be no escaping a sentence. She was going down for murder, and there was nothing anyone could do about it.

As the weight of that certainty bore down on her, Scarlet suddenly felt her lungs deflate. She sucked at the air around her, trying to draw some of it in but failing. She pulled again and again in short, sharp bursts, feeling the blood rush through her temples and behind her eyes, the pulse of her soaring heart rate hammering inside her head. She stumbled over to the hard concrete ledge with the thin roll-out mattress that she'd slept on the night before and sat down, closing her eyes and trying to calm her frantic gulps.

She leaned forward and forced her head between her legs, squeezing her eyes closed, praying for the panic attack to end. She wasn't in control of much right now, but she should at least be able to control her own body.

The seconds passed and finally her jagged breathing began to even out. The pounding inside her head dulled, and her heart stopped trying to beat its way out of her chest. She opened her eyes and sat up, exhausted suddenly by all that was going on.

She stared at the door and balled her hands into fists, her nails biting into her skin. It wasn't prison itself that scared her. She was a Drew. That name alone should command her enough respect to survive. And she was tough enough in her own right. But the thought of not returning home to her family – to never again sitting at the table on a Sunday with them all around her – tore her up in ways she couldn't bear.

Footsteps thudded down the hallway, and she tensed as they stopped outside her cell. The grate slid open, the metal screeching irritably, and a pair of eyes glanced through before the door groaned open.

'Come with me,' the officer said curtly.

With a deep breath, Scarlet steeled herself and stood up. She exited the cell and accompanied him down the hallway. 'Where are we going?' she asked.

'Your lawyer is here.' He didn't elaborate beyond that, and she didn't bother probing further. She'd wait and find out for herself.

She was shown to the interview room that was now more familiar than she'd have liked and waited for the officer to leave and shut the door before she sat down opposite Robert. He pushed a tall takeaway cup towards her.

'Here, thought you might like a decent coffee,' he said. Scarlet was about to refuse, knowing the last thing she needed was caffeine right now, but then he continued as if reading her mind. 'It's decaf.'

She gave him a tired smile of thanks and took the cup, wrapping her hands around it to soak up the warmth.

'Are you OK?' he continued, subtly appraising her. 'Your mother sent in a few essentials and some more comfortable clothes. Once they've checked them, they'll bring them to you.'

'Thanks. I'm...' She trailed off. She'd been about to say she was OK, but she wasn't. 'I'm not OK. I'm fucking terrified.'

Robert just nodded. 'They've scheduled your initial hearing in for tomorrow morning. Jennings will present the evidence against you and you will submit your plea.'

'Which is?' Scarlet asked.

Robert rubbed the bridge of his nose distractedly before answering. 'Your aunt wants you to submit a plea of not guilty so that it can go to a trial. But like I told you yesterday, even if we force a trial, you stand no chance of getting out of this. There's just too much evidence against you. It would likely prompt them to impose an even longer sentence in the end, for wasting their time.'

His eyes met hers and she saw the mixture of defeat and

sympathy in them. Her blood ran cold and she fought to stop herself from crying.

'My personal advice would be to plead guilty. You could tell them that it was an act of self-defence—'

'Which it technically was,' Scarlet interjected.

'Which it technically was,' Robert agreed. 'Use the self-defence point and also throw in a heat-of-the-moment angle too. Jasper killed your father and then came after you. You acted to defend yourself as he tried to kill you, and at the same time, he was taunting you about your father's death. You weren't yourself.' Robert painted the picture. 'You had a moment of madness, a red haze descended, it was fight or flight. You'll still get time, but I think that if we really press this home, you could get a reduced sentence.'

Scarlet nodded and lifted the coffee cup to her lips with shaking hands. She took a sip and placed it back down on the table, willing the shaking to stop, then sniffed and held her chin higher. 'You think that's really my best shot?'

'I do,' Robert said. He bit his lip and looked down. 'I think that's the best we can do with regards to *your* situation. The other thing we need to focus on is protecting the rest of your family.'

'What do you mean?' Scarlet replied sharply.

'You were all each other's alibis the night Jasper died. Even if you claim you killed him and set up his suicide alone, that doesn't explain why they covered for you. So, if we're going to protect them now, your story has to start after the hours their story covers. And it has to be absolutely infallible. Because if it isn't' – his gaze bored into hers – 'then not only will *you* be going down, but so will your aunt, your cousins and your mother, for accessory to murder.'

TWENTY-SEVEN

Ruby ran her fingers down the ravaged side of her face gently, wincing at the pain, then lowered her hands and closed her eyes with a look of shame. She'd never been particularly vain, coming to terms fairly early on in life that with her sharp nose, wild uncontrollable curls and thin angular frame she was never going to be a particularly great beauty. But she'd at least felt comfortable being in her own skin. Now, with the angry red burns down one side of her face and neck, she looked monstrous. They doctors had said it would heal over time, but it would still leave scars. Wherever she went, people would stare – she knew they would.

She sighed and walked across her bedroom to the window, looking down over the street below. Nothing much was happening at this time of the day. Most of the local residents had gone to work and their kids to school. Before the fire, she'd have been up and going about her day too. She'd finally been getting her act together. For once she hadn't been flailing through life as though she'd been swept up in a hurricane. She'd had her feet on the ground and was finally walking a path towards a stable routine. But then she'd got caught in the fire and everything had changed.

The calm she'd reached had disappeared and had been replaced with anxiety and bitterness. Why had this happened to her? Was it punishment for the years of drug abuse? Was it payback for the stress and heartbreak she'd put her family through as she disappeared off into some self-destructive hole again and again? Perhaps it was. Perhaps this was karma. But she'd been ready to change. She'd settled into her job working at the salon, she'd stayed clean, she was rebuilding her broken relationship with her family.

What was she supposed to do now? She couldn't walk back into the salon and start work as though nothing had happened. She couldn't ignore the stares from the customers and avoid their inevitable questions. Even the thought of that made her heart quicken with anxiety. She wouldn't just be Ruby anymore, she'd be the girl who got burned. She didn't want to be around anyone. It was hard even being in the same room as her family now. As much as they tried not to look at her burns when they spoke to her, they couldn't always hide their expressions. And she couldn't bear the sympathy and patience she kept seeing in their eyes.

She sat down in the armchair that faced the window and stared into the sky bleakly. She couldn't just stay up here in her room forever though. And she couldn't give in to the one thing she did feel like doing. When Ray had kidnapped her and forced her to go cold turkey he hadn't been messing around. He'd let her go with the warning that should she ever turn to drugs again, he'd kill her. And he'd meant it too, she knew. He'd kill her and make it look like an accident. In his warped view, this would be a kindness to her mother. The way Ray saw it, it would be better for Lily to mourn her daughter but be thankful that she was at rest than spend the next few years watching her self-destruct and waiting for the day she finally killed herself. So

losing herself in a druggy haze was off the table too. She sighed
and resigned herself to another day of going round in circles in
her head.

A movement in the street caught her attention and she
watched as her aunt Cath pulled up outside. Cath stepped out
of the car and leaned wearily against it for a moment, taking a
minute to breathe before she came in, assuming she was unobserved. She looked tired, deep lines of stress etched into her
usually clear face. Her smiling mouth was down turned and her
whole body seemed to sag as if she hadn't slept. She probably
hadn't, Ruby realised. She'd likely have been up all night
worrying about Scarlet again. And with good reason.

A seed of pity took root as she watched her aunt, causing
her feelings on the situation to mix. Ruby's first reaction, when
she'd overheard the news, was to feel bad for Scarlet. There was
little love lost between them, but she was still family. However,
since then, after having so much time to sit and think about that
situation, she wasn't sure she felt that bad at all. In a way, it
might even be a good thing for her, in the long run.

Scarlet had always been a thorn in her side. Hogging the
limelight from an early age, she'd always manipulated situations
to suit her, and Ruby had always seemed to end up fading into
the background. When Ruby had come back and Lily had sent
her to work in the salon, Scarlet had made no secret of her
disdain for her. She'd bossed her about and treated her like she
was an inconvenience. Even when she'd uncovered a thief
stealing money from the till, Scarlet had acted as if her
discovery was an annoyance. She couldn't do right for doing
wrong. Since she'd walked back in, Scarlet had held her down
firmly with one hand, whilst using the other to shine the limelight on herself. Without her there, perhaps Ruby finally stood a
chance of making her own mark within the family. Perhaps with
Scarlet out of the way, and once she'd worked up the courage to
join society once more, *she'd* finally have the chance to shine.

Down below, Cath gathered what little strength she seemed to have left and stood up straight, opening the back door of the car and leaning in to pick something up. Ruby blinked and frowned, squinting to see more clearly as Cath straightened back up.

What the hell was she carrying?

TWENTY-EIGHT

Lily hiked the heavy dish up higher with one arm and inserted the key in the door to the flat with the other. She turned it and pushed the door open, careful not to upset her cargo, then entered the large open-plan living space beyond.

'For Christ's sake, Mum,' Cillian remarked irritably as he stepped out of the bathroom, dripping wet with a towel around his waist. 'Ain't you heard of knocking?'

'I'm your mother, not the fucking postman,' she replied drily. 'Anyway, I've seen it all before,' she added, walking through the room towards the kitchen area.

She moved around the island breakfast bar that separated the kitchen from the lounge and placed the dish down. As she did so, the bathroom door opened wider behind Cillian and a similarly soaked Billie emerged, holding her towel wrapped tight against her chest. She shot Lily a small smile before slipping into the bedroom. Cillian gave his mother a look and she shrugged.

'I've seen all that before an' all,' she remarked.

Cillian tutted and rolled his eyes with a sigh then padded over towards her. 'What's that?'

Lily pulled the foil back to show him. 'Your aunt Cath couldn't sleep, so she made lasagne.'

'Didn't you want it?' he asked.

'She made five,' Lily answered wryly.

'Ah.' He switched on the coffee machine then pulled out three cups from the cupboard. 'You're staying for coffee, yeah?' he asked.

Lily debated it. Her natural aversion to sharing her sons with other women pushed her to refuse, but the more sensible side of her brain made her pause. She'd caught the look of hope in his eyes. He wanted her to stay and make an effort with Billie. It wouldn't be her first choice of activity, but then again she had sworn to try, seeing as Cillian was so taken with her. The last thing she wanted was to be at odds with him because she wouldn't accept someone he cared about. Plus, after their last meeting, she grudgingly had to admit that Billie wasn't all that bad.

'OK. Just a quick one though, as I've got a lot to do today.' She took the cups out of his hands. 'I'll make these – you go and get dressed. You also have a lot to do today.'

He nodded his understanding and left to get dressed, while Lily set about making the three cups of coffee. She had no idea how Billie took hers, but she didn't particularly care. The girl would take what she was given. She might have given in to giving this new girlfriend of Cillian's a chance, but that didn't mean she was going to go all out and bend over backward to do so.

The bedroom door opened behind her and Lily could tell by the softer footsteps that it wasn't Cillian. She poured the milk into the three mugs with a tight-lipped expression and stirred them before turning around and handing one across the counter to Billie, who had sat on one of the stools.

'Thank you,' Billie said politely, taking a sip.

Lily saw Billie's gaze flicker towards the sugar pot, but to her credit she said nothing and continued drinking the unsweet-ened coffee. Lily's shoulders relaxed and she leaned back against the counter, sipping at her own.

'How's Ruby doing?' Billie asked.

'Physically she's healing well,' Lily replied.

'I guess mentally takes a little longer when you've been through something like that,' Billie replied, sympathy in her tone and in her clear blue eyes. 'Did you give her that oil, for her burns?'

'I did, yes,' Lily replied.

Billie smiled, looking pleased.

'She said to tell you thanks. That she appreciates the kind gesture.'

She caught the look of disbelief on Cillian's face as he came out from the bedroom fully clothed and looked away towards the window. Ruby hadn't really said that of course. It wasn't her style. But she'd felt rude not saying something along those lines.

'Hopefully it will help. Should ease the tightness of the skin at the very least,' Billie replied.

Lily nodded and then turned to pass Cillian his coffee. 'Connor tells me you had a set-to with Luca Romano yesterday.' She wouldn't usually discuss something like this in front of one of their girls, but she knew Billie had been there. 'Why am I hearing this from him and not you, and today instead of yester-day?' she asked, lifting an eyebrow in accusation.

It was unusual for her to go almost a whole day without speaking to her sons, but she'd been so swamped and distracted by the position Scarlet was in that she hadn't had time to catch up with them.

'It was nothing major,' Cillian said dismissively. 'Just gave him a reminder that we aren't to be fucked with.' He sipped his coffee and looked at his mother over the rim. 'They've been sniffing round the protection clients, trying to get an in.'

Lily frowned. 'But they don't do protection.'

'That's what I said, but I guess they're looking to expand.' He sipped his coffee again. 'Word on the street is that we're vulnerable. Our factory's been burned down with no sign of retribution, Ruby's taken a hit, Scarlet's banged up, Uncle Ronan ain't been gone that long.' He pulled a grim expression and shook his head. 'We're looking weak.'

'We're not weak,' Lily snapped.

'It don't matter whether we are or aren't, what matters is that we look it,' Cillian said seriously.

Lily went to say something then snapped her mouth shut. Cillian was right. There was no sugar-coating it – the firm looked weak right now, broken and brittle. It was the perfect opportunity for rival firms to leave the sidelines and jump into the game. From the outside it looked like there would be little resistance. But there *would* be resistance. Lily Drew wasn't giving up so much as an inch of their turf without a damn good fight.

She wiped one hand down her face in stress. They had to nip this in the bud. Stopping a war from starting, keeping their rivals too wary to attack, would be a hell of a lot easier than overcoming them once they made a move.

'We need to make a show of strength,' she said without turning around. 'Something big. Something that will remind them who we are and make them back off.'

'Yeah, but what?' Cillian replied.

Lily bit her lip. Her jacket pocket began to vibrate and she reached in and pulled out her phone. Glancing up at Cillian, she gave him a meaningful look and he tilted his head to one side in question. Catching the exchange, Billie stood up.

'I'm going to go put some make-up on. See you in a bit,' she said tactfully, leaving them to it.

Lily answered the phone. 'Yes?' she asked, her tone calm and level.

'I've considered your offer,' came the cool response. 'Gather your team and meet me tomorrow night at the airfield we were supposed to meet at last time. We'll trial one job and see how it goes. I'll bring all the details.'

'No,' Lily replied, shaking her head. 'You can meet us on our terms. We own a salon by Snaresbrook Tube station. I'll send you the address and time.'

There was a long silence on the other end of the line and Lily tensed as she waited to see what Grace would do.

'Fine,' she finally answered. 'I'll be there.'

There was a short click as the call ended and Lily slipped the phone back into her pocket.

'It's agreed,' she said, locking gazes with Cillian. 'We meet her tomorrow night and get this started.'

'And then what?' Cillian asked.

'And then,' Lily replied, 'we make the kind of move we need to remind people just how strong we really are.'

TWENTY-NINE

Scarlet stared at the cell door. It was crazy really that the only physical thing between her and the outside world, between her and her life, was a tall sheet of metal, held to a frame by hinges. Something so thin, so unimpressive. And yet so effective.

Her hearing was in two hours. Right now, she knew the legal team would be gathering everything together to put before the judge. Soon, before she was escorted to court, she would be taken back to the interview room to write her statement. Her confession. She closed her eyes as a wave of sickness threatened to overwhelm her. She couldn't believe that it had really come to this.

They would be surprised to hear her confess, after all this time so vehemently denying her involvement. She'd decided to keep the admission of her crimes to herself until the last possible moment, unable to bear Jennings' unavoidable triumphant gloating for a moment longer than absolutely necessary. He'd make sure to rub in his victory, she knew, after the runaround she'd subjected him to. But much as she hated it, he *was* the victor. For the first time in the history of Drews versus the police, the Drews had lost. Unlike the rest of the family who'd always stayed a step or two ahead, she'd fallen at the first real hurdle, and for the first time since he'd died, Scarlet was glad her dad wasn't around. Glad that he hadn't lived to see the downfall of his only daughter.

Standing up, Scarlet shoved her hands into the pockets of the oversized hoodie she was wearing over leggings. It was an old one that she'd used while playing netball at school, not suitable for much in the outside world. Her mother must have dug it out from the back of her wardrobe, choosing it for comfort. She was glad of that. A small comfort in this living nightmare.

She paused at the other side of the room and closed her eyes, going over the story she'd worked out in her head one more time. It had to be just right. If she made a mistake – if her timings were off or she missed a detail – her story could be torn apart. And if it was torn apart it wouldn't just be *her* life that was over – the whole family would be sent down. The firm would cease to exist, their lives would all be ruined. Everything her father and aunt had worked so hard for would have been for nothing. That was something she couldn't allow to happen. Whatever else happened today, she couldn't watch her father's legacy disappear.

Footsteps sounded in the hallway, and she opened her eyes. Her heart rate quickened as the door opened and swung back.

'Scarlet Drew, come with me,' said the officer.

Scarlet bit back her fear and clenched her fists to stop herself shaking as she walked out of the holding cell. They took the long, clinical-looking hallway to the interview rooms and she tried to regulate her breathing. She needed to keep her head straight, now more than ever. As they reached the first of the doors, she began to slow then frowned as they passed it.

'Where are we going?' she asked. 'I'm supposed to write my statement before the hearing, aren't I?'

The officer didn't reply, and she pursed her lips. Whatever was going on, clearly she wasn't important enough to know the details. Is this how it would be from now on? Once she became an officially incarcerated criminal, would she just be pushed from pillar to post, decisions made about her life without her ever being told?

They turned a corner and walked down a slightly busier hallway, with posters on the wall and busy offices off to the sides. They turned again and Scarlet realised they were nearing the area where they'd initially booked her in. Her frown deepened. Were they taking her straight there? Without her lawyer? Surely they couldn't *still* be trying to trip her up? If they were, it was a wasted exercise, she thought bitterly. She was about to give them everything they needed to put her away.

The doors opened and they entered the custody suite. Scarlet bit her upper lip as they stopped by the front desk and the officer who'd accompanied her exchanged a look with the female officer behind the counter. She hissed out a long, sour breath and glared at Scarlet through the glass, pushing a clipboard through towards her. 'Sign here,' she ordered brusquely.

Scarlet peered down at the clipboard warily. It was the list of her personal belongings. So she was heading straight for court then. Clearly, they didn't expect to see her back. She'd have to tell her story in court without writing it all down first, it seemed.

She swallowed, silently praying that she didn't mess things up, then reached over and looked down into the bag, checking that everything on the list was there.

'Well?' the officer pushed. 'Sign, if that's all correct.'

Leaning over, Scarlet signed the papers, not bothering to read the print. As she lifted the pen, the woman reached forward and flicked the page up to reveal another beneath. 'And here,' she said, pointing.

Scarlet paused. She glanced down at the words, then up to

the officer. She glanced down and then up again a second time, completely confused. There had to be some mistake. She frowned warily. Was this a trick? She lowered her pen to the paper, signing slowly as she tried to work it out.

The officer sighed irritably. 'I haven't got all day.'

The door behind her suddenly flew open and banged loudly against the wall as Jennings stormed in. She turned as he marched towards her, her frown deepening. His face was contorted and red with anger as he leaned down menacingly towards her.

'How'd you do it?' he roared, spittle flying out of his mouth as he shook with fury. 'How did you fucking do it?'

It took Scarlet all the strength she had not to cower away from his rage. His eyes were wild as they stared into hers, and for the first time she found herself feeling afraid of him.

'What are you talking about?' she asked, trying to keep her voice steady.

'The evidence,' he spat. 'How did you fucking do it?'

'Do *what?*' Her heart beat faster as she tried to catch up. What was he talking about?

'Hey...' The officer that had accompanied her down stepped between them, gently forcing Jennings back. 'Not here,' he warned, glancing up at the camera.

Jennings followed his gaze and stepped back, running both hands back through his hair and pulling a deep breath in through his nose. 'I don't know how you did it, but I'm sure as hell going to find out,' he said, his voice low and threatening. 'And when I do, I'm going to make damn sure you never get the chance again.'

For a moment Scarlet tensed, sure, by the look in his eye, that he was going to reach forward and hit her. But with one last growl of frustration, he turned on his heel and stormed back out of the room, leaving her alarmed and confused.

What the hell had just happened?

The female officer who'd instructed her where to sign took the paperwork out of her hands.

'You have been released from custody without bail,' she said brusquely. 'You can leave freely, but be aware that should any new evidence come to light, or should you be suspected of another crime, you can and will be re-arrested.' There was a long silence. 'Off you go then,' she prompted. 'Unless you want to go back in.'

Scarlet blinked and quickly grabbed her bag of things from the counter. 'Right,' she said, her tone heavy with disbelief. How had this happened? She was all set to go to jail. There was enough evidence to send her down, even if she hadn't been about to confess. So how was she suddenly free? It didn't make any sense.

Her eyes flickering warily towards the door Jennings had left by, Scarlet walked away from the desk and out of the building. No one followed her. No one stopped her. It was no trick. She was truly free.

Scarlet squinted up at the sky then took in her surroundings. She was at the back of the station in a small, enclosed car park. With one last tense glance over her shoulder, she quickly exited the car park through the side gate and emerged into the street beyond.

She reached into the plastic bag as the gate swung shut and pulled out her phone, breathing out a sigh of relief when it came to life. She quickly scrolled to her aunt's number and pressed dial.

'Scarlet?' came her aunt's surprised tone.

'Yeah, it's me,' Scarlet replied.

'How are you calling from your own phone?' Lily asked.

'They let me out,' she replied, her words still tinged with disbelief.

There was a short pause. 'Why?' Her disbelief was echoed by her aunt.

There was an even longer pause as Scarlet tried to work out the answer. She raised her free hand to her head and turned in a tight circle, checking she was still alone. 'I don't know,' she said. 'I have absolutely no idea.'

THIRTY

Cath picked up one of the many plates of food from the large coffee table in Lily's lounge and wafted it in front of Scarlet's nose. 'Come on, have one more – you must be hungry still.'

'Mum, I'm fine,' Scarlet replied, pushing the plate away gently but firmly. 'Honestly, I'm fit to burst.'

After she'd called, her aunt had picked her up and instructed the rest of the family to congregate at her house. Two minutes after they'd arrived, Cath had screeched up the road and almost crashed into the back of Lily's car as she swung onto the drive, before stepping out and promptly bursting into tears. She'd clutched Scarlet to her chest and squeezed her so tightly she could barely breathe.

Once she'd calmed down a bit, Cath had gone straight to the kitchen, declaring her disgust at the way they'd clearly starved her daughter. Lily had stepped aside and watched, bemused, as Cath proceeded to cook every item of food she had in the fridge. They'd all been picking at it for hours on and off.

Cillian frowned at his phone. 'I've gotta see a man about a dog,' he said, standing up.

'Just don't be late tomorrow,' Lily warned.

'I won't. Catch you later.' He tipped his head to Connor, who kissed his mother on the cheek and followed his brother.

'Glad you're back on the right side of the bars, Scar,' he said with a grin as he passed her.

'Me too,' she replied with feeling.

The twins walked out and the front door shut behind them.

Scarlet turned back to her aunt. 'What's going on tomorrow?'

She was glad of the change of subject, tired of going over her own strange situation. The entire family had talked it through from every angle, but they were still no nearer to figuring out why they'd let her walk away when they were so close to sending her down.

'Grace accepted our proposition,' Lily replied.

Scarlet grinned, her eyes gleaming. 'That's good news,' she said.

'Grace?' Cath interjected. 'As in *the* Grace?' She glanced between her daughter and sister-in-law. 'What proposition? Why would you propose anything to *her*?' she asked incredulously. 'Actually, no. I don't want to know.' She pursed her mouth and lifted her chin. 'Yes, I do,' she argued with herself. 'No, I don't,' she ended, flustered. 'Oh, for God's sake.' She stood up and exhaled loudly through her nose, then picked up two of the plates and tipped the contents together, taking the empty one out to the kitchen.

Scarlet caught Lily's eye and hid a smile. Cath had always steered clear of the business. Through all her years married to Ronan, she'd kept firmly away from it, other than to protect him and act as his alibi when he needed it. But now that he was gone and Scarlet had taken her place within the firm, she was finding it harder and harder to keep her attention turned away. Her natural need to protect her child pulled her towards knowing what was happening, but she fought against it for the most part, always struggling with the delicate balance of knowing just enough to help guide her and just little enough to avoid having a heart attack.

'No, I do need to know,' she said, coming back into the room with her fists planted on her hips bracingly. 'Come on then – tell me why the hell you're propositioning the psycho that tried to kill you all.'

'We're going to work with her.' Lily crossed her slim legs and leaned back in her armchair as she lit a cigarette. She inhaled deeply and then blew a long plume of smoke out across the room. 'To steal paintings.'

'You're...' Cath's eyebrows shot up accusingly. 'You're teaming up with her? She burned down the factory and *nearly killed* Ruby, Lil. And you're going to work with her? That's what you're telling me?'

Lily stared back at her levelly across the room, a ghost of a smile on her face as she took another drag.

'Right,' Cath said, pursing her lips. 'Brilliant. Fucking brilliant.' She picked up another two plates from the table with sharp angry movements and marched back out to the kitchen.

'When are we meeting her?' Scarlet asked.

'*We?*' Cath shouted from the kitchen. She reappeared quickly. 'Surely you're not going, Scarlet?' she asked in alarm. 'You've just got out, though Lord knows how. You need to lie low for a while. Why don't you just focus on the salon and the normal stuff for a little bit, eh?' Cath glanced at Lily beseechingly. 'Don't you think, Lil?'

Scarlet looked to her aunt for support but found her expression torn. Her heart dropped. 'Lil...'

'I think your mum's right, Scar,' Lily replied. 'Until we figure out why they let you go, we don't know what game we're in. It could be some sort of trap, letting you out to condemn yourself somehow.'

'How could it be a trap?' Scarlet pushed. 'They *had* me.

They had me for murder and still they let me go. What more could they think they'd get?'

Lily sat back and squeezed her gaze, taking another deep drag on her cigarette.

'I get what you're saying, but I just can't see a worthwhile angle for them,' Scarlet continued. 'I'm not even on *bail* – they just let me walk out.' She shrugged. 'I don't know why, but I can't just sit around here doing nothing.' She looked up at her mother in despair. 'Mum, this is what I do. It's who I am.'

Cath looked up to the heavens and bit her lip with a shake of the head but said no more. She picked up the last of the plates and headed out to the kitchen, leaving them to it.

'Plus, you know you need me on the Grace job,' she added, lowering her voice. 'And I *should* be involved.' She stared at Lily across the table, and Lily held her gaze with an unreadable expression. 'This all started with me, remember? You can't side-line me now.'

She nodded. 'Let's go forward as planned. We'll see it through to the end together. As a firm.' She took one more drag and slid her gaze to one of the photos on the wall. 'As a family.'

Cillian watched the flat from the alleyway across the road. His phone rang and he glanced down at the screen before answering.

'Mum,' he said quietly.

'Is he there?' she asked.

'No. Still no sign. Fucker's been sleeping elsewhere since we paid him that visit.' He balled his free hand into a fist, frustrated.

He heard his mother's sigh hiss down the phone. There was a short silence and then the click of a door closing as she moved to another room to speak in private.

'You'll have to have him followed from the station again,

find out where he's going. She's free now, somehow, but he was the cunt that sent her there,' she said in a low deadly tone. 'He needs taking care of. But we need to work out how first. Make sure there's no way it can ever be tied to us.'

'We will. I'll sort it.' He ended the call and slipped the phone back in his pocket, melting back against the wall as someone passed the mouth of the alley.

His brooding gaze darkened once more as he looked up towards the window – no signs of life in the small flat beyond. John Richards was going to rue the day he ever went after Scarlet. And Cillian was going to make sure of it.

THIRTY-ONE

Scarlet cast her gaze around the street warily as Cath pulled up on their drive. There didn't seem to be any cars that she didn't know, or any suspicious-looking people that could be undercover watching the house. She wasn't sure whether this made her feel more or less confident of her newfound freedom though. It was all just incredibly strange.

She stepped out and rubbed her forehead, tired suddenly. After two nights on a thin roll-out mattress that had done nothing to buffer her body from the cold, unyielding concrete beneath, she was desperate to lie down in her own warm, comfortable bed.

'I think I'm just going to head straight up,' she said to Cath as her mother unlocked the front door.

'Yeah, 'course,' Cath replied. 'You must be knackered.' She glanced at her watch. 'I'm going to go catch up on my programmes for a bit before I hit the sack.'

'OK.' Scarlet leaned in and kissed her mother on the cheek before climbing the stairs. ''Night.'

The TV came on as she reached the landing, and Scarlet

heard her mother settle into the sofa and begin to flick through the channels. She was glad to see her relax. It had been a difficult few days for all of them, but Cath would have dealt with it the worst.

The sound of the TV faded to almost nothing as she reached her room at the back. She walked in and flicked the light switch, pushing the door shut behind her and heading towards the desk where she usually undressed.

The sense that something wasn't quite right raised the small hairs on the back of her neck just a millisecond before she caught the movement behind her in the mirror. She opened her mouth to scream, but a large hand covered her mouth and an arm pulled her upper body backward into a tight grip. She frantically struggled and kicked out, but whoever held her was bigger and stronger.

'Don't scream – it's me,' came the low urgent voice. 'It's me.'

He moved her forward and she stared into the mirror, realisation dawning. She stopped struggling.

'I'm going to let you go now,' he said, his tone calm and clear. 'Please don't scream. I just want to talk to you.'

He let go and she turned around to face him, fire in her eyes. 'What the *hell* are you doing in my room?' she demanded. 'How did you even get in? It's *illegal* to break into someone's house, you realise that, right? I mean, I'm no expert, but I imagine they teach that sort of basic law at police school.' Her sarcastic tone was paired with a withering look as she faced the man she hated more than anyone else in the world right now.

John exhaled heavily as he stared back at her. 'Yes, they do. Thank you for the reminder,' he replied, his sarcasm matching hers.

'What are you doing here?' she asked. 'Did my cousins not make it clear enough to stay away?' She held her head high and looked down her nose at him in contempt. 'Because next time they'll make it *crystal*.'

Ignoring her threats, he reached into the pocket of his casual black jacket and pulled out a couple of small plastic bags and some crumpled sheets of paper. He dropped them on the bed beside them and stepped back, gesturing for her to take a look.

Warily, Scarlet reached down and moved the papers aside. Her eyes widened and her mouth opened in surprise. Inside the two bags were the knife and what she assumed were the floor scratchings, along with the paperwork detailing them as evidence. Her mind began to swirl, and dots began to tentatively connect.

'What is this?' she breathed. 'I don't understand.'

'I told you I wasn't after you,' John said seriously. 'I meant it when I said I didn't know who you are. I was never after you. I've never wanted to see you go down. Especially not for this.'

'So, what? You stole the evidence?' She looked up into his eyes with a frown. 'But you barely know me. And this would have been a big credit for you. This is what you *do*. You put people away.' It didn't make sense.

'Bad people, yes,' he replied earnestly. 'But I don't think you're a bad person.' His bright green eyes flickered with a range of emotions as he held her gaze. He broke off and ran his hands up through his hair, turning in a circle before facing her again. 'This is crazy, I know. And it goes against everything I vowed when I joined the force. I'm not a bent copper; I've never done anything like this before.'

Scarlet watched the struggle in his face as he spoke, and she felt her anger wane. Had he really done this? Had he really turned rogue for *her*?

'When we met, and we got to know each other, I felt like there was something... I don't know, *more*, I guess. Something deeper than a normal connection. I felt like I really *saw* you. I thought you saw me.' He paused and looked away. 'Whether you did or didn't, when I found out who you were and what Jennings was pinning you for, I just knew you didn't deserve to go down. You don't deserve to lose your life for killing someone in self-defence.'

Scarlet bit her lip and sat down on the bed slowly, looking down at the papers in her hands and back up to him. 'And you didn't trust in the judgements of the jury?'

'Usually I would, yes,' he replied. 'But I've seen your file. The rest of it, I mean. Your family connections.' His eyes met hers. 'They'd have given you maximum penalties because of that.'

Scarlet nodded slowly. She'd thought as much. 'You could go down yourself, if they ever find out what you've done,' she said.

John closed his eyes, the weight of what he'd done showing in his frown. 'I know. But once I realised I couldn't just let it happen. I knew I had to find a way.' He opened them again and looked up to the ceiling, sitting down on the bed a little way away from her. 'So I found a way. And here we are.'

'Here we are,' Scarlet repeated in wonder.

There was a long silence as she processed everything. All this time he'd been genuine. When he'd cornered her by her car and begged her to listen and she'd pushed him away, when her cousins had gone round and warned him with a beating. She closed her eyes, guilt flooding in. But how could she have known? That was their way of life. They *had* to be careful; they *had* to assume the worst of men like John. It was what kept them out of prison. Usually anyway.

But now here she was, unexpectedly freed by the last person on Earth she'd have thought would help her. And he'd put his career and his own freedom at risk to make it happen.

'Were you careful not to leave a trail?' she asked, her concern for him now overriding her previous anger.

'Yeah,' he replied. 'It was actually pretty easy, given my level of access.' He sounded a little sad as he said this, and

Scarlet could understand why. It couldn't be easy going against everything you stood for, even for someone you care about.

She frowned as more and more questions began to resound in her mind. 'Why did they let me go so quickly?' she asked. 'They didn't even question me about it, or not really anyway.' Jennings' furious outburst replayed in her mind and suddenly made sense.

'I faked a demand from your lawyer,' he admitted. 'I needed them to find out before the trial, before you could say anything condemning. I claimed I'd had a call demanding fresh copies of all the evidence immediately. I passed it to Jennings and made sure I was around after he discovered it was gone. He threw a fit. I don't think I've ever seen someone lose it so hard. I said I'd deliver the news to your lawyer as I had the number, and that I'd try and buy us some time. Then I went back shortly after and claimed he'd demanded your immediate release following the lack of evidence. He had no choice but to let you walk.'

'Wow.' Scarlet blew out a long breath.

She thought back to where she'd been mentally, just seconds before her release. She'd been ready to confess. If they'd questioned her even for five minutes before they'd let her go, they'd have had her, evidence or not. She swallowed, realising how narrow her escape had been. Jennings would never know just how close he'd been. Or at least she hoped he wouldn't.

'I don't know what to say. Thank you, I guess. And I'm sorry, for, you know... My cousins.' She winced.

'I don't need your thanks. I chose to do it. And I did it because I feel a lot for you, Scarlet. I can't even really explain it.' He turned to her, raw honesty in his eyes. 'Look, I love what I do. I can't pretend I don't. When I put people away who really deserve it, it makes me feel good. It makes me feel like I've made a difference, and that's why I chose this career. But something

I've realised over time, and more so since meeting you,' he added, 'is that people who are bad and people who break the law aren't always the same thing.' He rubbed his head. 'My hands are bound by the law, and because of that I've put people away who I think weren't actually that bad. And that's just the downside of the job. But I just couldn't do it to you.' He sighed. 'I couldn't let it happen. You mean too much to me. And I'm hoping...' He twisted his body to face her. 'I'm hoping that now you realise I'm not a threat and that my feelings are genuine, that we can give this another try.'

Scarlet turned to face him too but moved no closer. 'John, you say that you can see I'm not a bad person,' she said, her expression grave, 'but you do realise that the evidence was right, don't you? I did kill Jasper.' Her eyes flicked down towards his chest as she wondered for the briefest moment if this could be an elaborate set-up. Was he wearing a wire? Was this all to get a clean confession?

John nodded. 'OK,' he said levelly.

Scarlet pushed the suspicion away. He'd more than proved himself tonight. 'And my family,' she continued, 'we're a firm. You understand what that means, don't you? We run all sorts of illegal businesses. And I am very much involved in that.' Her heart began to thump hard in her chest as she laid the truth bare between them.

John was quiet for a few moments and he wiped his hands down his face. 'I should care about that. Every moment of my life has wired me to care about that, but right now, honestly, all I care about is whether you and I are going to make it past this point. Because I really, really hope that we are. Since the day we met, I haven't been able to stop thinking of you. All our talks, everything we began to build... I don't want that to be gone. That's all I know, right now.'

He looked up at her and she saw the ravaged expression of a

man who'd thrown his soul to the wind to be close to her. Her heart slowed and her fear disappeared.

'You realise we'll have to hide our relationship. Indefinitely,' she warned. 'If they ever found out you were dating me, they'd put two and two together.'

He nodded. 'I know. I can't imagine being with me will do your reputation much good either.'

'No,' she agreed. 'It won't.'

His gaze pierced hers across the bed as they came to a silent understanding and he reached his hand out towards her face. She moved closer and he pulled her towards him. Their lips met, and as Scarlet melted into his embrace, it was as though a weight had been lifted from her heart. John's arms felt like home in a way that surprised her, in a way she couldn't understand. She didn't particularly need to understand though, she realised, so long as she could remain there.

Eventually, he pulled away and pressed his forehead to hers, grasping her hands in his. 'This is going to be dangerous for both of us,' he said.

'We'll figure it out,' she replied, squeezing his hands. They would need to. The ins and outs of this kind of relationship would be messy.

Ignoring the hard road they had ahead of them for a moment, she marvelled at this unexpected turn of events. An hour ago, she'd hated the handsome man in front of her. She'd hated him so much it had hurt. But it hurt that much because underneath the rage were feelings that had been scorned.

To now learn that she'd been wrong, that her first instincts had been right – and on top of that to learn that he'd been the one to save her from a life sentence – felt incredible. It felt too good to be true, but somehow it was.

'I'd better go,' John said, regret in his tone as he began to stand. 'I'll sort out a pair of SIM-only phones tomorrow that we can use. Then I guess...'

'Oh no,' Scarlet said firmly, pulling him back down to the bed and towards her. 'I think we've been apart enough. Don't you?' She kissed him deeply on the mouth and then ran her lips down his jawbone to his neck as he gave in and pressed his body to hers. 'You're not going anywhere tonight. Everything else can wait.'

THIRTY-TWO

Lily paced around her home office as she held the phone to her ear, the hold music on the other end irritating the life out of her. Robert was in a meeting and apparently couldn't be disturbed, but she had insisted his secretary pull him out to talk to her. She couldn't wait any longer – she needed answers. She needed to know why Scarlet had been freed. And she certainly didn't pay him as much as she did to be unreachable.

There was a quiet knock on the door and she turned to see Scarlet slipping in. 'Hey, you free for a chat?'

'Yeah, 'course. I'm just on hold for Robert. Hopefully he can shed some light on what's going on,' she said.

'I know what happened,' Scarlet replied. 'That's what I'm here to tell you.'

She dropped two small plastic bags down on the desk along with some papers. Lily looked down at them with a frown, then as she registered what they were, her eyebrows shot upwards. She sat down and leaned forward on the desk, propping one elbow up and covering her mouth with her hand as she continued to stare.

'How?' she asked.

'John,' Scarlet replied, sitting down opposite her.

'*What?*' Lily asked, flabbergasted. 'Why would he do this? What game is he playing?'

'No game,' Scarlet said simply, shaking her head. 'We were wrong about him. *I* was wrong.' She rubbed her forehead and sighed. 'He was never undercover. He really didn't know who I was. The time we spent together, everything we shared, it was all real.'

Lily made a sound of disagreement and disapproval. 'It can't have been. He's a copper,' she said. 'He's a copper and you're a *Drew*.'

'I know,' Scarlet replied, looking up at her. 'It's crazy but it's true. I wouldn't be sat here if it wasn't. He had no idea who I was until that day in the interrogation room.'

Lily looked down at the evidence bags in front of her in amazement. 'But why help you?'

'Because he couldn't see me go down. It wasn't easy for him,' she added defensively. 'He's risked a lot. But he really does care about me. And now I owe him everything.'

For Lily, this certainly changed things. Her plan for John, for starters. She'd been about to issue him his ticket to the next life. But now, like Scarlet had said, they owed him. It certainly was the most unexpected turn of events. What was she going to do about him now?

'You shouldn't have carried that over here. If they'd arrested you on your way and found that, you'd have been done,' she said.

'I couldn't exactly keep it in the house,' Scarlet replied.

Lily conceded with a tilt of her head and then pursed her lips, studying her niece. Scarlet looked away, but she couldn't truly hide what she was thinking. Not from Lily.

Scarlet liked John, and obviously from his recent heroics, he must be pretty taken with her too. But this unexpected heroic act was borne from the initial burst of romantic feelings between them, and whilst they may be strong right now, those feelings wouldn't last forever. She cast her eyes down to her cigarette packet and slowly pulled one out.

'He's done you an incredible favour. All of us really.' She placed the cigarette between her lips and sparked the lighter. 'But you know it can't go any further.'

Scarlet's cheeks flushed and there was a long silence. Lily inhaled the smoke and blew it back out, studying her. No agreement was forthcoming.

'Scarlet,' she said a little more strongly. 'It *can't*.'

'I don't agree,' Scarlet replied, shaking her head. 'I *won't* agree.'

Lily took another drag, twisting her mouth to the side as she exhaled sharply. 'Scarlet, he's a copper. It don't get any more taboo than that. Listen,' she cut her niece off as she opened her mouth to respond. 'I get it. I really do. He saved you and that's something. It is. But dating him is a risk, not just for you, but for all of us. We can't have a copper getting that close to this firm. Even if you say nothing, just being with you, seeing your comings and goings, hearing your phone calls, it reveals too much.'

'Hasn't he proved just how much he *isn't* a risk already?' Scarlet argued. 'He hasn't let me off a parking ticket, Lil – he stole evidence to get me off a *murder* charge.' She lifted her eyebrows at her defiantly.

'*You*, yes.' Lily rubbed her forehead. 'But what about your cousins, Scar? What about me?' She looked up, her dark brown eyes holding Scarlet's gaze. 'We aren't people he cares about, people he wants to protect. He's still Old Bill. He still disagrees, down to his core, with everything we do. And when he starts to realise the extent of that, then what?'

Scarlet opened her mouth and shut it again. Lily watched the cogs turning in silence.

'What if...' Scarlet began, her tone reluctant. She sighed.

'What if you made sure you had something over him. Privately of course. But something you could use as leverage, should you need to. Not that you *would* need it,' she added. 'But as protection. Perhaps condemning footage of him with us, talking with us. Maybe he could even be useful to you, down the line.'

Lily raised one eyebrow in interest. There certainly was an element of opportunity here. It would be helpful, having a pocket plod. The twins wouldn't like it. But perhaps with some conditions they would be able to work this to an advantage.

'If I did agree to that,' she said carefully, 'this still wouldn't be easy for you. You'd have to hide him from the public eye. No one in our world could ever know you're together, other than those closest to us.'

'I'm aware of that,' Scarlet replied.

'The family, partners, George, Andy and Sandra. That's it. Those are the only people who could know your secret.' Her gaze pierced Scarlet's, willing her to understand what a dire existence that would be.

Scarlet cast her gaze downwards. 'I know it's mad,' she admitted. 'I know it makes no sense. But there's just something between us.' She lifted her gaze back up to meet Lily's and a defeated acceptance now filled them. 'And after all he's done to keep me free, after all he's risked, I can't not fight for that.'

'I'm telling you now,' Lily sighed, 'I think it's a bad idea, for many reasons. But so long as he understands that we'll throw him to the wolves if he ever puts us in danger, then I won't stop you.'

'Thank you,' Scarlet replied, a tinge of relief in her tone.

'I'm not saying the others are going to be happy about it,' Lily warned. 'You've got more than one battle ahead of you.'

'I know.'

Lily blew out another plume of smoke and then tapped her ash gently into the ashtray on the desk. 'We need to focus on business now,' she said, changing the subject. There had been more than enough talk of John Richards today. 'I have a premises I think will work for the new factory which I want you to come look at, then we have the meeting with Grace tonight. You need to hold off talking to anyone in the family about John until tomorrow. We don't need Connor and Cillian distracted tonight.'

'OK. Where are the premises?' Scarlet asked.

'There's an industrial unit going down near Beckton gas works. Tucked away, it has a few metres of scrub at the back which backs onto the river.'

'That could be useful,' Scarlet mused.

'It could. It's the right size to set the main factory floor up pretty much exactly how it was before, but with much more spare space,' Lily continued. 'Couple of offices inside, better parking.'

'Basement?'

'No.' Lily took one last drag on her cigarette then stubbed it out. 'That's the only issue.'

'Where would we host the poker nights? And deal with, you know, less savoury business.'

'Less savoury business, I believe there's room enough there for that. As for the poker nights, I have a possible solution.' Lily leaned forward. 'There's a pub up for sale not far from this site, just up the road by Greatfields Park. It's called the Spoiled Pig. I thought we might buy it.'

'Buy a *pub*?' Scarlet asked, surprised. 'You want to run a pub?'

'No, but I have some people in mind who might want to run it under our employ. Trustworthy people. People who'll keep quiet about the second floor, which will be closed off for regular poker nights – much *more* regular than we were running before. And there's another set of offices out the back, which would probably suit us better outside factory hours.' Lily sat back.

'That sounds interesting,' Scarlet replied, nodding. 'When can we view them?'

'Now, if you like,' Lily replied. 'Then we need to head over to the salon and make sure everything's set up for tonight.' She stood up and smoothed down her knee-length black leather skirt. 'Because I wouldn't be surprised if Grace tries something.'

'You think she will?' Scarlet asked, standing to join her.

Lily's expression darkened. 'I think where Grace is concerned, we need to make sure we're ready for anything.'

THIRTY-THREE

Ruby's hand paused on its way up to her face as she heard the knock on the front door. She waited and cursed as she realised that no one else was in the house. Who was knocking on the door in the middle of the day? She peered out her bedroom window. She couldn't see who was at the door as the porch blocked her view and she didn't recognise the car. Was it a delivery? Lily didn't usually send deliveries to the house as she was never there, but perhaps now the factory was gone she had no choice.

The person below knocked again and Ruby sighed. She walked back to the mirror and tentatively rubbed the line of concealer in as best she could, wincing at the pain, then made her way downstairs. Whoever it was began to knock again as she reached the door, and she snapped in annoyance.

'Yeah, alright, I'm here! Christ!'

She opened it and blinked in surprise at the pretty smiling blonde on the other side. 'Oh. Sandra.'

She wished she'd stayed hidden upstairs as Sandra's gaze immediately took in her scars. She turned her head, embarrassed. 'Mum ain't here.'

'I'm not here to see her,' Sandra replied.

'Oh.' Ruby shifted awkwardly. 'Why *are* you here then?'

'I'm here to see you, silly!' Sandra laughed lightly and rolled her eyes, stepping into the hallway, forcing Ruby to move back out of the way.

Ruby closed the door and straightened her oversized jumper, feeling self-conscious. 'So, what do you need?' she asked, wishing Sandra would just leave.

Sandra's smile softened and her eyes moved down to the concealer stick still in Ruby's hand. 'You trying to do a cover job?' she asked, pointing down to it.

Ruby immediately slipped it under her sleeve and her cheeks flooded with red. 'What's it to you?' she asked brusquely.

'I ain't judging or anything – you don't have to be defensive. Not with me,' she added. 'I just thought maybe I could help. I'm good with make-up. I mean, look at me. This mug don't start out like this in the mornings, I promise you.' She grinned.

Ruby bit her lip. 'I've never been much good with make-up,' she admitted grudgingly. 'Never saw much point with my face. You can't polish a turd.'

Sandra screwed up her nose. 'That's disgusting for one thing and bollocks for another.' She stepped forward and took the concealer from Ruby, then took a closer look at her face. 'You've actually got amazing bone structure.'

Ruby cast her eyes down and pinched her lips together, unsure how to respond. She wasn't very good at taking compliments, on the odd occasion she received them.

'Here, come to the mirror.'

Sandra led her across the hallway and positioned her so that she could see what she was doing. She placed her large handbag down on the sideboard beneath and rummaged around for a few pieces of her own make-up.

'See, if you use a bit of contouring, like this...' She gently patted on some foundation which immediately did a better job of covering the redness. Ruby clenched her teeth, trying hard not to flinch at the pain even her soft touch triggered. 'And bring attention to the front of your cheekbones, a bit like this.' She carefully brushed some subtle bronzer into shaded lines and Ruby's face began to change before her eyes. 'Then add a little shimmer just here.' She dotted something onto Ruby's cheeks just under her eyes and rubbed it in lightly with her finger. 'You can see already, it's not as noticeable at all.'

She stepped back and pushed Ruby closer to the mirror. Ruby's eyes widened at the change in her face. Even those small changes had transformed her whole face. And Sandra was right. Although it didn't entirely hide the puckered skin – nothing short of a miracle could do that at this point – it had certainly softened it and made it much less obvious.

'Wow, thanks, Sandra,' she said shyly. The make-up burned the new raw skin but she didn't care. She hated to see it more than she hated the feel of it, so she'd suffer it. She glanced up at Sandra in the mirror and saw a strangely sad look in the other woman's eyes.

'You know, I really didn't like how that Nat used to speak to you,' she said. 'It was uncalled for.'

Ruby nodded. 'Yeah. She was a real bitch.' She said the words casually, but her feelings on the matter ran much deeper.

Natalie had been Scarlet's best friend for many years. When Scarlet had opened the salon, she'd hired Natalie as the manager, and when Ruby had been sent there to work, Natalie had treated her horribly. She'd spoken to her rudely, made her do twice the work that anyone else did, tripped her up, mocked her at every opportunity and went out of her way to make Ruby miserable.

Sandra worked in the salon too and there had been many times she'd quietly stuck up for Ruby. She'd never joined in with Natalie's nastiness despite the fact she'd often tried to involve her. Ruby had been grateful for that. When Ruby had found Natalie had been scamming money from the business, she'd been elated to out her to Scarlet and Lily. The cruel young woman had been fired and ejected from the local area with warnings never to return.

Now, Sandra saying the words out loud as she stood there trying to help her feel better about her scars made Ruby feel a real warmth towards her. Ruby had never really had friends. Not real ones anyway. The people she used to hang around with in their mutual hope of scoring more drugs as a team were never friends. But perhaps that was what this was. The beginning of a friendship.

'Do you fancy a coffee?' Ruby asked tentatively.

Sandra smiled. 'I'd love one.'

Ruby led the way through to the kitchen and set about making a pot, whilst Sandra sat on one of the barstools at the kitchen island.

'When do you think you'll come back to the salon?' she asked.

'I'm not sure,' Ruby said, uncertainty clear in her tone.

'What, because of your scars?' Sandra asked bluntly.

Ruby glanced at her and then turned back to the coffee, her shoulders hunching tensely.

'Sorry, I don't mean to upset you,' she continued. 'But I can see it's bothering you, and I get it. I'd feel the same.' Ruby's shoulders dropped. 'But you can't hide away forever. You need to get back out there, get back on the horse.'

'Why do you even care?' Ruby blurted out. She turned and handed Sandra her coffee.

Sandra took it and wrapped her hands around the mug with a smile that didn't reach her eyes. She looked away for a few moments.

'I grew up in an orphanage, me,' she said after a pause. 'Moved about a bit to and from different foster homes until I aged out of the system. You learn a lot about people, growing up like that.' She turned back to Ruby, her gaze sombre. 'You learn to recognise the others like you. The lost ones who fight like they ain't got no other choice. And when you see them, you grab on to them and you stick together. It was the only way to get through back then. Still is now sometimes.'

Ruby's eyebrows shot up. Sandra always seemed so bubbly and sure of herself. It was a surprise that she'd had such a lonely, unstable upbringing.

She stirred some sugar into her coffee. 'Surely you don't see an orphan in me,' she replied curiously. 'I mean, we're in my family's house right now.'

'I didn't say that people like us were all orphans,' Sandra said, taking a sip of her coffee. 'But I see you.' She took another sip and gave Ruby a brief smile over the top of her mug.

Ruby didn't respond, unsure exactly what to say to that. She took a sip of her own coffee and the pair sat in silence. In one way, what Sandra had said didn't make sense, but in another weird way it did. Perhaps deep down they were the same. The thought was pleasant, whether or not it was true.

Sandra glanced up at the clock. 'I can't stay too long – your aunt Cath is holding the fort. It really would be good to have you back soon. You know all the stock is in total shambles now. The stylists just chuck everything anywhere, and your aunt, well, she does make it nice and tidy but she hasn't got that little system like you had. That works so well.'

'Well...' Ruby felt torn. Part of her wanted to stay hidden away forever, but she knew that wasn't realistic. And she was beginning to go mad, cooped up here. Her hand rose to her neck and she touched the scars there.

Sandra noticed the action. 'I can do your make-up for you,' she offered. 'Make you feel a million dollars.'

'You can't do it every day though,' Ruby replied.

'What if I teach you?' Sandra said suddenly. 'Why don't

you come by tomorrow afternoon towards closing and I'll bring my make-up and we'll go over everything. Yeah? Then I'll give you a list of what to buy so you can put it on yourself going forward. How does that sound?'

Ruby's hopes rose. Maybe that could work. 'OK,' she agreed with a nod. 'I'll do that. Thanks.'

Sandra grinned and hopped off the stool, taking one last sip of her drink. 'Great. I'll see you then. I'd better go.'

'I'll see you out.' They walked back through to the hallway and Ruby opened the door.

'Your aunt will be pleased to see you back,' Sandra said as she stepped out onto the porch. 'So will your cousin.'

Ruby's smile froze and she forced it to remain there despite the reminder of her cousin. 'See you then.' She waited for Sandra to reach her car then closed the door, her face dropping to a sour expression.

For a brief wonderful moment, she'd thought the universe might have been giving her a break. Scarlet had been set to go down for murder, and if all had gone to plan the rest of the family would have been home free. It would have been perfect. Princess Scarlet would no longer have hogged the limelight and everyone's attention all the time. She'd have been out of the way in what would have been Ruby's personal happily ever after story. The road would have been clear for her to step up and finally show her mother and brothers what she was made of. It would have been their family – their *immediate* family – as one whole unit, fierce and strong. She'd allowed herself to picture it, to feel the elation.

But somehow Scarlet had slithered out of it, like she always did. Somehow she'd walked away from a murder charge smelling of roses and with no loose ends, and Ruby's happy ending had shattered like the fragile fantasy it was.

Back in the kitchen, she picked up Sandra's mug and poured the coffee down the sink, and she felt the bitterness settle back in. Her chances of thriving had once again been thwarted and it was all because Scarlet just couldn't stay down.

She turned and began to pace, agitated. Everything that was wrong in her life had one common factor. Scarlet.

Scarlet had muscled into the heart of her family, leaving no room for her.

Scarlet had taken what *should* have been her place in the firm.

Scarlet was the reason Grace had burned the factory down with her inside, leaving Ruby scarred and broken.

Everything bad that happened to her always seemed to have Scarlet at the root of it. And she'd had enough.

The unfairness of the situation suddenly overwhelmed her, and with a roar she turned and hurled Sandra's cup into the bottom of the sink, smashing it to pieces.

THIRTY-FOUR

Connor watched from the shadows as the man across the road disappeared down the dark alleyway opposite. He took one last drag on his cigarette before flicking it away and crossing over. Checking no one else was headed their way, he slipped down after the man, careful not to make a sound as he quickened his pace to catch up. He reached the corner and paused, then hurried on as the man disappeared from view again. He slowed to a stop at the end of the alley and peered round.

It opened up into a backstreet car park, tall crumbling walls surrounding it, save for the entrance and row of buildings at the front. The man he'd followed stood in the middle staring at these buildings for a moment, as if assessing them. He reached into his inner jacket pocket and pulled out a gun, holding it loosely to his side.

Connor's jaw locked grimly, but he moved forward anyway. He hadn't come unprepared.

Silently closing the distance between them, he approached from the back. His fingers wrapped around his own gun for a moment, held tight against his back by his belt. But then he pulled his hand away and reached into his pocket instead, swiftly flicking up the Swiss army blade he kept there. A gun could be knocked away without too much risk of damage at close range. A sharp knife against soft flesh, on the other hand, held a much more immediate risk.

Creeping forward over the last few feet with cat-like precision, Connor finally reached his prey. Suddenly aware that someone or something was behind him, the man tensed and began to turn, but it was too late. Connor wrapped his arm around his neck and pressed the blade to his throat.

His eyes flashed in the darkness and his voice dropped to a low, menacing growl. 'Give me the gun and keep your fucking mouth shut, if you want to keep breathing.'

Lily watched through the glass as Grace and two of her men approached the front door of the salon. Grace wore a haughty smirk which set Lily's teeth on edge, but her expression did not betray her as they entered.

George stepped forward and checked her over for a weapon, whilst Andy did the same with her two men. 'We're not carrying,' Grace said witheringly. 'It would be a bit of a risk somewhere like this, wouldn't it?' She pointedly glanced at the busy road through the wall of windows. 'Far too public. But that's why you picked it, right?'

Satisfied, George and Andy let them pass and stepped back, keeping a watchful eye on the newcomers.

'You found the place OK then?' Lily said with a tight smile.

'Clearly,' Grace replied in a low, sarcastic drawl.

Lily bit down to stop herself from responding. Grace slowly circled the salon, looking around with vague interest and subtly checking out who was there.

'You have the upstairs too?' she asked.

'No, they're private flats,' Scarlet answered from her seat across the room. 'It's just this and the back room.'

Grace turned her nose up, apparently unimpressed. 'Not exactly the most appropriate place for a meeting,' she declared.

'Well, our usual meeting place is currently little more than a pile of ash,' Lily snapped. 'So you'll just have to make do.'

Grace turned to her with an icy smile. 'Then make do we shall. And firstly, we'll be renegotiating our terms.' She picked something invisible to anyone else off her perfectly pressed dress and sat down in one of the styling chairs, crossing her legs to one side. Both of the men who'd walked in with her stood close behind, watching the rest of them warily.

Lily looked out of the window, not quite hiding her smile. 'We won't be renegotiating anything,' she said firmly.

Grace made a quiet sound of amusement. 'It wasn't a question. Did you really think I'd come here with just two men and no weapons?' Her cold blue eyes flashed dangerously. 'I'm not new to this game, and I certainly don't intend to be dictated to by the likes of you when I'm playing it. You might run this area, but I'm a bigger fish and I swim in a much bigger pond. *I* call the shots.'

She stood up and walked over to Lily, looking down at her with a steely gaze. 'You caught me off guard at my home and that was unfortunate. I still could have had you taken care of there and then. I had more men inside – they'd have come at a shout and you'd have been sorely outnumbered within seconds. But' – she twisted her head and raised her eyebrows – 'I wanted to hear what you had to say first. Your idea has merit and I'm willing to give it a try. But it will be *me* who makes the plans, *me* who decides which part *you* have to play in them, and ultimately *me* who decides who gets what. I could take this to any old firm in London. It's not like you're the only thieves I can make connections with. I don't actually need *you* to carry this idea of yours out.'

She rested her hand on the top of one of the chairs and

began to drum her fingers. Lily didn't answer, instead waiting for her to finish her whole spiel.

'Now that I've gained your attention, I'll explain how it's going to go,' Grace continued. 'You can work this job. Mainly because you've proven your skills to be more than adequate, which saves me time and hassle testing people elsewhere. You'll take *ten* per cent of the profits, not forty. And you'll use only *my* specified locations for storage.'

'And what makes you think that's going to happen?' Lily asked calmly. 'Why would we accept that?'

Grace grinned, baring her teeth like a snake might bear its fangs at its next meal. 'Because right now I have a man in that alley across the road pointing a gun at your head. And if I decide to signal him, he'll pull the trigger. You could of course run, but I have another man covering the back door. And he has instructions to shoot at anyone leaving other than me.' Her grin twisted into a nasty smirk and then dropped completely. 'You'll agree to my terms, and we'll lay those plans tonight. And should any of the agreed steps be messed around at any point, they'll be back to pay you a visit.'

Lily nodded sombrely then slowly walked forward towards the window. She pointed at the alleyway Grace had indicated across the road. '*That* alleyway?' she asked. 'That's where your man with the gun is?'

'Yes,' Grace answered, lifting her chin higher.

'Huh.' Lily pulled a face. 'That's funny. Because I thought that was the alley where my son had *disarmed* your man and knocked him out earlier.' She frowned as if unsure. 'Hold on, one sec.' She held a finger up to silence Grace, who had blinked and opened her mouth to reply. Pulling out her phone, she clicked on a picture and then smiled. 'Oh, that's right. It is.' She held the picture up and showed Grace the proof Cillian had sent over just minutes before the other woman had arrived.

'And as for your backstreet insurance...' She walked over to the door to the back room and pushed it open, revealing Grace's second man strapped to a chair with tape covering his mouth. Connor stood silently behind, leaning against the counter with a hard look on his face.

Lily slowly walked back and sat down facing Grace, watching as a red flush of anger crept up her face.

Then Grace smiled, a swift, cold smile, throwing daggers at Lily.

'Well, well,' she said. 'One step ahead again, it would seem. Though I guess I shouldn't be surprised. This is your kingdom, after all.' She looked around with an expression of distaste. 'It was worth a try.' More composed now, Grace smiled once more, almost in good humour.

'Shall we discuss the job now that we're all back on the same page?' Lily asked icily.

Grace nodded. 'I have an old acquaintance who throws a few dinner parties a year. Lavish events, anyone who's anyone is invited, so it's fairly crowded and the household staff are always overworked.'

As Grace settled into setting the scene, Lily exchanged a look with Scarlet. Grace was going to try to double-cross them at every opportunity and, whatever they did, they couldn't let her win. Because so much was at stake here.

So much more than even Grace knew herself.

THIRTY-FIVE

John followed Scarlet towards the front door of the large, beautiful home where her aunt lived and tried to ignore the unease in his stomach. As he took in the many windows, the sweeping drive and perfectly manicured gardens, he had to stop himself from shaking his head. The house was twice the size of the home his mother and father had worked so hard to pay the mortgage on their whole lives. It seemed that crime really *did* pay after all.

Looking down at the beautiful young woman beside him though, he pushed those thoughts away. He'd crossed the line himself now, for better or for worse. He'd waded into the murky waters of evading the very laws he upheld, in order to protect her – in order to keep her out of the prison that would slowly eat away at her soul until nothing was left but a bitter shell. As he watched her now, her thick dark hair bouncing in the breeze, her pale skin flushed from the cool air and the bright eyes that seemed to forever dance with colourful spirit, he knew he could never let that fate become her. Prisons were there for good reason, but they were places for much darker beings than Scarlet Drew.

She slowed as they reached the porch and looked up at him, uncertainty now in those bright grey-blue eyes. 'Listen...' She bit her full bottom lip and he had to stop himself from mentally replaying the feel of it on his own. 'My cousins will give you a hard time.'

'Hey, don't worry about it,' he said, eager to allay her worries. 'I'm a big boy.'

'I know, but—'

'Seriously,' he cut her off and reached for her hand. 'I'm harder than I look. I have to be, in my job.' He grinned at her and was glad to see a little relief colour her expression.

'OK, well...' She hesitated and stared at the door for a moment. 'It's now or never, I guess.'

Reaching forward, she twisted the handle and pushed the door, stepping inside and leaving him to follow. Trepidation overwhelmed him for a moment, but he pushed forward, reminding himself that he could handle anything.

Inside, Scarlet veered to the side through an archway that led to a large open-plan kitchen. Her aunt Lily stood behind a wide counter, stirring milk into a coffee and watching him with a hawk-like expression. Her two sons hung around the far end of the room, also watching. An angry flare shot through him as he remembered his last meeting with the pair, but he suppressed it. That was in the past now. It had to be, if they had any chance of moving forward in peace.

One of the twins had a brooding yet disinterested expression and the other watched him almost as sharply as his mother, a hard, unforgiving glint in his eye. This one grabbed a peanut from a nearby bowl and threw it into his mouth, not moving his gaze for a second.

'Well, if it ain't DI Dickie come to pay us a visit,' he sneered. 'How's life on the other side of the line treating you so far, *Dick*? They discovered you're a turncoat yet?'

'I'm sure DI *Richards* has been careful enough to ensure that doesn't happen, Cillian,' Lily responded with a loaded look.

Cillian smirked and picked up the peanut bowl, taking it over to his brother, where he leaned back against the windowsill beside him.

Connor eyed John from across the room. 'That's gonna leave a nasty scar, ain't it?' he said, looking up at the gash that was still healing on his head. The gash that he and his brother had inflicted. 'You'll have to be more careful, Dickie.'

Scarlet tutted and shot them both an angry look but pursed her mouth, leaving John to fight his own battle. And he needed to, he knew. The underworld worked much the same way as prison or the jungle. The strongest came out on top and the weak were quickly devoured.

He nodded, with a forced smile of amusement. 'I've had worse,' he replied, looking from him to Cillian. 'Bigger wounds from bigger men. Though I repaid all of *them* with a new home behind bars.'

'That a threat?' Connor asked, standing up and balling his hands into fists by his side aggressively.

'Not at all,' John said, stepping forward and holding his gaze to show he wasn't intimidated. 'Because we're all friends here, right?'

'Yes, we are,' Lily cut in with a glare at Connor. Connor backed off with a sniff. 'For now.'

The glare was turned on John as she added the last two words and he was reminded of the warnings in her police file. Lily was the dangerous one here, the one he had to watch at all times and never get on the wrong side of. She was the one who would ruin him or even end his life, should the tables turn. The sons, for all their big words, were just the muscle.

'Would you like a coffee?' Lily asked.

'Sure, thanks,' John replied, stepping back next to Scarlet as the tension began to dissipate.

'So here we are,' Scarlet said, her tone level but tense as she stared her cousins.

'Yes, here we are,' Lily repeated quietly, pouring out a fresh mug of coffee. 'And I guess thanks are in order. You saved Scarlet from a lifetime behind bars when we weren't able to. We're exceedingly grateful for that.'

'Don't mean we owe you nothing though,' Connor added sharply.

'Actually, it means exactly that,' Lily corrected. 'But I'm sure Mr Richards here is wise enough not to hold that over our heads.'

'Nah, DI Dick's smarter than that,' Cillian added with mock sincerity. He pulled a toothpick out from somewhere and stuck it between his teeth.

John narrowed his eyes, then, hiding his annoyance, turned to Lily. 'Please call me John, Ms Drew.'

'Lily,' she offered in return. She passed him his coffee, and he gave her a smile of thanks.

'Oh, come on,' Connor said with a tut of annoyance. 'Let's stop dancing around it, shall we? Why'd you do it? What do you actually want from all this?'

Both Cillian and Lily turned to stare at him too, clearly curious as to the reasons themselves. John felt the weight of their scrutiny and almost glanced sideways at Scarlet, but still aware he needed to hold his own, he stared Connor straight in the eye without faltering.

'I already got what I want,' he answered simply. 'For Scarlet to be free.'

'How gallant,' Cillian murmured, clearly not buying it. 'I think what my brother's getting at is whether or not you're interested in compensation for your troubles.'

John shook his head. 'I'm not after your money. Your coffers are safe from me.'

'I'd be more than happy to add you to our payroll actually,' Lily cut in. 'As a thank you.'

She smiled at him. The action was friendly enough, but John wasn't fooled. He knew there was a cold, hard viper behind that smile, and nothing that viper ever did was without good reason.

'You've taken a great risk in doing what you have,' she continued smoothly. 'You might as well enjoy some of the benefit.'

John returned her smile as politely as he could, but underneath he felt a ripple of unease. He knew what he'd done the moment he'd picked up the evidence bag. He'd aligned himself with the Drews, with a criminal firm. There was no going back now. But going onto their payroll, accepting money from them, was a whole other level. One he wasn't prepared for.

'There's no need. Really,' he stressed. 'I have all I need.'

Next to him, Scarlet reached for the coffee Lily had just poured her. 'Now we're all here, I just want to go over our situation,' she said, changing the subject. 'John and I are seeing each other now, but it's on the quiet. No one can know, other than us and those closest to us. If it gets back to the station, they'll put two and two together, and none of us need that.'

'Least of all you, eh, *John*?' Cillian said, using his actual name for the first time.

'It wouldn't exactly go in my favour either,' Scarlet snapped, clearly tired now of her cousins' jibes.

Cillian's expression darkened. 'Yeah, exactly, and it's an unnecessary risk. Look, you like each other and that's all well and good right now, but when you get caught – and at some point you *will*,' he added, 'the fallout ain't gonna be pretty. Why don't you save yourself the hassle of all that and part ways now, as friends, before you get in any deeper?'

'Why don't you back off and get on with your own love life, Cillian,' Scarlet burst, outraged. 'It ain't your place to suggest that or anything else. That's *my* decision, and whether or not it's complicated is *my* concern, not yours.'

'And where do you think this is going to go, Scar?' Cillian snapped, the underlying concern for his cousin clear in his tone. 'How's this going to end? You sneak around together, fall in love maybe, then what? Marriage? Kids? *No.* You can't have that with him – not now, not ever. Because like you just pointed out, if people ever see you together then they'll figure out it was him who took the evidence. However long it's been, a year, a decade, there will be *someone* who pieces together the fact you're a couple with the fact he was *there* the day the evidence that could have sent you down went missing. That he was on the fringes of the case the whole time.'

John felt a weight settle on his chest. It was something that had been pushing at the sides of his mind and so far he'd ignored it. But it was true. What future could they really have together, if they were both to stay out of jail?

'I don't know where this is going to end up,' Scarlet shot back at him. 'And maybe our options are limited, but that doesn't mean you get to dictate what I should do about it and how. John and I are dating, and that's the situation. Nothing other than us keeping this to ourselves matters right now.'

'And what about you, John?' Cillian asked, turning towards him. 'Are you happy putting yourself at risk for something that don't have any real future? You happy putting *her* at risk?'

John opened his mouth to reply, but Scarlet cut him off.

'He doesn't have to answer you,' she snapped. 'He doesn't work for you. He doesn't owe you jack shit.' She grasped John's arm and began pulling him back towards the hallway. 'Come on, we're done here. Lil, I'll see you in a bit.'

John gently pulled his arm from her grip and put his untouched coffee back on the counter. 'Thanks for the coffee. It was nice to meet you,' he said to Lily.

She stared back at him thoughtfully and he wished, not for

the first time this visit, that he could read what was going on behind her deep brown eyes.

'Take care, John,' she said. Her gaze intensified and bored into his. 'We'll talk again very soon.'

He kept his smile fixed on his face, but inside, his heart sank as he turned to follow Scarlet, and a ripple of cold foreboding made its way down his spine.

THIRTY-SIX

Ruby pushed her hands deep into her jacket pockets and hung her head as low as she could without blocking her view, as a couple of young women walked past chattering excitedly. Neither of them looked up at her as they passed, and even if they had, they wouldn't have been able to see much through the thick scarf she wore, but still she felt as though the ruined skin on the side of her face and neck was some sort of giant homing beacon for every judgemental gaze in the Western world.

It was the first time she'd ventured out of the house and her heart had pounded through every second of the journey. She was nearing the salon now, and as she peeped up and saw the sign, she felt an overwhelming wave of relief wash over her. She hurried her pace and was soon pushing through the door.

She sagged as it closed behind her and the familiar surroundings greeted her. Her aunt Cath was tidying the waiting area to the side and Roxy was blow-drying a client's hair. Roxy smiled at her in the mirror and Cath immediately dropped the magazines she was straightening and hurried over to give her a warm hug. As Cath's arms wrapped around her, she immediately tensed, partly from habit and partly because of the pain the motion caused around her burns, but Cath was careful to avoid touching these directly and Ruby forced herself to relax.

'Oh, it's so good to see you, love,' Cath gushed. 'Up and about, I mean. How you feeling?'

'OK, I guess,' Ruby replied, looking away.

It was true on a physical level. The burns were still raw, but she'd been taking painkillers and applying the various oils and ointments she'd been given, and so long as she was careful, the pain wasn't too bad. Mentally she felt like a total wreck. Every night she still woke up in full-on panic, drenched in sweat, convinced she was back in that room. Trapped, choking, dying.

Every time she closed her eyes she drifted back there. She'd become afraid to sleep, but sleep was something she couldn't avoid for very long. Her body was still healing, still tired. Try as she might to stay awake, sleep always claimed her in the end. And the nightmares inevitably followed.

Her waking hours didn't bring much of an improvement. Time seemed to stretch on endlessly, and memories of the night of the fire circled around and around in her brain, causing her to melt down into little more than a nervous wreck.

She needed a distraction, anything to bump her mind out of this endless loop. And that was why she was here now. Sandra's visit had given her hope, bolstered her courage to give the world another chance. Her new friend was a magician with make-up, and having someone who seemed to genuinely want to spend time with her had lifted her spirits. She'd already made her mind up to put herself out there and invite her to go for a few drinks. She was nervous, as having a girlfriend to go for drinks with was a new concept, but she was also excited. It would be fun to have someone outside of her family to hang out and have laughs with, who didn't just put up with her because they had to.

'Do you fancy a coffee?' Cath asked, still smiling from ear to ear.

Ruby managed a quick smile back. Her aunt had always been pleased to see her, even when she'd been an absolute nightmare. 'Nah, I'm OK.' She pushed the side of her face deeper into her scarf self-consciously. 'Is Sandra here?'

'I thought I heard you come in,' Sandra said in a jolly tone as she came out of the back room, a bowl of freshly mixed colour in her hands. She popped it on a trolley and rolled it over to one of the stations. 'I'm glad you came. I brought all my stuff today.' She grinned at Ruby with a sparkle in her eye.

'What are you two up to then?' Cath asked.

'Sandra's going to teach me how to properly fix up me boat race,' Ruby replied.

'Oh, that's nice.' Cath smiled. 'Not that you need it, but it's always nice to get dolled up.'

'Come on then,' Sandra said, clapping her hands. 'I'm about done now. Let's use the end chair – we won't be in anyone's way there.'

Ruby followed Sandra to the chair at the back of the room and settled in, watching eagerly as Sandra popped a large make-up box on the shelf in front of her and began taking things out. This was already fun, she realised. And they hadn't even started.

'OK, so I think this foundation would go quite well with your skin tone. It's my winter one for when the sun hasn't tanned me up for a while, but I think it would suit you now.' She pulled Ruby's arm forward. and Ruby watched as she squeezed a bit out on the side of her wrist and rubbed it in. 'Yes. That'll do. I think when you buy some, though, go just one shade lighter. You're more a porcelain.'

'Oh, OK,' Ruby replied, mentally noting it down. *Porcelain*. It had a nice ring to it. It was the prettiest way she'd ever heard someone describe what she just saw as her pale, lifeless skin before.

She sat quietly as Sandra worked away on her face, occasionally replying when she asked a question but otherwise just enjoying this time being pampered and groomed by her new friend. The door opened at the other end of the salon, but Ruby didn't bother to look until she saw Sandra roll her eyes and irritation flash over her pretty features. She frowned, turning her head to see who it was.

'Alright, Rubes?' Connor smiled. 'What you up to then? Christ, look at you! You actually look quite pretty.'

Ruby scowled. 'You don't have to sound so surprised,' she snapped.

'I'm not surprised,' he replied. 'Sandra's got a real knack with beautifying. Proper talent.'

Ruby shook her head in disbelief as she glared at him in the mirror, but he was no longer looking at her. His wistful gaze was set on Sandra. But Sandra either hadn't noticed or was steadfastly ignoring him, as her gaze was intently set on Ruby's face. She added more bronzer to Ruby's newly contoured cheeks with a few more flicks of the brush.

'There,' she said, standing back to assess her work. 'I think that about does it. Now we just need to finish it off with the right lippy.' She continued rummaging in her bag.

'You off out somewhere special, are ya?' Connor asked Ruby, constantly glancing at Sandra as he talked.

'No. What do you want?' Ruby asked bluntly.

'Do I have to want something to talk to my favourite sister?' he exclaimed, apparently offended somehow.

'I'm your only sister,' she replied flatly, 'and far from your favourite sibling. Why you in here anyway?'

'I had to drop something off to Auntie Cath.'

'OK. See you later then,' Ruby pushed. This was *her* time right now. Clearly, he was here trying to butt in on her time with Sandra, and Ruby wasn't in the mood to play second fiddle.

'Alright,' he replied with a tut. 'So, Sandra, how's things?'

'Yeah, good,' she said in a short tone. She still didn't look at him, and Ruby couldn't help but feel pleased. She hid a smile.

'Ah that's good, that's good...' He ran his finger over the back of the next chair, hovering awkwardly. 'I was just wondering if maybe you'd had a think about that restaurant I was telling you about the other—'

'I'm washing me hair that night, sorry,' she said, cutting him off.

'But I haven't even suggested a day yet,' he replied, a frown falling over his face.

'It don't matter what day it is. I'll still be washing my hair,' she replied airily.

'Do you wash your hair every day?' he asked slowly, looking confused. 'OK. It could be a late dinner, like, for after you're done?'

Ruby couldn't contain the snort of laughter and quickly hid her amusement with a cough. Neither of her handsome brothers had ever had to deal with rejection, so the fact it wasn't clicking with Connor shouldn't have been a surprise. But somehow it still was.

'Connor, piss off,' she said, butting into the exchange in her usual blunt style. 'Can't you see we're busy?'

'We really are very busy right now,' Sandra added in a no-nonsense tone. 'Thanks for popping by.' She gave him a tight smile and moved around to the other side of Ruby.

Connor scowled at Ruby in the mirror, and she shot him a defiant look back. He rolled his eyes, locked his strong, prominent jaw and walked off, leaving them to it. Sandra found the lipstick she'd been looking for and applied it to Ruby's lips as Ruby watched Connor say goodbye to their aunt and leave the salon.

'What was all that about?' she asked as Sandra pulled the lipstick away.

'Rub your lips together,' Sandra ordered. 'And that – eugh.' She rolled her eyes dramatically. 'Your brother won't stop asking me out. I've told him to jog on a few times now. Especially after one of the things he said to me! Honestly, you wouldn't believe it.'

'What did he say?' Ruby asked, intrigued.

Sandra glanced behind them. 'I'll tell you over a drink sometime. It ain't really a very salon-appropriate conversation.'

Ruby felt a little flutter of excitement in her belly. This was her moment, her opening to invite Sandra out for some girly drinks. She took a deep breath and let it out again slowly, working up the courage to ask the question. Next to her, Sandra began to pack away all her bits and pieces of make-up, and her heart rate rose. This natural window of opportunity would only be open for so long. She licked her freshly painted lips and went for it.

'I was thinking actually...' She tried to level her voice out, to sound more casual. 'About maybe if you might want to grab a drink now, after work? In the pub down the road. Or wherever.' It was clunky, but she'd asked the question. She'd taken the leap and suggested after-work drinks like any normal person might. Her nerves tensed as she waited for the response.

'Ahh, I'd love to,' Sandra replied.

Ruby felt her heart lift with joy.

'But I can't tonight.'

As swiftly as it had lifted, it dropped in disappointment.

'I'm meeting Scarlet to go over this course I'm about to join.'

And then it plummeted.

'Oh, I see. No worries,' she replied, trying to keep her tone light when her feelings were anything but.

'Defo up for drinks another day though,' Sandra added.

'Sure, sounds good.' Ruby swallowed the lump of disappointment that had appeared in her throat. 'Thanks for the face,' she added, forcing a smile. 'I'd better go.'

'Oh, OK then,' Sandra said, clearly surprised that she was hurrying off so fast. 'Here, take this.' She gave her the lipstick she'd just applied. 'It really suits you. You can keep it.'

'Thanks.' Ruby gathered her jacket and bag. 'I'll catch you later.'

Waving goodbye to her aunt as she hurriedly left, Ruby felt her cheeks burn as she struggled to keep containing her feelings. The fresh air outside helped a little as it hit her face but not enough to stop the spiral of hate and frustration from growing as she stormed down the street, suddenly desperate to get away from the salon she'd earlier found such comfort in.

Of *course*, Sandra had plans with Scarlet. Of *course*, Scarlet had already swooped in ahead of her – just like she always did. It seemed that before she'd even made a decision herself, Scarlet was already ten steps ahead in every single part of her life, just *there*, lurking and stamping all over whatever small thing that Ruby had wanted to claim for herself. She didn't even have to be around her for it to happen.

Ruby had barely even seen Scarlet since she'd woken from her coma. Her cousin had been there to welcome her home, which would have been down to Lily's orders, and that had been it. A quick, obligatory 'glad you're home' comment and nothing more. Not that she'd expected much more. They'd never liked each other, so tears and emotional reunions would never be their thing. That didn't bother her. But this, the constant overshadowing of her life was getting to the point she could no longer bear it.

And now, as usual, just as she had found the courage to step up and brave the world on her own, to reach out in genuine friendship for the first time in her adult life, Scarlet had thwarted her plans once again.

She pushed her wild red curls back off her face in frustration, ignoring them as they bounced straight back. No matter what she did, no matter what direction she tried to grow in, Scarlet would always be there in the way.

Still marching down the busy high street, Ruby suddenly slowed as she reached the pub. Forget social drinks, she needed a strong vodka to take the edge off and to stop her hands from itching to murder her oh-so-perfect younger cousin. Reaching the door, she hesitated then walked in and made a beeline for the bar. She ordered a double vodka and Coke, quietly trying to calm herself down as she waited.

She'd never really murder Scarlet, however many times she dreamed about it. Murder wasn't her thing, and she didn't fancy a stretch behind bars for doing it either. But one day she was going to teach that bitch a lesson. She promised herself that as she sat watching the bartender pour.

One day she was going to take it all back from Scarlet. Everything she'd ever taken from her. And she'd leave her cousin feeling as lost and hollow and as worthless as she'd made her feel all these years. She'd make her suffer and pay, if it was the last thing she did.

THIRTY-SEVEN

Two hours later, Ruby stared at the bottom of her empty glass feeling deflated. She'd lost count of how many she'd had; she'd just kept ordering one after another, never letting herself run out of the alcohol she was trying so desperately to drown her sorrows in. Except it wasn't working. Her sorrows had not been drowned – if anything they'd been magnified. Her anger had subsided, but a deep wallowing wave of self-pity had taken its place and she enjoyed that even less than the rage.

'Same again?' the bartender asked, noticing her empty glass.

Ruby weighed up the odds of yet another one having a different result to all the others. 'Nah,' she said after a few moments. 'This ain't doing it tonight.'

She sighed, her heart feeling heavy. Her phone lay in front of her, silent as usual. There were no friends in her life to message her or call her up for a chat. No boyfriend lurked in the background, not even a booty call who might fancy his chances. No one in the world knew or cared about where she was. Not even her mother had called this evening. She could disappear off the edge of the world and no one would even notice.

It was a sobering thought, and suddenly what little fog the

vodka had blanketed her heart in vanished. She swallowed, trying to dislodge the pain from her chest, but it didn't work. It was a simple truth, and truth could not be pushed away.

The bartender wandered back over, casting furtive glances towards the customers further down the bar. He leaned in with a conspiratorial whisper. 'If drink ain't doing it for you, I could get hold of some things that might.' He gave her a meaningful look as she pulled her gaze up.

Immediately the pull of the whispered promise caught her right in the gut, the memories of a thousand trips hitting her with full force. But she dismissed it, with difficulty, muttering through gritted teeth, 'Nah, I'm good.'

He shrugged and wandered back to the glasses he was stacking on the shelf at the back of the bar. Turning down the chance of the only relief she'd ever known was the hardest thing in the world. But she had no choice. Ray Renshaw had made sure of that.

If anyone else had threatened to kill her if she returned to her druggy ways, she might have called their bluff, but not Ray. The man was as ruthless as they came and his word was law. There would be no second chances, just the deliverance of that promise. And there wasn't a club or pub in the city he didn't or couldn't have eyes in.

But what else did she have? No friends, no passions that she could follow, no real purpose in life. Every moment of her life was harder than ever after the fire. She was filled with anxiety and nightmares – she wasn't really *living* at all, when she thought about it. She was merely existing, rather painfully, perched on the edges of everyone else's lives.

Tears blurred her vision as she felt more alone than ever before. What was the point of it all? What was the point of even being here? Suddenly, she didn't care anymore. She didn't care about Scarlet, or Ray, or anyone else. She was done being in pain, done feeling low. She was going to go and find some relief, some small window of happiness and she didn't care what happened to her afterwards.

'Hey,' she called to the bartender. 'I've changed my mind.' She sniffed and blinked away the tears. 'What can you get hold of?'

THIRTY-EIGHT

'I know it's a push, but I need the furnace finished and delivered within a week. I'll pay whatever it takes.' Lily turned her head and put her hand over the ear that didn't have a phone against it in an attempt to drown out the noise of the busy pub around her. 'I need it three times the size of the last one. Yes, three – why? Because that's what I need, Reg, what else can I tell ya?' A small crease appeared in her forehead. 'Made to measure? That's fine. Price is no object, I just need it that size and I need this pushed through as priority to be here in a week. Can you do it or do I need to shop about?' There was a short pause and then she smiled. 'Good. See this is why I always come to you, Reg. I'll send you the new address. Keep me updated.'

She put the phone down and quickly typed out a text, sending him the address for their new factory premises as promised. Ray put his arm around her and gave her a nudge.

'All work and no play makes Lil—'

'A rich woman,' she finished, cutting him off with a tight smile.

He threw his head back and laughed heartily. 'I can't argue

with that, I suppose,' he replied in good humour. '*But,*' he continued, sliding her untouched glass of wine towards her, 'it also means this rather fine glass of Chardonnay is dangerously close to growing warm, and we can't have that.' He shook his head. 'What sort of reputation would my pub have, if it got round my woman was drinking warm wine?'

Lily laughed, a genuine laugh that made the skin at the corner of her eyes crinkle attractively. 'Your pub's reputation has absolutely nothing to do with the wine at all, and you know it,' she said.

'Very true, but I still think you should drink up and forget work for a while. Or is there something else I need to do to get your attention.'

Ray's gaze darkened and twinkled as it bored into hers, and she felt the familiar pull of electricity between them. His large muscular body was turned towards hers and her eyes flickered down to the top of the well-defined chest and smattering of dark hair showing through the open buttons at the top of his shirt. His fingers began massaging her shoulder, and she leaned back into the protective arc of his arm, enjoying the feeling.

'There's nothing you need to do to get my attention, Ray,' she said in a gentler tone than usual. She laid her hand on his leg and squeezed. 'Sorry. Just distracted with getting everything in place for the new factory.'

'What are the new digs like then?' he asked, reaching to the table for his packet of cigarettes. He lit one and handed it to Lily, then lit himself a second.

In any other pub there would have been gasps of outrage that they were smoking inside, but this was Ray's pub. The most notorious pub in South London – indeed probably in the entire city – it was frequented only by those who resided in the many layers of the underworld. Police no longer came to call-outs here, marking it as a no-go zone, and anyone who came knew that what happened here stayed here. Narks and gossips were not dealt with gently, and there were no rules or laws that counted, other than Ray's.

She blew out the smoke she'd inhaled. 'They're pretty good. Probably a better set-up than the old one actually. It's bigger, which we needed. Plus, the location's better for dealing with the other stuff. More out of the way.'

'Makes sense,' Ray replied. 'When you first set up there you weren't where you are now. You couldn't have known what you'd need down the line. It'll be good to get a fresh start in that sense.'

Lily nodded and took another drag, lowering her gaze to hide the stab of grief that always came when she thought back to the factory. It wasn't really the factory she missed. It was just a building, bricks and mortar. But the memories that had echoed through the halls had kept Ronan close since he'd died. It was the place they'd built up together, with blood, sweat and tears. They'd outgrown it long ago, but they'd held off moving through sentimentality. After Ronan had died, the sentimentality had doubled. She never would have given it up if she'd had the choice.

'I'm looking forward to your poker nights restarting,' Ray continued.

'Yeah, actually, they won't be held at the new factory,' Lily replied.

'Oh? You're not restarting them?' he asked, clearly surprised.

'I will be, but not there. I'm buying the leasehold on a pub just round the corner from it – I'll hold them there.' Lily took another drag on her cigarette and looked to Ray for his reaction.

'You're buying a pub?' he asked, his thick eyebrows rising up almost to his hairline.

'I am. It's a run-down shithole, good for laundering. No brewery ties. It has a flat above that I'm going to knock about to make a gambling floor with a couple of offices where I can run everything else. It means I'll be able to run them more regularly and people won't have to be so careful coming and going. Nothing looks odd about people disappearing into a pub now, does it?'

Ray nodded, seemingly impressed with the idea. 'What's it called, this new pub of yours?'

'The Spoiled Pig. But I'm going to change it. I figured the Blind Pig was more apt, considering.' She let her smile curl upwards slowly.

Ray chuckled. 'I like it. You always did like to call things as they were, Lil.'

Her eyes twinkled as she took a sip of her drink. 'The blind pig' was the less commonly known term for a speakeasy, back in the twenties during America's prohibition. A place where illicit alcohol was served in secret, where dark deeds went on behind dark doors. If drinking with friends could be called a dark deed. Well, her alcohol would probably be fairly legal, but the other things that went on in her new pub would most definitely not be. It was the perfect name.

'I'm glad things are looking up for the firm,' Ray continued, his brows knitting together into a frown as he stubbed his cigarette out in the ashtray on the table before them. 'You need this.'

Lily caught the tone and her attention sharpened. 'What do you mean? What you hearing?'

'You know what I'm hearing, Lil,' he replied. 'They're saying you're losing hold.' He looked up at her steadily, not sugar-coating it. She didn't expect him to. They knew each other far too well to pussyfoot around things like this. 'There's been a lot of gossip, one thing after the other. A few people are thinking of taking a chance.'

'They'll fucking regret it if they do,' she hissed, anger flaring up at the thought of another smaller firm daring to try and topple them.

'Which is exactly what I've had my boys tell them, wherever they've heard a sniff.' Ray shifted in his seat and cast a glance over the busy pub from where they sat in the slightly elevated area he favoured. 'But my word alone won't hold them back for long. You need to put on a show. Remind people how strong you are.'

'That's exactly what I am doing,' Lily replied, sitting back with one arm crossed over her middle as she took another drag. 'I've got something in the works that will remind them all *exactly* who we are.'

'What's that then?' Ray asked curious.

She blew out the smoke and watched it waft away through cold, narrowed eyes. 'You'll see, when it's done,' she replied. 'In fact, I'll make sure you get a front-row seat.'

THIRTY-NINE

Ruby swayed and moved to the music, her hands in the air and her face to the sky as she closed her eyes, letting the lights and sounds wash over her. The smile on her face was calm and genuine, and for the first time in a long while she moved freely without a care in the world.

Just a few hours ago she'd been so unhappy and bogged down by the grey dismal weight of her world that she'd wanted nothing more than to fall asleep and never wake up again. Every breath and every thought brought forth more pain, but the pills the bartender had sourced for her had changed all that. As they'd kicked in, she'd physically felt the weight lift from her body, like a dark, heavy cloak being removed from her very soul. The sadness, the loneliness, the sheer despair she had been drowning in had been banished by the light of the ecstasy that now ran through her veins.

After taking the drugs, she'd jumped on a bus and travelled into the centre of the city, away from her usual haunts where people she might know could appear. She'd walked, then, allowing the drugs to soothe her ragged system whilst she cast off her worries and troubles. Before they took over completely, she'd found a busy club to hide in, full of bodies dancing together in the dark. A swarm of strangers. It was the safest place to be, one being in a large herd. Less noticeable.

She opened her eyes and watched the lights dance around the room, and a laugh escaped her lips. It was a light, joyful laugh, and it lit up her face in the way only true happiness could. As her eyes travelled down, they met with another pair across the dance floor. A tall man with dark eyes and a broad smile was dancing, watching as she enjoyed herself so freely. She smiled even wider, feeling nothing but love for this complete stranger, and he danced his way over.

'Hi, I'm James,' he said, leaning into her ear so as to be heard over the music.

'That's lovely,' she breathed back into his.

He laughed, amused at her comment. 'What's your name?' he asked as he continued dancing with her in time to the music.

'Ruby,' she answered, her promise to not reveal herself to anyone this evening totally forgotten.

'Pretty,' he replied. 'Like your hair.' He gestured up towards her wild bouncing curls. Attention drawn to her hair was something she usually hated, but right now she was incapable of hate, so instead she beamed.

'Thanks. Dance with me, James,' she demanded, throwing her arms in the air as the song changed to one of her favourites. 'I want to dance.'

She'd forgotten the half-drunk bottle of beer in her hand, which then flew through the air, hitting someone nearby and spilling all over the floor. James, spurred on by her invitation and joyous mood, stepped forward and wrapped his arms around her waist, grinding into her as they danced together to the music.

· · ·

Unnoticed by Ruby, two men stood watching in the shadows on the floor above, their interest caught by the flying bottle.

'The girl there,' one of them commented with a frown. 'The redhead – is that who I think it is?'

The other peered down, squinting to get a better look. Recognition flashed across his features and a grim expression settled over his face. 'If you're thinking that's Ruby Drew, then yeah, it is. And she's off her nut.'

Ruby swayed around, not even slightly in time with the music, her eyes closed and her mouth gurning as the drunken letch next to her held her up.

They exchanged a look. 'You know Ray Renshaw put word out to deliver her to him if she's seen geared up like that. There's quite a hefty reward in it too.'

Down below, Ruby fell to the floor and her leery companion quickly pulled her up, holding her against him and pulling her over to one of the tables, keeping carefully out of sight of the bouncers. She seemed to rouse herself and he handed her a drink, which she tipped back and gulped down without question.

As a couple of people began to look over, the man she was with grabbed his jacket and hooked his arm around her waist. Pulling her towards the exit, he led her away from the heaving dance floor and on to whatever plan he had next.

'Go and tell the boss,' the first man said.

'But he's in a meeting,' the other replied.

'It don't matter. He'll want to be interrupted for this. Trust me.'

FORTY

Scarlet stirred the last of the three cups of coffee she was making in the back room of the salon then dumped the spoon in the sink and walked carefully through to the front with the tray. Cath took it off her as she reached the reception and handed one back to her, one to Sandra and grabbed the last for herself before sitting down behind the desk.

'Let's have a look at the books,' Scarlet said, her tone all business. She took a sip and then placed her coffee out of the way. It was early, the salon wouldn't open for nearly another hour, making it the perfect time to go over the things they didn't want the stylists or clients observing.

Cath pulled out two sets of identical books and opened them on the corresponding pages, sliding them round to face her daughter. Scarlet's critical gaze scanned the lines, marrying up the false accounts with the figures they'd been pushing through, then she nodded slowly.

'And this is all up to date before my arrest?' she asked.

'It is,' Sandra confirmed. 'After that your aunt pulled the loads off somewhere else. Said it would be safer not to push anything through with so much attention on you.'

Scarlet ran her finger down the columns to the last few days. 'The problem with that is that there's a clear drop-off in income. We'd be better sticking to the usual amount.' She stood up straight. 'I'll speak to Lil later. The last thing we want is to be caught out for actually running straight.'

Just then, there was an almighty crash as two bricks smashed through the two main windows at the front of the building. Glass shattered and flew through the salon, and Scarlet instinctively turned away and raised her arms to cover her face. Cath and Sandra ducked behind the desk, and one of them let out a small scream of surprise and fright.

As the last of the glass settled, Scarlet whipped her head back round, shock and hot fury running through her veins. Her eyes searched for whoever had dared attack her salon, and they landed on the culprits with no trouble.

Luca and Riccardo Romano bowled through the front door, the only glass pane they'd left untouched, two heavies filing in behind them. Scarlet felt her insides clench at the sight of the group of large hard men. They clearly meant business, and she was outnumbered and unprepared. But she was not about to let them know how intimidated she felt. She thrust her chin forward and glared at them with as icy a look as she could manage.

'What the *fuck* do you think you're doing?' she demanded in a harsh bark.

Luca marched forward and leaned over her with a dark look. 'I'm smashing your salon windows, Drew,' he sneered. 'Or was that not clear enough.'

Scarlet forced herself not to move, though every muscle ached to pull back as he pressed almost against her in his bid to terrorise her. She couldn't. That was a show of weakness and she wasn't going to give them even the slightest hint of that.

'Oh, that part's clear,' she hissed back at him. 'I'm just wondering what you think that means exactly. You come over here throwing stones and your weight around, and for what, eh? All you've earned yourselves today is a nasty comeuppance down the road.'

'Yeah?' he said with a mocking laugh. 'Why? What you gonna do about it?'

'Me? Nothing.' She smiled coldly. 'You've outmanned me. Too scared to come and smash my salon on your own, you've left me no choice but to deal with this later, when I'm more prepared.'

'That a threat, is it?' he asked, flexing his muscles as he stared her down.

Scarlet pushed her face even closer to his, not missing a beat. 'It's a promise,' she said smoothly.

'Scarlet?' Cath's voice was quivering. With fear in her eyes, she slowly approached the pair.

'It's alright, Mum,' Scarlet said, keeping her gaze on Luca's. 'He can't touch me.' A dangerous look crossed her face. 'He's already made a big enough statement here, most likely in retaliation for the kicking the boys gave him the other day. He knows there will be comeback and he'll be ready for that, but he can't touch me, because as big an idiot as he is doing *this*, there's a chance he might still walk away. If he touches *me* however, he knows his chances of breathing in an ongoing capacity are severely limited.'

There was a minuscule flicker in Luca's eyes and Scarlet knew she'd hit the spot. She narrowed her gaze and withdrew from their stand-off.

'You've made your mess,' she said, her head held high. She walked back to the desk and crossed her arms. 'Now get the *fuck* out of my salon.'

Luca sniffed and smirked. 'I ain't interested in you. But you'll pass on my message.' He gestured towards the smashed glass that littered the floor. 'We're done watching you Drews make a mess of things. You're on your way out, and we're going to help you towards the door.'

He turned and walked out of the salon. 'Your glory days are over,' he called over his shoulder. 'It's time for some new blood to run things around here. You tell your cousins that. And that we'll be ready for them next time.'

FORTY-ONE

The thick, heavy thudding that reverberated through her brain was what ultimately woke Ruby. She groaned, squeezing her eyes shut against the light that was forcing its way through her eyelids. She tried to roll over, but her head felt as though it was about to split in two, so she swiftly decided on staying put.

With difficulty she opened one eye just a crack instead and looked around, trying to work out where she was. She quickly closed it, the daylight from the partially open curtains doing nothing to help her headache. She didn't recognise the room she was in at all, and with rising trepidation she tried to piece together her memories of the night before.

Her heart sank to the bottom of her stomach like a stone as she recalled buying the ecstasy from the barman. She'd been doing so well, staying off drugs for much longer than she had ever managed before, so a big part of her felt disappointed in her lack of control. But she also didn't regret it. That wave of relief from the pain that had washed through her had been more than welcome. She'd needed it. She just wished that she could remember the rest of the night and how she had ended up here. Wherever *here* was.

Another feeling suddenly crept forward. Fear. Last night she'd reached such a low she hadn't cared what happened to her. But now, in the cold light of day, as she suffered from a comedown and her arrival back to reality, Ray was suddenly once more a very real threat. Who had seen her last night? Where had she even gone?

She could remember going into a club, dancing to the music, drinking way too much. She squeezed her eyes shut harder as she tried to focus. A dim recollection of a man walking over to her appeared. They'd talked, she remembered. The lights had been mesmerising though, distracting her when he'd said his name. All she could remember was the smell of his aftershave as he held her close. Very close. That was right, she thought, they'd danced. She replayed the hazy memory in her mind, shrouded as it was by the misty haze of the drugs she'd taken. She'd felt relaxed, laid her head on his chest as he wrapped his arm around her.

This must be his place, she realised. She must have hooked up with him. She let out a groan, wondering what exactly she'd done. Forcing her eyes open once more, she lifted the covers and looked down. All she was wearing was her underwear. She looked around the room and clocked her clothes on the chair, neatly folded. She frowned. Had she really folded them the night before? That wasn't like her, not when she was tripping.

As she looked around again, she noticed how tastefully the room was decorated. Pale blues and beiges complemented each other, and pretty details stood out everywhere. A dressing table sat on one wall with a jewellery box on top. This wasn't a man's room. Her natural instincts kicked in and her senses sharpened. Ignoring the screaming ache inside her head, she pushed herself up into a seated position and rubbed the sleep from her eyes before staring warily at the closed door.

Where the hell *was* she? She closed her eyes for a moment as nausea hit. Every part of her ached to lie back down and sleep off this horrific mix of hangover and comedown, but she knew she couldn't. She had to get out of here, get somewhere safe, somewhere she could hide and work out whether or not Ray knew yet. But where could be safe from Ray?

Gingerly, she slipped her legs out over the side of the bed and stood up on the thick carpet. She swayed, then clamped her jaw determinedly. She had to get herself dressed.

Reaching the chair, she sank into it and shoved on the black cigarette trousers and white satin shirt she'd had on the day before. Standing up, she tucked the shirt in quickly and picked up her tan slingbacks, then padded softly over to the door.

Here she hesitated and cocked her head to the side, listening out for any signs of life beyond.

After a few seconds of silence, she decided to brave opening it, praying to the heavens that it wouldn't make a noise and potentially alert anyone to her presence. She wrapped her fingers around the handle and slowly pulled it down, thanking her lucky stars as it swung open silently and with ease.

She peered out and looked around. She was near the end of a long hallway. A couple of doors led off on the other side, and further down this side the wall opened up into an open-plan living area.

Tiptoeing forward, she held her breath and made a beeline towards the front door. It was so close, just a few feet. She only had to reach it and she'd be out. But as she neared it, the living area came into view, and with it, the two people sitting waiting for her. She froze as she locked gazes with the solemn, attractive woman perched on a bar stool by the kitchen island, but it wasn't until her eyes moved over to the smartly dressed man in the armchair, watching her with a dark expression, that her heart plummeted.

'Hello, Ruby. Remember me?'

FORTY-TWO

Ruby licked her lips, trying to calm her racing heart. 'I remember you,' she said, slightly breathless in her fear. 'I'd be pretty stupid not to.'

He nodded, his steady, serious eyes not leaving hers for a second. 'Yeah, you would,' he agreed. 'But it seemed a valid question, seeing as somehow last night you managed to forget who Ray Renshaw was,' he continued, his tone hard. 'And I'd always thought of him as a pretty unforgettable person.'

The man facing her exuded danger, and every tiny hair on her body stood on edge. It was a natural reaction, she supposed, to a man like Freddie Tyler. He was the biggest fish in the London pond. The firm he headed ran everything in the West and through Central, and he had fingers in many pies through the rest of the city too. He made Ray's firm look small, not to mention their own. He was the ruthless and powerful king of the jungle. And somehow, she'd ended up in front of him on the one morning she needed to hide from the rest of the underworld. This was not good. Not good at all.

'I didn't forget,' Ruby answered him, drawing in a deep breath. 'I can never forget who Ray is.'

'So you're on a death wish then? That was a suicide attempt?' he asked harshly, one eyebrow arched over his cold handsome face.

Ruby swallowed. *Did* she want to die? she asked herself. Last night the thought had crossed her mind. But now, in the cold light of day, her survival instinct was waking back up. Was it too late though? Freddie had close connections with Ray, that was common knowledge. Had he already called him? Was Ray on his way over now?

'No. I don't want to die,' she said, holding her chin a little higher as a spark of defiance broke through.

Freddie stared at her for a long few moments, tapping his fingers on the arm of the chair. Ruby swallowed once more, her worry growing. Then she cast her eyes down, suddenly exhausted with everything. Maybe this was a good thing. Maybe if Freddie did pass her over to Ray and he did snuff her out, it would be best for everyone.

'Hey,' Freddie said, his tone less brusque than it had been before.

She looked up unhappily and saw him staring at her with a small frown.

He exhaled heavily through his nose. 'You're lucky it was *my* men who found you. They brought you straight to me before anyone else saw you.'

Ruby blinked and her brow furrowed. Freddie stood up and exchanged a look with the woman at the breakfast bar.

'People make mistakes. And I think that last night was a mistake, for you. ' He eyed her, his expression unreadable. 'I go way back with your mum, and I have a lot of respect for her. Get yourself straight, and then go *home*. Don't speak about last night to anyone. As far as I'm concerned, you were never here – I could do without pissing Ray off. And do yourself a favour: don't repeat this again. Because Ray ain't a forgiving man, and we both know what he's likely to do to you if you fall back into your old ways. He ain't put the word out on you for nothing.'

Ruby just nodded, not sure what to say. She'd known Freddie and her mum knew each other, she'd seen them talking once at a funeral, but she hadn't realised that they were that close. Realising suddenly that she was staring, Ruby cleared her throat. 'Thanks,' she said. 'I'll do that.'

'Seriously, you were lucky last night,' Freddie stressed. 'You won't be that lucky twice.'

Ruby nodded. 'Yeah, I know.'

Straightening his jacket, Freddie gave her one last stern look then turned to the woman still sitting at the bar drinking her coffee. 'Thanks for this – I owe ya.'

'Yes, you do,' she replied with a smile. 'Tell Anna I'll meet her at Heaven Above, around lunchtime, to go over those plans.'

'She's just taken Ethan to football practice – can you text her?'

'Yeah, OK. Catch you later.'

The front door shut behind him and Ruby was left alone with the glamourous woman. The woman sat watching her over her coffee as she took another sip, her long tanned legs crossed to the side below the tight beige dress that encased her perfectly proportioned body. As she subtly studied her back, Ruby couldn't help but envy her hair for a moment. It was red, like hers, but the other woman's curls were soft and shiny, instead of coiled like springs the way Ruby's were.

Another wave of nausea hit and she closed her eyes for a brief moment, reaching out to steady herself on the wall.

'What did you take?' asked the woman, in her wide East End accent.

'What?' Ruby asked, confused.

'Drugs – which ones?'

'Oh, um...' Ruby had to think back to the night before, her

brain only working at about half the speed it usually did. 'Ecstasy of some sort.'

'Come, sit down,' the woman replied. She stood up and gestured for Ruby to move to one of the comfortable chairs that adorned the lounge.

Ruby did so gladly, relaxing into the big taupe armchair now that she knew she wasn't in any immediate danger. The woman walked back to the kitchen and then returned with a large glass of orange juice.

''Ere,' she said, handing it over. 'Drink this. It'll make you feel better quicker.'

'Really?' Ruby asked, feeling doubtful.

'Yeah, I had a client years ago. Doctor, he was. Liked a few trips on the weekend, always had a truckload of OJ on hand for after. Helps to replenish what the drugs have stripped from your system, he claimed. Halves the comedown time.'

'Yeah?' Ruby took a couple of sips. 'What kind of client? What do you do?' she asked curiously. She couldn't place this woman. She wasn't Freddie's other half, that much she knew. His other half was a dark-haired woman he'd been with for years.

The woman gave her a strange half-smile. 'Not the same sort of things I did back then,' she replied. 'These days I part own a couple of clubs, among other things. Drink up. It really will help. I'm Tanya, by the way. This is my place. Freddie brought you back here last night.'

'Oh, are you two a thing?' Ruby asked. Perhaps she was his mistress.

'Nah, not us,' Tanya replied with a smile of amusement. 'He's with my best mate. But we all work together. We're family really.'

'Ah, I see,' Ruby replied. And she did. You didn't grow up in the underworld without understanding what a close-knit firm was like. 'What happened last night exactly?' she asked. 'I'm a bit hazy.'

'I wasn't actually there, but from what I gather you were rolling round the dance floor off your face and gaining a lot of attention,' Tanya said, sitting down in one of the other armchairs and twisting to face Ruby. 'Simon – he works for Freddie – he recognised you and remembered that Ray had put word out.'

Ruby took another sip of her orange.

'He asked Freddie what to do and Freddie insisted you were picked up and hidden. He actually went to great lengths to make sure no one who'd seen you would say a word.' Tanya gave her a hard look. 'Some chancer was trying to take you home, but he was sent off with a flea in his ear. He didn't seem to know who you were, from what they could gather. At that point you pretty much passed out in the office before anyone could get any sense out of you. And then Freddie brought you here to sleep it off.' Tanya shrugged and grinned. 'Can't say it was the biggest surprise he's ever turned up with, to be honest.'

Ruby nodded. 'Thanks for putting me up,' she said awkwardly.

Tanya shrugged again. 'Didn't really have a choice. Couldn't exactly leave you on me doormat.'

Ruby was about to suggest that she could have said no altogether, but then she remembered who she was talking about. No one said no to Freddie Tyler. Not even family.

'Can I give you some advice?' Tanya asked.

Ruby looked back at her warily. Everyone always wanted to give her advice on how to live her life. *Be a good girl, stay clean, work hard, play nice.* It was all the same self-serving suggestions. The sort of stuff that made life easier for them. She nodded anyway, realising she was in no position to decline.

Tanya leaned forward towards her, an earnest look on her face. 'There are lots of things in this life that can give you a high. Not so easy perhaps. Not the same. But if you're looking to stay ahead, stay off Ray's radar and still find something worthwhile to wake up for every day, maybe you should look at switching addictions.'

'Switching addictions?' Ruby asked in surprise. This was a new one.

Tanya studied her for a moment, her pillar-box-red lips twisted to one side as she appeared to be considering something. 'Years ago, I worked in a really shitty club, the kind that girls who have no one end up in. The kind where most drown in their own despair, to be honest.'

Ruby blinked, surprised. The cool, collected, together-looking woman in front of her didn't match in her mind a girl who could have come from the pits of a seedy club.

'I got into some recreational drugs. Never slipped down the slope hard, but it took the edge off when I needed it to,' Tanya admitted. 'Some of the girls around me though...' she lamented. 'After a while I began to be able to tell the difference in the skag heads, between the ones who'd turn it around and the ones who would be overtaken by it and fade away. You see, they were weak. The ones who faded and never made it back. They'd go past the point of return and just give up. They'd end up dying on the streets or worse. One girl I knew was found dead behind a dumpster right by her back door.'

The picture Tanya was painting hit home. Ruby knew the ones. Being on the scene so long herself, she'd seen it too. They were too weak to handle it and stay in control. But she'd always stayed in control. At least, that's what she'd told herself.

'The others, though, the ones who turned it around, I admired them.' Tanya's bright, piercing eyes met hers. 'Not many people do, but not many people appreciate that there are reasons girls like that end up on the gear. The same way I'm sure you had your own reasons. And once you're on, that pull is almost impossible to break away from. But the other ones, the strong ones, they do. And in my experience, the ones who stay off for good go either one of two ways. Either they find strict sobriety and focus on containing their addictive natures in a little box – which I imagine can't be much fun. Or they accept that they will always be an addict and they channel that addiction elsewhere. I knew some pretty amazing girls who did that and absolutely thrived. They didn't let the addiction own them – they owned their addiction and made it work for them. That's strength.'

'Everybody always seems to want to cure my addiction, like it's something that will go away,' Ruby said.

Tanya shook her head. 'You can't cure it. It's part of who you are. But you can control it. And not just by stopping the urges, by rerouting them.'

Her gaze flickered up and down Ruby's body and she began to feel a little self-conscious.

'I don't know you. I don't know what you're likely to find solace in. But from what I gather you're a fighter. So *use* that. Some people channel it into fitness, some people try to help others, addicted to saving as many as they can.' She stood up and ran her hands down her dress. 'Some end up switching to gambling. Healthier, but it leaves them broke. Some become addicted to power, working their way up the chain to the top. I don't know what will float your boat, but whatever it is, you should give it a try. What can you really lose?'

Tanya gave her a challenging look then walked out into the hallway, beckoning her to follow.

'Come on. I'll drop you back home. You can think up a cover story on the way. Because he's serious, you know,' she continued, her voice developing a sharp note. 'You were never here.'

'I was never here,' Ruby agreed, standing up to follow.

Putting on her shoes, she turned their conversation over in her mind. It was probably the best piece of advice anyone had ever given her. She was what she was, and despite everyone's desperate wishes, there was no changing that. But perhaps she could harness this deeply rooted fault of hers. Perhaps she could turn it into something useful.

Maybe, if used in just the right way, her addiction was the weapon she could finally use to take back her rightful place by her mother's side and overtake Scarlet for good.

FORTY-THREE

The sound of high-heeled shoes marching across the concrete floor echoed around the large, empty warehouse as Grace made her way towards the Drews, who were gathered around a large trestle table in the middle of the room. As she approached, her men trailing closely behind, she looked around with cold interest.

'This is to be your new factory?' she asked, her roaming gaze resting on Lily.

'Yes,' she replied. 'Somewhat bigger than our last place.'

'Quiet, this area, isn't it?' Grace asked coolly, a spark in her eyes. 'You'll have to think a little more deeply about security, I imagine.'

'Actually, that's already arranged,' Lily replied with a smile that didn't quite reach her eyes. 'Luckily we know someone who's very good at all that. Plus,' she added, as she walked around the table towards Grace, 'we're getting guard dogs that will live on site. They're in training right now, learning our specific needs. They'll barely twitch if any of us arrive, but a stranger—' She blew a loud breath out through her cheeks. 'They're being taught to go for anyone trying to get near this place after hours. Viciously. Especially tall blondes.' Her smile grew as she watched Grace's expression sour momentarily.

Grace's gaze moved over each member of the family behind her in turn. Cillian, Connor, Scarlet and finally back to Lily, before she smiled a polite practised smile.

'We really need to start putting all this banter behind us if we're going to work together successfully, don't you think? It's tiresome,' she said.

'True,' Lily agreed. 'Let's get down to it, shall we?' She gestured towards the empty table.

Grace clicked her fingers, and one of her men stepped forward with a folder. She took it and placed it on the table, pulling out a thick wad of papers. She spread these across the table as the Drews gathered around to see.

Lily's gaze sharpened as she took in the details. They'd asked Grace to put together all the details they'd need for the upcoming job and she'd certainly delivered. Photos, copies of the building's blueprints and the housekeeping schedules were all there.

'Marie is a trust-fund baby who spends most of her time on a yacht in the south of France. With more money than she knows what to do with, she grew bored of her usual investments and began to look elsewhere for a lucrative thrill and that's how we initially became acquainted. She's a friend of a friend really but still invites me to her parties. And as I told you before, they are quite extravagant events. The Fall Ball is always held in the large ballroom at the back of the house, here...' Grace leaned forward and pointed to a rectangular space on the blueprint. 'It opens out onto the back terrace which will house some sort of entertainment. This does count out a large area across the back and sides for movement.'

'That doesn't matter,' Lily said with a dismissive wave of the hand.

'Marie's artwork is kept over here.' Grace pointed. 'This

long hallway is wider than it looks on here, and she has all her prize pieces on display there. The room off the end, here, is where she keeps her illegal findings.'

'That doesn't look particularly hidden,' Scarlet remarked.

'It's not. It's not even got any kind of security on it, other than a basic lock,' Grace replied. 'But that's Marie's way, you see. I think she enjoys the thrill of the possibility that she could one day be caught. A fantasy more than bravado,' she continued with a wry smirk. 'It's not like anyone would go out of their way to pick a lock in a random room in another person's house.'

'Other than us,' Connor commented.

'You *can* pick the lock, I take it?' Grace asked, as if the thought had suddenly occurred to her.

'We could pick a lock with our eyes closed by the time we were twelve,' Cillian replied curtly.

'You're sure there's no security to worry about, once we're inside?' Lily asked. 'What about cameras?'

'Just one camera on that main hallway which is linked to the rest of the household CCTV. That's on an internal loop which is all collected over here in the network room.' Grace pointed to a small area under the main stairwell.

'That's in full view of the party,' Connor pointed out, looking to Lily.

'It is,' she said, twisting her mouth to one side. 'We're going to need a window of opportunity where no one will be walking that way and the doors are closed if we're going to be able to get in there to turn the system off.'

There was a silence as everyone thought it through. Lily considered all the possible angles. She could see from the blueprints and one of Grace's photos that the double doors to the ballroom were only a few feet away. There would be no chance of getting in there without being seen and questioned unless the entire party was out of the way. But how, when that room was to be the centre of it all? She frowned, looking at the lopsided photo of the doors.

'Grace, how did you get this photo?' she asked.

'I popped over to offer my help with the planning. A ruse just to get inside so I could take these. I was taking photos without looking at the phone, which is why they're a bit squiffy.'

'And you were friendly?' Lily pushed.

'Obviously,' Grace replied with a withering look.

Cillian made a sound of discomfort and Lily glanced over towards him. He was rubbing his neck and pulling a face. She turned back to Grace.

'Did she seem to enjoy this sudden interest?'

Grace considered it for a moment. 'Yes, I think she's quite lonely.'

'Yeah, must be tough with all those parties and piles of gold,' Cillian commented sarcastically. He twisted his neck again with a groan.

'Money doesn't cure loneliness,' Grace replied. 'And neither, necessarily, do people.'

'Perhaps you could cultivate this new friendship,' Lily said as the idea slowly came together in her mind. 'Maybe you could be so thrilled about this new friendship that you want to put a surprise together for her, an entertaining treat partway through the evening.'

Lily saw Scarlet's eyes light up as she caught on to her train of thought.

'Some sort of circus act perhaps?' Scarlet suggested. 'A fire breather or something, in her honour as host. You'd tell her that all the doors need to be shut and everyone has to be inside for the big surprise.'

'Even if I did consider that, where on earth would I find a circus act?' Grace asked, clearly not sold on the idea.

'I have some contacts,' Lily replied.

Grace pursed her lips and exchanged a look with Duffy.

'Look, whether you like the idea or not, we need those doors closed and a decent window of distraction to close off the cameras or we can't pull off the job. It's as simple as that.'

Grace stared down at the picture of the doors, her expression grim. She nodded, grudgingly. 'If it has to be done.'

Cillian groaned once more and arched his back, twisting his neck to the side as far as it would go.

'It will also help your alibi,' Lily pointed out, eying her son suspiciously as she continued her conversation with Grace. 'You're supposed to stay front and centre – how much more front and centre can you get than playing the role of her new best friend and taking over the show to surprise the host?'

'It's really not the done thing,' Grace complained.

'Neither is stealing paintings, but there we go,' Lily replied in a matter-of-fact tone. 'Now, what next? The doors are closed, we turn off the cameras, pick the lock and take the painting. If this distraction can last long enough, we should be able to do that all fairly quickly. And if that's the case we should be able to just walk straight out of the front door. So, Cillian, if you sort the cameras, Scarlet and I can get the painting, then Connor you meet us out front—'

'No,' Grace cut in sharply with a shake of her head. 'You'll forgive my mistrust, but considering our history, I would rather Duffy be the one to take the painting from there to a secure location of *my* choosing.'

'And how do we know you won't just do *us* out of things there?' Connor shot back.

'Connor, you'll drive the van *with* Duffy to the front of the building,' Lily said, before the stand-off could develop further. 'Duffy can then take the painting from us and sit with it in the back whilst you drive to this place of Grace's choosing. The rest of Grace's men can fall in behind the van from wherever they're waiting in the wings and follow you back. We will follow shortly afterwards and pick you up.'

'And the painting stays there?' Connor asked, surprised.

'It does.' Lily lifted her chin. 'After all, that was the deal, right? We steal it, Grace sells it, we split the profit sixty-forty. And as tempting as it would be for Grace to keep the money, she knows as well as we do how lucrative it is to keep this partnership going.' She turned to Grace. 'Isn't that right?'

'Indeed,' Grace answered wryly. 'That's settled then. After that point, when you're safely away, I'll ask Marie how her collection is doing. I'll let her lead me over, ask after the Picasso and when she opens the room, I'll be as shocked and outraged as anyone else.'

'And you'll have an alibi for the whole time. They won't suspect it of being taken after you're gone, if they see it missing while you're still there,' Lily confirmed.

She eyed Cillian once more as he grimaced and swore. 'Cillian, are you OK? What's the matter with you?' she asked.

'It's me neck, it's killing me. Don't know what I've done.' He pulled a face at Grace across the table. 'You know when you just wake up like it?' he continued. 'I need to find someone decent to sort it out. Anyone got any suggestions?'

'No, not really,' Connor replied immediately with a shrug.

Scarlet frowned but stayed quiet, shooting Lily a subtle look of suspicion.

'What about you, Grace? You got any gems hidden away?' he asked.

'No,' Grace said, looking down her nose at him in disdain. 'The only masseuse I know is the lady at my local day spa. But she only works on women, I'm afraid.'

'Oh, I see. Never mind then,' Cillian answered, turning his attention back to the pictures on the table.

Lily narrowed her gaze at him then reached down and pulled all the photos and paperwork together. 'We'll go over these and the plan in more detail then come back to you with timings and all that. It's probably best if you keep busy that day too, for accountability. Maybe use that day spa of yours, book in some treatments, anything that leaves a financial trail. Just to be on the safe side.'

'Good idea,' Grace replied. She stared at Lily for a moment and then moved her gaze across the group. 'Let's make this happen, and let's make it smooth. I'll contact Marie shortly and start making plans with her to get closer. Let me know when you have my big surprise organised.'

Turning around, Grace clicked her fingers at her men and they swiftly fell in behind her. Lily watched as the small group marched back out of the building and the door closed, leaving them alone once more.

'Come on, Scarlet,' she said, still staring at the closed door, lost in thought. 'We have a lot to do.'

Turning to the task at hand, she slipped the paperwork back into the folder and tucked it under her arm before pointing at Cillian with a hard glare. 'I know what you're up to, mister. With all that aching-neck bollocks,' she said, her tone hard. He froze and waited warily for her to continue. 'Or at least I think I do,' she admitted. She narrowed her gaze and then suddenly relaxed it. 'And it's bloody brilliant.'

Cillian breathed a sigh of relief and Connor grinned. Lily walked off with Scarlet falling in beside her.

'Just whatever you do,' she called back over her shoulder, '*don't* fuck it up.'

FORTY-FOUR

Cillian stared up at the sign swinging above the door. Half the letters had come off, but he could still just about make out the words.

'The Spoiled Pig?' he asked, looking sideways at his mother.

'Soon to be the Blind Pig,' she replied. 'I'll have the works started tomorrow. I only got the keys today. It's a mess inside, but you'll see the potential.'

'Well this is certainly a new adventure,' he replied, a touch of disapproval sneaking into his tone as he exchanged a look with Connor. He clamped his jaw shut to refrain from saying more.

They had a lot of trouble knocking at the door right now, and he wasn't sure it was the right time to delve into new waters. But he wasn't the one running this firm, his mother was. So there was no point in sharing this opinion. He rolled his shoulders and pulled his jacket straight.

'Go on then – show us the new palace.'

Lily stepped forward and unlocked it, and the three of them filed into the dark, dusty bar beyond. She closed it behind them and he squinted, waiting for his eyes to adjust. The place smelled musty, as though no one had been inside for a long time, and as he walked over to the bar and ran his finger along the top, the dust only added to this belief. The carpet was threadbare, and everything around the room was cheap and outdated.

'This is a total dive,' Connor said from the other side of the room.

Cillian nodded in agreement.

'It *was* a total dive,' Lily corrected. 'Which was why it was so cheap. But we're going to refurb it and spruce it up. Make it somewhere for our kind to go. Somewhere they can relax. Somewhere *we* make the rules.'

'Do we really need that on our plates right now?' Cillian asked, unable to hold back any longer.

'It won't be on our plates. Once it's up and running I'm getting Tommy Harding in to run it. He wants back in the pub game and he's someone we can trust to look after our best interests.'

Cillian pulled a face of grudging approval. Tommy had run a couple of pubs that had been frequented by members of the underworld for years. He'd decided to try early retirement a few years back but had quickly grown bored and had run jobs for several firms as and when he could get the work ever since. He was a fearsome man, as crooked as they came, but one who ran a tight ship. He held no respect for the laws of men, displaying loyalty only to the sacred laws of the underworld, and any establishment he ran reflected that. No one caused trouble in one of Tommy's pubs. Not if they wanted all their bones to remain intact.

They followed Lily through a side door and up some stairs. Above, there were several doors, and she walked through the first.

'This will be the main office from now on,' she said. 'The next room will be Scarlet's, then the rest of this floor we'll knock through to be a regular gambling den.'

Cillian nodded. There had never been any need for him or Connor to have an office. They avoided the paperwork side of the businesses like the plague and were forever thankful that their mother, and now Scarlet, dealt with all of that.

'Sounds good.' Cillian eyed his mother and waited. There was something else she wanted to discuss, he could tell.

Lily took a deep breath. 'I didn't want to mention this until after the meeting with Grace, but this morning the Italians hit the salon.'

'What?' Connor demanded in an incredulous tone.

'What do you mean "hit"?' Cillian asked.

'Scarlet went early to meet Cath and Sandra to go over the books and they put bricks through the windows, both sides of the door.'

'Motherfuckers!' Connor exclaimed, balling his hands into fists.

'They made it clear that they plan to oust us and take over.'

'They ain't taking nothing,' Cillian snarled, flexing his muscles under his sharply fitted suit and turning away from his mother as he tried to contain his anger. 'We've let those fuckers run around unchecked long enough. It was fine when they kept to their own ground, but that's a step too far. That's several steps too far. And they need to be taught a lesson.'

'I couldn't agree more,' Lily replied. 'You know the chip vans? Round up enough muscle, organise a timed attack. Flip them over, all at the same time.'

The Italians were a small firm, only able to keep their fingers in a few pies at a time. One of their biggest sources of income was the string of fish and chip vans they had dotted around the East End. These vans violated everyone's rules. They were illegal, because they'd never obtained the permits required to sell food on the street. Most of the police turned a blind eye in return for a free lunch, and when they didn't, the Italians just accepted the fine and moved on for the day. They had been trading on Drew territory for years and the Drews had allowed it, as these vans didn't rival any of their own businesses, but that had been before they'd smashed the salon windows and threatened to take over. Now the vans being here was just taking the piss.

'Don't do anything else,' she warned. 'That will be a statement enough and ruin their equipment. Then take Luca. No need to break any more of his bones than you have already. Tie him up and wait. Once he's visibly pissed himself, dump him on the old man's doorstep with a note telling him he needs to add nappies to his shopping list, and not to let his kids stray into our yard again. That should be enough to put them back in their box. They've pushed to see whether they'll be met with resistance or not, but their old man's not daft. He'll pull back.'

'And if he don't?' Cillian asked.

'We need to stay on alert, keep tabs on them. Maybe we should get some of the younger lads on watch.'

'We can't watch all of them,' Connor pointed out.

'We don't need to. Luca's the sore one. He's the one leading this little strop. We only need eyes on him and maybe his brother. See to it,' she ordered, her gaze darkening. 'And get the rest done too. I want all those vans out of business before the end of the week.'

FORTY-FIVE

John straightened his tie and walked out of the lift and through the busy office. Phones rang, voices chatted and somewhere nearby someone cursed and hit the side of a broken photocopier. But John didn't hear any of this. He was concentrating on his game face.

He'd been avoiding Jennings since he'd manipulated Scarlet's release. He'd seen him just once when he'd delivered the news – the performance of his life – and after that he'd steered clear. Guilt didn't plague him, the way he'd thought it might, afterwards. But fear did. Fear that Jennings would figure it out, fear that he'd let slip in his expression or that Jennings would question him harder than he was ready for. But there was only so long he could avoid his colleague. His new *friend*.

He'd had to befriend the man to get close enough to the case to undermine it. Favours and coffees and lunchtime chats had all been handed over freely, despite the fact the entire time he'd rather have been doing *anything* else. The man was a boor, brutish and angry, out for the win at any cost. And whilst this was a respected behaviour in the police force, John found it tiresome. He just wanted to get on with his own workload and look after his own team, rather than continue to indulge Jennings and his self-absorbed rantings and ravings. But it would be odd for him to suddenly drop the other man now that he'd achieved his goal. Suspicious, even. So for now he had to make an effort.

Reaching the glass-fronted office, he knocked twice and pushed the door open, leaning in. 'Alright? Free for lunch?' he asked, hoping he sounded more enthusiastic than he felt.

Jennings sat facing the back wall, playing with a stress ball, but he swivelled in his chair to face him once he heard the voice. 'No, but come in,' he replied.

John entered and shut the door behind him, taking a seat casually. 'What's up?' he asked, gesturing to the ball.

Jennings looked down at it as if only just realising it was in his hand and put it down in the paperclip pot where he kept it. He rubbed his forehead and sighed frustratedly. 'Just this Drew case. It's haunting me. We *had* her. She was there in the palm of our hands, no way to escape sentencing.' He groaned and ran his hands down his haggard face.

'You've still not got her back?' John asked, feigning surprise. 'Surely we can just grab more evidence from the site?'

He knew this wouldn't be possible. The night he'd taken the evidence he'd snuck onto the site and detonated a small explosive in the basement, bringing the ceiling down and smashing what little evidence would be left on the floor to nothing. It was due to be done anyway – he'd checked the demolition schedule. All he'd done was speed up the process. As it was under street level it had barely caused a scene above, and it was so late that no one had been around to notice what little there was to see. He'd walked away and left it for the builders to figure out the next morning.

'The idiots brought the bloody roof down before I could get back in,' Jennings replied angrily.

John made a sound of frustration. 'Typical. Is there absolutely no way of getting anything from the rubble?'

He was pretty sure there wouldn't be, but he wanted to hear the defeat from Jennings himself. The last thing he needed was some fluke find off the back of the other man's perseverance.

'No, no.' Jennings shook his head. 'It's ten feet of debris – anything down there is either gone or unreachable now.'

There was a sharp knock on the door behind him and Jennings signalled for whoever it was to enter.

'Sarge.'

John turned at the familiar voice and found himself looking up into Ascough's keen pixie-like face.

'What is it?' he asked.

'There's headway on the Jackson case. You'll want to see this,' she replied, an excited twinkle in her eye.

'OK, I'll come now. Sorry, Paul,' he said to Jennings. 'I'll catch up with you later.'

'Sure. Maybe drinks one night after work?' Jennings asked.

John pulled a face. 'Evenings I'm usually a bit tied up. Lunch though, definitely,' he offered.

'Oh yeah?' one side of Jennings' mouth turned up into a curious smirk. 'Caught yourself a lady already, have you? You've only been in London five minutes.'

'Oh, no, it's just—' John began to protest.

'It must be a bird, to keep you busy in the evenings. They're the only things strong enough to keep a man away from the pub with his mates, at least. Come on, spill the beans, Richards,' Jennings pushed jovially. 'Who is she?'

John stood and forced a grin, feeling cornered. 'Oh, it's nothing serious. Very casual.' He shrugged and pulled a face. 'Nothing to write home about just yet, which is why I keep it on the down-low, but er, yeah, just spending some time.'

Jennings rolled his eyes, looking disappointed. 'Christ, a married man can't live vicariously through you much, can he? That was about as juicy as a slice of day-old bread.'

John forced another grin, partnering it with a chuckle. 'I'll catch you later.'

Turning back to Ascough, he followed her out and through the office to the hallway with the lifts. As they waited, she glanced up at him.

'You've dipped your toe in the local dating pool,' she said in an upbeat tone. 'Good luck.' She leaned in conspiratorially. 'It's an absolute swamp, to be honest, but I'm told there's supposed to be a few diamonds in the mud if we keep looking long enough.'

He laughed, this time genuinely, at her dire account. Glancing over his shoulder as they stepped into the lift, he quickly checked Jennings hadn't followed them out.

'I'm actually not dating anyone,' he said. 'I just didn't fancy wasting what little social time I do have with that sour old git.' He grinned to turn his last few words into a joke. 'Don't tell him that though.'

She laughed. 'Your secret is safe with me.'

It was a fine line he had to tread, to keep the people around him off the subject of his dating life. It had been easier to keep Jennings at bay with the tale of a casual romance. Something that would keep him too busy to go out, but not something serious enough to delve into details. When people were married to their work the way most of the police force was, it was only natural to want to share and discover personal details with those around you. With Ascough though, it was safer to pretend that there was no one at all. She was too astute, noticed too much. And Scarlet was the one thing he didn't need anyone asking about down the line, as she surely would.

'Well, you know, if you ever fancied a drink with someone who wasn't a sour old git, I could show you around a bit. I know a few places that do particularly nice cocktails.' She looked up at him a touch shyly for someone who was usually so confident and smiled as she tucked her short hair behind one ear.

If he hadn't been sure before, he was now. Ascough had a

thing for him, and this was her way of subtly trying to find an in. He didn't want to hurt her feelings but needed to shut down her tentative interest.

'Yeah, maybe we could get the team together or something one night after work. I've been meaning to suggest that for a while actually.' He didn't look back at her, but he could almost feel her disappointment in the air between them.

'You live Tooting way, don't you?' Ascough asked after a few moments, as the lift stopped to let someone else in.

John froze. How did she know that? He kept his personal life strictly private and he knew he'd not let something as personal as where he lived slip. His silence and expression must have given his feelings away as she hurried to continue.

'I only say because I noticed you got the same Tube home as me the other night. We got off at the same stop but you were a couple of carriages ahead. I saw you do the same once before, too, when you first started. I figured you must live around there.' Her face flushed. 'Sorry, that sounds super weird. I wasn't following you or anything.' She laughed, clearly embarrassed.

'Oh, no, I know,' John replied. 'Obviously not. You just caught me off guard. Yeah, I have a flat there. It's just a crash pad really.'

He tried to calm the alarm bells ringing in his head with difficulty. What if he'd been with Scarlet when she'd seen him? Not that she would meet him at work, but she could easily have met him at the Tube station the other end. What if Ascough had seen them together?

The threat had been real from the moment he'd decided to steal the evidence and align himself with Scarlet. It had been real when they'd agreed to give things a go in secret. It had been real when he'd met her family and had jumped in with both eyes open.

But right now, the reality of the risks he was taking was starker than ever.

FORTY-SIX

Standing in the shadows of the entrance to a small church across the street, Connor and Cillian watched in silence as the man in the food van served the short queue of customers. Just a few buildings further up the high street was a clock tower and Cillian's eyes flickered over to it. There was about a minute left to go. One of the men beside them started to move but Cillian's arm shot out, stopping him.

'Not yet,' he murmured, moving the toothpick in his mouth to one side with his tongue. The last customer stepped forward. As he gave over his order, the clock chimed. At that, the brothers marched into the sunshine and crossed the road, the two men behind them quickly falling in line.

The man in the food truck serving glanced their way. He was just turning back to the food when he froze and did a quick double take at the menacing group approaching him.

'Oh, shit,' he cursed, the panic clear in his eyes. He looked around and disappeared for a moment before reappearing with a baseball bat, brandishing it with both hands. The customer who'd been waiting for his chips stepped back and quickly scarpered, his lunch forgotten.

Cillian turned to his brother with an amused smirk. Clearly the guy recognised them, but the bat wasn't going to do him much good. They weren't going to hurt him. Not directly anyway.

'You might want to get out, mate,' Cillian called as the small mob surrounded the van.

'You might want to fuck off,' came the reply. His words were brave, but the wobble in his tone gave away his fear. 'Don't you know who this truck belongs to?'

'Actually, I do, as it happens,' Cillian replied. 'And I'll say it one more time: you really might want to get out now.'

'I ain't going nowhere,' came the stubborn reply. 'But you might wanna run before I call my boss, cause he ain't going to be happy. You're gonna pay for showing your mugs here like this, you stupid cunts.'

Cillian nodded at him, his expression turning cold. 'I think he might be a bit busy actually. I imagine his phone's going all kinds of crazy right now.' He held the other man's gaze for a few moments, watching the confusion and fear and anger and bravado all play out. 'Oh well. You were warned.'

Giving the others the signal with a sharp tilt of his head, they all began to rock the van back and forth.

'Eh! Eh, what you doing?' the man inside screamed. 'Oi, stop it! What the fuck are you doing? I— Argh!' He screamed out as the hot oil in one of the fryers splashed his arm. 'Shit! Stop it right now. I said, stop it right fucking now!'

The van rocked further and further as the four of them built up the momentum. The shouts quickly began turning to screams of panic and pain as the oil splashed out everywhere inside the food truck.

'Come on, put your back into it,' Connor yelled at the two men they were with. They redoubled their efforts, and within a few seconds, they finally managed to get it to a point where it could tip.

'Get back,' Cillian yelled as it groaned at the top and then carried on over with a loud resounding crash to the ground.

The screams inside reached a crescendo as the fryers completely tipped over, their boiling contents burning the man still inside. The bloodcurdling screams were chilling, but Cillian's expression didn't so much as flicker as he turned and walked away.

'Come on,' he said curtly. 'We need to get out of here.'

As the man's screams and curses filled the air around them, the sound of sirens began wailing in the distance.

FORTY-SEVEN

Connor crept around the corner of the building to the edge of the window. He peered in, careful not to be seen, then pulled back to where his brother was waiting by the car.

'Well?' Cillian asked.

'Still sat there, just chatting. And the other three are still with him. We're outnumbered, I don't think this is gonna be our window.' He pulled a grim expression and scratched the back of his head, looking back towards the corner. 'And to be honest, if they see us here, we're fucked.'

Cillian pulled a face and looked around before nodding reluctantly. They were in a dead-end side road with nowhere to go but the way they'd entered. If Luca and his men came out and spied them, they'd be sitting ducks. And Luca would definitely not pass up on the opportunity to return the kicking they'd given him.

'Alright, come on then,' he said. 'We'll sit down the road and follow him.'

After they'd tipped the van earlier – and confirmed that the others had all been overturned too – they'd spent the afternoon trying to track down Luca. At first they'd watched from a distance as he and all the other main faces within the Italian firm gathered together at one of the family houses. Clearly, they were discussing the attack and how to deal with it. When Luca had come out, his face had been thunderous. He'd sped off in his car, and for a while they'd lost track of him, but then he'd resurfaced at the restaurant.

It was a popular spot for the members of that particular firm, owned by one of their cousins, and when they'd done a drive-by earlier in the evening, they'd been in luck. Luca had just been walking in with three of his men and had sat down for a meal. Since then, they'd waited it out, hoping for an opportunity to grab him. But it would be foolish to try something when he had so much backup.

As they turned to get into the car, there was a sudden increase in volume of the chatter from inside the restaurant. They paused and stared at each other over the roof, then Cillian tilted his head towards the noise.

Connor turned and jogged to the corner then pressed his back to the wall and inched closer until he was close enough to peep round. Just a few feet away, Luca stood alone, his hand cupped around a lighter as he lit his cigarette. Connor's eyes widened. This was their chance. He turned and frantically gestured for Cillian to join him.

As Cillian made his way over, Connor peeped round once more. Luca was turned away from them, staring down the road with the phone to his ear. He was silent for a moment, then whoever he was calling picked up.

'Eh, yeah, it's me. Listen, that Irish guy you told me about, the one who's good with the car bombs. Set up a meeting,' Luca said.

'Where are the others?' Cillian whispered.

'Still inside. What do we do?' He looked at his brother, waiting for his decision.

This was a prime opportunity to grab him, but it would be

tight. The men inside could come out at any moment or spot them through the window. If they were going to do it, they had to act fast.

Cillian glanced around the corner at Luca once more with an undecided grimace. 'Where's your blade?' Connor touched his belt. 'OK. Fuck it, let's do it. I'll circle to the front, you kick his knees out and take his fall, I'll grab his legs. We shove him in the back and you keep him there against the knife while I drive.'

'Got it,' Connor confirmed.

'Good. Go.'

Connor twisted and they rounded the corner together, swiftly descending on the unsuspecting Luca Romano.

'...tell him I pay cash, no trace. And— Hey, what the...'

Just as Luca recognised Cillian, Connor booted him hard in the back of the knees, forcing him to fall backward. He caught him under the arms as Luca's phone clattered to the floor. As the other man began to struggle, he felt Cillian take the burden of his legs.

'What the fuck are you *doing*?' Luca yelled, outraged. 'Alf! Stan!'

Connor's head whipped round to the large window of the restaurant and he locked eyes with one of Luca's men, watching as he registered what was happening with surprise.

'Quick,' he shouted to Cillian across the struggling Italian between them.

They picked up the pace, running awkwardly with Luca around the corner to the car. Slamming back against it, Connor shifted Luca's weight and fumbled with the door handle.

'Any time now,' Cillian said in an urgent tone.

'Got it.' Connor pushed back off the car and pulled the door open, still holding Luca up with difficulty.

'You two have got to be fucking joking,' Luca spat as he continued to writhe, very nearly twisting out of their grip before Connor steadied him again.

'Nope,' Cillian said before they shoved him quickly into the back.

Connor pulled the blade out of his waistband and held it to Luca's neck as the other man righted himself, grabbing hold of his arm tightly.

'Move and I'll slice your fucking throat,' he growled as Cillian slammed the door shut and jumped in the front. He quickly turned the key and locked the doors just as shouts sounded in the road behind them.

'He's down here!'

Cillian slammed the car into reverse and shot back, the car weaving all over the road as he tried to right it against the sudden speed. Connor looked through the back window at the three men, who were now quickly diving out of the way.

'Hold on,' Cillian said heavily.

Connor braced himself against the passenger seat, careful to keep the knife against Luca's neck. The Italian was now silent, watching everything play out with a tense expression.

As they swerved through the mouth of the side alley and onto the main thoroughfare, a taxi that had been making its way down the road veered to the side and managed to just miss them, blasting his horn angrily as he passed. Screeching to a halt, Cillian switched into first gear and squealed off as fast as he could.

The men who'd jumped out of the way began chasing them, and for a moment, as Connor watched with bated breath, he thought they might actually catch up. But as Cillian put his foot down and the engine roared to life, they were left behind, growing smaller and smaller as they slowed to a defeated stop.

'Ah, Jesus,' Connor muttered through a huge deflating sigh of relief. 'That was fucking close.'

'It certainly was,' Cillian agreed, sounding equally as relieved.

'You two cunts have got some nerve,' Luca snarled. 'When my father—'

Connor punched him in the face hard, with a roll of the eyes. 'Shut up, you prat,' he replied as Luca held his hands to his bloody nose with a sound of pain. 'Your *father's* going to think you're an idiot. Honestly, this is twice you've been caught out by us now.'

'Plus, anyone who needs to start a threat with "when my father", ain't a man a father can be proud of in the first place,' Cillian continued.

'Yeah?' Luca shouted, spitting out the blood that was running into his mouth. 'And how would you fucking know?'

Connor pulled his fist back and punched him again in the same spot, even harder this time. The sickening crunch of cartilage shattering resounded through the air, confirming that this one had broken his nose again. Luca wailed in agony and doubled over.

'Now, that's just rude,' Connor said. 'I don't really mind that we don't have a dad, meself, but my brother here gets a bit touchy about that. And I ain't having you upset my brother.'

'He couldn't upset a stomach,' Cillian said from the front seat.

The words were dismissive, but Connor still picked up the tightness in his tone. The subject of their dad had always been a difficult one for Cillian.

'Mum did say no broken bones,' Cillian added, changing the subject.

'Yeah, well.' Connor shrugged. 'He was asking for it.'

They travelled mostly in silence for the next ten minutes until they reached a quiet industrial estate. Cillian drove to one of the darker roads at the back, and they stopped briefly to secure Luca properly. They cable-tied his wrists and ankles together and bound him to the chair through the boot with a rope. As they fed the rope through the chair, Cillian paused.

'Hold up a minute.' Reaching into a bag in the boot, he pulled out a pack of what looked like padded white sheets.

'What the hell are they?' Connor asked.

'Puppy pads,' Cillian replied.

When Connor frowned, he continued. 'Puppy pads, to put under him. We've got to wait till he's in the right state to drop back, but that don't mean we have to dirty the motor.' He tutted and took a sheet through to the back of the car, moving Luca around until it was positioned underneath him.

'Why are you using them? How long we gonna fucking be here?' he asked indignantly. 'You can at least let me out to do me business. I ain't a dog.'

'You are today,' Cillian replied, slamming the door shut as more expletives came hurling out. He sighed and slipped into the driver's seat.

Connor closed the boot and had a quick cigarette before he joined his brother. It was one of the worst things about Cillian giving up smoking the way he had. Other than the bloody toothpicks he kept finding everywhere. He was no longer allowed to smoke in his car. Which, considering how many hours they spent together in a day, was seriously inconvenient.

'Bloody health freak,' he muttered moodily under his breath as he flicked the butt away.

He walked down the side of the car and got in, sitting in the passenger seat beside his brother now that Luca no longer needed to be held at knifepoint.

'Where we going?' he asked as Cillian pulled back onto the road.

'We'll go for a drive, head out of the area. They know it was us, so they'll be looking in our usual places,' Cillian replied.

'What about one of the storage barns?' Connor asked.

'What, and let him see where they are? Nah.'

It was a good point. They *were* only holding him for a fairly brief amount of time, so making secure arrangements was more hassle that it was worth. He settled back into his seat and prepared himself to wait it out. Surely it couldn't be that long before Luca pissed himself. He'd watched him knock back a fair amount of wine at the restaurant.

'You tried your hand again with Sandra lately?' Cillian asked.

'Yeah, but she's still playing hard to get,' he replied glumly. 'I don't get it, I really don't.'

'Me neither,' Cillian replied. 'And you took my advice?'

''Course. I told her straight, time and again. Now she ain't an escort anymore, I wouldn't treat her like one. I want to take her out proper. For free. Not offering her money for her time.'

There was a snort from the back and Connor glared back at Luca. 'Shut it, you.'

'I think you should keep telling her that. Maybe she just don't believe you yet,' Cillian said sincerely.

'Maybe,' Connor replied, looking out of the window. His feelings for Sandra wouldn't be quashed. Since he'd first met her, he couldn't get her out of his mind. And now that she was finally free to date as just a normal bird, and not as someone whose time he paid for, he really wanted to set things on the right path.

The chuckling from the back continued, and he turned to glare once more. 'You want me to have another go on that nose of yours? Because I *will*.'

Luca shook his head. 'No, I don't, but I just can't believe you're falling for this. Your brother here can't be serious. That's the worst advice I've ever heard.'

'And what would you know?' Connor shot back.

'Plenty. I get more pussy than a cattery. You can't talk to a woman like that and get results. You're telling her, an ex-escort, that you want to bed her but not pay. It's insulting. You're reminding her you used to pay for it and that you still think of her like that, then tell her you want the same goods for free.

Why would you even bring it up? What's *wrong* with you? No wonder you can't get anywhere.'

Connor thought it over and frowned. 'He's right,' he said, as the realisation dawned. 'Why would you tell me...' He trailed off and his frown deepened as the smile Cillian had been hiding crept out. 'You bastard!' he exclaimed. 'You fucking bastard. I really like Sandra and you've been fucking me over this whole time.'

Cillian laughed and tried to dodge the punch Connor threw towards his arm. 'Ahh, man.' He looked in the mirror accusingly at Luca then sideways towards Connor. 'Come on – that was funny though, you have to admit. I had you going for weeks before the leaning tower of piss-takers here ruined it all.'

'*No*,' Connor declared. 'It *wasn't* funny. I'm serious, Cillian – she's the one.'

'The *one*?' Cillian's eyes widened.

'Well, the one I can't stop thinking about anyway. It ain't funny at all. Imagine me doing that to you with your Billie, eh? How would *you* like it?'

Connor scowled and looked out the window, clamping his mouth shut before he could say anything else. He couldn't believe Cillian had done that to him. He couldn't believe he'd fallen for it. He felt like a total idiot. He felt his cheeks colour in embarrassment and fury and turned his face so that neither of the others would see. What must Sandra think of him? He guessed she'd made that pretty clear. She wanted nothing to do with him now. And all thanks to his stupid joker of a brother.

'Ahh, come on, Connor,' Cillian said, the laughter finally gone as he began to realise how much upset he'd caused. 'Look, I'm sorry. I'll make it up to ya. I'll go speak to her tomorrow and straighten it all out.'

'I think you've done enough,' Connor said tightly. 'Just leave it alone. And don't fucking talk to me.'

'Don't talk to you?' Cillian asked. 'Well, that's lovely, ain't it? What we supposed to do for the next few hours if we ain't talking?'

'You can talk to me,' Luca interjected from the back. 'For starters you can start talking about why the fuck you've—'

'Shut up, Luca,' the twins yelled in unison.

'Look, just drive,' Connor said with a sigh. 'This ain't over, but I don't want to talk about it anymore. We're in for a long night so let's just get through it, yeah?'

'OK.' For once Cillian didn't have a quip or comeback, and Connor was glad.

How was he going to win Sandra's affections after all of this? He needed to figure it out, because she was the only girl he could think about. And Connor Drew was anything but a quitter.

FORTY-EIGHT

Scarlet pulled the oven door open and checked the dish inside. It was bubbling away nicely and she gave a short nod of approval before shutting it again. The doorbell rang and Cath made a squeak of alarm behind her.

'Oh my God, he's early,' she exclaimed, aghast. 'I haven't even taken me rollers out yet. He can't see me in me bleedin' rollers! Jesus H. Christ.' She wrung her hands together in despair and made a run for the stairs. 'Wait until I'm out of sight, Scarlet – I'm not ready.'

Scarlet watched her mother hurry off. 'You do realise you're not actually invited, don't you?' she challenged. 'You're supposed to be going to Lil's.'

'Well, obviously, Scarlet,' Cath called back with a withering tone. 'But I have to make a good impression when I meet him. You did introduce him to the *entire rest of the family* before me.'

The reminder was the fifth that day and Scarlet rolled her eyes. She was being made to regret that decision significantly.

'Which is fine, you know. I'm only your *mother!*' Cath's voice disappeared as she went through to the rear of the house and Scarlet went to open the front door with a sigh.

She put her mother to the back of her mind and put on a smile, expecting to see John waiting on the other side. Her face fell when she saw it was Cillian.

'Oh. It's you,' she said, stepping aside to let him in.

'Don't act too pleased about it, will you?' he replied sarcastically.

'Sorry, was just expecting someone else.' She glanced out at the street in case John suddenly appeared then closed the door regretfully when he didn't. 'Is it quick?' she asked, unable to hide her impatience as she turned to her cousin. 'Only I've got John coming for dinner and he'll be here any minute.'

'Actually,' Cillian began, 'that's what I've come to talk to you about.'

Scarlet frowned. 'Oh, OK. What about him?'

Cillian pulled back his suit jacket and shoved both hands down into his trouser pockets before walking into the kitchen and looking out of the window towards his car. Scarlet's gaze followed his.

'Is that Connor? Why's the engine running?'

'Oh, we've got a hot pizza in there, can't stay long,' he replied in a strange tone.

Scarlet pulled a face and went to stand behind the large kitchen island where she'd been cutting thick slices of fresh sourdough. She picked up the knife and continued slicing, watching him warily across the room as he paced by the windows.

'Look, I know you're going to tell me it's none of my business,' Cillian started, taking a seat opposite her on one of the island bar stools. 'But this guy you're dating—'

'John,' Scarlet reminded him sharply.

'John. He's a fucking copper, Scar.'

'I'm aware of that, Cillian,' she replied tersely. 'Everyone is.'

'And no one's happy about it, not really,' he replied.

'What are you talking about? We've gone over this. Your

mum's OK'd it.' She put the knife down, annoyed now. 'He got me out of *jail time*, Cillian. He risked his job and his own freedom. I think he's more than proved himself.' Glaring at him, she picked the knife back up and continued hacking away aggressively at the bread.

'And that's why mum accepted him. That and the fact she now wants to turn him into her pocket plod thanks to you.'

Scarlet shrugged. 'I did what I had to do to get Lil's approval and it worked. And that's that. We're a couple now, and you need to start getting used to it.'

'A couple...' Cillian rolled his eyes and shook his head. 'You've known him five minutes.'

'About the same amount of time you'd known Billie before you blew up the sacred Sunday lunch,' Scarlet shot back hotly. 'But did I come and lecture you on your life choices? No, I didn't.'

'Billie ain't one of our natural enemies, Scar. We haven't spent our whole lives avoiding and outsmarting masseurs; we've been avoiding and outsmarting *coppers*. And now you're fucking dating one.' He let out a frustrated sigh as Scarlet glared at him across the island. 'How do you think the others in our world are going to take that, eh? They're going to see him as the threat he is to them – and he *is* a threat,' he quickly continued, seeing her open her mouth to argue. 'Maybe not to us, but to everyone else in our world he is. And being with you is like an open door to the goings-on in this world. You're making them vulnerable and they ain't gonna take that lying down. When they find out, and they *will,* the other firms will close us out.' He beseeched her, begging her to listen. 'They'll stop doing business with us; we'll be blacklisted.'

Scarlet felt her fear and her anger rise at his words. She knew what he was saying could potentially be true, but she didn't want to hear it. He had no right coming to her and trying to tell her to get rid of John.

'We won't *be* found out,' she snapped. 'I know all this and so does he. What we have is private and it will stay that way. And whatever that means down the line, we'll deal with it then. But that's for no one to decide but *us*.'

Cillian shook his head, and his lips formed a hard line. 'This ain't the Scarlet I know. The Scarlet I know wouldn't put the firm at risk like this just for a bloke.' He held her gaze, suddenly looking tired. 'What would your dad have to say about it, eh? If he was still here.'

Scarlet felt the words hit her in the heart as if they'd been daggers, and her insides turned cold. She locked her jaw and balled her hands into fists at her sides to stop the knee-jerk tears from falling. Swallowing hard, she blinked them away and nodded slowly, grim-faced.

'You know, I think you were right,' she said coolly. 'It *ain't* none of your business. Get out.' Her last two words were quiet but hard, and after a moment or two of holding her gaze, Cillian sighed and stood up.

'I didn't come to fall out with you,' he said.

'Could have fooled me,' she replied, crossing her arms across her middle defensively.

'Just think about it, Scar,' he asked. 'Think about what you're doing. What you're asking of the rest of us. We have to put the family first in our world, *always*. It's how we survive. We don't get to stop just because we found something shiny we like the look of.'

With one last long look at her, he turned and walked back out. Scarlet heard the door close and her resolve crumbled. Hot painful tears escaped and ran down her cheeks, and she sniffed loudly, looking up to the sky before blinking them back.

It was a low blow, bringing her dad into it like that. No, her dad had never liked coppers, and they wouldn't have exactly been high on his list of favoured suitors for her, but even he would have seen the merit in someone who'd risked it all to save his daughter. She was sure of that.

She ripped off a piece of kitchen towel and carefully wiped under her eyes, removing any evidence of her bout of emotion. The last thing she needed was her mother's concern or for John to notice she'd been crying. Tonight was about *them* and nothing else.

Carefully inspecting her face in the mirror, she decided that there were no telltale signs. Her pale cheeks were perhaps a touch pinker than usual, but that wasn't a bad thing. She fluffed her thick black hair and ran her hands down her casual burgundy dress. It was unfussy and flattering, perfect for a romantic evening in like the one she had planned.

The doorbell chimed once more and she turned towards it, this time more hesitantly. She hoped it was John and not another family member come to share their opinions. As she opened the door, her smile grew and she felt herself relax.

John grinned at her, his bright green eyes sparkling in the way that always mesmerised her. He brandished a bottle of wine in one hand and a bunch of pink roses in the other. 'These are for you,' he said.

'Thanks.' She stepped back and he walked in, looking around the large hallway with interest.

His gaze landed on the big family photo that hung in pride of place. He looked as though he was about to comment then closed his mouth and turned back towards her. She was glad. She really didn't need another conversation about her dad right now.

'You look lovely,' he said, moving towards her.

She pulled him closer and wrapped her arms around his waist, looking up at him with a smile.

'So do you,' she said, reaching up and lightly kissing him. Her heart lifted as their lips touched, reminding her exactly what she was fighting for. There was something deep and raw between them, something she cherished in her heart already. He kissed her back warmly then pulled away, his gaze lingering on her face.

'Well, thanks, it's my best dress,' he joked.

She laughed and took the wine and flowers from him. 'I'll put these in some water and then—'

'Oh, hello!' Cath exclaimed in a fake tone of surprise as she floated down the stairs in a manner not unlike some of the stars in the old black-and-white films she liked to watch. 'Is it that time already? You're John, I presume?'

Scarlet just about stopped herself from rolling her eyes. Her mother was dressed to the nines in her favourite two-piece she used to keep for what she called 'posh restaurants', with her hair set in loose curls and her bright red lipstick on.

'Going up the West End tonight then, are you, Mum?' Scarlet asked in a sarcastic tone.

'No, just your aunt Lil's – I told you that,' Cath replied.

'I know,' Scarlet replied flatly, looking down at the outfit purposefully.

Cath gave her a sweet, fixed smile, but her resentment at being called out was clear.

'Hi, yes, I'm John.' John stepped forward and held out his hand politely.

'Oh, we ain't that formal around here, John. Come on, in you come.' Cath reached forward and grabbed him, pulling him towards her and kissing his cheek.

Scarlet's eyebrows shot up, and she had to bite her lip to stifle a giggle at John's face. He straightened back up and smiled back at her mother politely.

'It's lovely to meet you, Mrs Drew.'

'Cath – you must call me Cath,' she insisted.

'Cath. And you look lovely this evening,' he continued.

'What, this old thing?' she asked with a dismissive wave. 'I haven't even had time to change since I've been in from work,' she lied, avoiding Scarlet's gaze. 'I work at Scarlet's salon, you see. You know, helping to run things.' She took John's arm and tucked it into her own, turning him towards the kitchen. 'No rest for the wicked, eh, John? Not that we're wicked,' she added hurriedly. 'Not that wicked anyway.'

John laughed. 'You really don't have to worry about all that,' he said awkwardly. 'I know... enough.'

Scarlet followed behind the pair, thoroughly amused.

'Yes, you're a good boy from what I hear. Or is it bad? My Ronan, he was never a fan of pigs – policemen, I mean – on the whole. They were always after him, you see. And I can't say I was ever fond of them for that meself either. But at the same time, I never saw things as black and white. Because I think you lot are brilliant for certain other things. I mean, there are some real bastards out there, John. Nasty bastards who like to knock their old women about. *And* their kids. They're the *real* criminals. You know what I mean?'

Scarlet zoned out as her mother prattled on, watching John move around her home and her mother make the effort to bond with him. It was so unnatural, their conversation, how uneasy Cath clearly was. And that was because they really were from two very different worlds. Worlds that clashed. Worlds that should never be blended.

Was Cillian right? Was she being selfish trying to make this work?

John caught her eye and she quickly smiled. But as he looked away, the warmth that his gaze had planted in her heart turned cold. Was this all worth it, or was she really just pushing her family firm towards devastation and ruin?

FORTY-NINE

The leaves on the old oak tree outside the run-down café rustled as the wind blew through the branches. Several leaves snapped at the stem and softly spiralled towards the ground in the weak evening light. One perfectly golden example rocked backward and forward, landing gently on the ground before the closed glass door. Barely a second passed before it was blown violently away by the force of the door smashing open and the body that was promptly thrown through it, onto the pavement.

George leaned out and snarled as the man he'd just launched scrambled to his feet. 'Now *fuck off*,' he ordered.

Inside, Lily waited until George had closed the door and was once again by her side. On her other side, Andy stood, staring menacingly at the two men left still sitting at the table in front of them.

'Now, Mani, is that really any way to greet a visitor?' She was referring to the knife the eager young man who'd been by his side had pulled on them when they'd walked in, not five minutes before.

Emmanuel Romano – known more familiarly as Mani –

sighed heavily and picked his napkin out of the top of his shirt, throwing it down on his half-finished dinner.

'You can't exactly blame him, after what you did to our food trucks,' he replied, his tone irate.

'That was just business, Mani, nothing personal,' Lily replied in her cool, calm tone.

'And my son?' Mani asked, lifting one eyebrow and looking up at her with disapproval.

'Well, that was probably a bit of both,' she admitted. 'I take it my boys reminded you to keep your children in your own backyard in future?' she asked, lifting her chin as she stared down at him with a polite, fixed smile.

Mani's look would have made most men quiver in their boots, but Lily's defiant gaze didn't falter. He picked up his water and took a deep drink before continuing.

'What do you want?' he asked bluntly.

'To put an end to this little squabble, before it gets out of hand,' she replied lightly.

'Squabble?' Mani shook his head. 'You put our entire fleet of trucks out of business. Not to mention two of the men who work them in hospital.'

'You smashed up our salon and threatened my niece. Not to mention our entire business,' Lily replied, tilting her head with an accusatory look. 'What did you expect?'

Mani sighed and sat back, studying her in a strangely detached way for a few long moments. 'You know, I took a step back from a lot of the business, a few years ago.' He tapped his chest. 'The old ticker. Ain't what it used to be. The doctor says it's too much good living, but' – he shrugged – 'better to live right than exist wrong, eh? It's my sons and their cousins who run things mainly now.'

'Oh, come on, Mani,' Lily replied, her tone bored. 'We both know you still pull the strings, even if you no longer do the dance yourself.'

'Perhaps on some things. But where those boys want to take this firm, that's up to them. It's their future now. And if they see fit to expand when another firm is toppling, topping, toppling down...' He made small hand gestures to go with his words. 'Then that's up to them. I can't say I blame them. Perhaps I should have tried doing that a long time ago, now I see you are so worried.' He smirked, believing himself to have hit the spot.

Lily sighed. 'We aren't worried, Mani. We could crush you tomorrow,' she replied simply. 'But that's messy. And it doesn't particularly serve anyone. You know, you used to be too scared to make a move on us. Which was wise.'

Mani chuckled. 'That was back when the things you did were scary. But lately all you've done is take blows instead of delivering them. Something tells me you aren't what you used to be.'

'Is that right?' Lily asked in a deadly tone.

'It is,' Many responded, holding her gaze.

Lily nodded and made to move towards the door. 'Watch this space, Mani. You may see something that could change your mind.'

'Perhaps you should take a leaf out of my book, Lily Drew. Take a step back, let the kids take things where they will.'

'I'm nothing like you, Mani,' she said, pausing at the door with a small smile. 'But then again that's why I'm on top, and why I'll damn well stay there.'

FIFTY

Looking into the mirror one last time, Ruby cast a critical eye over the area she'd covered with her new make-up and forced herself to relax. She hadn't done quite as good a job as Sandra had, but it was close enough. Unless you were looking for them, the burns weren't too blatantly obvious.

The chatter from the rest of the family downstairs wafted up the hallway and into the room, Scarlet's laugh shattering her fragile calmness like an elephant stamping on an egg. She gritted her teeth and forced a deep breath.

'Keep your eye on the prize,' she muttered to herself.

Since she'd returned from her narrow escape and had slept it off, she'd done nothing but plan. Working her way backward from her ultimate goal, she'd set herself a series of small steps to get to what she wanted to achieve. That Tanya woman had been bang on the money. Ruby couldn't change who she was – it was too deeply ingrained. But she *could* harness those weaknesses and turn them into strengths. She could find her highs in other ways and channel her addiction towards the things she needed to do to get there.

To get what she wanted, what she *really* wanted – Scarlet

knocked off her precious throne – she needed power within the firm. To get that sort of power, she needed to make herself indispensable, to be the one her mother called upon to get things done. And to do that she needed to integrate herself in the day-to-day running, in *all* areas, not just the salon. Which meant she also needed to start taking part in the social things they did as a family.

Not much of a people person at the best of times, Ruby had always found it tiring to be around them all. But it was all part of this journey, and so today, for the first time in many years, she was going to be part of the Sunday family lunch.

Stifling the reluctant sound that seemed to bubble up from the back of her throat, Ruby walked out into the hallway and down the stairs. The sound of general chatter died down as she walked through into the kitchen and opened the drawer where she knew her mother's aprons were. Selecting one, she wrapped it around her waist and tied it quickly with deft hands then turned towards the sea of shocked expressions and gave them a brief accusatory glare.

'Don't stop on my account,' she said, her tone bolshy as she attempted to cover her feelings of awkwardness.

The twins exchanged a look of surprise but turned back to their conversation with Scarlet. Cath grinned like a Cheshire cat and handed her a fresh chopping board.

'It's lovely to have you join us, Rubes,' she said happily, glancing over at Lily.

If Lily was surprised then she didn't show it the way the rest of them had. Though this wasn't unexpected. Her mother had always had a good poker face. Instead, she just handed Ruby a punnet of tomatoes.

'Here, these just need slicing up for the caprese salad.' Lily shot her a warm smile and for a moment Ruby caught the joy behind her mask.

She smiled back and picked out the largest tomato, then

began slicing at the kitchen workstation between her mother and her aunt. Although the action felt odd and unnatural, it also felt quite nice. And that surprised her.

'Fancy a drink, Rubes?' Connor asked, breaking off from his previous conversation and walking over to the kitchen island.

'Yeah sure, what we got?' she replied.

'These two are on the wine, but there's beers or...' He trailed off, seeing his mother's face. 'Or, um, squash,' he finished lamely.

'Booze was never my poison,' she said, glancing at her mother. 'I'll have a beer.'

'Coming up.'

'How you feeling now, Ruby?' Cath asked, chucking the carrots she'd been chopping into a mixing dish and pouring some honey over the top. 'Your burns and things, I mean.' She began to toss them gently as she waited for Ruby's answer.

Ruby wished she didn't have to talk about it. It was all still there – the pain, the scars, the nightmares. All the reminders of the horrific trauma she'd gone through.

'I'm OK,' she mumbled.

The night before she'd woken twice in cold sweats, screaming, sitting bolt upright clasping her sheets in her fists as she was shaken awake by her mother. After the second time, her mother had sat in the chair by her bed and settled in for the night, so that she wasn't alone. She glanced at Lily now, wondering if she was going to bring it up. Her mother shared a look with her that promised it was just between them, and she felt grateful for that. Her aunt Cath meant well, but that sort of vulnerability was hard to even share with Lily, let alone anyone else.

'You're looking great,' Cath replied. 'I like that lippy on you, by the way.'

Connor handed her the bottle of beer he'd just got her from the fridge and she took a deep swig, savouring the sharp, icy bubbles. Scarlet wandered back in and sat down on the other side of the island, picking at a piece of bread from the bread bowl that was supposed to go in with the starters.

Ruby quashed a scowl with difficulty. It was always the same with her, no matter how big or small the situation. There were the general rules and then there was whatever Scarlet chose to do.

'She looks lovely, doesn't she, Scarlet?' Cath continued.

Ruby felt herself bristle as Scarlet looked over towards her reluctantly. She didn't need a pity compliment from her hated younger cousin. She didn't need anything from her.

'Yeah,' came the half-hearted response. 'Really n—'

'I'm finished with these tomatoes,' Ruby butted in quickly. 'Where's the mozzarella?'

'In the fridge,' Lily said levelly, glancing between the two.

Ruby busied herself with getting the cheese and grabbed the pesto whilst she was there. She really didn't know why Scarlet had felt the need to sidle over. It wasn't like she was coming to help. As that thought settled, it planted a small seed of satisfaction inside her.

It was a minor point and most likely no one would consciously notice it today, but this was one thing she was doing that her cousin wasn't. She was standing with her mother and her aunt, helping to feed the family. Standing on the adult side of the island. When they'd been just kids, it had always been the adults who cooked while the kids played. And it seemed the habit had continued as the rest of them had grown older. But not for her. She was back and she'd placed herself firmly on the authoritative side of things.

As she noticed this, so, it seemed, did Scarlet. Her cousin sat up straight suddenly and her gaze flickered between the three of them as Ruby placed the mozzarella on the chopping board.

'Do you need any help with anything?' she asked.

Ruby's heart constricted and her hand faltered as she reached for the knife.

'No, we're OK,' Lily replied. 'Everything's covered.'

Ruby picked up the knife and sliced into the cheese with a smug smile. Placing the small rounds on the plate next to the tomatoes, she then lifted her head and pushed her curls back off her face.

'I've been thinking,' she said brightly. 'It's been great easing in with work at the salon, but I want to get more involved with the rest of the business.'

Scarlet's face adopted a look of shock which she hurried to contain, but her body remained tense. It was clear that this was the last thing Scarlet wanted, which just made Ruby want it all the more.

Lily tilted her head as she considered it. 'You've worked hard at the salon and *have* proved yourself very reliable. Especially with all that Natalie business.' She nodded slowly. 'If you're serious then you can start by learning the factory side of the business.'

Ruby felt the elation swell up inside of her, and it almost doubled at the sight of Scarlet's disappointment. Her cousin looked at her with a fixed smile, but her disapproval still lingered behind her grey-blue eyes. Ruby held her gaze with a look of triumph and smiled back – a wide genuine smile.

'Sounds good,' she replied to her mother, not moving her eyes from Scarlet's. 'I look forward to that.'

And I look forward to all the trouble I'm going to cause you, Scarlet Drew, she thought venomously. *It may take time, but I'll overtake you one day. And you won't even see it coming.*

FIFTY-ONE

Scarlet stood by the newly restored salon front window and stared out at the busy street beyond, not really seeing the cars as they whizzed by or the people who hurried past to the nearby station. She crossed her arms and chewed one of her fingernails anxiously.

'Ain't you just had them done?' Sandra chided as she walked past.

Scarlet lowered her hand and looked at the nail with regret. 'Yeah. Never mind.'

'What's up with you today? You seem worried. Everything OK?' Sandra eyed her with concern as she tidied up one of the workstations.

Scarlet bit her lip and then went over to the reception desk. 'I don't know. Ruby's decided she wants to get involved in the main side of the business. And Lil's all for it.' She pulled a grim expression.

'Well, that don't seem like it's a bad thing,' Sandra replied in her easy, sunny way. 'It might be just what Ruby needs right now. Something new to sink her teeth into and distract her from everything.'

'It might be what *Ruby* needs, but that don't mean it's what the business needs.'

Sandra opened her mouth to reply, but then the door opened and Cillian entered with Billie, putting an end to their conversation.

'Cillian, what are you doing here?' Scarlet asked. 'Hi, Billie.' She smiled.

'Yeah, what are we doing here?' Billie echoed. 'Hey, Scarlet.'

'It's Billie's day off and I've just been called to go deal with something, so I had a bright idea,' Cillian said with a winning smile.

'That'll be the day.' Ruby's voice suddenly joined the conversation as she walked into the salon behind him.

Cillian gave her a withering smile then continued, ignoring the jibe. 'I thought that while I'm busy, you girls could pamper *my* girl and make her feel like a million dollars. A nice blow-dry or something. Whatever you think.'

'But I just washed my hair this morning,' Billie said with a frown. 'You were there—'

'Yeah, but, you know...' Cillian smiled again and clapped his hands together, rubbing them and nodding as if hoping everyone else would join in.

Billie turned her confused gaze to Scarlet, who returned it with equal force. Ruby, who'd been about to walk through to the back, paused and exchanged a look with Sandra. This was very out of character for Cillian. Not that he didn't like to spoil his women, but he usually did it with finesse and in a well-planned manner. He was known for it. This clunky attempt didn't make much sense to any of them.

'You're in luck, as it happens...' Sandra said slowly, 'as Rox's next client just cancelled. But try and book next time, yeah?'

'I really don't need my hair done though,' Billie protested, still sounding utterly confused.

'OK, well, what else do you do here, Scar?' he asked, looking at Scarlet expectantly.

Scarlet blinked. '*Nothing*, Cillian. It's a hair salon. I mean, Sandra makes a mean tea, but I wouldn't say it warrants a special visit.'

Billie snorted with laughter and quickly covered her mouth. 'Honestly, babe—' she began.

'Nah, come on. I want to get you a blow-dry and then I'm going to take you out tonight. OK? Yeah?'

Billie shook her head with an amused grin. She caved in. 'Alright. If you insist.'

'Good stuff.' Cillian's gaze darted towards Sandra. 'Now, er... while I happen to be here, I did have something I needed to talk to you about actually, Sandra.'

All four women made sounds that indicated the penny had dropped in unison.

'There it is,' Scarlet said.

'Knew it,' Ruby muttered.

'What?' Cillian cried, holding his arms out in a gesture of innocence. 'Listen...' Not waiting to be called out further, he followed Sandra over to the station she was headed towards and began talking. 'I fucked up. I did something which I really need to put right.'

Scarlet laughed silently as he began to tell his tale and Rox led Billie away to the wash. She turned back to what she'd been about to do and saw Ruby rummaging behind the reception desk. She exhaled and fought to resist her natural aversion to her cousin.

'I didn't think you were in today,' she said, standing away from Ruby.

'I'm not.' Ruby was blunt. 'Just grabbing my bits before I head over to the pub. I'm starting there with Mum today.'

Scarlet caught the glint of triumph in her eye. 'Great. Good luck,' she said, hoping the words sounded more positive than she felt.

Ruby looked up at her coldly with a tight smile as she closed the reception-desk drawer. 'I don't need luck,' she replied. With that, she turned and swept out of the door and didn't look back.

Scarlet watched her go with a heavy feeling of dread settling over her. She didn't like Ruby, she never had, but that wasn't why she didn't like the idea of her entering the mainstream of their business.

Ruby was a liability – she had been from the start. It was all very well now, while she was playing happy families and enjoying this new game, but what would happen when the novelty wore off? Ruby hadn't stuck to one thing – good *or* bad – for very long through her entire life. And when she finally grew bored or lost her patience with this latest fad, she would leave a trail of destruction behind her, the same way she always did. What then? How bad would the fallout be, and how on earth could they even predict it? Ruby was the most unpredictable force on the planet, and that scared Scarlet, even if it didn't scare Lily.

And on top of that, there was something about Ruby's attitude lately that didn't quite sit right. The little looks, the undertones. There was something going on behind the scenes with Ruby, she was sure of it. And that didn't bode well for anyone.

Sandra's voice broke through her thoughts, and she half tuned in as her mind still lingered on Ruby.

'You're not getting it,' Sandra said with a sigh. '*Yes*, that was probably the most stupid and offensive thing I've ever heard him say, but that ain't why I'm not interested.'

'You're right, I don't get it. He really does have a thing for you, you know. It's genuine,' Cillian replied.

'And that's lovely. Any other girl would be lucky to have him feel that way, but I just ain't into him.'

'Why not?' Cillian sounded put out. 'He's a handsome bloke, top of his game, smart dresser.'

'Just ain't my type,' Sandra replied simply.

There was a short silence as Cillian tried to find an argument, but it appeared he couldn't. 'You're mad,' he said in the end.

'Maybe. Now go on, piss off,' Sandra said in a good-natured tone. 'I've got work to do.'

'Women,' Cillian muttered, walking towards the door.

He paused by Scarlet. 'What's up with you?' he asked as he noted her expression.

Scarlet sighed, frowning deeply. 'Why does everything that comes out of her mouth sound like a threat? Like, literally, *everything*.'

'Who, Rubes?' Cillian asked. He glanced out of the window at the retreating figure of his sister halfway down the street. 'Probably because it is.' He pulled a face and then walked out, leaving Scarlet to ponder that thought.

FIFTY-TWO

Lily stepped out of the way of the carpenter who was bringing through one of the panels for the wall at the end of the bar. The electrician balanced precariously on a ladder in the middle of the room, muttering under his breath as he looked at the mess of dangerous-looking wires that were tangled up where a cheap chandelier had once hung. One of the builders whistled a toneless tune as he hammered away at the rotting wood of the old bar, and behind him one of his workers ripped down the heavy old curtains that were hanging off the rails. As they fell, a cloud of dust escaped into the air, coating the pair of them.

'Oi, watch it!' the builder by the bar exclaimed.

Ruby walked over, looking down at a notebook as she scribbled something down quickly. 'The plumber says the pipe's backed up and he needs to go grab a part quickly, but he'll be back soon and it shouldn't take more than a couple of hours.'

'Good. Who was that on the phone?' Lily asked.

'The flooring guy. He wants the payment up front before he lays out for the materials. Say's that's his policy on this estate.'

Lily shrugged. 'Fair enough. When does he want it?'

'He said he'll be over in an hour to collect,' Ruby replied.

'Ah. I need to go out in a minute and I won't be back in time.' Lily pulled a face. 'The furnace is arriving at the factory and I need to make sure everything is in order.'

'I could go get the money out of the home safe and pay him?' Ruby suggested tentatively.

'Um...' Lily bit her lip as the usual warning bells went off in her head.

For years they'd avoided giving Ruby access to the family's money at all costs. She'd been too reckless, too hell-bent on destroying herself. She'd lied and conned them more times than Lily could count to get enough to feed her habits. But that had been before. Ruby had changed. And whilst Lily wasn't a fool – she knew that things could all change again in an instant – she realised that she was going to have to show more faith in Ruby if she expected her to keep going the way she was.

Ruby looked at her now, the familiar wariness behind her eyes of someone used to being rebuked.

'Yeah, that makes sense,' she said with a slow nod. 'I'll give you the invoice and the code and you can take out enough to cover it. Just make sure you note down how much you've taken out in the notebook just inside the door.' She eyed her sharply. 'That's how we keep track, whenever anyone needs to take any.'

'Sure thing,' Ruby replied, holding her head a little higher, the wariness gone now that she'd been trusted the way anyone else in the family would have been.

'If you could do that and then just stay here today, oversee the refit and deal with anything that comes up, that would be really helpful,' Lily added, glancing down at the phone in her hand. 'Sorry, I know we were supposed to start on the factory stuff today. It will have to be tomorrow.'

'No worries,' Ruby said with a shrug. 'It's all part of the business, ain't it? That's what I'm here for. To learn all sides, not just one.'

Lily felt a flood of warmth wash through her as she looked

at her daughter. Ruby really was trying. For the first time in her life, she was stepping up and making a go of things, the way she'd always wanted her to. Looking up to the heavens, she sent up a silent prayer that this was it. That Ruby would stay on this path now. That she was back in the family fold for good.

Her phone beeped – a message from Ray. She turned so that Ruby couldn't see her screen then opened it up. She hadn't exactly lied to Ruby about the fact she and Ray had patched things up. But she hadn't exactly told her either. She knew she'd have to eventually, but right now Ruby already had so much to cope with, she didn't want to upset her and set her back in any way.

Dinner tonight? the message read. She smiled fondly and typed out an acceptance then slipped her phone into her pocket.

'All set for tonight?' Ruby asked.

'Hm?' Lily responded, her eyes widening with alarm. Had she seen the message?

'Tonight. With Grace?' Ruby stared at her as if she was going mad.

'Oh!' Lily exclaimed, the light bulb above her head finally switching on. 'Right. Grace. I still need to call her. I'll do that now.'

'OK. Text me the code and that,' Ruby responded, walking away and getting back to her notes.

Lily was amazed that she'd managed to forget. She'd have to cancel Ray after all, she realised with regret. But he'd understand. She pulled out her phone and dialled Grace's number.

'Grace, I've sorted your distraction for the party. Can you meet me tonight? Great. I'll text you the address – meet me there at eight thirty. Just us, no need for anyone else.' There was a pause and then Grace accepted the proposal. 'I'll see you there.'

She ended the call and bit her lip as she stared down at the phone. After a few moments of pause she opened her messages and tapped out another text to Ray.

> *Change of plan, I need a favour. Go to Club Anya tonight with your men. Don't interact with me, just familiarise yourselves with my guest. I may need someone down the line she won't see coming.*

FIFTY-THREE

Grace stepped out of the taxi and met Duffy's gaze. He stood across the road watching. She nodded and he entered the nearest bar, heading towards a table at the window. Lily had suggested they both come alone, and whilst she was fairly sure there was no ulterior motive, it didn't hurt to have eyes on the situation. She pushed a stray lock of hair back into her neat updo and smoothed down her black chiffon shift dress before walking confidently through the doors and into the smart-looking West End club.

Inside, the lights were dimmed around the dark glitzy bar. There were tables and booths, which were mainly full, and a large stage in the middle which was currently empty. She walked towards the hostess table and gave her name to the girl there, who promptly showed her to the booth where Lily was waiting.

'Grace,' Lily said, nodding in greeting. 'What will you have to drink?' She raised one eyebrow and the hostess hovered, awaiting her response.

'I'll have...' She picked up the drinks menu on the table and cast her eye down the cocktail list. 'An espresso martini. Will you join me, Lily?' she asked, glancing at Lily's almost empty wine glass.

'Sure, why not,' came the reply.

The hostess disappeared, and Grace slid into the semi-circular booth. They were facing the empty stage, quiet music playing in the absence of entertainment.

'So what's the grand plan of distraction?' she asked, cutting straight to the point.

'You'll see her soon.' Lily pulled up her sleeve and checked her watch. 'She'll be on in a couple of minutes.'

Grace subtly assessed Lily from the corner of her eye. As usual she was dressed all in black, a long-sleeved turtleneck top tucked into a slimline knee-length leather skirt. It suited her, but surely the woman got bored of always looking the same, she thought. She was an attractive woman, in her own way. Her tight golden curls stood proudly to attention, as wild as ever, around a pale, well-defined face. The only colour to be found was in the deep red lipstick she wore. The overall look the woman went for didn't appeal to Grace; it was too harsh for her liking. But even she had to admit it was striking.

Lily turned and it was obvious she'd been caught staring. She smiled. 'I do admire that top on you,' she lied smoothly. 'Turtlenecks are underrated, in my opinion.'

Lily turned back towards the stage, the lie clearly accepted. 'I've always thought so too,' she agreed. 'But anything too far above the nipple has died out in the younger generation. A lost subtlety.'

'So true.'

The hostess came back over with their drinks and placed them on the table between them. Grace lifted hers and held it out to Lily, who did the same and chinked the glass.

'Cheers,' Grace said with gusto.

They both took a sip and Lily offered a wry smile. 'You know I can't remember the last time I came out and had cocktails with another person and just enjoyed it. Every time I'm out I'm either *at* work or doing something *for* work.' She twiddled the stem of the glass. 'I mean, obviously this is work too, but... it's nice to get out and do something different.'

Lily sounded quite wistful as she spoke, and Grace felt a barrier drop between them. She sipped at her cocktail again. Her plan, it seemed, was working. The false sense of security she was counting on lulling the Drews into was beginning to come together. She returned Lily's smile as warmly as she could manage.

'I totally get that,' she replied. 'You know, although my social diary is fairly full, I rarely get to relax. Either I'm hosting a charity event or people are watching just waiting for any tiny slip-up.' She pulled a face. 'Society events are quite tiresome really. So sitting here with no responsibility or eyes watching your every move is a breath of fresh air for me too actually.'

Lily's smile widened fractionally and she looked down at her drink.

'Here's to enjoying cocktails together,' Grace continued, lifting her glass. 'Perhaps the payday isn't the only benefit to this new partnership of ours.'

Lily tilted her head to the side in consideration. 'Perhaps not,' she agreed.

The music suddenly stopped and the lights dimmed further. A hush fell over the place as people stopped their conversations to look with anticipation towards the stage. Grace's gaze followed everyone else's as new music began to play and a spotlight appeared in the centre of the stage. She searched the wings and across the back curtain for signs of a performer entering, but nothing moved. As she frowned, a shadow appeared in the centre of the spotlight, and as it grew bigger, she suddenly realised that whoever was arriving was coming from above.

A large ring fell into view and the tall, slim woman standing inside it arched back, her long blonde hair flicking into a perfect arc across the light as she began to contort. She moved in time with the music, swinging and swaying and balancing in precarious positions. The silver sequins and beads on her corset glimmered with every movement, and Grace found herself utterly transfixed. The graceful, daring creature in the spotlight reminded her of a Cirque du Soleil show she'd been to once in Paris. She had never seen such talent here in London.

'She's incredible,' she exclaimed quietly, not wanting to break the quietness around them.

'Isn't she?' Lily replied. 'She's going to be your grand gesture to Marie.'

'How do you know her?'

'Through a friend of a friend,' Lily answered vaguely. 'She'll expect payment, but the price is fair and we'll hardly miss it from the profits.'

'Of course,' Grace agreed. 'Does she know?'

'About the heist? No. She's a straight hire,' Lily replied. 'It's cleaner that way. Less to cover.'

Grace nodded in agreement. They were resourceful, the Drews, she had to give them that. In another world, had they not crossed every sacred line she held dear by stealing her retirement fund and breaking into her home, she may even have stuck at this little partnership with them. But they had. And Grace was not someone who easily forgave. Not even for the kind of money they could make together.

She sipped at her cocktail and shot Lily another faked friendly smile. 'You should serve these in your new pub,' she said, pretending to take an interest.

'Perhaps I will,' Lily mused.

'How's all that going anyway?' Grace asked. 'The pub and factory and everything. Are you all set to get things back up and running soon?'

Lily took another sip of her cocktail before answering. 'It's going OK,' she replied, her tone level and unreadable once more. 'The pub works are underway and the factory refit, though that's a bit slower. A lot has to be custom made.'

'You know, my father's family were in manufacturing. They sold off the company years ago, but not before he showed me the ropes. I remember him explaining the ins and outs of why the layout always worked best in a certain way. Workplace psychology.' She smiled, genuinely this time, as the memory took her back. 'He was quite a stickler for it.'

Lily looked sideways at her and studied her face for a moment. 'You'll have to pop down sometime then, see what we're doing and give us your opinion on the placement of our new equipment. I've just had the furnace set up. It's integral – it really does need to be just right.'

Grace hid her elation as Lily offered a tentative branch of friendship. People were so easily manipulated at times that it almost hurt. Grace wouldn't have to break down the doors to get the Drew family defences down. Lily, the head of the family, was already leading her in.

'That would be lovely,' she said pleasantly as her dark thoughts began to warm her heart. 'I truly look forward to it.'

FIFTY-FOUR

Scarlet pulled out of John's embrace and tidied her hair with her hands. They were sitting in his car in the car park behind the salon, grabbing a few stolen moments together between life's responsibilities. He groaned and pulled her back towards him, raining kisses over her mouth and down her jawline.

'Don't go yet,' he murmured.

She closed her eyes and melted back into him for a moment before gently pulling away. 'I have to. I have so much to do today,' she said regretfully.

He accepted this with a nod. 'I know.' He stared out of the front window and squinted against the sun. 'We need to find some proper time. I know you've got a lot on this week. Why don't I take you out for dinner somewhere next week? Maybe get a hotel, make a night of it.'

Scarlet hesitated, torn by his suggestion. 'We might be seen.'

'We'll go somewhere outside the city, somewhere no one will recognise us,' he replied, turning to face her.

Scarlet looked up into his green eyes and felt the familiar warm tug inside her chest. She wanted to spend more time with him too. Already they had grown so close. So much so at times it was like they'd never not been together, as if it had been like this between them for years. But despite that, the world they lived in was against them in every single way. And not only the world but her family. No matter how she tried to ignore Cillian's words, they seemed to be burned into the walls of her mind.

She sighed, unhappily. John leaned forward and lifted her chin with his hand. His gaze was serious as it met hers. 'I know it ain't easy, all this,' he said, as if he'd read her mind. 'But it's worth it.' He smiled sadly. 'We'll figure it out down the line, but for now, let me just take you for dinner?'

His simple plea was so heartfelt, Scarlet couldn't help but smile. She took his hand from her chin and squeezed it. 'Yeah, 'course,' she replied. 'Somewhere far out of the city.'

'I'll make it practically abroad,' he promised.

Scarlet leaned in and kissed him slowly and deeply, one last time. 'I'll call you later,' she promised.

She stepped out of the car and made her way back into the salon, waving back at him as he drove off. Inside, she unwedged the door and closed it, straightening her dress and looking in the mirror to check her hair. She jumped as she saw Ruby behind her, glaring at her reflection.

'Jesus Christ, Ruby,' she exclaimed. 'You gave me the fright of me life! What are you doing here anyway?' She frowned. 'Ain't you supposed to be at the factory?'

'Ain't *you* supposed to be working instead of making out with lover boy in the car park?' Ruby shot back sourly. 'I'm here dropping off the wholesale order. We were running low on colour,' she added.

Scarlet bit back the retort that played on her lips for Ruby's first comment and instead took a deep breath in and out. 'I could have done that,' she said.

Ruby continued stacking the small boxes of colour in their correct places. 'You wouldn't have the first clue what we need,' she sneered rudely.

Scarlet's eyes narrowed. 'No, I probably don't. But I'm glad *you* do, because that's exactly the sort of thing you were hired for,' she snapped. 'Because while the rest of us are busy running *multiple* companies, keeping all our clients happy, pulling off heists, laundering the money and keeping the other firms at bay,' she reeled off, counting their many responsibilities on her fingers, 'we needed someone here to make sure we didn't run low on colour.' The last few words dripped with sarcasm as she glared with disdain at her cousin.

Ruby glared back, her cheeks reddening, and she dropped the boxes she'd been holding, turning to face her square on. 'You know they say the most successful leaders in life are the ones who weren't afraid to get their hands dirty at the bottom of the ladder before they climbed it.'

'Well it seems you've got that end of the ladder all sorted, don't it?' Scarlet shot back, tired of this exchange already. She had enough on her plate without Ruby starting another point-less fight. 'Good for you.'

'Yeah, it *was* good for me,' Ruby replied, her eyes flashing dangerously. 'In fact, it taught me a lot. About the salon, about the business, about *you*.' Her gaze bored into Scarlet's.

Scarlet's eyebrows shot up and she barked out a laugh. 'About *me*? You don't know the first thing about me. You don't know how hard I work, the shit I do to keep this all going, the late nights, the sacrifices, *nothing*. You don't get it and you never will. Because while I was here dealing with the fallout after Dad's murder and picking up the reins, you were where you always are. Shooting up and checking out of reality. Taking the easy road.' She looked down on her in contempt. 'You think a little stint playing hairdressing assistant teaches you anything about us? About this firm?' She made a derisive sound. 'You know nothing.' She glanced at the last few boxes on the side. 'But I'll remember who to come to when I'm looking for the price of bleach.'

Ruby stared at her for a moment, the hatred she felt almost burning the air between them, then she stepped forward. 'I know enough to bring you down, Scarlet Drew. And I'll do it too. Not today, not tomorrow. But one day. And when I do, there won't be nothing you can do about it.'

With those last deadly words, Ruby turned and walked out through the salon, leaving Scarlet to stare after her with a sudden and deep feeling of foreboding.

FIFTY-FIVE

Lily stood in the mainly empty factory, staring up at the large metal furnace, marvelling at its size. It was an ugly-looking thing, but it was incredibly efficient, being three times as big as their last one. The metal grated stairs had been put in place, along with the walkway all around the edge above the areas where the other machines would be installed. One or two of the smaller ones had already arrived and the pipework was partly connected, but there was still a long way to go.

The muffled rumble of a car pulling into the car park outside reverberated through and then stopped as the engine was switched off. A car door slammed, and then after a few seconds, the door opened behind her. She didn't bother to turn, instead waiting for Ray to reach her.

He stood next to her, eying the large machine. 'That's some serious business right there,' he commented with a low whistle.

'She's a beauty,' Lily replied.

Ray repositioned himself behind her, wrapping his arms around her waist and nuzzling into her neck. She leaned back into him and closed her eyes for a few moments.

'So that was Grace, huh?' he asked, settling his chin on the top of her head.

'It was. You got a good look?'

'We did. And at her mate across the road pretending he weren't with her too. He was about as subtle as a stripper in a nunnery,' Ray replied.

'Tall, lanky, floppy brown hair?' Lily asked.

'That's the one.'

'Duffy. Good. You might need to remember him too.'

She felt Ray frown. 'What's the play?'

Lily bit her bottom lip. 'Maybe nothing. It depends on how things go down. I'll keep you updated, but be ready tomorrow night. OK?'

'Anything for you,' he replied, squeezing her a little tighter.

His words were casual enough, but Lily knew how pleased he really was to be invited in on a plan. She usually kept staunchly in her own lane as far as business was concerned. Ray had offered his help often over the years, but she could count on one hand the times she'd actually accepted. Independence was very important to Lily. In her view, if she couldn't protect and drive her family standing on her own two feet, then she didn't deserve to be there at all. But allowing him in now and again to lend a hand was OK.

'Do you want to come and see the pub?' she asked, turning to face him and wrapping her arms around his waist.

'What, check out my new competition?' he said with a loud gravelly laugh.

Lily grinned. 'What's the matter, old man? You worried mine will be better?'

'Less of the "old", thank you. I can still throw you around the bedroom for a few rounds more than any youngster could.' His blue eyes twinkled in his rugged face and Lily nuzzled in closer, savouring the musky scent of his aftershave.

'You'll have to remind me sometime,' she said.

She pulled back and stared him out with a half-smile for a few moments before turning to the door. 'You coming?'

They took both cars to the pub, which was only a few minutes' drive away. Really, they could have walked, but time was something Lily could ill afford to waste. She parked up and waited for Ray to do the same before leading him inside.

The noise was almost overwhelming as all the contractors she'd hired went about their jobs. Music blasted from somewhere, shouts and curses flew around the room, drills and chainsaws screamed and a loud banging reverberated through the whole downstairs from somewhere.

'Taking things slow, I see,' Ray joked loudly over it all.

'Come upstairs,' she replied, with a gesture towards a door at the side of the room.

It was quieter above with the door to the stairs closed behind them, and they could finally hear themselves think.

'This main area here is where the poker nights will be held. Weekly, once we're up and running.' Lily cast her eye over the space. It was even bigger than she'd estimated, now that it was all knocked through.

Ray walked slowly, his hands in his trouser pockets, his jacket pushed back. He nodded approvingly. 'It's a good space. You'll need to frost the windows so no one can see in.'

'Already arranged,' Lily replied.

'And you'll have to figure out a way to hide your equipment. If you ever get raided—'

'Ray.' Lily stopped him. 'This ain't my first rodeo. Don't try and teach me to suck eggs.' She grinned to take the edge off her words.

Ray held his hands up, suitably reminded of his place. 'Where's your office?' he asked, changing the subject.

'This way – come see.'

They walked through to one of the newly decorated offices, and Lily looked around at the freshly painted walls. These rooms hadn't needed much done to them, other than a general sprucing up, so she'd already been able to start moving the files in that they'd saved before the fire. She walked around the new desk that had arrived the day before and sat down in the leather swivel chair that had arrived along with it. Ray sat down in the guest seat opposite her, and she ran her hand across the desk absentmindedly.

'You don't like it, do you?' he observed.

Lily tried to look positive, but she knew she wasn't fooling anyone. 'It's smaller than my old office. And it doesn't have any windows. And it don't oversee the factory floor.'

'And it ain't the office you and Ronan built everything up from,' Ray added quietly.

Lily swallowed, a lump threatening to rise in her throat. 'No,' she admitted in a heavy whisper. 'It ain't.'

She took a deep breath and let it out slowly, sitting back and slumping into the chair for a moment. It took all the strength she had to keep the company running and the family together every day. And she loved it – it wasn't something she'd change for the world. But a year ago it had been the two of them holding it all up together. And although the rest of the family had stepped up to help with the load, nothing could ever fill the void that he'd left.

'Nothing can bring the old factory back now,' Ray said quietly. 'But that don't mean you can't carry him with you here. He's still with you, every step of the way. And he's probably moaning about the fact there ain't no window too.'

Lily laughed, a smile forming even through the pain. 'You're right, he probably is.'

'How on earth are you going to smoke?' Ray asked suddenly, as the thought occurred to him.

'They're putting a heavy-duty air filter in the wall tomorrow,' she replied. 'I'm already way ahead of you on that too.'

Ray grinned. 'You've always been a step ahead of me on everything, Lily Drew. As I'm sure you always will be.'

Lily smiled back fondly and reached forward over the table for his hand. Although she kept him at arm's-length, Ray's love had been her anchor over the years. He had always been there for her, come hell or high weather. And she knew he always would be.

The door opened and Ruby walked in, her nose in her notebook the way it usually was these days, breaking the moment between them. 'Mum, there's been a letter redirected from the old factory about the— Oh.' She stopped short as she looked up and saw Ray.

She paled, her eyes widening, and her gaze darted over towards her mother. Locking her jaw, she pulled herself to full height. 'What's *he* doing here?' she asked through gritted teeth.

Lily pulled her hand back and stood up, cursing herself for not checking Ruby's whereabouts before they'd headed over. This wasn't the right time for this to be discussed, not with the heist coming up tomorrow, but it seemed she was left with no choice.

'Ruby, I thought you were sorting out salon business this morning?' she said calmly.

'I was, and I did. But then I swung by home and saw this, figured I'd bring it to you and carry on going through all the factory procedures. What is he doing here?' she repeated, not put off her question.

'Ray is here to see me, and the pub,' Lily answered simply.

'It's good to see you working with your mum, Ruby,' Ray interjected. 'It suits you.'

'Don't patronise me,' Ruby snapped, barely looking in his direction. Her burning gaze was trained on her mother. 'How could you see him still, after what he did to me?' she asked accusingly.

Lily looked into her daughter's eyes. 'Look, Ray forcing you through cold turkey the way he did was not OK. We had a serious falling-out over it, as you know. I don't expect you to forgive him or to like him for it. But though he went about it in a bad way, even you must understand that he was just trying to help.'

'Trying to *help?*' Ruby exclaimed in disbelief.

'Yes,' Lily insisted. She eyed her hard. 'You might not like to be reminded now that things are different, but you were *running* towards an early grave. I worried, every time I saw you, that it would be the last time. When I could even *find* you that is.' For the first time in years, Lily laid it bare on the table. She loved Ruby fiercely and hated hurting her, but if they were all going to keep moving forward, they had to start being totally straight with each other.

She ran her hands down her face. 'I don't agree with how it happened, but I can't tell you that I'm not glad it did. You can hate him and I'll accept that. I'm angry on your behalf, because it wasn't his place, and I'll protect you from ever having to suffer something like that again. But I can't hate him for it.'

Lily prepared herself for an onslaught, for Ruby to scream and curse and spit fire, as she was so famed for. But the onslaught never came. She just shook her head at her mother with a long, hard look.

'I thought...' she floundered. 'I don't even know what I think anymore.' Turning around, she walked back out of the office.

'Ruby!' Ray called after her.

'No, leave her,' Lily ordered, staring after her as she turned out of sight. 'Let her go. I'll speak with her later.'

She knew Ruby better than anyone, and stopping her right now, trying to force her to listen when she was still reeling, was a bad move. It wouldn't make her hear them; it would just bolster her resolve not to. No, Ruby responded best to action. To being shown. And Lily was going to show her just how much her family had her back. Much sooner than she realised.

FIFTY-SIX

Billie drove her little blue car up the long, sweeping driveway and looked out of the front window in awe. 'Bloody Nora,' she breathed.

As she reached the turning circle in front of the impressive entrance to the Jacobean manor she paused and bit her lip, wondering where to park. She eyed the line of sleek-looking cars parked to one side – a Mercedes and two Range Rovers – and deliberated for a moment. Then she shrugged and pulled up next to them.

'Don't feel intimidated,' she whispered to her little Toyota as she locked the door. 'You're just as good as them.'

Slinging her bag over one shoulder, she hoisted her folding massage table under the other arm and dragged it over to the entrance. The door opened as she approached, but the man who opened it just watched her with mild curiosity as she puffed and panted with the table all the way up the stairs. When she finally reached him, he stepped back to let her in.

'She's in the drawing room,' he said in a bored tone, gesturing towards one of the doors.

'Thanks,' she said in a clipped sarcastic tone with a wide, fake smile. 'Arsehole,' she muttered as she walked away.

Putting the massage table down in the hallway, she knocked on the drawing-room door and then walked in when a female voice bid her to enter. The drawing room was as impressive as everything else she'd seen so far and she tried not to look around with wonder. She was here on a job and it was an important one. She needed to focus. Walking over to the elegant, tall, slim blonde lady sitting in one of the armchairs, she held her hand out with a smile.

'Hiya, I'm Billie, the masseuse the day spa sent over.'

'Yes, I figured,' Grace replied with a cool smile. She glanced at Billie's outstretched hand and then ignored it. 'Shall we get on then?'

'Yeah, OK.' She withdrew her hand and fiddled with her bag, looking around the room. 'Where do you want to go? It's very bright in here – a bit too bright if you want to really see the benefits of the full relaxation package.'

'Oh, is it?' Grace frowned at the tall windows that edged the room. 'Yes, I suppose it is. Usually, I go down to the spa, so I've never actually had one here before. Where would you suggest? The bedroom?'

'Hmm, you don't want to be so relaxed you want to go to bed though,' Billie said, trying to think of a worthy excuse. 'And actually the massage bed is a bit bulky to take upstairs,' she added. This part was true. 'Is there somewhere else down here out of the way with less light?'

'Er, I suppose... There's an old games room we hardly use. Well, not much of a games room now, since my husband passed away.'

'I'm sorry,' Billie replied.

'Why?' Grace asked, distracted.

'About your husband,' Billie reminded her.

'Oh, yes. Tragic. Taken from us before his time by a drunk

driver,' Grace replied, clearly trying to force some sort of saddened emotion. It fell short, but Billie acted as though it hadn't.

'Such a shame,' she said, shaking her head sadly. 'Let's try in there then, shall we? If you're ready.'

'It's right this way,' Grace said, standing up and walking out of the room.

Billie followed her out, quickly grabbing her massage table as Grace swept off down the hallway. She hurried after her and fell into step, keeping note of where they were going. She silently counted the doorways as she passed them until she found the one she was looking for. She eyed it, making note of the artwork on the wall just outside, then followed Grace to the games room which was luckily not much further along.

With a smile, she set up the bed and her oils and the calming music she always played her clients, then left Grace to get undressed in private. As she stood outside in the hallway, she peered up and down, checking for any activity. There were two male voices in the distance discussing something but nothing close enough to worry about. After a minute or two she knocked and walked back in.

'OK. Are you comfortable?' she asked.

'As much as one can be with their face in a hole,' came the reply.

Billie tapped some of her lavender oil onto her hands and rubbed them together, holding them under the table by Grace's face. 'Breathe in for me,' she ordered.

Grace did so, and she pulled her hands back and poured out some more oil, rubbing it straight into the woman's back. 'And now I want you to just relax and unwind and I'll wake you in ninety minutes when we're done.'

'Oh, I won't sleep,' Grace responded.

We'll see about that, Billie thought.

She'd been surprised when Cillian had first asked her to get involved with this job. She hadn't been sure at first. Not that she was bothered by what they did at all, but she'd always liked to keep her professional life separate from her personal life. Mixing the two had always seemed like a very foolish idea. But when he'd told her about Grace and all she'd done to their family, she hadn't been able to say no.

He had been the one to arrange for all the staff at the day spa to come down with a terrible case of food poisoning. Not that it was really proper food poisoning. They'd be fine in twenty-four hours. But that was long enough for the place to be closed and for the manager to quickly outsource as many of her appointments as possible.

Billie had met that same manager a few nights before by chance – or at least that's what the manager had been led to believe – and after several merry drinks which Cillian had kept providing all night, she'd taken Billie's card and promised that if she ever had any extra work in the area, she'd send it her way. It was all said as no more than a polite gesture at the time, but of course she'd called just days later, asking Billie if she could take on some of her higher-maintenance regulars for the day.

Grace stuck to her promise of staying awake for the first hour, as Billie worked hard undoing all the tense knots running riot through her body, but as she moved on to the reflexology, her breathing began to slow. Carefully, she went to work on the pressure points in the feet and above the ankles which would push Grace over into a deep, peaceful sleep. After a few minutes, she began to softly snore and Billie gently lowered her foot to the table with a smug grin. No one could escape her expert manipulation of the pressure points.

Backing away from the sleeping figure, Billie quietly opened the door and peered out down the hallway. It was still empty so she slipped out and crossed over to the door she knew led to Grace's study. The room was smaller than the others she'd seen so far, the dark panelling on the walls making it appear even more so. She quickly moved around the large wooden desk at the back of the room and tried all the drawers. Grace's address book was in the third one she opened, and she quickly flipped through the pages. Running her finger down them as she went, she paused as she found the right one and pulled out her phone to take a picture.

Satisfied she had what she needed, she closed the book and placed it carefully back. As she did, her eye caught something underneath and she drew it out to have a closer look. It was the details of Grace's husband's life insurance. She was about to lay it back down when she noticed something interesting. The payout amount had been upped significantly only six months before. Her eyebrows shot up, and after a moment of debate, she took photos of this too. Something told her Cillian might be able to make use of it later on.

She closed the drawer and cast her eye over the desk to make sure she hadn't knocked anything, then made her way back out. As she pulled the door closed behind her, a voice shouted up the hallway.

'Hey! What are you doing, going in there?' the man asked with a frown.

Billie froze and then turned, fear rising. He reached her, frowning in accusation. Billie smiled apologetically.

'I was just looking for the kitchen,' she lied, pushing her phone deeper into her pocket. 'I need some water for Grace. Massage pushes so many toxins round the body, it's important to—'

'Yes, yes,' the man replied, uninterested. 'The kitchen is that way. This room is off-limits.' He continued to glare at her until she moved away from the door.

'Oh, sorry, my bad. It's like a maze – I'm not used to being in a house this big.' She excused herself with a light laugh.

'Clearly,' he said rudely, looking her up and down.

Through gritted teeth, she shot him as sweet a smile as she

could manage and then turned to go and find the kitchen. As she walked, she wrapped her fingers around her phone with a feeling of deep satisfaction. They could look down their noses at her as much as they wanted. She'd got what Cillian needed, and that was all that mattered.

FIFTY-SEVEN

The tension in the air was palpable as Scarlet, Cillian and Connor all met at Lily's house as per her instruction, and they waited in silence while she laid out their new heist gear.

For every job they did, they all wore nondescript black outfits with a generic ski mask. No tags, no coloured trim, no unusually placed pockets, no defining features whatsoever. And after each job was pulled they would burn the outfits until nothing was left of them but ash. If ever the police came snooping, they didn't want to risk the discovery of their heist outfits to be the evidence that finally took them down.

'Right, has everyone got everything?' Lily asked, standing back and looking at the piles she'd just created. They all checked and agreed that they had and Lily nodded. 'Good.'

In just under an hour they'd be on their way and there would be no turning back. They'd gone over the plan a hundred times, though it was simple enough. All they had to do was wait for a text from Sophie, their talented dancing distraction, telling them that the doors were all shut and she was about to enter the room, then they had a ten-minute window to walk in, kill the security feed, steal what they'd come for and leave. There was only one lock and it would take them no longer than thirty seconds to pick it. The only real risk was someone walking out of the room before the show was over. But Lily was betting on the odds being in their favour. Sophie was so entrancing there wouldn't be a person in that room who wasn't stunned to a standstill.

Lily looked at each of them in turn, her face solemn. 'Tonight's a big night. First and foremost, we must be on our guard. Although I don't think she'd be stupid enough to pull something while we're actually on the job, you need to keep your wits about you. If you see anything at all that has you spooked, you call it and get out.' She eyed them hard. 'But if things go well then just stick to the plan and get it done. We only have a small timeframe – we can't afford to mess about.'

'Of course,' Scarlet agreed.

Lily regarded each of her sons in turn as they remained silent. 'I'm serious, boys,' she warned. 'Not one step out of the agreed process. Too much rides on tonight. *This* is what's going to put us back on the map. *This* is what's going to remind people who we are – the Italians and any other fuckers who've suggested we're weak lately.' She began to pace, still watching them. 'Do you hear me?'

They were so close now, so close to being securely back in the game. Back on the up, instead of tumbling in freefall as they had been lately.

'Yeah, we hear you,' Connor replied.

Lily nodded, but as they glanced at each other, communicating in that secret way that she'd never been able to unpick, she felt a churn of unease settle in her stomach.

FIFTY-EIGHT

The car door opened and Grace took the hand that was offered by one of the footmen greeting people as they arrived. She shot him a broad smile as she pulled the voluminous train of her carmine red ball gown out behind her. It was an unusually bright choice for her, but on this particular occasion she wanted to stand out more than usual. She needed to make sure her whereabouts were accounted for at all times. She'd accessorised the statement gown with a pair of large diamond chandelier earrings. They were one of the few items of real value her mother had left to her and always drew remarks, which helped with her secondary goal of the evening. Making sure people believed she was so rich she couldn't possibly need the money from a stolen painting. If only they really knew how much her financial situation depended on it. But the fact they didn't was what would keep her in the game.

'Thank you,' she said graciously to the footman, stepping away as he moved to help the next guest out of their car.

Warm dazzling lights and the sound of music greeted her as she swept through the hallway towards the ballroom. As usual Marie had gone to great lengths to decorate for her annual Fall

Ball, with extravagant displays of autumn flowers and leaves covering almost the entire hallway. It was an impressive sight.

As she reached the ballroom, she paused to look pointedly around, her head held high and her shoulders back. Many eyes turned towards her with an appreciative glint, but she ignored them all except one. A short brunette in a burnt-orange satin gown came hurrying towards her with a huge smile wreathed across her face.

'Grace, darling, you look incredible!' she exclaimed.

'Marie, I was about to say exactly the same thing to you. I *adore* that tone – it's so autumnal,' she gushed back.

'Oh, do you think?' Marie asked, delighted. 'I do like to tie in with the theme, you know.'

Grace did know. Marie was incredibly predictable. Predictable and boring.

'How clever,' she enthused, hiding her real thoughts.

'And this colour on *you*, Grace,' Marie replied, turning the conversation back to her guest. 'It's absolutely *gorgeous*. I don't think I've ever seen you in something so daring before.'

'I had it made specially to match the red of my Porsche,' Grace said with a gleam in her eye. 'I *had* planned to arrive in that tonight, but then the darn thing ended up having to go in for an MOT!' She rolled her eyes dramatically. 'I mean, can you believe that this happened today, of *all* days.'

Marie burst out laughing, loud guffaws of amusement. 'Oh, Gracie, you *are* funny!'

Grace kept her smile up and laughed along through gritted teeth. She *hated* being called Gracie, and if it had been anyone else tonight, she'd have made them regret their mistake. Instead, she wove her arm through Marie's, pulling her close and walking along to the drinks table, smiling at the people she knew on the way.

'You really have outdone yourself this year,' she said.

'I hope so. I do want everyone to have the best time,' Marie answered anxiously. 'I doubled the fireworks this year. I felt as though they were over too quickly last time. Did you think they were over too quickly?' She waited to see what her new closest friend thought.

'I remember them being fabulous, and I can't recall much about the length of the show, to be quite honest,' Grace answered tactfully.

'As long as everyone is happy, that's all that matters,' Marie replied.

Grace saw her opportunity. 'They will be – you needn't worry. But what about you? You always spend so much time making things wonderful for everyone else that you rarely seem to actually enjoy these things yourself,' she admonished.

'Oh, but I do...' Marie tried to assure her.

'Nonsense, I've seen how you worry.' She gave her a knowing look. 'But I wanted to do something special for *you* this year. Especially since we've recently grown so much closer.'

She reached over to the table full of espresso martinis and picked two up, handing one to her host.

'I hope you don't mind.' She smiled in what she hoped was a sheepish manner. 'But I've arranged a surprise for you. A special performance in your honour, along with a toast for your guests to celebrate *you* for a change, instead of just the changing seasons.'

'Oh, really?' Marie asked, surprised.

'I know it's not the done thing, but I just really wanted to do something nice for you. Is that OK?' Grace pushed.

'Ahh.' Marie blushed and smiled bashfully. 'That's really lovely of you. No one has ever arranged something in my honour before. You're a good friend, Grace. I look forward to it, whatever it is.'

'I'll just need to give a few directions to your event manager,' Grace replied.

'Of course, whatever you need.' Marie's smile widened. 'It's been so lovely spending more time with you recently and growing so much closer. I wonder why we didn't do this years ago?'

Because I have better things to fill my time with than simpering prats like you, Grace thought viciously.

'I have no idea,' she lied, returning the adoring smile.

'What does it matter?' Marie offered a wave of her hand. 'We're here now. And I do so value our friendship.'

'As do I, Marie,' Grace replied with total honesty this time. Her smile darkened as she looked back towards the doorway. 'As do I.'

FIFTY-NINE

The doors were finally closed and the front of the grand-looking building was deserted. Grace's enticing and insistent announcement over the loudspeakers had ensured that everyone, down to the last footman, had disappeared into the ballroom. Lily watched the proceedings with bated breath from her hiding place in the bushes fringing the wide driveway.

Sophie climbed the steps and entered the hallway in the distance. Stepping to the side, she found an empty chair and put down the cases that held all she needed, then shed her long black overcoat, revealing her shimmering, almost translucent, bodysuit beneath. She pulled her phone out and sent a text.

Lily felt the vibration in her pocket as it arrived, then Sophie disappeared further into the house out of sight.

Standing up, Lily pulled her balaclava down and gave the others the signal. They moved up to join her, and together the three of them jogged towards the entrance, covering the ground within seconds. Connor was still half a mile or so down the road with Duffy in the van, which he'd pull round once Cillian told them the CCTV cameras were all off.

As they passed the first of the cameras, Lily lowered her

head and the others followed suit. She tapped Cillian on the arm and he forked off with a nod as they reached the top of the steps.

'Shit, which way was it?' Scarlet asked in a low whisper, hitching the case they'd brought to transport the painting in further under her arm.

'Here,' Lily replied, leading the way.

Everything looked vastly different now that they were actually here and not just staring at photos and blueprints, but that didn't make a difference to Lily. They passed through the ornately dressed halls, past statues and other frivolous decoration, and before long they reached the long wide hallway where Marie displayed her artwork.

Lily paused, putting her hand up to stop Scarlet going any further. While the CCTV outside would have caught them going in, it would be too dark and grainy to make out much detail. The camera on the inside, though, would pick up much more detail. There was only one, just ahead of where they now stood, trained on Marie's precious hallway of art. Lily focused her gaze on this, watching the small red dot that showed it was still connected. After a few seconds there was a soft clicking sound and the red light disappeared.

'OK, go,' she ordered, her tone urgent.

Their ten-minute window was already well underway, and whilst Grace had promised to try and buy them as much more time as she could, it wasn't guaranteed. They needed to move fast.

They ran down the long hallway, Lily prompting Scarlet just once as she paused in awe at one particularly ugly-looking painting.

'You wouldn't believe what that—'

'We don't have time,' Lily said in a hard tone, cutting her off. 'Focus.'

Reaching the door, Lily pulled a pouch out of her pocket

and opened it up. She offered the contents to Scarlet. 'Do you want to do it?'

'Pick the lock?' Scarlet asked, her whispered tone surprised.

'No, make a cup of tea... Yes, pick the lock,' Lily replied sarcastically with a sharp tut.

'I don't know how,' Scarlet admitted.

'*What?*' Lily asked, astonished. 'How can you not know how to pick a lock? I taught my boys when they were ten.' She stared at her niece in the darkness as though she'd never seen her before, but of course Scarlet couldn't see her expression through their masks any more than she could see hers.

Scarlet shrugged. 'Dad was never allowed to teach me things like that, was he? You know what Mum was like.'

Lily tilted her head to the side with a nod of acceptance. Cath had been hell-bent on turning Scarlet into a straight-shooting model member of society before she'd grown up and taken her rightful place in the firm.

'Just hold this,' she ordered, handing her the pouch and taking out what she needed. 'We're going to have to revisit your education once we're through all this,' she added as she bent down and pushed two long pins into the lock.

There was a short silence as she manipulated the inner workings until they gave way, then she twisted the handle and pushed open the door. As it swung open, the Picasso came into view, a single painting mounted on the far wall, lit up in all its achingly chaotic glory. Sharp black lines scratched abstract shapes into a background of burnt orange and beige hues and the word 'café' was scrawled across the top. It didn't look like much to Lily, but Scarlet let out a reverent breath of wonder.

'Bingo,' Lily muttered, walking over to it. 'Come on – let's get it down.'

Scarlet laid the case down on the floor and opened it, then joined her. 'You know they call this piece *The Pigeon with Green Peas*,' she said as they gently lifted it off its mount.

'That makes no sense,' Lily replied, shaking her head. She would never understand art.

They moved the piece into the case and clipped the sides shut. 'How long have we got?' she asked, glancing back at the door.

Scarlet checked her watch. 'Four minutes.'

'OK, let's finish up what we need to do here and move.'

Grabbing a handle each side, the pair walked quickly back through to the long hallway where the rest of Marie's collection looked down upon them eerily in the shadowy light.

A couple of minutes later, they were approaching the front of the building and were about to round into the main hallway when a dark figure suddenly swooped round the corner, pushing them back roughly. Scarlet began to gasp, her reaction automatic, but Cillian swiftly silenced her with a hand over her mouth. He guided them back against the wall, and Lily and Scarlet pulled their cargo in tight, trying to melt into the shadows as much as they could, as they heard someone walking through the hallway beyond.

The footsteps stopped and an indignant grunt made its way through to them. Lily froze, looking sideways at her son. He shook his head, gesturing for them to stay still.

'*That's* where I left it.' Whoever it was tutted loudly. 'I knew I wasn't imagining things. I definitely *did* pick it up...' The footsteps restarted and echoed off into the distance.

Lily breathed a sigh of relief and moved forward, peering round the corner. 'Come on,' she said as a loud round of applause erupted from the ballroom. 'We're running out of time.'

With Cillian's help, they ran the case out of the building and down the steps. In the distance, Connor was making his way down the drive towards them in the van they'd set up with fake plates earlier that day. Lily and Scarlet lowered the case to rest on the ground for a moment. As they did, Lily noticed Cillian was making his way back up the steps.

'Cillian?' she called quietly. She looked at her watch. 'Cillian!' she hissed more loudly when he didn't respond.

'I'll be quick. I'll catch you up,' he called back over his shoulder.

'Cillian, wait!' she called.

But he was already gone.

SIXTY

Sophie took one last bow before her adoring audience and then with a twirl through the air, she leaped gracefully across the ballroom floor and made her exit.

Immediately, the crowd began chattering excitedly about the incredible performance, but Grace quickly drew their attention back to her with the microphone.

'Excuse me, ladies and gentlemen. I hope everyone enjoyed that wonderful performance, a special last-minute addition to the evening, in honour of our very generous and rather fabulous host, Marie.'

She gestured towards Marie, who stood just a couple of feet away from her, and everyone applauded once more. Marie blushed and thanked them all repeatedly, though no one could hear her as Grace still had the mic.

'I have been coming to these balls for several years now and each time Marie works *tirelessly* behind the scenes to welcome the new season in with the utmost elegance, opulence and charm. We are all so very lucky to be able to be part of it, and so I just wanted to thank you, Marie,' she gushed, 'from the bottom of my heart. And not just on my behalf but on behalf of all of us, if I may be so bold?' She raised an eyebrow at her audience, and they all cheered in agreement. She smiled and lifted her glass. 'To Marie,' she finished.

'To Marie,' came the chorus of jolly replies from the merry men and tipsy ladies.

There was a few more moments of cheer, and then that cheer slowly turned back to chatter as Grace handed the microphone back over to the tight-lipped event manager.

'That really was something,' Marie said to her now, her eyes glistening with a mixture of emotion and too much vodka. 'You really are so sweet to have arranged all that.'

'Oh, it was nothing,' Grace said, waving it away dismissively. 'Now, why don't we get back to our drinks and catch up, shall we?'

'Yes. Though I probably should just do a quick round to make sure I've spoken to everyone and they've had a good time,' Marie replied, looking around with a slight look of concern.

'Yes, of course – go, go,' Grace urged. 'I'll speak to you again in a bit.'

She watched Marie walk off and picked up another glass from a passing tray of champagne. Taking a sip, she cast her gaze over towards the double doors that led out into the hallway. They were just being opened again now that the entertainment was over. She wondered if everything had gone smoothly on the Drews' end of things. Not that it particularly mattered if it hadn't. If all had gone to plan then she would be pocketing a nice payday very soon. But if it didn't and they got caught, then she could throw them under the bus as easily as throwing a bucket of water – because she had an alibi for this evening and no ties to them that could be proved. And if they got locked up for the foreseeable future then that saved her the job of killing them and disposing of their bodies for a while. Prison time wouldn't be as satisfying as seeing them dead, but it would certainly be a more efficient way of dealing with them.

And Grace had always prided herself on being fabulously efficient.

Two hours later, Grace found herself stuck with a companion who had taken a rather annoying liking to her as she'd made her way around her various social circles.

Ted Cavendish was a tall, fairly attractive and consistently positive man in his forties who had infamously never managed to get anyone suitable to marry him, despite his family's wealth and their best efforts to help him pass on the family name. This was mainly because, although at first he appeared to be a potential prospect, the moment any woman with half a brain started talking to him, it became painfully apparent that he was as empty-headed as a sheep. And that was being slightly unkind to the sheep.

He was accepted and invited to everything because he had been born into so high a societal rank that they couldn't not. But once at the event, everyone avoided him like the plague, trying their hardest not to get locked into babysitting him for the night. Unfortunately, Grace hadn't been paying close enough attention at one point in the evening to escape before he approached, and he had attached himself to her ever since.

'But isn't it just *so* lovely though,' he slurred drunkenly, having had far too much red wine.

'Yes, you said already,' Grace replied with a clipped tone as she looked around once more for a possible escape route. As expected, everyone was now avoiding eye contact.

'And the leaves on the decoration, all the golds and the reds, they're so apt considering this is the Fall Ball. Do you think she realised when she ordered them?'

Grace spotted Marie crossing the room close by and sprang forward to get her attention. 'Marie, there you are, darling. I quite thought I'd lost you,' she said, reaching forward to squeeze her arm.

Ted followed, delighted to be approaching their host. 'Marie, hello!' he cried.

Marie gave Grace a look that showed she did not thank her for bringing him over. Grace returned one of apology.

'Hello, Ted,' Marie said politely. 'Are you enjoying the evening?'

'Oh yes, very much so,' he enthused. He paused as if trying to remember something. 'My mother says I should ask you about your new painting. She says you've acquired something quite special.'

For the first time since he'd ambled over, Grace found herself pleased that Ted was around. His mother's conversation prompts had worked to her favour.

'Oh, Marie, do tell? What have you bought?' she asked with a broadening smile.

'Something rather interesting actually, from an up-and-coming German painter. I had a tip-off that his work was going to skyrocket in value over the next decade or so,' she explained, giving Grace a knowing look.

'You *must* show us,' Grace pushed.

'Yes, please do,' Ted added, his tone full of joy at just being involved. He knew nothing about art, Grace knew.

Marie's excitement began to visibly bubble. She glanced back at the ballroom and then made a decision. 'Come on then. No one will miss me for a few minutes.'

They slipped out of the room and made their way towards Marie's art collection. She chattered away, telling them the story of where she'd bought the piece and how she'd won the auction hands down. Grace smiled and nodded, though she couldn't really focus. Her anticipation was growing by the second. What would Marie do when she saw the Picasso gone?

She wouldn't notice straight away, as it wasn't in the main hall-way, but Grace would find a way to get Marie to check up on it.

They reached the hallway and Grace had to stop the smile of excitement from curling up her lips too much. Would Marie scream? Would she cry? She quickly practised mentally how shocked and upset she would need to show herself to be in response.

'What a lot of paintings you have, Marie,' Ted said, stating the obvious. 'Some of them are very pretty.'

'Thank you, Ted. This is the one, Grace...' Marie pointed to her latest addition and began rattling off the details.

Grace cast her eye over it critically and then dismissed it. It was nothing unique, and she could tell by several factors that it was unlikely to go up much in value at all. Most likely, the artist would shine dimly for the next five minutes and then fade from the art world's memory like most of them did. Whoever had sold it to Marie had been a better conman than she was.

Bored, she looked across to the other pieces in Marie's collection that she actually liked. As her gaze rested on an empty spot near the door where they'd walked in, she frowned slightly.

'Marie, didn't you have the Hofmann hanging there?' she asked. 'Is it being cleaned?'

Marie turned to look and gasped loudly. She looked at Grace, her eyes widening in horror. 'It's not being cleaned,' she said with panic in her tone. 'It was there this morning – I remember looking at it. Where the hell has it gone?'

She began to look around the room, her head swinging wildly. She paused as her gaze came to settle on the door at the end of the hallway and Grace watched as her stricken face paled to almost grey.

'That door was locked too,' she said, dread in her tone. She stood there frozen for a few seconds, seemingly too scared to check, then slowly walked towards the room.

Ted looked from one woman to the other, the entire exchange having gone over his head. 'What's happened? Someone forgot to close the door?' he asked.

Grace watched Marie enter the room and heard the strangled cry of despair as she saw the Picasso was gone. Her own eyes had widened in shock and fear, though she hadn't had to fake it the way she'd imagined. She slowly turned back and stared at the empty space where the Hofmann had hung.

The stupid fools were only supposed to take the Picasso. Marie couldn't report the Picasso as missing. They would have been home and free. But now they had stolen a genuine registered piece of art. An expensive piece of art. Now they were not home and free at all. For the Hofmann, Marie would call the police. Not only the police, but every PI going, every newspaper, every single outlet that could spread the word that it had been stolen. Every authority in the country would be searching for that painting. And each of those bloodthirsty authorities would be desperate to bag the culprits and throw them behind bars.

The Drews had just created the biggest shitstorm that the art world had seen in a very long time. And she was right at the very centre of it.

SIXTY-ONE

It was three in the morning by the time Grace finally reached home, and she kicked off her high heels angrily as soon as she stepped in the door.

'Get me a burner,' she roared at the men milling around her. 'And get Lily Drew on the line. I'll be back in two minutes and she'd *better* be waiting to talk to me.'

She stormed upstairs, holding up the voluminous skirts of her dress. In her bedroom, she angrily tore the dress off her body, almost ripping one of the seams in the process, but she didn't care. She pulled the diamonds off her ears and flung them into the jewellery box that she usually placed them in with great care, glowering at her own reflection in the mirror above. Wrapping her most comfortable dressing gown around her, she tied it as she nimbly jogged back down the stairs. One of her men was waiting for her, the phone in his outstretched hand. She snatched it off him and put it to her ear, clicking her fingers towards the drinks trolley as she marched into the day room.

'What the *hell* did you *do*?' she demanded down the line.

'Grace,' came Lily's calm response, 'I am as livid as you are.'

'What do you mean?' Grace spat impatiently. 'What happened?'

There was a heavy sigh. 'It seems my son saw what he thought was an opportunity,' she said, anger now colouring her tone.

'It *was* an opportunity,' she heard one of the twins argue in the background.

'Cillian, *not now*,' Lily growled. 'Look. I thought we were all on the same page. Clearly we weren't.'

'Clearly not!' Grace yelled. Someone handed her a neat Scotch and she downed it in one. 'I've just spent the last four hours being grilled by the bloody police! By morning this is going to be all over the news!'

'We can fix this,' Lily resolved.

'How on *earth* can we fix *this*?' Grace screeched, throwing her hand up in the air in frustration.

'I have the painting here with me now. The one that wasn't supposed to be taken. I'll have the boys drop it to you and then we'll figure out a way to anonymously—'

'No you will not!' Grace replied indignantly. 'I can't have that painting *here*! I can't be around it at all. The police could pull me back in or search my house at any moment.'

There was a pause. 'OK, we'll keep it then and think about how to deal with it later down the line.'

'No,' Grace responded curtly, closing her eyes and pinching the bridge of her nose. She couldn't trust them to hold on to it – she needed to regain some control while she still could. 'Have your sons meet my men with it, somewhere discreet. I'll have them take it to where I'm storing the Picasso.'

'Tell your men to meet them at the new pub at noon tomorrow. And can you meet me at the factory to discuss what we're going to do about this?' Lily asked.

Grace considered her options. She would have to be careful

from now on, have a reason for wherever she went in case the police began tracing her movements.

'Perhaps if you drove to a nearby housing estate,' Lily added, as if reading her mind. 'Legally those roads can't have any ANPRs, so even if you're tracked, they'll lose you going in. I'll have Scarlet pick you up and bring you here so we can talk discreetly. Then she can drop you back to your car afterwards.'

Grace nodded. That made sense. 'I'll text you a location at eleven forty-five,' she agreed. With nothing left to say, she ended the call and sat forward with her face in her hands.

'What's happening?' Duffy asked.

She thought it all over for a few moments, holding her empty glass out to be taken and refilled.

'We have the Picasso safe in the vault, yes?' she checked. He nodded. 'Good.'

She looked around at all the men in the room. Her men, loyal men who'd worked for her for years. 'Tomorrow you'll go together to collect the stolen painting – the *other* stolen painting – from the Drew twins at their new pub.' She eyed them all again, reviewing her options.

The twins were dangerous men. Vicious, hard, brutal men. And they were efficient when being directed by their mother. They would be ready for any surprises tomorrow. Lily would have made sure of it.

'Just take the painting to the vault and then come back here,' she ordered, making her decision.

'And what about you?' Duffy asked.

Grace took the refilled glass of Scotch and took a deep sip, savouring the burn it trailed down her throat and into the pit of her stomach. 'Lily is hard, but she's not as clever as she thinks she is. Nor as safe, without her muscle. I'll find an excuse to send Scarlet out of the building, then pretend to discuss the return of the Hofmann until I'm right up next to her. And *then...*' The darkness inside Grace glowed viciously through her eyes. 'I'll stab her with the knife I'll have up my sleeve, over and over until she bleeds out on the floor. Without Lily Drew, the rest of them will fall apart. And as they do, we will pick them off piece by piece until no one is left.'

Lily pushed the phone back in her pocket and sat down in her favourite armchair in her home study. Cillian yawned and she glared at him.

'Did you really have to argue with me on the call? She's wound up enough,' she snapped.

'I think she needed to hear it,' he replied, defending his comment.

Lily tutted and stood, too irritated to remain sitting. She turned to Connor. 'I need you to do something for me tomorrow. Pick up Ruby before the meets and bring her over to the factory. She ain't talking to me right now and I need to get that straightened out.'

'No problem,' Connor replied.

Lily checked the time. 'Now go home. All of you. Or crash here if you'd rather. But either way, get some sleep. Tomorrow is a big day.' She looked at each of them in turn, her expression serious. 'We need to be on form. Because we have a hell of a lot to do, and how our future turns out very much depends on it.'

SIXTY-TWO

The sun beamed down through the chilly autumn air as it came around to twelve o'clock and Lily watched from the window, her arms folded across her chest, as Scarlet drove up the road and into the car park at the front of the building. Her niece stepped out of the car, her sleek black hair shining in the sun. Grace got out the other side in a wide-brimmed hat and large sunglasses. She hurried towards the door ahead of Scarlet, and Lily braced herself for what was to come.

Ruby stood sullenly to the other side of the room next to Connor and Cillian, and the tension radiating off her was palpable. She caught her mother's eye.

'Why am I here?' she asked in a tone that left no one in any doubt of her feelings on the matter.

Lily stared her down hard for a moment, and Ruby had the sense to purse her mouth and look away. After a moment Lily decided to answer her. 'You're here because you're my daughter,' she replied quietly.

Ruby's brow puckered at the vague reply but she chose not to pursue it, deciding instead to go back to ignoring Lily.

The door opened and Grace swept in. As well as the hat

and glasses, she wore a long, oversized raincoat that seemed out of place on her lithe figure. All part of her disguise, Lily supposed. She marched confidently forward across the floor, the heels of her shoes echoing off the walls, but her footsteps slowed as she noticed that Lily was not alone. She peeled off the glasses and glanced at the twins with a frown of deep concern.

'Why are they *here*?' she demanded abruptly. 'They're supposed to be at the pub handing over the painting to my men. Where's the painting?' She looked around as if hoping to find it, but there was nothing.

Scarlet quietly closed the door and moved to stand with Lily. Grace stared at her, glanced back at the twins and Ruby, then turned her gaze back to Lily.

'Well? What's going on?' she prompted.

'The painting is in a safe place, for now,' Lily replied.

'Eugh...' Grace rolled her eyes and turned in a small circle, looking up to the heavens with her hands on her hips. 'Are we really going back through all this again? *You* not trusting *me*, *me* not trusting *you*. This is a partnership. One that *your son* totally fucked up last night. But yet here I am trying to sort it out with you. Can we not move past all of that tiring nonsense and just get on with it?'

'Sure,' Lily replied. 'But while you're here, I was hoping to get your opinion on the factory, like we talked about. You were going to give me some advice,' she reminded her.

Grace blinked and stared at her as if she'd gone mad, then shook her head with a sound of frustration. 'Fine. You want me to look at the layout. OK, let's see.' She turned towards the few machines that were already in place and gestured at the large amount of empty space around them. 'I mean, you've hardly started filling the place up, but where are you planning to put the main walkways?'

'Come up here – you'll get a better view,' Lily suggested, pointing at the metal walkway overhead.

Grace shot her a sly calculating glance and Lily wondered what was lurking behind it. As she began to walk over to the stairs, the front door creaked open and Ray walked in, followed by one of his men, who slipped to the side wall and stood there silently. Grace paused, and Lily waited as Ray approached them.

'All sorted?' she asked.

'All sorted,' he confirmed.

'Who's this?' Grace asked with wary suspicion.

'A very close friend,' Lily replied. 'Ruby, you stay right there,' she ordered sharply, seeing her daughter's attempt to slink off.

'I'm not staying here with him. *Or* her,' she added with an accusing glare.

'You'll stay where I tell you,' Lily responded, her tone hard. 'I need you here.' Her voice softened as she implored Ruby with her eyes.

She could see the flicker of conflicting emotions behind her daughter's gaze, but Ruby reluctantly stepped back to where she'd been leaning against the wall before.

Grace reached into her pocket and pulled out her phone. 'I'm not sure what's going on here,' she said, 'but I'm done.' She made to move towards the door but stopped when Scarlet blocked her path. 'Get out of my way,' she ordered.

'Who are you calling, Grace?' Lily asked, her sing-song tone deadly.

'My men,' Grace replied, not deterred. 'They're only round the corner at your pub and they didn't come unprepared. They'll be here within a few minutes, and unless you want there to be a problem – a very violent problem – I suggest you ask your niece to move the *hell* out of my way.' She glared at Lily, the domineering action not successfully masking her fear.

Lily's face broke into a smile and she chuckled low and loud.

'What's so funny?' Grace hissed, her glare filled with venom.

'You, Grace,' Lily replied. She stepped forward towards her. 'Your men aren't coming. They're a little tied up at the moment.'

'Literally,' Ray added with an amused smile.

'Which means you're here all on your lonesome,' she added, tilting her head as she studied her.

Grace's chest began to rise and fall faster as she started to panic. Her gaze darted between Lily and Ray. 'OK then,' she said carefully. 'What is it you want? A higher cut? Perhaps I *was* a little hasty in our initial bargaining. A fifty-fifty share would be fairer, all things considered. When I sell the Picasso, I could split it with you equally. If we part ways cordially of course.'

Lily smiled indulgently. 'You don't *have* a Picasso, Grace. We do though.'

Grace frowned. 'You handed it to Duffy. He checked it.'

'He checked *something*,' Lily corrected. 'The case we gave Duffy held a framed print.'

'He had to check quickly because time was running out and it was very dark, so you mustn't be too cross with him for not noticing,' Scarlet added, scrunching up her nose.

'What?' Grace asked, aghast.

'We swapped the cases,' Cillian said slowly, as if trying to explain to a small child.

'My men *saw* you go in. They were watching. You only had one case. Do you really think I wouldn't check that?' Grace asked, getting angry. 'You're calling my bluff.'

'Actually, I *did* think you would check that,' Lily answered. 'Which is why Sophie took the other box in, along with the rest of the stuff she needed for her performance. She left it in the hallway for us to switch on the way out.'

Grace paled and swallowed, stepping backward.

'And if we're getting everything out in the open, it wasn't Cillian who took the other painting, it was Scarlet and I,' Lily admitted. 'We grabbed it at the same time as the Picasso – the case was deep enough to carry them both. I just needed you to think we'd messed up so that you'd come here today. And you came so helpfully alone.'

'Well, you've shot yourself right in the foot stealing that Hofmann,' Grace shot back. 'They'll never give up searching for that. It's worth a fortune and it's *legitimate*. You might have been able to pull one over on me, but you should have stopped there. Your greed is what will inevitably end you.'

'Not at all. You see, we're not keeping the painting. They're going to find it, very soon, locked away in Duffy's garage inside that dented car he used to kill your husband for you.' She watched the look of horror creep over Grace's face and felt a stab of satisfaction. 'Did you think we'd forgotten?'

Harry, Grace's husband, had been the reason they'd stolen her painting in the first place. Their meeting had been the catalyst that had started off the entire chain of events that had led to today. In her rage at his stupidity at letting them see the painting, and at putting himself in a position vulnerable enough that they'd been able to so easily steal it, she'd murdered him, staging a hit-and-run. The police had bought the story, but the Drews had known better. And when Billie had tracked down Duffy's personal address, they'd scoped it out and finally found the evidence they'd been looking for.

'Yes, it's going to be such a juicy, scandalous story, once they piece it all together,' Lily continued, clasping her hands behind her back and beginning to slowly pace. 'Let me frame it for you. You and Duffy have been having an affair for years.' She ignored the snort of disgust. 'He killed your husband so that you could claim the life insurance you very recently upped in value. But that wasn't quite enough for you, so you had him assist you in the theft of the Hofmann too. Which you intended to then sell on the black market.'

'It will never hold up,' Grace declared. 'Aside from the fact I'll throw you under a bus if you try to aim it my way, it's all circumstantial. There's no evidence whatsoever. And I have an alibi.' She shot her a smug glare.

'Actually, there *is* evidence,' Lily replied. 'You see, after we came out with the case, Cillian went back in and turned the cameras back on. We were all suited up, but *Duffy*, he got out of the back of the van to check and take the case with nothing over his face at all. And on top of that, right now Sophie is down the station giving her statement and explaining – rather tearfully – that she hadn't understood the partial conversation she over-heard you have about making sure the painting was hidden quickly, until she'd seen the news this morning. And I can tell you, she's as good an actress as she is a dancer.' Lily pulled an impressed expression and nodded sagely.

Grace was now as white as a sheet, and her breath was ragged with rage and fear. 'You won't get away with this. I'm not going to prison without a fight. I'll tell them everything about you.'

'You won't be telling anyone anything,' Lily replied, staring at her with the full force of the hatred she'd spent so much time hiding. 'And you won't be going to prison either.'

Grace recoiled with a gasp as the realisation that Lily didn't intend to let her leave here finally dawned.

'Grab her,' Lily growled.

SIXTY-THREE

The twins grabbed hold of Grace's arms, and she gasped then struggled to get out of their grip.

'Get off me,' she screeched. 'Get off me *now!*'

As she writhed and twisted, something clattered to the ground and they all looked down at it. The little blade rocked back and forth on the rounded handle until it came to a gentle stop. Lily smirked up at her.

'What were you planning to do with that?' she asked, amused. 'It wouldn't even carve a small chicken.' She heard Ray chuckle behind her.

'You need to unhand me this *instant,*' Grace demanded.

The twins staunchly ignored her and she turned her pleas towards Lily.

'Think about what you're doing, you fool,' she hissed. 'I thought you were smart when you approached me about these jobs. I thought you had what it took to move up to the big leagues. And that's where this would have taken you. It still *could* if you stop this stupidity *right now!*'

Grace's tone turned desperate. '*Look* at me, Lily. Look at everything I have. You could have this life too. With my help, you could set yourselves up the way I have and make this sort of money all the time, without anyone else. I'll help you do that. I'll give you all my connections and set you on the higher path. If you just let me go.'

Lily looked up to the twins, across to Scarlet and then rested her gaze on Ruby. 'We don't need *you* to move anywhere. If we want to change circles, we could make that happen in a number of ways. But we've always been grafters. People who enjoy variety and the freedom that swimming in our own waters affords us. Grace, we wouldn't want to be like you for all the money in the world.'

Turning around, Lily glanced towards Ray. He was silent and reserved, watching her with an interested glint in his eye. She'd asked him to handle Grace's men at the pub. They were holding them there until Ray gave them the signal that Lily was done.

'But we've got off-track,' Lily continued. 'You were going to come and give me your expert opinion on the layout of our new factory.'

She sidled up to Ruby and wrapped her arm around her shoulders protectively. Ruby was observing the entire exchange with wide serious eyes.

'I want you to watch this up close,' Lily said quietly.

Pulling her along with her, she walked over to the stairs, her warm grip firm and secure around Ruby's arm.

'Come up here with me, my love,' she told her.

Scarlet stepped to the side with Ray, and the boys began to follow Lily and Ruby, forcing Grace up the stairs between them.

'No,' she cried out. 'No!'

'It's so kind of you to offer your opinions on our new factory,' Lily called back over her shoulder. 'Considering you were the one who laid our last one to waste.'

'No! Stop this. Get *off* me, you filthy *rats!*' Grace raged, wriggling and writhing and trying anything she could to get out of their grip. But they were strong and there were two of them. They barely faltered against her best attempts.

'What are you going to do?' Ruby asked her, her tone no longer filled with the anger and accusation it had been before. 'Throw her over?' She glanced down over the railings at the concrete floor below.

'*This?*' Lily asked surprised, following Ruby's gaze downwards. 'She'd barely break a wrist. No. I'm going to give her what she deserves. What she's *earned.*'

They had reached the top of the stairs and covered the length of the walkway, coming to a stop on a small platform at the end next to one of the machines. Here she turned and faced Grace as the boys forced the other woman in front of her. Her expression was now wild with fear, and her usually perfect hair was slipping out of its clips, flyaway strands falling forward over her face.

'We never planned to meet you,' Lily said, looking her up and down, her dark brown eyes hard and unforgiving. 'We wouldn't have been here at all if it hadn't been for your drunken letch of a husband. And you took care of him, which we were grateful for at the time. It saved us a job. If you'd left it there you could have still been living that *oh so wonderful* life of yours.'

'What are we doing up here, Lily?' Grace demanded through gritted teeth. 'Come on, what is this?'

'*This* is what happens when you mess with the wrong people.' She let go of Ruby, who stepped back quietly to the side rail, and her voice turned low. 'You burned down our factory. Our *home*, really, as a firm. That hurt. But *nothing* came close to the hurt that came from realising my baby girl was locked inside.' A dark and wild expression flashed across her face for a moment before the cold, hard mask returned with her control.

'You don't have kids. Or a heart, I don't think, so I doubt you could ever understand the way in which your very soul burns like it's trapped in the inner circle of hell when your child is hurting and you can't help them.' Every word that fell from Lily's lips dripped with heavy emotion. 'Add to that the sheer fury that comes from knowing the person hurting them is *enjoying* it, and that mixture is the seed you planted in me that day.'

'Lily...' Grace's tone faltered with fear. 'It was business.'

'It wasn't business, Grace. It was revenge,' she replied sharply. 'Call it what it is. Go on, say it.' She stepped forward and grabbed Grace's face with her hand, viciously sinking her nails into her cheeks. '*Say it*,' she ordered. 'It was *revenge*. Setting that fire and sealing all the exits so that no one could escape was *revenge*.'

'Fine, it was revenge!' Grace shouted back through sounds of pain.

Lily threw Grace's head to the side with a curl of her lip and stepped back from her. She took a deep breath, regaining control, then nodded slowly. 'The thing about revenge, though, is that you have to execute it just right. You have to find the right balance or it becomes just one of a series of back-and-forth actions between two parties.'

She began to pace from side to side as she spoke. 'Either you dole out retribution that asserts your authority at a fair level that the opposition can grudgingly accept as their due and bow out from – like the factory, for instance. If you'd just taken the building, we'd have accepted that. We did steal your painting, after all. Or if you want to take revenge to the *next* level, if you want to start burning people's family members alive...' She stopped pacing and looked Grace in the eye. 'Then you'd better make sure you burn the whole family and see it through to the bitter end. Because they're the only two ways to keep revenge as revenge and not just another battle in an overall war.'

Lily paused and then walked slowly over to the machine at the end of the wide platform on which they all stood.

'I had this custom-made for the new premises. It's three times the size of the last one. Do you know what it is?' she asked Grace.

Grace opened her mouth to answer, but the words died on her lips as she suddenly realised where all of this was going.

'At the *old* factory we had an induction furnace for the steel and an incinerator for the industrial waste.' She shrugged. 'Standard equipment. But both were a bit small, and each took up a lot of space. I had them build this as a hybrid.' She looked up at it proudly. 'It's both in one. It can be switched like that.' She clicked her fingers. 'I can't fire the steel in just an incinerator – it doesn't get hot enough. Steel needs temperatures of up to eighteen hundred degrees, you see. But you probably know that. Handy bit of machinery.' She turned to Grace with a cold gleam in her eye. 'I thought you could give us your expert opinion on it,' she said casually.

'No,' Grace uttered, terror in her tone. 'You can't be serious. Lily, I'm begging you...'

'Surely begging is beneath you, isn't it?' Lily said cuttingly. 'You're far too highbrow for that, Grace.'

'Lily, *please*, stop this. I'll do anything. *Give* you anything!'

'You can give me your screams,' Lily replied. 'You can give me your *fear*, the same things my daughter gave *you*. And then you can give me your last excruciating breath. I want your final few moments to be the worst of your toxic, pitiful life. And I want them to be that bad because of me.' Looking up to her sons, she gave them a nod.

'No! Noooo! Please! No!' Grace's screams grew frantic as the twins lifted her off her feet between them. She screeched and fought wildly, but it was no use.

They climbed the last steps up to the top of the furnace and then hoisted her up onto the chute that led down into it. She grappled and tried to hang on to the edge as they forced her in, but they unhooked her fingers and shoved her down hard.

'Please, no!' she screamed up.

'Close the chute,' Lily ordered.

The twins did as they'd been asked, pulling down the heavy metal hatch and securing it tightly. Immediately the screams muffled to almost silence and the only sound was the dull banging of her fists on the metal of the inside drum.

Lily moved to press the button that would fire up the flames.

'Wait.' Ruby laid her hand on her arm, stopping her.

Lily turned, a question in her eyes. Surely Ruby didn't want to let the woman live?

'Let me,' she said with a steely tone. 'She nearly killed me. She scarred me for life.' Her lip wobbled and she clamped her jaw. 'I want to be the one.'

Lily nodded and stepped back. Ruby took her place and bowed her head for a moment, as though the weight of the world was on her shoulders. Cillian looked to his mother enquiringly and she shook her head. Ruby needed to do this in her own time. And hopefully, when she did, when she finally took revenge and took the power back from Grace, it would start to help her heal.

Lifting her head, Ruby pressed the button, and as the rumble of the fires started up, the frantic banging from inside turned to silence.

SIXTY-FOUR

The following morning, Lily stirred her tea and checked her messages, feeling more peaceful than she had in a long time. She wondered how Ruby would feel this morning. Would she feel lighter, the way that she did? She certainly hoped so. Her inner demons might still haunt her, but the one who'd caused all her recent trauma had finally been slayed.

She checked her watch and then took a sip of her tea. It was early, which meant she still had time to herself before everyone else either woke up or arrived. Sunlight filtered through into the large kitchen, and a light breeze played across her face from the open window, and she closed her eyes, enjoying the feel of it on her skin for a few moments.

They were due in for questioning today, following Duffy's arrest the evening before. He'd sung like a canary, shouting their names all over the shop. But that didn't worry her the way it would have done in the past. Not now they had John watching their backs from the inside. It had already been arranged. There was no proof of their involvement anywhere, and Lily had made sure they all had tight alibis. They'd be let go and Duffy's claims dismissed. This was merely a formality. It would still be an open case, and Grace's face would be plastered across the news for the foreseeable future as they searched far and wide for her. But Grace was gone. It would ultimately find its way to the cold files and be forgotten.

It had been a particularly successful job for Lily, all in all. Not only had she gained a Picasso and got rid of Grace, but she'd got Ruby back onside and John in her pocket too. Not that he fully realised it yet. But his successful recapture of the painting had been down to her. As had Duffy's murder charge. It wasn't that he now owed her exactly, as his involvement in getting Scarlet off her murder charge more than outweighed those things. But he *was* now quite deeply entwined with the family. Should she ever need to use or threaten him, all she'd need to do is remind him of the reasons he'd closed those two high-profile cases. He'd have no choice but to do as she wanted. And that was more valuable than anything money could buy.

The sound of the rubbish truck entering the end of her street came in on the breeze, and she took a seat at the table by the window. She watched it approach and had a sip of her tea.

She'd thought about what to do with Grace's ashes long and hard over the last few weeks since she'd first come up with this plan. The furnace had burned her down to nothing but ashes and tiny bone fragments, then she'd carefully collected them and got Andy and George to clean everything down overnight to make sure not an atom of her remained behind. She'd considered scattering them in a flower bed at first, but after some thought, she'd decided the remains of such a toxic creature would probably only feed the weeds. Plus, Grace didn't deserve to be laid to rest somewhere that pretty anyway.

As the bin men picked up the pile of bin bags and threw them into the back of the truck where rotting food and dirty toilet paper lay scattered from spillage, she took another calming sip of her tea. The truck drove on down the street, and she watched with a smile as the smallest bin bag of her pile jiggled and rolled around in the back, eventually disappearing under the mass collection of rubbish.

'Rest in peace, bitch.'

SIXTY-FIVE

John walked back into his office and was stopped in his tracks by an eruption of cheers and applause by his team. He laughed, surprised.

'Crikey, what's this all for?' he asked, though he suspected he knew.

'The record time in which you cracked this case, guv,' Ascough replied, her pixie face gleaming with admiration.

'*We,*' he corrected, hiding how pleased he really was at the praise. 'It was a team effort, and don't forget how much that anonymous tip helped us along. A disgruntled employee, I suspect, who wanted the ship to sink.'

'Most likely,' Ascough agreed. 'No one we've interviewed who worked at that place likes her, you know.'

'Any update from the borders?' John asked, walking back towards his desk.

'Not yet. There's still a chance she could slip through on a fake passport, but we've got the face recognition cameras searching all ports for her, and Border Control have her face.'

He nodded and sat down behind his desk. 'It's been thirty-six hours since the painting was taken, then the cameras tracked her to where she dumped her car around eleven thirty yesterday morning where the trail goes cold, so she could be anywhere by now. She was clearly planning to disappear. But we're still in the initial seventy-two-hour window, so I'm not giving up hope yet.'

He smiled encouragingly, but in truth he already knew they wouldn't find Grace. Scarlet had told him as much. She hadn't gone into detail, and he didn't want her to, already ill-at-ease with the knowledge he did have.

Sophie's statement had been all they needed to get a search warrant for Grace's estate. And the anonymous call telling them she'd had an affair with Duffy and to search his property – not only for clues but for the car that had ended her husband's life – had led them straight to the painting. They were checking the painting now for DNA and fingerprints, then it would be processed through the system back to the owner. A happy ending to a dramatic case.

Duffy, on the other hand, was not getting such a happy ending. He'd been arrested and charged with the murder of Harry Chambers and his involvement in the art heist. He'd accused the Drews of being involved, but John knew they'd been careful to leave no proof, and after he led them through standard questioning, he'd pass their alibis as clear.

'I think you deserve a drink, guv,' Ascough said, pushing her short red hair behind her ear. 'And I'm buying. I won't take no for an answer,' she said in a jolly tone. 'Come on.'

He hesitated and she hurried to continue. 'All of us, or anyone up for a drink anyway. Come on – who's in?' she asked, turning back to the team.

A few of them piped up to accept and she turned back to him with a grin. 'Shall we head?'

'I can't,' John said with a regretful smile. 'I need to meet someone. But another time for sure.'

Trying to ignore the crushing look of disappointment on her face, he grabbed his phone and keys from the desk drawer, picked up his jacket and headed out with a friendly wave, before anyone could ask him where he was going.

SIXTY-SIX

The door of the newly decorated Blind Pig opened and John slipped in, walking over to Scarlet where she sat propped up at the bar and giving her a deep kiss before settling in on the stool behind her. The place was still closed, not technically opening until the following weekend, but Lily had decided to throw a small pre-opening party for those they all held nearest and dearest.

She stood behind the bar – this being the one and only time she intended to act as a server herself – and looked around. At the table nearest to Scarlet and John, Cillian sat with Billie, their hands entwined and their heads together as they discussed something privately. To the other side of her, George and Andy sat watching the rest of the room, sipping their pints. Ruby and Sandra perched by a taller table near them, chatting quietly, and Cath stood up at the bar laughing as Ray regaled her with his latest joke. The inner circle was growing. It was something she'd actively fought against for years, but the children had grown up and had earned the right to bring their own people in. And to their credit, everyone they had brought in had more than proven themselves to be loyal and trustworthy.

She lifted a glass and tapped it with a spoon until everyone had fallen silent. 'Now that I have your attention, I'd like to make a toast.' She lifted her glass. 'To family,' she said in a heart-felt voice. 'In whatever form it comes in. Whether we're bound through blood, friendship or loyalty, you're all here tonight because you're part of this extended family.'

Would the newer faces last? she wondered. She hoped so. For all their sakes.

'It's been a hard graft, this last job. All of you helped and I'm grateful to you for it. Every little thing each of you did helped us get what we went there for, and it also helped us give that bitch what she deserved. No one crosses one of our own and gets away with it. It's an eye for an eye in this family.' She smiled at Ruby, her love flowing freely through her gaze. 'No one will ever hurt you again and get away with it, Ruby Drew. *No one.*' Her gaze wandered sideways and rested on Ray.

His eyes met hers and she held them for several moments. She saw the question and then the dawn of realisation that the subtle threat was for him. His realisation turned to surprise, then a hard look and finally a subtle nod of accep-tance. No one else in the world would have got away with threatening him the way she just had, but she didn't care. Her family were the most important thing in the world to her, and though she loved Ray with all her being, she'd give her last breath for her children. Even if that meant turning him into an enemy.

It had been the real reason she had invited him along on their last job. She hadn't needed his men, not really. But she'd wanted him to be there to observe her wrath, to see how dangerous she could truly be. Over the years, he'd watched her rise up to the position she was in today. He knew who she was better than most. He'd heard the stories, listened to her prob-lems, advised and supported, but he'd never actually watched her roll up her sleeves and do the dirty work that got her there.

But yesterday he had. And the reminder was there to serve as a warning. He was never to touch Ruby again.

'To family,' she repeated, lifting her glass.

'To family,' they all cheered.

Ruby watched Ray's face and her eyes twinkled with amusement. She should never have doubted her mother. Through thick and thin, Lily had always had her back. Ray had undermined her and she hadn't ousted him from her life for it, but as was her unique and clever way, she'd laid a very dark and dangerous threat at his door without even raising her voice. He was in no doubt now that he was not allowed to overstep the mark again, the way he had when he'd kidnapped her and forced her to go cold turkey.

It wouldn't stop him from carrying out his threat, of course. She knew that. He'd told her straight that if he ever found her back on the gear, he'd kill her and make it look like an accident. He'd fix it so that Lily would never know he'd been involved. But the fact her mother had taken a stand made her feel better all the same. She was telling Ray that when it came down to it, her daughter came first. And that meant a lot.

The irritating sound of Scarlet's laugh drew her attention to the other side of the room, and the familiar feeling of hatred snaked its way through to her stomach. She took a deep breath and reminded herself to stay focused. Ruby had her mother onside now and was quickly picking up everything Lily was teaching her about the business. It wasn't going to be easy, and it wasn't going to happen overnight, but she had her goals in sight now, and with every encounter she had with Scarlet, her resolve only grew.

As Scarlet threw her head back once more, Ruby looked away towards Cillian. Assuming he was unobserved, his expression was unmasked and she was surprised at the hatred and darkness she saw there. She followed his gaze and her eyes landed on John. Suddenly she understood. John sat relaxed and at ease, watching her cousin with a wide smile. He was handsome in an unusual way and from what she'd seen so far was a really nice guy. She could see why Scarlet liked him. But she also understood exactly why her brother hated him. He was a threat. He was a problem.

She tilted her head as her gaze wandered to their hands nestled together in Scarlet's lap, a dark seed of an idea taking root in her mind. They were so happy. So in love. Even despite the glaring differences between them. They could never work, not in the long run. Only the people in this room were even allowed to know they were together. There were so many ways it could go wrong. In an instant, it could all come tumbling down around them, breaking their hearts and forcing them apart. He was Scarlet's first love, so it would be the most devastating too, when it finally happened. A cold smile began to creep up on her face, and as Scarlet glanced her way, she hid it by taking a sip of her drink.

Oh yes, there were so many different ways Scarlet's happy little set-up could be shattered. And Ruby was going to make sure it happened at the worst possible moment, causing the worst possible damage to her oh-so-perfect cousin.

A LETTER FROM EMMA

Dear readers,

Thank you so much for reading this book and I hope you enjoyed it. If this is the first of mine you've picked up then welcome to the world of the Drews! And if you've been on this journey with me from previous books: welcome back, friends. If you would like to hear more about the series, sign up here. Your email address won't be shared and you can unsubscribe at any time.

www.bookouture.com/emma-tallon

This has been an interesting one for me, not least because of the two very contrasting sides to Ruby. I would imagine for those of you who've read this series from the beginning that your feelings about her have changed and flipped, perhaps even a few times. I know mine have. She has so many layers that even I often have a hard time unpeeling them. I'd be interested to know your thoughts, so please do mention them in your reviews.

I've really enjoyed writing *Her Betrayal* and I'm glad it's been fun as this particular one is an amazing milestone for me. Just a few years ago, the thought of being a genuine full-time published author was one of my greatest dreams, but one I didn't think would ever actually happen. Now here I am releasing my tenth novel into the world. It feels incredible and humbling, and I just hope that I've done the writing justice.

Now I'm busy writing the next book in the Drew series, and as always there are some challenges and twists in the road ahead. I hope you'll come along and join me through that book too, but in the meantime, stay safe, stay well and stay happy.

All my love,

Emma xx

 facebook.com/emmatallonofficial
twitter.com/EmmaEsj
instagram.com/my.author.life

ACKNOWLEDGEMENTS

First of all, a huge, heartfelt thank you to all my readers. You are the reason I'm able to lock myself away in the cabin at the end of the garden and continue writing these books. Thank you for every copy you buy, every post you share, every review or recommendation you make. I appreciate it more than I can express.

Secondly, I want to thank my wonderful friend and editor, Helen. Without her, these books wouldn't be what they are, on so many levels. And my days wouldn't be half as fun without her on the other end of my emails either.

And lastly, there are too many to list, but thank you to the amazing family and close friends around me who make my life better every day. You know who you are. Without your love and support, I wouldn't be able to put my heart and soul into my writing, and I'm so glad to have each and every one of you.

Printed in Great Britain
by Amazon